Mary Lee Demarest

Verse and prose writings of Mary Lee Demarest

Mary Lee Demarest

Verse and prose writings of Mary Lee Demarest

ISBN/EAN: 9783337374037

Printed in Europe, USA, Canada, Australia, Japan

Cover: Foto ©Andreas Hilbeck / pixelio.de

More available books at **www.hansebooks.com**

VERSE AND PROSE

WRITINGS

OF

MARY LEE DEMAREST,

AUTHOR OF "MY AIN COUNTREE AND OTHER VERSES."

GATHERED AND PUBLISHED BY HER HUSBAND.

" A gentle, loving, trustful heart ;
  A woman's wit, with childhood's grace :
The pure soul shining in her face—
  A nature above art."
                              —*Page* 355.

———————

PASSAIC DAILY NEWS OFFICE,

PASSAIC, N. J.

1888.

T. MOREY & SON,
Electrotypers and Printers,
Greenfield, Mass.

CONTENTS.

	PAGE
LINKS,	3
CHAMOUNY AND THE MER DE GLACE,	83
HOW GERTY MORSE SAID "YES,"	106
SOUTHERN VIOLETS,	121
THE JOYFUL SUFFERER,	127
THE STORY OF ADJAI,	146
ANDREAS HLAVERTI,	152
A MORNING IN THE HOMES OF CHINA-TOWN,	156
THE ACID TEST,	165
CASTING, OR CARRYING,	170
CHRIST IN ART,	175
HE CARRIES THEM UP HILL,	177
HOPE ARCHER'S PARABLE,	180
HOW A CHRISTMAS CARD SAVED A LIFE,	185
AN INCIDENT OF THE WEEK OF PRAYER,	188
I SURRENDER,	192
A NINETEENTH CENTURY BARREL OF MEAL,	195
REDEMPTION OF STRAYS,	202
SPENDING-MONEY,	204
SPIRITUAL MALARIA,	214

	PAGE
A STORY FOR LITTLE NAN,	216
PRAYER-MEETING VARNISH,	221
ENGLAND AT GARFIELD'S GRAVE,	228
GUY FAWKES' DAY,	238
GIFFORD'S WIFE,	241
THE WIND AND THE WHIRLWIND,	258
WHEN THE EVEN WAS COME,	275
A DOMESTIC MISSION,	280
THE SOLDIER'S COMFORT,	289
SOLDIER, A LETTER FOR YOU,	294
INDELIBLE INK,	299
PINE KNOTS FROM OLD CAROLINA,	306
FOREIGN FRAGMENTS,	311
MARBURG ON THE LAHN,	311
THE FACKEL ZUG,	312
THE JERUSALEM CHAMBER,	314
LORD MAYOR'S DAY,	316
HYDE PARK,	317
FROM RIO TO PETROPOLIS,	318
BUENOS AYRES,	319
SUNNY MEMORIES OF MENTONE,	320
REFLECTIONS,	324
MY JOY,	324
UNTO YOU, GENTILES,	326
HE SAVED OTHERS: HIMSELF HE CANNOT SAVE,	328
ONE FAITH,	331
LITTLE HELPERS,	331

REFLECTIONS—*Continued*.

THE LION AND THE ADDER, . . . 333

GIVE PLACE, ... 334

I AM NO POET, ... 335

THY HOMESICK CHILD, ... 336

HOMELESS, ... 337

LIFT UP THE CHRIST, ... 338

MY JERICHO, ... 339

WHO AND WHENCE, . 340

THRO' MY SKYLIGHT, . . 342

SYRIAN CHILDREN, 343

THE RIFTED CLOUD, . 346

SPES SALUTIS, .. . 346

CUM SCUTO, VEL SUPER, . . . 348

1865, ... 349

GARFIELD, . . 351

AT EVENTIDE, ... 353

MINISTERING, ... 353

A CHRISTMAS CAROL, ... 354

BALSAM—BALM—EVERLASTING, . . . 354

GOLDILOCKS AND SILVER HAIR . . 355

MY LOVE, ... , . 355

MY REST, ... 357

A NIGHT WATCH, ... 358

THE LAST THING, . . . 360

THRO' GLOOM TO GLORY, ... 362

IMPOTENCE, ... 364

DUMB, ... 365

PAGE

PEARLS AND PEBBLES, ... 365

UNDER THE SNOWS, ... 366

BONNY DOON, ... 368

POPPIES GROWING ON THE RUINS OF A ROMAN VILLA, 369

OUTWARD BOUND, ... 370

TWO SUNSETS, ... 372

FOREIGN MISSIONS REPORT, . . . 374

FOR THE MASTER'S USE, . . 379

HAMPTON-COURT VINE, . . 383

Y. M. C. A., . 385

CENTENNIAL, . . 386

BACHELOR'S SOLILOQUY, . 387

DOUBLE ENTENDRE, . 389

THE TROOPER'S DEATH SONG, . 390

APPENDIX (WAR LETTER), ... 391

EDITOR'S NOTE.

IN compliance with numerous requests, some of the writings of the late author of " My Ain Countree " have been collected in this volume. In searching among the manuscripts, many were found, in which her dear pen had been laid down, before completion, —never to be resumed. Several of these have, however, not been omitted. Pleasure is experienced in acknowledging, here, the courtesy of Publishers, who have kindly permitted the reproduction of articles heretofore printed. Their names are given at the close, wherever known. With a special feeling of calmness, are committed to the hands of many friends these echoes of the loved voice of One at rest. The reviewer's shaft may speed, but not perturb.

T. F. D.

N. Y., Aug., 1888.

I

GATHERED WRITINGS

OF

MARY LEE DEMAREST.

LINKS.—PART FIRST.

CHAPTER I.

AT THE OAKS.

All linked together in an endless chain,
For life or death, for blessing or for bane:
Dear God, so lead us that our lives may be
Strong links to bind some other souls to thee!

"VERY well, do as you wish, wife—Catskill, Lebanon, Narragansett, or Richfield. But to an old-fashioned man like me, it does seem like tempting Providence to leave a home like this, in such blazing hot weather, and pitch ourselves in among a crowd of strangers, in a big hotel."

Mr. Norris and his wife were standing by the bay-window of the library, one summer evening in the end of June.

The grand old trees, which had rightly given their name to the place, stood out clear and bold in the soft moonlight, and cast their massive shadows on the beautiful lawn, sloping down to the margin of the silver river.

"I know, George! I'm sure we couldn't have a lovelier home than The Oaks; but I do think a little change is beneficial once in a while, and you know Jessie is fond of society, and is so pretty"—

"Yes, yes, between Mrs. Hammond, Saratoga and Washington, the silly child has nearly lost her head. But remember, wife, two things are settled: Where one goes, all go. I won't have the children and Hope Archer shipped off to some farm-house, or left here without us again. And another thing,— Jessie must do without a French lady's maid this summer. I'm not made of money; and what's more, if I could afford it, I wouldn't. It's high time she should learn to be of some use to herself and others."

"George, I do think you are hard on Jessie"—

"No, I am not. You spoil her by giving in to her nonsense too much, wife. I know one thing: she'll never be the beautiful woman her mother was—and is," said Mr. Norris, affectionately putting his arm around the wife, of whose beauty he was still as proud as when he married her twenty-two years before.

He was ten years older than his wife—a hale, hearty, silver-haired man of fifty, whose influence in the community was due far more to his character than to his culture. Much to the disgust of his daughter Jessie, he was known throughout the country as "Squire" Norris. Though not a Christian himself, he respected those who honored Christ as much as he despised those who he thought were shams. Affectionate and kind, as he was, to all his children, Jessie was the only one with whom he had little sympathy. Carroll, Isabel, Grace, Harry— all were nearer to their father than his beautiful eldest daughter.

On account of the extreme heat, Mr. Norris had vetoed any further study on the part of Grace and Hal until September; so Hope Archer's occupation, for the time, was gone. One morning, a few days before they were to leave for Narragansett, Jessie suddenly entered her mother's dressing-room, where Mrs. Norris and Isabel were in busy consultation over sea-shore and mountain wardrobes.

"Mamma, of course you are going to take Estelle! I cannot possibly get along without a maid. You know I cannot do up my hair in that new way my-self, and I want her to drape my dresses every evening. Isabel said something about Estelle's not going. I think it would be a downright shame!"

"My dear, your father does not understand such things; he says he cannot afford it. There are so many of us, and you are not contented to go to a quiet house. He wishes Hope Archer to go with us this summer. I suppose she *does* need the change."

"I think it is too mean," said Jessie, angrily,— "the fuss my father makes over that girl! Well, if she is to go, mamma, you must just tell her she is to help me dress every evening. She is quick enough, and knows how things ought to look; and then, it will keep her out of the way, too."

"I do think you are too bad, Jess," broke in Isabel. "You know Hope is always ready to help us. She often makes me ashamed of our selfishness. There! I don't care if you are angry. She never puts herself forward; you know *that*, very well; and if people like her, it is because they cannot help it, she is so bright and lovable."

"Hush, girls! I do wish you would not dispute so. I dare say Hope will be only too glad to make herself useful; probably will feel more free to go if she understands that there is something definite for her to do."

A quick knock at the door announced the little governess herself, who had come to speak to Mrs. Norris about her own plans for the summer vacation. In the adjoining room, perched up in the wide window seat, sat Hope's pupil, Grace, busy in exploring "Nellie's Silver Mine;" and yet with ears and eyes wide open to everything that concerned her dear Miss Archer.

"My dear," said Mrs. Norris, "we are just talking of our plans. We shall be away at Narragansett and Catskill for six or seven weeks, and Mr. Norris wishes the children—and you—to have holiday until September; so we shall be glad to have you go with us, and you can find little ways to make yourself useful to the girls and myself" ("Not to me, mamma, if you please," interrupted Isabel, with hot cheeks), "if you feel delicate about going otherwise. We are not to take any maid; there are so many of us we can get along by helping each other, and I suppose you will not care to go down in the evenings very often—I mean when there is anything special going on—on account of your mourning, my dear!"

Hope stood quietly until Mrs. Norris ceased. " I thank you, Mrs. Norris, for thinking about me," said she, simply. " But I would much prefer to remain in Norriston until your return."

" But, my dear, we could not leave you at The Oaks with only Griffin, you know. She is a good old soul, but no company for you. My son and his friends will be coming and going until his vacation, and it would be quite, quite unpleasant, and out of the question, you know."

Hope's color rose, as she unconsciously drew her figure to its full height, and looking steadily at Carroll's mother, said, quietly : " You quite misunderstand me, Mrs. Norris. I could not possibly remain at The Oaks. You forget Miss Winchester's claim upon me, and that I must stay with her, if you do not need my services as governess. I came to speak to you about it."

" Very well ; oh ! very well, my dear. It is strange I had not thought of it before, and I am glad "—her manner had lost the tone of patronage—" she will have the pleasure of your company, since we must forego it."

Hope's lips wore a proud smile as she left the room, saying, to herself : " How *could* she ask me in that cold-blooded way ! It was Jessie's work, I am sure. And then to think I could possibly be willing to stay at The Oaks ! If she could only believe I can't *bear* her darling Carroll—but she is so proud of him, the poor mother, she cannot think that possible." Hope stopped short in her soliloquy, startled to find in her heart a wicked little wish to punish Car-

roll Norris for being the occasion of such a mortification.

When the sun was low that afternoon, she started to
walk down to see Miss Winchester, her dear "Cousin
Bess," the only friend who had proved faithful during these later years of her lonely orphan life. Her
pride had not yet recovered from its wound, but she
had a brave spirit, and was not in the least degree
morbid. She had thought sometimes it would be
very hard to stay at The Oaks, except for the steady
fatherly kindness of the old Squire, who had known
and admired her own father, and for the loyal affec-
tion of Grace and Harry.

Since Isabel's return from school, Hope had been
much happier, for her pleasant companionship was a
great relief after Jessie's arrogance and Carroll's persistent attention. Conscious of her own uprightness,
she could bear even Mrs. Norris' occasional slights,
for they were always traceable to her evident desire
to prevent Carroll's "foolishness." But now her
heart was sad and sore, and she felt very forlorn and
homeless.

As she walked along the sheltered wood-path, thinking of her troubles and trying very hard to "cast her
burden on the Lord," a carriage came down the drive,
and Squire Norris' hearty voice called out : "Why,
Miss Hope! are you running away? So—jump in,
my dear. Going to Miss Winchester's? All right,
I'll take you there and bring you back. Are you
nearly ready for the sea-shore and the mountains,—
bathing suit, mountain-dresses, and all that sort of
thing? What! not going?"—as Hope told him she

was going to stay with Miss Winchester. "Nonsense; you need a change, child. You're not used to all this confinement and bother of teaching."

"I do thank you very much—don't think me ungrateful, please, dear Mr. Norris; but you know every thing is so different. It would be very hard to go to Narragansett now. We used to go." Hope's flushed face and trembling voice pleaded well for her.

"To be sure; yes, yes, I understand. Wonder I didn't think of it! That's all right. Well, you must go somewhere. Miss Winchester will take you, I am sure. You shall have a check—that's the square thing of course, since you won't go with us; and mind now, you don't give the money to the missionaries, child, instead of going off somewhere, to get the roses back."

"You are very, very good, sir," said Hope; "but please, *please* don't! I have plenty of money."

"You have? Well, you're the very first woman I ever heard say so. Now, remember and tell Miss Winchester that I say you need a change, and it will do her good, too; see if it doesn't."

Hope did not return to The Oaks that evening. Miss Winchester sent a little message to Mrs. Norris, begging that she might stay with her until the morning, and the Squire's hearty assent promised that everything should be pleasant for Hope, as far as he could make it.

"Stay as long as you like, my dear; only we do all miss you, whenever you are away."

"I will come up in the morning to help pack; there will be so much to do if you go on Thursday."

"Very well, my dear. Good-night."

CHAPTER II.

THE SAME.

MRS. NORRIS received Miss Winchester's message coolly, saying: "Oh! very well." But Jessie exclaimed in open ill-temper: "I wish, to goodness, her dear Miss Winchester would keep her forever! Then perhaps we might afford to take a lady's maid, like other people."

"What's all this? Jessie, if you cannot speak more properly, you must be silent! What has Hope Archer to do with a lady's maid, wife?" asked the Squire, rather sharply.

"Why, nothing," said Mrs. Norris, uneasily; "except that I said, when I asked her to go with us, that we were not to take any maid; that we would help each other—"

"And that she might be lady's maid to Jessie," interrupted Grace, saucily; "and that she couldn't stay at The Oaks while we are gone, because of Carroll. But didn't she look pretty when she heard that! She looked just like a queen," said Grace, recklessly.

"Go to your room, Grace! Your insolence is insufferable. It would be well if Miss Archer had taught you to honor your mother and behave yourself." Mrs. Norris' voice trembled with anger, and her face flushed painfully.

"Oh! mamma, I am sorry," said Grace, the tears filling her eyes. Miss Hope does tell me how bad it

is to speak so, and I do try to keep my tongue still ;
but I haven't now! Do forgive me, mamma —
please." Grace stood a moment, waiting for some
gentler word from her mother ; but she only repeated :
"Go !" and the child, turning, rushed up stairs, and
flung herself sobbing beside her bed.

When she had gone, Mr. Norris said, gently (he
was respectful to his wife, even when most angry) :
"We will talk this matter over by-and-by, wife," and
left the room.

Then Carroll turned to his mother, and said, indignantly : "If there is any truth in Grace's statement,
you can scarcely expect a lady—and Hope Archer
is a lady—to be willing to return here. But, if she
goes, I go, too !" So saying he walked out of the
open window, and, lighting a cigar, strolled away
through the shrubbery to the river.

Poor Mrs. Norris burst into tears. Carroll was
her idol.

"Much ado about nothing," said Jessie, scornfully,
as she swept into the adjoining room, and began to
play one of Chopin's Nocturnes.

Isabel came up to her mother, and put her arms
around her. "Mamma, don't feel so bad. I think
Hope will stay. I am sure I should be sorry enough
to have her go. Grace was very naughty to-night,
but she is entirely different from what she was a
year ago. Carroll is silly about Hope ; but she
snubs him so, I think he must soon see that it is of
no use. He was angry, and Grace did exaggerate.
I'll tell him so, by-and-by."

"My good, helpful child !" said her mother affectionately. "I am going to my room now. No, I don't need anything. My head aches, but I shall be best alone."

Isabel walked into the music-room, where Jessie was playing in the moonlight. Isabel was the only member of the family, except her father, for whom Jessie had any respect, and the few plain home-truths which the beautiful, haughty Miss Norris ever heard came from the lips of her younger sister.

"I am ashamed of you, Jessie," said Isabel, slowly. "After getting mamma into trouble, it would have been only honest to have borne your share of the blame. You know mamma will do almost anything to please you."

"I am not to blame for that, am I?" said Jessie, coolly. "I have a strong will, and she has a weak one; that's all."

"No," said Isabel, "that is not all. Mamma wants to do right, but you almost always get her to do wrong. She is so fond and proud of you, it is all the meaner if you don't own up and tell papa and Carroll what you said to mother about Hope's waiting on you. If you don't tell, I shall."

"Very well. I shall do no such thing. Papa has never been good to me since Mrs. Hammond was sent away, and I am not going to make any confessions to him. Besides, you will remember the pretty little speech which made Carroll particularly angry was not of my suggestion," replied Jessie, triumphantly.

"I do wish, Jessie," said Isabel, slowly, "you would try to help mother instead of harming her."

"Nonsense! I am not one of your goody sort of people. But you are a better girl than I am, Issy," said Jessie, relenting a little. "I might try not to get mother into scrapes, I suppose, just by way of variety, and to oblige you :"—with which rather negative admission Isabel was obliged to be content. Indeed, it meant more than it seemed.

Two years ago, a Mrs. Hammond had come to The Oaks as governess, on the recommendation of some friends of Mrs. Norris. She was, as they described her, a very attractive and accomplished person. She was also an unprincipled, strong-willed woman, and soon held the household—the Squire and Carroll being absent on business—in almost entire subjection to her will and ways. Isabel distrusted her from the first, and bravely resisted her influence, striving to open her mother's eyes, but in vain. Mr. Norris had not been at home a week before he quietly dismissed the lady, with salary up to the full term of her engagement. Jessie stormed and raged in vain. She had been especially charmed by Mrs. Hammond, admiring her from the first, and had adopted, with almost fatal facility, the views of the older woman.

So it was not strange that, when her father summarily installed Hope Archer as governess to the younger children, Jessie determined to make her life as uncomfortable as possible, nor that she succeeded admirably for a while. In her arrogance she had been ready to class Hope and her mother with the "weak-minded," for whom she felt the deepest contempt. Yet there was still in Jessie's spoiled nature a true instinct which recognized goodness ; and

Hope's brave and faithful life was beginning to influence her unconsciously. "Mamma is fond of ready-made clothing—in morals; anything to save trouble. But Hope is different. There is nothing shabby or slipshod, or that doesn't *wear* well about her," at last owned Jessie, one day, to Isabel. "Don't imagine I am fond of her! I am not; but I am sure, if her position had been mine, I should have shirked and cheated and been revengeful many a time."

Hope, however, was very far from imagining that Jessie had watched her so closely. It would have amazed her greatly if she could have heard this honest verdict on her life. She told Cousin Bess, in the quiet talk they had that evening, that Jessie sometimes was very provoking, sometimes very pleasant; but generally she treated her *as if she weren't there.*

When Hope returned in the morning, she was conscious of a subtle, exhilarating change of atmosphere at The Oaks. The social thunder shower had cleared the air, leaving the sunshine brighter, and the earth fairer, than it had been before. To speak without metaphor, Mrs. Norris was affectionate and Jessie was civil, while Isabel, Grace and Hal were warmer than ever in their welcome. Mrs. Norris felt relieved and grateful to Hope for being forgiving, and coming back pleasantly; and, with the readiness of an impressionable nature, was glad to make amends, as far as she could, for the slights of the previous day.

Grace was eager to be with her dear Miss Hope as much as possible during the two days that were left, while Harry openly declared he wished Miss Hope were going instead of Jess. He wanted her to show him all the jolly places she had told him about; and *he* would take her out beyond the breakers if she'd go— he wasn't a bit afraid! "Which was not at all astonishing," Hope told him, laughing, "since he had never been within sight of the surf!"

While Hope was busy in Grace's little room, sorting clothing and packing the sea-side trunk, Grace found a chance to confess that she had been very naughty to mamma last night—"dreadfully saucy and mean;" and had been sent up to her room in disgrace.

"After I had been trying so hard to get the better of my horrid tongue! Wasn't it dreadful, Miss Hope? I did think mamma never would forgive me, and I couldn't do anything to let her know how awfully bad I felt. Then I just remembered what you told me the other day when we were reading about Peter in prison—how he was lying between two soldiers bound fast with two chains, and the keepers were before the door. Don't you remember? You said that no one could ever be so miserable, in such a strong prison or under such heavy chains, but that God could set him free, and that Peter's deliverance was in answer to prayer. So I *did*—I mean I asked God; and oh! Miss Hope, do you know *mother came to my room before she went to sleep*—she had a dreadful headache, too — and kissed me and said — said some lovely things to me! I know I never loved her so much as I do now. Do you think it was wrong to be sure God had forgiven me when he made mamma come and say she forgave me, and to kiss me good-night?"

CHAPTER III.

BESIDE THE SEA.

GRACE and Harry Norris cared for the sea and
the rocks, not for the society of Narragansett.

"The boys and girls are too grown-up for us," remarked Grace in a letter to Hope Archer. "I do
think it is horrid, Miss Hope, the way almost all the
children talk and flirt and carry on. They don't like
me one bit. I don't care much—except that I am
afraid it's partly because of my horrid tongue, you
know. It's awfully hard for me to speak the truth in
love. I do get so boiling over, when people say
mean things, and then I don't think or care what I
say; and so I have to be sorry afterwards. I do
wonder if the apostle James had a great deal of
trouble with his tongue! I read a verse in his epistle
that discouraged me dreadfully yesterday. You know
it says that all savage beasts can be tamed, but 'the
tongue *no* man can tame.' Then I remembered you
told me to be sure that, if I loved and trusted the
Lord Jesus, all God's strength was mine—all ready
and waiting for me to use, I mean; and that Christ
had fought the battle, and won it for all who love
him; so I have picked up courage again. . . . I was
dreadfully afraid for a while that Harry was going to
'be friends' with those foolish boys, but now he is
disgusted with them, and stays with me and two or
three very nice children—Blanche and Paul and
Mary Harvey. We went, with them and Isabel and

Captain Harvey, over to Wakefield the other day, and had such a jolly time, and had our pictures taken, too., I like Captain Harvey better than any other gentleman here. He is splendid-looking, and it seems to me he likes children better than young ladies. But all the young ladies admire him ever so much. Jessie was dreadfully provoked that she didn't go along with us, instead of Issy ; but you know Jess *never* goes with us children anywhere, and Issy does, whenever mamma can spare her. Oh ! dear Miss Hope, how I do wish you were here ! You don't know how much I love you ! "

Hope could not read "between the lines," nor guess the secret of the chivalric devotion of little Grace for herself, nor the very good reason there was for relief that Harry had become "disgusted " with Ben Howard and his friends. It happened in this wise :

One morning, during the second week of their stay at Narragansett, Grace and Harry were together on the beach. The tide was low, and they were walking towards Indian Rock.

" I say, Grace, isn't it just jolly down here? Oh ! there comes a stunner."

The children rushed out of the way of the in-rolling breaker, laughing and excited.

" Harry," said Grace, with unconscious pleading in her tone, "isn't this better than being with Ben Howard and those other boys ? I don't think they're a bit nice."

" May be it is," replied Harry, cautiously. " But, Grace, I want to tell you something—it's an awful secret, and you must never tell as long as you're a mortal man—woman, I mean."

"Nonsense! Harry, what do you mean? You do like mysteries so, 'and I can't bear them."

"Very well, if you don't choose to promise," said Harry, offended. "But it's something about somebody you love very, very much. It's about Miss Hope."

"Oh! well," said Grace, relenting as far as her thirteen years cared to yield to Harry's eleven. "If it's nothing I *ought* to tell—that mamma ought to know about—I promise."

"All right," said Harry, mysteriously. "Ben Howard says his sister Hetty flirted awfully with Mr. Wayne Halsey, when he was engaged to our Miss Hope, and she told him that Miss Hope liked our Carroll; and then—I forget it all, but there was a—a —devilish row."

"Stop! Harry Norris. Don't you say another word! You're talking just like that bad boy, Ben Howard, swagger and all! Oh, Harry, I didn't think you'd ever swear!"

"I didn't," said Harry, stoutly, though Grace's sorrowful face made him uncomfortable. "That isn't swearing. Swearing is taking God's name in vain. I'm sure 'devilish' isn't that, by a long shot! It's just—the opposite," replied he, triumphantly.

"Harry," said Grace, quietly now,—for she had asked God to help her say what was right and true, and to keep HER tongue from speaking evil,—"Harry, perhaps I can't quite tell you why it's wrong, if

it isn't really swearing. But you know you wouldn't
say it before papa, or mamma, or Miss Hope!"

"Well, what if I wouldn't!" said Harry, gruffly.
"Mrs. Hammond used to say it, and I heard Jess
say it once, too!"

"Don't, Hal, dear! You know what's right, and
it's mean to make excuses that others do such things.
I think *this* is the reason why it's wrong," said Grace,
slowly: "God tells us in the Bible that the devil is
strong, and hates God and hates us; that he goes
about as a roaring lion, you know; and God means
us to resist him, and to hate all his evil ways. Now,
when Ben said the trouble his sister had made for
Miss Hope was—*that* kind of a row—he didn't mean
that he hated it because it was a cruel, fiendish thing,
but only that there was a very great deal of trouble.
So it seems to me, it's a kind of contempt of God to
treat lightly, or make sport of something he says is
wicked and awful."

"All right, Grace, I won't say it any more. But
it's true, I tell you, about Ben's sister. I said I
thought it was a mean thing, but Ben said it was all
square; that 'everything was fair in love and war;'
that his sister liked Mr. Halsey and couldn't bear
Miss Hope, and meant to get Halsey away from her;
but Ben said 'Hetty didn't quite come it that time,'
for Halsey found out she told lies and flirted, and
then he was so awfully sorry and ashamed he went
off, and nobody knows where he is."

"And Ben Howard told all that about his sister!"
said Grace, her face glowing with scorn and anger.

"He ought to have been so ashamed of her that he could never speak of it to a living soul."

"Well he wasn't," said Harry. "He seemed to think it was smart."

"It isn't; it's a mean, wicked, cowardly thing, Harry. I don't think children have any business to be talking about such things; but I'm sure it isn't any more right or *honorable* to steal a girl's lover than it is to steal her money or her watch, and it's *ten thousand* times worse and meaner," said Grace, indignantly. "Poor, dear Miss Hope! Oh,"—

Harry and Grace turned the corner of a projecting rock, and suddenly came upon Captain Harvey lying on the sands with a book beside him. The quick color rushed to Grace's cheeks, and Harry, too, was a little uncomfortable. Captain Harvey looked up, took off his cap, and said, quietly:

"Won't you sit down, Miss Grace—and Harry?" The children seated themselves silently. "I didn't wish to hear what I was not meant to," said he, looking with his frank, kind eyes at the flushed face beside him. "I only heard a few sentences; but, Harry, my boy, let me tell you, you cannot do better than remember, all your life, what this little sister of yours was telling you."

"Then it isn't true—what Ben Howard said?" asked Harry, eagerly; "everything *isn't* fair in love and war?"

"No!" answered Captain Harvey, emphatically. "Right and honor are the same, the world over, to an honest man. That bad proverb has been made an excuse for a great deal of trickery and treachery, of which no honorable man, soldier or civilian, would be guilty."

"Grace says that we children oughtn't to talk about such things," said Harry, reluctantly ; "but I don't see why not ? "

"Perhaps your sister will tell us why," said Captain Harvey, gently.

"I don't think mamma and Issy would like it, one thing," said Grace ; "and then it seems somehow mean to be talking and listening to things, even if they are true, about grown-up people that we wouldn't dare to do before them."

"Perfectly right," said Captain Harvey, with a bright smile ; while he thought within himself : " An honest, honorable little girl—not a bit like the gay Miss Jessie. I wondered if Miss Isabel has the same nice notions ? "

One afternoon, a week after this little episode, Captain Harvey noticed a sail-boat about to put off, and heard Grace's eager voice calling : "Oh, Captain Harvey, won't you come with us ? "

Jessie added a more dignified but very cordial invitation, and Captain Harvey replied courteously: "With pleasure, if I can find some one to carry a message to my sisters. I was on my way to see if they wanted to walk to the post-office with me."

As Captain Harvey joined the party, Jessie introduced him to her friends, Miss Marvin and her brother.

Mr. Marvin, or "the Hon. Philip Marvin, of Liddegate Hall, England," as he subscribed himself in the hotel register, was a good-looking, somewhat supercilious Englishman, who, in spite of his insular belief in the superiority of everything on "the other side," was very much charmed with the beautiful Jessie. The addition of another gentleman to the party, especially "one of those handsome West Point fellows," as he grudgingly admitted to himself, was not very welcome to Mr. Marvin.

Captain Harvey turned to the skipper as they sailed away: "Aren't we going to have a blow before sunset? I'm not much of a sailor, but it looks to me like it." The man muttered something in a surly manner, and Mr. Marvin volunteered the remark that there were "enough *sailors* on board to manage that little craft," and proceeded to entertain Miss Norris with an account of his cruises in his yacht, "The West Wind."

Grace was delighted to have a talk with Captain Harvey. "I only wish Mary and Paul and Blanche were here! Did they bathe this morning? You don't know how stupid it is; papa went to New York yesterday and won't be back till Saturday," said Grace, confidingly, "and mamma is so afraid; she said she would have no peace if we went to bathe without papa."

"If she would trust you with me, I should be very glad to take charge of you—one at a time "—said Captain Harvey, pleasantly.

"Oh! I think she would. That would be splendid. But I didn't mean to *hint;* I never thought of it!" Grace looked up frankly, to meet his amused smile.

"I never should imagine you guilty of hinting, Miss Grace. But tell me," said he, in an undertone,—"this is not the boat and the skipper your father employs?"

"No," said Grace, in the same tone. "I don't know anything about it, except that Jessie asked me to go, and said it was all arranged, and mamma said I might go and sent my thick jacket. The *old* skipper was cross, and wouldn't take us this afternoon. He is a very old bear sometimes, but I like him better than this one."

Captain Harvey thought to himself he was not at all sure "it was all right," Miss Jessie's assurance notwithstanding.

Jessie was in high spirits, chatting gaily with Miss Marvin, a fair, pretty English girl, and her brother, and was evidently anxious to make it pleasant for all the party.

She explained to Captain Harvey: "My friend, Miss Marvin, threatens to forsake us to-morrow for the gaieties of Saratoga and the sublimities of Niagara, so we wish to show her all we can of this little nook this evening." The conversation digressed to English sea-shore places, Highland hunting lodges and the Princess of Thule. Still, Mr. Marvin held aloof in a rather ungracious manner, to the evident discomfort of his little sister sitting beside him.

Suddenly the sky blackened, a squall struck them, broadside, the men sprung to the sails, but too late. No one knew how, but the little boat tipped over, and all were in the water.

Mr. Marvin rose to the surface and grasped the edge of the boat. The skipper was alongside. Annie Marvin was clinging to her brother.

"Any chance of righting this confounded boat?"

"Not in this squall," growled the man.

"Here, my good fellow," said the Honorable Philip, "take my sister ashore safely and I'll give you twenty pounds. I shall have all I can do to take care of myself in this sea!"

On the other side, swept further and further away from the boat, Captain Harvey was struggling to hold up Jessie and Grace.

"Grace, Jessie, put your arms *over* my shoulder— so. Don't clutch me, Jessie, or I can't hold you. They'll see us from the shore and send boats."

"Oh! it is my fault," moaned Jessie. "We shall all be drowned. I deserve it, but I'm so afraid to drown."

"You can't hold us both," said Grace. "And oh! this is the arm that was hurt. Your poor little sisters!"

"You can take care of Jessie, I am not afraid— not much—and I can float, and if I don't get ashore—"

"Oh, no, no! save Grace and let me go," cried Jessie, without relaxing her hold.

"Jessie, don't mind—too much—about me if I don't get ashore. My love to everybody. Oh, if they only would send help!"

"Hold on, Grace! I can stand it a little longer, child."

"No, no, dear Captain Harvey, good-bye. The Lord—Jesus—knows I am here. He saved—my soul—he'll take care—good-bye."

She let go. A great wave swept her away from Jessie's agonized sight.

------◆------

CHAPTER IV.

THE SAME.

WHEN Captain Harvey's little sisters and Paul received their brother's message, that he had "gone for a sail in the *Sea Gull*, with Miss Norris and Grace, and hoped to be back to walk with them after supper, they, as usual at such times of absence, perched themselves up in their sky-parlor window, spy-glass in hand, just to watch the boat that held their dear, big brother. He was father, brother, hero to them—all in one. And they could scarcely be sorry for the wounded arm that had sent him home to them to stay until he was well and strong as ever.

"Why, there's Harry Norris!" cried Paul. "I'll get him to come up here and watch, too."

Before Paul could mount the stairs again with Harry, came a shriek of grief and horror from the children who were watching the little boat on the sea.

"Oh, it's upset! It went right over. Brother Aleck! Oh, help!"

They tore down the long stairs,—the story told by their white faces and quivering lips.

"Aye, aye, little misses. We'll have a boat out there as fast as strong arms can take her." It was the old skipper, Ben Harding, that spoke. "I wouldn't take them out myself this afternoon for fear of this squall ; but this is another matter. Bad luck to the feller that did take them, just for the sake of the money !"

"Let me go along "—" and me !" cried Paul and Harry.

"No, no, boys ! It's work for men, not for children. There's summat you can do ashore, if it's true that there's a good God up there looking after folks in trouble. And you go home and keep your mother and your sisters from going crazy over them that's out there in danger, boys !"

A sad group it was in that big "sky-parlor" of the Harveys. Close to the large windows were gathered Mrs. Norris, Isabel, Harry and Captain Harvey's little sisters and Paul.

"Oh, if I hadn't let them go !" groaned Mrs. Norris. " I never thought of their going with any one but Ben Harding. What will your poor father say? Oh, if he only were here ! It is my fault, my fault ! He told me to be careful ! "

"Mamma, mamma, it is not your fault ! " Harry's voice spoke up, sharp and clear. " Jessie knew what she was about. She heard papa tell me we were not to go with any one but Ben Harding, and in his boat. Ben wouldn't take her this afternoon. I wanted to go, too ; but he said it looked squally, and he was really cross about it. So then—she must have got that other fellow's boat. It's just like Jessie ; and now Grace is there, too, and she'll be lost !"

Harry burst out crying. Grace was his dear sister but he did not love Jessie very much.

"Hush, my boy! This is no time to have hard thoughts of your sister. Pray God to spare Jessie and all of them, and to make us better."

Harry looked in wonder at his mother. "It sounded more like Grace than like mamma," thought the boy.

Meanwhile another boat quickly followed Ben Harding's. The squall was over; again the sun shone out.

"Oh! there is somebody; there are three near where the boat went over. "Oh, God!" said Isabel, with a shudder. "How selfish I am! I never once thought of Annie Marvin or her brother; but they must be there—somewhere!"

Swiftly now the little boats sped over the waters, nearer and yet nearer to the black objects now appearing and again vanishing before the agonized eyes of the watchers.

"I counted seven a minute ago," whispered Isabel; "but now there are only six."

It seemed as if every one in the hotel and the neighboring houses were watching, too.

Careless, gay fellows, who had danced with Jessie and Annie Marvin; loving mothers, whose children were safe beside them; stout-hearted fathers and merry girls—men, women and children, were all steadily watching that little spot on the great ocean, where they knew well the struggle between life and death was waging.

Mrs. Norris held close and tight Captain Harvey's curly-headed little sister, Mary; poor Blanche was clinging to Isabel, and Paul and Harry stood together in their eager watch.

"Oh, I know how it will be!" cried Paul, at last. "Aleck'll be drowned *sure*, trying to save other people. Oh, dear! oh, dear!" and the boy gave way to a terrible burst of grief.

Isabel drew him close to her. "Paul, dear little boy, don't you think it is something to have a brother so grand and good and heroic—to know that he won't shirk anything in life or death that he knows is right? If he were my brother," said the girl, slowly, with her soul in her eyes: "I would thank God for him, whether he were in heaven or on earth; and—I would try to be like him, Paul!"

Paul turned and put his arms around her neck, and cried, "Oh, Aleck, Aleck!" Then, with a sob, he looked up and said: "I'll try! And may-be God will spare him to us "—

"Yes, yes," said Isabel, eagerly; "never, never, give up hope."

Blanche said, slowly: Oh! it seems years since yesterday. Don't you remember, Paul, Aleck had been reading about Jesus walking on the sea, and the disciples not knowing him? Gracie said she thought it was strange they didn't know the Lord. And Aleck said to remember it was early, early in the morning, in the twilight before the dawn; early morning for their faith, he said, as for their sight."

"Yes," said Paul, "and he said that afterwards, after the resurrection, the disciples were on the sea and Jesus stood on the shore in the early morning light. And then it was John, the one that Jesus loved so much who knew him first and said : ' It is the Lord.' "

" And then—Oh, Isabel ! I can't look at the boats any longer. It makes me feel so selfish. Isn't it just dreadful ? "

" Poor children," said Isabel, crying with them. " It is worse for you than for us. Only you know it is so dreadful to think it was our sister who led them all into peril, and "—

" Isabel, dear, don't ! " cried Blanche.

" I do believe God will save them all. Don't you want to know what Gracie said, and Aleck liked so much ? "

" Yes, dear," said Isabel, gently. " Gracie said some verses, something Scotch. I can't remember much except it was : ' We ken Thee not by the pathway o' the sea.' "

And Aleck said all troubles were like the sea sometimes, and we must remember the Lord is coming to us, even when we can't see him.

" I know," said Isabel, the tears standing in her eyes. " I remember the verses. Gracie found them in a paper last spring. It begins :

> " ' Our een, aft whiles, are howden, Lord
>   Tho' near we are to Thee,
>   But maist o' a', we ken Thee not
>   By pathway o' the sea.' "

" Yes that is it. But, oh ! see, see ! They have reached some of them. Oh, God have mercy and bring them all safe home ! " cried Blanche.

Ben Harding's boat found Mr. Marvin, and then his sister and the skipper of the *Sea Gull.* Notwithstanding the large offers of the Honorable Philip Marvin, if they would make with all speed to the shore, Ben Harding rowed on to find the others. "Is it the time for a man to be selfish when he's been saved from death himself and knows others are in the same luck he was. Here's blankets and brandy; wrap up the lady and yourself and you'll be none the worse for a half hour more trying to save other men's lives." Poor Annie Marvin, she was ashamed of her brother that day! Now the other boat came up, having picked up the missing sailor on the way. Mr. Marvin and his sister, with the skipper, were transferred to it and bidden hoist a signal of good news to those on shore, while Ben Harding's boat went on to find the others. Nothing to guide them over the trackless wave, no clue, no trace of any human form. But sailors' eyes are keen, their ears are sharp. Just in time to save them, they find —not all, but two.

Captain Harvey, when the strain was over, went off into a swoon. Both boats were well supplied with restoratives. Jessie recovered consciousness first, and, after a little, Captain Harvey revived. One thought, one longing now was shared by all: hope grew faint. Jessie, poor Jessie! "Oh! if Grace is lost, you know I am her murderess," moaned she.

"Miss," said Ben Harding in his bluff way, "it 'pears to me it's time you asked the Lord to help. We're doing all that mortal man can do. But I've hearn tell, and I reckon it's so, that life and death are in the hands of God."

"Oh, Ben, I do! I've been a wicked, selfish girl,

and don't know how to pray, but I know God can help, and I do ask him for Christ's sake—Oh! there —there!" shrieked Jessie.

She was right. Over another wave, another, and now they have reached her sister. "Oh, oh! is it too late?" cries Jessie's heart.

They have lifted her into the boat, chafed her lifeless hands and moistened the cold lips with brandy; but no sign of life! Back to the shore they pull, for dear life, truly, now.

A sigh—a quiver of the eyelids. Ah! thank God, thank God, she lives!" sobs Jessie.

Run up the signal! Joy! joy!

"So He brought them into their desired haven."

----◆----

CHAPTER V.

AT THE OAKS.

GRACE NORRIS was lying by the open window, the Sabbath morning after the accident. She looked happy and restful—not eager and buoyant, as she had been a few short days ago. Beside her, sat Hope Archer, who knew well how to give the gentle nursing and petting which the child's shattered nerves very greatly needed.

Grace held Hope's hand against her cheek, with her favorite caress, and said softly: "It was ever so good in Miss Winchester to come, Miss Hope. I haven't thanked *you* for coming, any more than I would think of thanking papa or Carroll."

"I should think not," replied Hope, lightly. "I could not possibly have stayed away."

"But how did you ever hear?" asked Grace, wondering. "I have been so stupid, it never occurred to me to think of it; I simply took your presence for granted, because you know you *do* belong to us."

"Jessie sent me a telegram," said Hope, quietly. "It was very good in her, for she didn't like me much at The Oaks."

"Poor Jess!" said Grace, tenderly. "It is awful for her. She hasn't had any rest or comfort, fearing that Captain Harvey would die, you know, for she feels so strongly that all the trouble came from her wilfulness."

"I know, dear; I feel more sorry for Jessie than for any one else; but the doctors think now that Captain Harvey is out of danger, although it may be a long while before he is well."

"How good God has been to us!" said Grace, earnestly. "It is so nice to have papa and mamma and all the others go to church this morning. You know they asked to have thanks offered in church, Miss Hope!"

"Yes, dear; Blanche and Paul told me their thanksgiving and yours were to be offered together."

"Yes. How close it brings us to each other, does it not? It does not seem possible that we had never seen Captain Harvey one month ago! Now he and Paul and Blanche and Mary are like our own family."

"Dear child, you must not talk any more just now. Shall I read to you a little while?"

So Hope read a chapter and sung a hymn, and

then, as in the old days at The Oaks, she preached a little bit, as Grace begged her to ; that is, she spoke from her own heart to Grace's, telling how God's blessed message comforted and helped her in her every-day need. Suddenly Grace looked up and said : "Do you remember that wonderful picture of 'Our Sin-Bearer?' You told Harry and me about it one Sunday at home, and Captain Harvey has a beautiful engraving of it here. You know Harry and I learned the verses in St. Peter about the Saviour's example, 'who his own self bore our sins in his own body on the tree.' Well, it was strange," said Grace, softly, "how that verse and that picture came up before me when I thought I never should see any of you again in this life, and remembered how bad and selfish and careless I had been. It seemed to me as if, before I had time to really feel how dreadfully wicked I had been, all the great heavy pile of my sins was resting on the Sin-Bearer, and the fear of dying was taken away I believed it would be all right with me, even if I should drown, and then I let go my hold of Captain Harvey. And after that I just floated, and floated, and I thought the waves were Christ's footsteps, and he was coming to me."

Grace paused, and a tender look, almost a smile, shone in her eyes with the remembrance. "The next I remember, was that I was in the boat, and Jessie was crying and kissing me, and I was ever so glad I hadn't drowned."

"There, dear," said Hope, gently, "don't think of it any more."

"It doesn't worry me to remember it one bit, but

it makes you feel bad, so I won't talk about it.   Don't
you like Blanche and Paul, Miss Hope?   Oh, I hope
you will see Captain Harvey before long !   He is—
beyond words," said Grace with her old sweet laugh.
"You used to tell me not to use extravagant expressions, so I think I am safe there."

"I am sure he is a brave Christian gentleman, and
as unselfish as he is brave ; and as for Blanche and
little Mary and Paul, I think, as you say, they are
'perfectly lovely,'" said Hope, smiling.

"Indeed they are," echoed Grace.   "You can't
think how fond they are of Isabel !   Mamma told
her if she didn't mind she had better stay at home
this morning to keep little Mary quiet.   She hasn't
recovered from the fright yet, and Isabel seems to
know just what to do with her—ever so much better
than Blanche does."

"Then that *was* Isabel singing a while ago; I
thought it was her voice."

"Yes, she was singing 'Rock of Ages' and 'Immanuel's Land,'" said Grace.   "She sings right into
my heart.   You don't know what a comfort Issy is to
mamma and Jessie now.   She always has been good
to Harry and me."

"Indeed, I can well believe it," answered Hope ;
"and Jessie is—"

"Very different, is she not ? " said Grace, supplying the words.   "It does seem as if it were almost
too good to hope for, for we haven't been a religious
family at all ; but I *do* think God is making Jessie a
Christian, though she doesn't take any comfort yet.

But she is so humble, and stops short when she begins to say something cross."

Hope's eyes filled with tears, as she leaned over and kissed Grace. "'For my thoughts are not as your thoughts, neither are your ways my ways,' saith the Lord," she whispered. "And now, dear child, you must take your medicine and go to sleep."

"Very well, dear Miss Hope. I do feel a little sleepy. It has been such a comfort to have this talk with you. It has quieted me, rested me, somehow. Now I'll go to sleep."

Hope sat beside Grace while she slept, and looked out on the sea from the same window where four years before, she had watched the ocean in a furious storm while her father and mother were beside her. But there was now no bitterness in her heart over the losses and sorrows which God had sent to her. It was even sweet to be once more where they three had been together, and yet was it possible it was only a few weeks ago that she had told Mr. Norris she "could never bear to go to Narragansett again?"

CHAPTER VI.

THE SAME.

WHEN Miss Winchester and Hope unexpectedly met Mr. Norris on the boat for Narragansett, his first greeting made it quite evident that he had received no telegram, and was still ignorant of the cause of their sudden trip.

"That's right, Miss Hope; going to the beach

after all !   Now I call this a really sensible move for
Miss Winchester and you."

It was very hard for Hope to answer, quietly, that
" Mrs. Norris had sent for her ; " but it was not until
they neared the landing that Hope felt she must speak
more plainly.   Poor Mr. Norris was completely
stunned.

" What does it mean ?   I have had no telegram.
I suppose I must have just missed it everywhere.
Grace ill ?   Why the child was merry as a cricket
Wednesday morning, and this is Friday ! "

Jessie and Harry met them at the wharf.   Putting
Miss Winchester and Hope in the carriage under
Harry's care, Mr. Norris and Jessie walked up, by
the nearer footpath, to the hotel.   In those few moments, for the first time in their lives, the hearts of
father and child met in confidence and sympathy.
Jessie's full and agonized confession of her self-will,
disobedience and deceit touched her father's warm
heart ; and while he hated the sin none the less, he
felt himself strangely moved to love and comfort the
sinner.

" Oh, papa," she said striving vainly to keep back
her tears, " do pray that I may not be a murderer !
God has spared Grace ; but if Captain Harvey dies,
it will be I who have killed him !   I never prayed in
my life before," said Jessie, humbly, " and I am so
bad I am not fit to pray ; but I can't do anything
else, and Issy says God is very merciful."

" My poor child," said her father ; " God help you
and all of us !   We have been a godless family, and

I am the most to blame ; for I knew better, and had a good Christian mother."

The days wore on,—the long bright summer days of watching and suspense ; for neither Grace nor Captain Harvey rallied as the doctors hoped they would. During those sad days, which Jessie never forgot in after-life, no one was able to comfort her as the father whom she had so lately learned to know and love. She said one day to him : " Papa, I think I have been trying to bargain with God all this while, promising to serve him if he would make Captain Harvey and Gracie well. Now I have given it all up, and want him to take me, if he can care for such a good-for-nothing girl ; and I am willing he should punish me as he pleases. But, oh, I hope he won't let others suffer so terribly for my sin ! " Another day she said : " Papa, do you know you have helped me to believe in God's love ? You have been so piti-ful and good to me in this trouble that I can understand a little how our Father in heaven feels towards us."

Ever since that dreadful day of the wreck, Blanche and Paul had clung to Isabel, and claimed her as their special friend. Little Mary Harvey was a very delicate, nervous child, and often it seemed to Blanche as if she would *never* go to sleep. Then Blanche in despair would beg Mrs. Norris to let Isabel come and sing to her, and soon the over-wrought, excitable child would close her eyes and sink into a quiet sleep. Once in these weeks of watching, Isabel had seen Captain Harvey. Paul had taken Blanche for a walk on the beach, and Isabel was on the balcony, where she had been sitting after little Mary had gone to sleep, when Mrs. Norris called to her, asking her to bring some ice and a bandage for Captain Harvey's arm.   She could not forget his white face and earnest eyes, nor the clasp of his hand as he tried to rise from the couch where he lay.

" How can I thank you for being so good to my little sister," he said ; adding, with his old smile : " You see I am a very good-for-nothing member of society now, and being so idle, I have taken to the naughty habit of stealing."

" I shouldn't have suspected you of such a thing," replied Isabel, with a smile in her eyes.   " How came you to be so bad ? "

" Well, the fact is, as your kind mother knows, I am very apt to get restless at the close of these long days, and sometimes I steal a share of little Mary's lullaby, and go to sleep while you are singing."

" Since you aren't polite enough to stay awake and listen," answered Isabel, with a quick blush and smile, " I suppose I must forgive you ; but it is a very bad habit, I assure you.   Good-night."

After that evening, little Mary learned to go to sleep while Isabel's sweet voice wandered on through wonderful bed-time stories, and when a few times the child begged her to sing instead, Isabel had an un-comfortable consciousness that she was singing for the big brother also.

At last the happy day arrived, when both patients were pronounced in a safe condition to attempt the journey to The Oaks.   For by Mr. and Mrs. Norris' urgent invitation, Captain Harvey and his sisters and

Paul went home with them. It was Grace's blunt speech that finally overcame Captain Harvey's reluctance, as he said, "to quarter such a family on them, and one of them such a helpless log as he was!"

"Captain Harvey, if you won't come home with us, I shall always think you haven't forgiven me for hurting your arm that day; and as for Blanche and Paul and Mary—*they belong to us now*, and you really mustn't take them away!"

The change proved very beneficial to the two invalids, who soon regained their former strength; while little Mary grew rosy and plump, as she had never been in all her short life. When Captain Harvey had grown strong enough to join in the out-door pleasures at The Oaks, he gradually became aware of a barrier of reserve upon Isabel's part. Grace and Jessie were eager to show their guests the beauties of the neighborhood; and, after Carroll sailed for Europe, Mr. Norris and his wife were always as ready as the younger members of the family to row, ride or drive, or to plan a day's pleasuring somewhere. But strangely enough, whenever Isabel could stay at home without notice, she was inclined to do so. Once Captain Harvey asked her laughingly, whether she really wore glass slippers, and had a fairy godmother all to herself.

Isabel scarcely dared to own to her own heart why she shrunk from joining the merry parties in those fair September days. Once when Harry and Grace went with Captain Harvey to watch the sunset from the top of High Rock, Harry was determined to grumble over Isabel's absence. Grace spoke out with her old sharpness: "Why can't you let Issy be, Harry? I think she doesn't feel quite strong since last summer, and you know she never will make a fuss. She always wants us all to enjoy ourselves. I think somebody might think a little bit about *her* feelings!"

"I am sure *you* do," said Captain Harvey, warmly. "You are a brave little champion, Gracie, and deserve a medal! Harry and I are concience-stricken, and very sorry we have teased your sister; but, of course, the fact is, we miss her when she isn't along with us. But we'll not tease her any more, will we, Harry?"

CHAPTER VII.

THE SAME.

BUT a few days afterwards, Paul, with a boy's unfortunate brusqueness and with an air of injury, expressed his disappointment at the change in Isabel: "You aren't half as good as you were at Narragansett, Isabel. You don't seem to care about Aleck or any of us, for you never will go along when we take a walk or row."

"Paul, my boy!" exclaimed Captain Harvey; and Paul felt himself rather unjustly rebuked.

Isabel looked up, laughing, while the color rose in her cheeks, and she looked so lovely Captain Harvey could not but watch her.

"What a stupendous accusation, and how very unjust, seeing I am taking a walk with you just now! If Carroll were here he would tell me to 'deny each and every allegation of the complaint,' isn't that the phrase? Then, you see, on the other hand, Paul," she said, merrily, "my collapse into my native inland badness is a very good reason for keeping my wickedness to myself."

"Nonsense," said Paul, very much ashamed of himself by this time. "I am awfully sorry I said that, Miss Isabel."

"I didn't mind it a bit, Paul," said Isabel, with her old frank look at the boy's flushed face; and then, turning to the older brother, she said quietly:

"We were proposing to go to Dingle Ridge this afternoon. You know there's a lovely view from the crest of the hill, and a pretty lake near the top."

"That's jolly," said Paul, delighted, as he was with any and every thing at The Oaks.

"That would be charming, if I could manage to write some letters first," said Captain Harvey.

They were walking in The Nook, a rough, rustic arbor, where the children were fond of bringing their books and games.

"Would you not like to write here?" proposed Grace. "The chairs are very comfortable, but the table is rather rickety."

"It's a good deal better than a drum head," said Captain Harvey, lightly. "This will be very comfortable, and far pleasanter than writing in-doors. Paul, will you bring me my portfolio, please?" Paul rushed away, eager to do anything for the big broth-

er who was his hero.   He returned with the portfolio, and, before Isabel could tell him of the inkstand under a beam in the arbor, he had gone off
again exclaiming : " I'll fetch the ink in a minute."

"I don't know how I shall manage," said Captain
Harvey, gravely, "but I may as well learn to do
without Blanche as secretary.   One hand should be
enough to write with, should it not?" said he, looking at Isabel, apparently struck by her silence.
Something in her face, in her wistful look, moved
him to give her two letters, saying : "Would you
mind reading them?   You'll see it is rather serious
business, for it concerns the children as well as myself.   Poor children! they don't know yet," he said,
with a quick sigh.   Aleck Harvey's grave eyes
looked past the fair, flushed face beside him, beyond
the far-reaching lawn with its grand old trees, beyond the shadows and sunshine on the broad, fair
river—off to the far horizon line where earth and
heaven seemed to meet.

"Such a good bye sort of look," thought Isabel,
with a heart-ache ; and inwardly thanked him for
never looking at her while she read those letters.
One was from his Colonel, in reference to his return
to his regiment, the other from his mother's sister,
offering to take care of the children if he would leave
them with her.

Isabel needed all the self-control of her nature, as
she sat there holding those two dreadful letters in her
hand.

"He would go back to his regiment," she thought
"and perhaps be wounded again and die."   She felt

like crying out wildly against the cruel fate before him, but, like many another woman, she sat still and gave no sign. "Oh!" she thought, "if something would happen to make it right for him to stay!" But she must speak—what would he think?

She slowly folded the letters and turned toward Captain Harvey. His eyes came back from their far-away look and rested on the sweet, flushed face beside him.

"Thank you, thank you very much," she said giving the letters back to him. "Do you really have to go back to your regiment?"

His hand closed over the little fingers that held the letters, while he answered, smiling: "I do really have to if the surgeons will pass me."

"But you will leave the children here—oh, please, do! We should miss them dreadfully, and it would seem as though we hadn't lost you entirely if we may have them still."

"You don't know how you tempt me," said he, suddenly. "It will be harder for me to go than you can possibly imagine. But I must do my duty."

"Yes," said Isabel, softly. "I know you will." She never guessed how much more her eyes said, as she looked up at him for a moment.

"God bless you for that," he said, hurriedly, lifting her little hand reverently to his lips. Then, rising suddenly, he walked to the arched doorway and looked again to the far horizon. As for poor little Isabel, she sat bewildered and half abashed.

"What had she said?" she thought to herself. "What ever had she said to make him thank her—

like that! Oh, dear! had she said anything dreadful?
But no, she was sure she had not. *Of course* they all
believed Captain Harvey would do his duty (her
heart throbbed gladly with true pride in her hero) and
she had only said so."

Then she became conscious that some one was
speaking to her.

"I did not know before that we could see the ocean
so plainly from this place. Look through my glass,
Miss Isabel. You can see the ships quite distinctly,
can you not?"

"I say," cried Paul, coming toward them on a run,
"it is too bad you've had to wait all this time for the
ink, but Blanche and everybody has gone off, and I
have just found them; and lunch is ready, and will
you please come, Mrs. Norris says, and write your
letters afterward."

"The mail closes at half-past five," said Isabel,
glad to speak of something ordinary, while her
thoughts *would* wander to the answers to be written
to those dreadful letters.

CHAPTER VIII.

THE SAME.

THE following day Captain Harvey went to Washington with Paul. Two days afterward, came a letter
to The Oaks, which, for a while, quite startled Mr.
Norris out of his self-possession. Suddenly, rising
from the breakfast-table with the letter in his hand, he

retreated to his study, exclaiming emphatically : Astonishing! Astonishing! Wife, come here, please, when you are through breakfast."

Mrs. Norris very soon followed him, and read Captain Harvey's straightforward letter, begging they would allow him to try to win their Isabel.

"Well, wife, what do you think? Confounded cool, isn't it? To put us under such obligations by saving the life of one girl, and then to come and ask us to give him another," exclaimed Mr. Norris, testily, manifesting a strong inclination to wipe his eyes in the midst of his indignation. Mrs. Norris laughed, "Oh! you blame him for not asking for Jessie? Is that it, George?"

"No, it isn't! I suppose I'm just as unreasonable as most fathers are about their daughters."

"It seems to me we have only ourselves to blame for it, if you don't like it, George," said Mrs. Norris, seriously.

"Oh, I like *him* well enough. He's a first-rate fellow, square and above-board, as his father was before him. But I don't enjoy the idea of sending off one of my girls to live among those wild Indians."

"Well George," said Mrs. Norris, slowly, "this has been a wonderful summer, and it seems to me we have come to look at things in a very different way from last year. For my part, I would rather have Isabel run the risk of life on the frontier, with such a man as Captain Harvey, than live with John Middleton in New York."

"Good land, Bessie, what has upset your notions so? I thought you liked Middleton ten times better than I ever did.　A good-enough man, but far too fond of fast horses, and show, and style for me! What has turned you against him?"

"I don't dislike him personally, George," said Mrs. Norris, speaking with some hesitation, "but I see what all this kind of life amounts to now.　If you want to know what has changed my views, I shall have to make quite a confession.　First, Hope Archer's influence over Grace convinced me that there was something in being a Christian that I didn't know anything about.　I have watched her a good deal this year past, and then this dreadful time this summer, and Jessie's repentance, and Captain Harvey's heartiness in serving Christ, and some things he said about his mother—take them all together, George, even *my* worldliness hasn't withstood the power of living Christianity!"

Mr. Norris drew his wife closer to him.　"I would give anything in the world to be a Christian, George," she whispered.　"I have been nothing but a sham, all my life."

*　　*　　*　　*　　*　　*　　*

Six months have passed away since the scene in Mr. Norris' study,—the six months which Mr. Norris insisted should elapse before Captain Harvey should seek to win their Isabel.　During that time Blanche, Paul and Mary had been with their aunt, Mrs Taylor, in Cambridge, with the exception of a fortnight in the winter holidays, which they had passed at The Oaks.　As Paul said, "It was too jolly for anything; if Aleck had only been there, too!"

But he was off in Arizona, and letters did not

arrive as regularly as his sisters, and perhaps some one else, wished they might. But Isabel kept her own little secret bravely, and in the many letters of her brother, which Blanche sent to The Oaks for their friends to read, there was never any special message to her.

Isabel had long ago told herself that it was only because it was she who had happened to be in the arbor that morning when he had been "so friendly" —she would have said, if she had tried to put that sacred memory into words.

"Mamma, how you do count the days!" said Isabel, laughing, as her mother said one morning:

"George, do you know it is *the third of April?* Do you think you will want me to come to your study this morning?"

Mr. Norris was standing by the open wood fire, for the mornings and evenings were still chilly at The Oaks. His arm was around Isabel, who was "helping him look up the news," as she said, gaily. He turned to his wife with a smile at her suggestive question. "You are an excellent calendar, Bessie. You've reminded me of the flight of time every day for the past month, haven't you, wife?"

A smothered exclamation of horror from Isabel's lips drew their attention to her. She stood white and still, with eyes fixed and finger pointing to a paragraph, headed:

"MORE INDIAN TREACHERY.—It is reported, though not officially as yet, that a detachment of United States troops, 5th cavalry, on the way to relieve a starving settlement, has been surrounded and nearly destroyed by Indians. The scout who brings this report states that Major Harvey and Captain Murray were with the party. Major Harvey received his brevet only a few weeks ago. It would truly be a sad fate for him if, after recovering from the wound of a poisoned arrow last year, this gallant officer should so soon fall by the treachery of another band of these Indian devils."

"It cannot be true! Oh, it cannot be true! Poor Blanche and Paul!" cried Isabel, bursting into tears and clinging to her father's arm.

"Of course it's one of those horrid political newspaper reports," said Jessie, with fine impartiality. "I don't believe a word of it!"

"It is not official. I'll telegraph immediately to the War Department. So, children, keep up a good heart," said their father, trying to speak cheerfully as as he left the room.

"Mamma," said Grace, "don't you remember Blanche wrote that her brother was to have leave of absence and come East very soon? so there's no good in our believing a word of it. Oh! it is *too* dreadful."

"Mamma, won't you write to the children?" said Isabel, still shivering, but trying hard to control herself.

"Yes, dear, and you write a little note, too; they are so fond of you," said Mrs. Norris, tenderly. "We will not send the letter until papa's telegram is answered. He thinks we can hear in two hours."

It was a sorrowful morning at The Oaks. Mr. and Mrs. Norris felt sadly sure that little Isabel's heartache was far keener and sorer than Jessie's or Grace's, yet all they could do was to sorrow and hope with her, and give no voice to the conviction which had come with the falling of the heavy blow.

"Oh, dear," cried Grace, "I do wish Annie and Will Russell were not to come to-day!"

"It can't be helped," said Jessie, shortly, "and we must make the best of it; but I *do* wish they'd send word they couldn't come."

Grace and Jessie left Isabel to write her note in quietness. After she had written it, she stole away to the arbor, to wait until some news should come. It was a lovely spring day. She had felt so happy that morning, for somehow the hope of Aleck's return had crept into her heart unawares. She sat with her head hidden upon her arms beside the little rickety table. Every word, and look, and tone came freshly back to her.

"O God! don't let it be so, please; or, if it must be, make me willing!" she cried. At last, a shadow of her old hope and courage came back to her, while she gave her poor, crushed, little heart into God's own keeping. "I suppose I ought to go back to the house now," she thought, wearily, as she heard a carriage drive up and the stir of an arrival reached her.

"There! I suppose Harry is coming to call me," as she heard hurried steps nearing the arbor. "Oh, I wish I hadn't cried!" She turned to the archway, where she had stood with Aleck, looking out on the far-off sea. Then—how it was she never knew—she heard his voice, looked up, and he was beside her. "Oh, oh! I thought you were dead!" she sobbed, covering her face with her hands.

"Thank God, it was a false report from beginning to end, dear child."

He drew her to a seat, and with a tremble in his own voice said, while he held her with his strong arm :

"Isabel, dear, won't you look at me ? Remember I haven't seen your dear face for six long months."

She took away her hands. "Oh, I must go !" she whispered, as she felt her cheeks flush under his earnest look.

"Isabel !"—He spoke the name as if it were very sweet to say it—"Isabel, your father and mother sent me to find you here. I cannot let you go just yet. If you knew how I had longed to see you,—how I have thought of this little arbor as the dearest place on earth because of my memory of you ! My little darling, how I have hoped for this day ! Isabel, dear, look up and tell me, do you think you could ever love me well enough to be a soldier's wife ?"

She slowly raised her face. A sparkle of her old spirit shone in her eyes, though her lips still quivered, while she said, shyly :

"That would depend altogether upon—who the soldier is—Aleck."

PART SECOND.

CHAPTER I.

THE OLD WINCHESTER HOUSE.

HOPE ARCHER drew a long sigh of relief when she had bidden good-bye to all at The Oaks, as she imagined, "until September," and was fairly at home again with her dear Cousin Bess.

"The Old Winchester House," as it was called throughout the country, was built before the Revolution by the great-grandfather of the present Miss Winchester, who had held large grants from the crown. The chronicles of those old days, preserved in letters between members of that long-perished generation in the mother country and in the colonies, were no small pleasure to this solitary woman, who loved the old homestead and honored her ancestors with a fidelity inherent in her nature.

The house stood on a sunny knoll, one side of which sloped down to the silver river, where, in the days when Elizabeth Winchester was young, many a boat was moored by the steps at the foot of the garden, while merry visitors gathered in the wide, low-browed rooms or lingered under the old trees on the lawn. Now, the children of those old friends of Elizabeth Winchester were made welcome to the pleasant home of her girlhood by the graceful, high-bred, simple-hearted woman, whom they were permitted to claim as "Cousin Bess." But Hope

Archer was the only one of them all who had even a far-away legal claim to kinship ; Hope's grandfather, Harry Archer, having been cousin to John Winchester, the father of " Cousin Bess."

When Hope's father, four years before our story opens, was ruined pecuniarily by the fraud of a trusted friend for whom he had indorsed, the blow, coming, as he owned it did, as the consequence of his careless confidence and folly, roused him to energetic action to retrieve his error. He flung himself again, with all the force of his nature, into the profession which he had given up when, by his father's death, he had become a wealthy man. His friends rallied around him, clients multiplied, and life seemed very sweet and good. His wife had secretly grieved over the indolence into which he had fallen in his prosperity, and now, with wifely pride, rejoiced in his success.

Swiftly fell the blow by which he was smitten down. A few days' painful illness, borne bravely with cheerful trust in God's faithful promises for himself and his dear ones, and Livingston Archer's place in the world was empty forever. Elizabeth Winchester's promise to her cousin to care for his wife "as her own sister," comforted Hope's father on his dying bed as no other human pledge could have done. When all was over, Mrs. Archer, with womanly independence, refused to be a burden to any one, although she gratefully accepted Miss Winchester's invitation to live with her in the old Winchester home. The interest of a few thousands, left to her by an uncle, together with her earnings as an artist with needle and brush, sufficed for the support of herself and

Hope. To her little daughter she was friend and teacher as well as mother, and so two years of widowhood passed, not without comfort and sunshine. Many a time Hope planned how, in the years to come, she would have a class, perhaps even a school of her own, and her mother should do nothing but paint lovely pictures and make their home with Cousin Bess, in the fairest old place in the world.

But suddenly the child was orphaned. Mrs. Archer died, after an illness as short and sharp as her husband's had been, and poor Hope seemed crushed and bewildered by the suddenness of the blow. It was a merciful Providence, though a strange one, that brought Hope back from her mother's grave to nurse Miss Winchester through a nearly fatal illness. The fever which had terminated rapidly in Mrs. Archer's case, ran a slower course in Miss Winchester's, and, after four weeks' loving and faithful nursing, Hope's heart was comforted by Dr. Butler's announcement that she was out of danger. The girl of seventeen had grown womanly and brave in those sad days. After Miss Winchester's recovery, when she told Hope she must never leave her except for a home of her own, Hope put her arms around her old friend's neck and said : " Dear Cousin Bess, I haven't any one but you now. Please scold me when I am bad, and let me teach if I have an opportunity, and I will always come home to you in my holidays. I am sure I shall be better and brighter if I am very busy."

So, when Mr. Norris asked Hope to teach Grace and Harry, Miss Winchester unselfishly consented ;

but the old homestead seemed very desolate without the girlish presence which had made such sunshine in the older woman's life.

Now, in the summer holidays Hope and Miss Winchester were together again, and, notwithstanding her longing for tidings from Wayne Halsey, the young girl was blithe and happy. The second day of her vacation, she came home at sunset with a letter for Cousin Bess, bearing Brazilian post-mark and stamps.

"Wayne!" exclaimed Miss Winchester.

"Yes," said Hope, with a little tremor in her voice. "That's his very own W. He always makes such funny capitals! Let me put my head in your lap while you read it, please. So Cousin Bess read and Hope listened.

Wayne told how he had sailed in the *Paranhiba*, bound for Bahia and Rio, of the long days in which, to keep himself from vain regret, he had studied Portuguese with Jack Howells, and navigation with the mate, "a kind, hearty, old man, who seems to have taken a fancy to me, somehow" ("Just like Wayne," thought Hope. "Who ever could resist his winning ways?") "I wish," he wrote, "you could see Jack Howells, dear Cousin Bess. He is such an earnest, straightforward fellow, full of life and fun, and a Christian, too, without a bit of sham or brag. He knows the story of my folly. Didn't he talk to me! He told me plainly that if Hope was the true, good woman I described her, I wasn't worthy of her; that I had behaved abominably, and if she ever forgave me it would be because of her goodness, not because of mine, and so on. Well, it is all true.

They had been in Rio only three days when Wayne wrote, and were stopping at the Hotel Estravieros, out on Botafogo Bay, only until they could get more reasonable quarters.

"How I wished for you and Hope, when we sailed into the harbor of Rio. You know I have no gift at descriptions." Then came a pencil sketch—"just to show how we entered. These giant mountain peaks, standing out in the sea, are like weird sentinels guarding the harbor. The two islands between which our ship is sailing are Pai and Mai (Father and Mother). On the mainland are Corcovado and Sugarloaf and Gabra, and the distant, perpendicular mountain shafts are the Organ mountains. We need no pilot for this harbor; it is very safe. We sailed in at midnight, the moon was not more than half-full; but, oh, how it shines in these tropic skies!

"You know we had to give up our familiar old friend, the North Star, some time ago—I think before we crossed the Equator. The Coal-Sack, the Magellan Cloud and the Southern Cross are on duty now. I wonder if you remember, dear Cousin Bess, telling me about these southern heavens, long ago, when Hope and I were children, and I had taken a sudden craze on the subject of astronomy! Hope would enjoy these new constellations and the wonderful glory of the tropical moonlight. If I could only hope some day—some day to stand on the deck with her, and we enter the harbor together!"

Cousin Bess read the last sentence to herself, and putting the letter in Hope's hands, she said: "There, child, you had better finish it. I think it is more

than half for you, at all events !   So you stay here,
dear, while I tell Sally about breakfast."

Wayne's pencil again supplied the place of lengthy
descriptions, as he sketched their quarters in the
hotel at Botafogo, and the immense, dreary, seven-
windowed *salon* which nothing less than such moonlight as was shining when he wrote could glorify.

" A forlorn, homeless looking place, with pictures
of Queen Victoria, Washington and Lafayette staring
at us from the walls—I suppose to remind us that we
are truly strangers and pilgrims, and don't belong
here.   The ' Praia do Flamingo '—the beach at the
back of the hotel—is a fine place for a swim.   Jack
and I take a bath at five o'clock in the morning, and
then go back and take an early breakfast before beginning our daily round, which, sad to say is not
quite as steady a round as we wished it to be.   But
you'll be glad to know that I have the partial promise
of work in the survey of a projected railway in the
interior.   I haven't been able to get hold of a map
of the locality yet.   These Brazilians are a rather
slow sort of folks, and quite jealous of the enterprise
of the aggressive Anglo-Saxon. •1 shall have the appointment, if any foreigner gets it, the Consul tells
me, and he seems to know how things happen here.

" Jack's affairs are no nearer settlement than mine ;
for the American partner in the firm of Riggs & Herrera, who sent for Jack and me to come here, is very
ill and unable to see any one, and Herrera is in
Paris.

" Under the circumstances, we can only ' bide a wee,'
as Hope used to sing ; and Jack and I are going to

stay together as long as we can. We are paying at
the rate of 50 milreas per week for our two rooms
(the dreary *salon* is thrown in, because we don't want
it!), with breakfast, and dinner, which is about twelve
dollars apiece ; but that is too much for men who
have to make their own fortunes.

" A friend of Jack's father, who is a sort of independent missionary among the Portuguese here, has
told me of comfortable quarters, and we are going
to have our trunks moved to-morrow, and quit the
dreary, forlorn splendor of the Hotel Estravieros.
. . . . I wish you could have been with us yesterday. This Mr. Richards is a peculiar man, but very
interesting. He asked us to come to a service which
he holds Sunday evenings in a large upper room in
the Casa da Biblia (which, you will guess, is a Bible-
house), on the top of a hill called the 'Morro do
Liveamento.'

" I did not suppose that I could understand a sermon in Portuguese ; but Mr. Richards' face and gestures are so expressive, that I had no difficulty in
following him.

" I confess, I never was so much interested in an
English sermon. And the text was : ' He that believeth, shall not make haste,' and the burden of the
sermon was about staying ourselves on God's promise, and being sure that nothing should fail of his
good pleasure—and so on. The hymns and music
were very fine ; the chorus of one hymn runs in my
head still : ' *Non si pressa, non si pressa,*' which is, of
course, ' Shall not make haste.' Well, I dare say it
was a comfort to Jack. He seems to have taken it

home to his heart; but the trouble with me is, that I
am not at all sure that *my* good pleasure is *the Lord's*
—in fact, quite the other way.   So I live in restless
anxiety, always afraid of some bad news, of something that would make an endless blank in my life.
Heigh ho! I didn't mean to write all this.   I wish I
were like Jack. *He* is not afraid of evil tidings.
Good-bye, dear, kind friend.   Write me all about
yourself and Hope, and never give up

Your affectionate boy
WAYNE."

CHAPTER II.

THE SAME.

"IT is quite remarkable, Hope!" said Miss Winchester, teasingly, a few weeks after Wayne's letter
came. "Your taste for Portuguese grammars and
Brazilian travels has developed amazingly!   I think
that patient old clerk at the library imagines you are
writing a 'History of Brazil, Past and Present,' at
the very least."

"I believe he does," said Hope, laughing. "He
told me yesterday I was the most enterprising young
lady who came to the library, and mentioned the
fact that 'Mrs. Darwin assisted her husband in his
studies and book on Brazil.' You remember it, don't
you?   I had hard work to keep my face straight, but
I managed to assure him that I had no ambition to
be a scientific explorer, and was reading only 'for
information.'"

The summer days passed rapidly by. Hope studied, read aloud to Miss Winchester, sung and painted during the day-time; and often in the twilight she rowed cousin Bess and herself to some neighbor's garden on the river for a friendly call. Wayne's letter was immediately answered by his old friend from the fulness of her warm, kindly heart. Of Hope she wrote frankly, saying she was the sunshine of the old place, and true and good as always.

"You have your honor to redeem, and your manhood and fidelity to prove, for your own sake as well as Hope's, my dear boy," wrote Cousin Bess. "It is a hard discipline for you; but your friend Jack Howells is right—you needed it."

After a few uneventful weeks came the startling telegram from Jessie Norris, their hurried departure for Narragansett, and stay there, and Hope's return with the family to The Oaks some time after Miss Winchester had left the sea-shore for Norriston.

Then Hope came home again to Cousin Bess, to stay until she was needed by her pupils at The Oaks. Meantime, Carroll Norris suddenly left for Europe. No one but Hope and he knew the story of those few moments one moonlight evening, while he lingered by the river.

When he came to bid Miss Winchester good-bye, the old self-conceit and assurance had so thoroughly given place to a quiet sadness, that Cousin Bess, whose heart always went out to all in trouble, felt drawn to him as she never had been since his boyhood.

"Dear Miss Winchester," he said, earnestly, "you

used to tell me when I was a boy that my pride would have a fall. Well," he said, smiling, "it has ; but it is all right. Take good care of yourself—and of Hope. She is my good friend, I know, but will never be more than that. Good-bye—good-bye ;" and he wrung her hand and rushed away in a manner very unlike his usual stately walk.

In September Hope returned to The Oaks, but it was indeed a very much sweeter life there than ever before. Jessie was so thoroughly changed that the memory of her old pride and unkindness vanished entirely from Hope's forgiving heart. Mrs. Norris, too, was very kind, though Hope did not know that her altered manner was partly the effect of a frank talk which Carroll had with his mother the night before he sailed.

On the 20th of each month Miss Winchester's Brazilian letter was duly posted from New York, and occasionally she wrote also by way of England, " so that the poor boy may be sure to hear from us," she thought, "and need not fancy himself forgotten." But it was long before another letter came from Wayne. And then two came in one inclosure, with a line, saying that the earlier one had been forgotten by the clerk, and had only been discovered when he had written the later letter. The first one Wayne wrote from Petropolis, where Jack Howells and he were having a grand, good time as guests of the American Minister, who had been a college class-mate of Wayne's father. Wayne wrote in excellent spirits, saying that the railway scheme was flourishing, and was really, he believed, the secret of his very cordial reception by so many delightful people.

"Everybody is as pleasant to us as if we were princes! But I assure you, I would gladly leave all these kind people to-morrow and go to work at the survey.

"How I wish you could see this gem of a summer home among the mountains! I haven't become quite accustomed yet to winter in June and summer in January; but after all, we free American citizens, from a republic north of the Equator, cannot expect to set the fashions and seasons for all the rest of the world."

Then followed a hurried sketch of their journey to Petropolis from Rio, by ferry-boat, rail and diligence.

"We enjoyed the thirteen miles in the *diligence*, drawn by relays of mules—four to each carriage—up the fine macadamized road to the top of the Serra. These mules—splendid creatures, having the speed and beauty of a horse, with the sure-footedness of a donkey—carry you up the mountain at a swinging gallop all the way. It seemed odd to see a hedge of century plants and cacti along this road. The vegetation here constantly surprises me, being such an exhibition of the flora of both tropical and temperate zones.

"Coming back this evening from a horseback excursion to Cascadina, we reached the plateau at the summit of the Serra just in time for a most gorgeous sunset and afterglow. Jack says, 'After this, we cannot call Turner's coloring extravagant.' Imagine great masses of richest purple, gold and crimson clouds fading away at the horizon to a most delicate tint : blue, and pink, and faintest tinge of green ; below, wild gorges, high hills, tumbled together like children in a frolic, the flash of a mad mountain torrent, sharp cliffs and fair valleys, and far away the dim line of the sea, while like a silver thread winding and doubling on the verge of precipice after precipice, now lost, again appearing, yet always ascending, shines the long road which led us up to these heights.

" ' Oh, if Hope could have seen it ! ' Mrs. Stuyvesant exclaimed. ' What a picture ! ' and Jack added, ' What a poem, too ! ' The natural consequence was—we turned our horses' heads and rode · back to dinner. Prosaic, but true !

" To-morrow we are permitted to call on Dom Pedro, as he has sent word to that effect. He is as pleasant at home as he was on his tour, and I suppose the subscriber will have a chance to answer some questions *in re* surveying, engineering, etc. I hope so."

The other letter bore date a month later. Wayne wrote with a heavy heart. " How can I tell you all that has happened since my last letter ! You do not know what a blessing your letters are to me. God bless you for them, dear, kind friends. Well, I must tell you briefly the story of these four weeks since Jack and I were at Petropolis—so happy and hopeful we were ! Well, nothing turned out as we hoped. Red tape and torpor, schemes and intrigues, hindered my appointment, though the Consul assured me still : ' if any foreigner is to have the work, you'll have it.'

Mr. Riggs, who had asked Jack to come here, offering him an interest in the firm, died, and the other partner, Herrera, is closing up the business. Both Jack and I were growing home-sick for letters, our pockets were pretty nearly empty, and things looked rather serious.

"Howells, however, had the offer of a position at Valparaiso, and I had made up my mind to go there with him, unless there was some definite word for me concerning the survey by the end of the month. I knew I could get money from the Consul if worse come to worst, but I had a little bit of pride in not using father's letter of credit. Jack had determined to go in a sailing vessel around the Horn, and of course if I went at all, I was going with him.

"Well, we waited till the last day, and no news. We were on our way to the *Santa Lucia*, to take passage by her, when Jack said : 'Try once more at the Consul's. I think the English mail came in last night.' 'All right,' I said.

"Well, I found a letter from you and my commission as surveyor, etc., etc. Jack had home letters, but no business news. So it was settled, you see, and I suppose you will be sure it was a plain interposition of Providence. It was hard to bid Jack good-bye and see him start alone. I cannot tell you what he has been to me—friend, counsellor, brother, all in one. And now—

"It is a week to-day since the *Santa Lucia* sailed, and last night the English steamer from Buenos Ayres came in. The captain says he saw a ship go down in the terrible gale three nights ago ; that it was impos-

sible to launch a boat; he tried and failed.   His own
vessel was in great danger, but he lay to, hoping to
pick up some of the passengers or crew, but did not
see one man.   They picked up some spars marked
with the name of the vessel, and reported accordingly
at this port.   I cannot believe that Jack is gone,
that I shall never see him on earth again.   He was
so ready to live, and yet he is taken and I am left!
My heart is very heavy.   It seems to me Jack is calling to me from his grave in the sea to finish his work
in the world, to live the life he would have lived.
And, Cousin Bess, it is impossible for me, for I am
not a Christian and Jack was.   That was the secret
of his happy life.   Oh, Jack, Jack! How can I be
good without him!   I can understand pretty well
David's lament over Jonathan.   * * *   Do write
about Hope and yourself.   I shall probably be far in
the interior, perhaps shall have no opportunity of
sending letters frequently, so do not be anxious if you
should not hear from me for months.   I am sure you
pray for me.   Don't give me up.

Your affectionate

WAYNE."

———•———

CHAPTER III.

THE GOLDEN SOUTH AMERICAS.

WAYNE'S next letter was sent by private hand from
the rough mountain camp where he and two English-
men were busy on the railroad survey.   He wrote
cheerfully, said he was well, but almost famished for

news from home. He begged Cousin Bess, if it would not be too painful, to write a little note to Jack Howells' sister, and he inclosed her address. "Of course I wrote," he said, "after there seemed no reasonable doubt that all on board the *Santa Lucia* were lost, but somehow, Cousin Bess, *I cannot believe Jack is dead*, and yet it would be only cruel to strive to give my groundless hope to others.

"I miss him every day, but I do thank God for those few months' companionship. * * * Please write me all you can about Hope. Tell me how she looks, what she does—anything you will. The distance between us seems immeasurable, yet I never doubt that she did love me once. Fool and wretch that I was to be jealous of her and turn to a false flirt for comfort! Howells is the only man I ever knew who was worthy of her. Dear, sweet, proud little Hope!"

Springtime came again, bringing unspeakable happiness to Isabel; and in the busy stir and excitement, half glad, half sad, of her wedding, for Major Harvey had only one month's leave of absence, and Isabel was to go to Arizona with him, Hope tried hard to forget her own anxiety at Wayne's long silence.

At last, in June, came a few lines, in which he mentioned several letters he had sent, but which Miss Winchester knew she had never received. He was hard at work, the survey was accomplished successfully, the plans reported and accepted, and now the practical, actual road-making was to begin. He had been down to Rio once or twice, and had persuaded Mr. Richards to return with him and do some missionary work in their camp. "You may imagine the need of it. The two hundred men with us now are virtually heathen. They are disgusted with the Roman Catholic priesthood here in Brazil, have sense enough to turn their backs on the mummery and pretended miracles which are rife wherever there are devotees of St. Joseph and the Holy Virgin, and yet they know nothing better. One of my assistants is a good man, and is gaining an influence over these rough fellows. But we need some one who has more time and is used to reaching the Portuguese, as Mr. Richards is. I wish very much you would send me some hymn books, Portuguese, if you can find them, but, if not, then English. We want the music especially. We have some excellent hymns of Mr. Richards—I inclose copies of two or three—but there is no music suitable for them. I don't want to bother you with this commission, dear Cousin Bess, but I know it is more in your line than mine, and you are the only one I can ask to do such a kindness for me."   .

By the next steamer, Miss Winchester and Hope sent to Wayne such a supply of hymn books and of music, copied by Hope and set to the words which Wayne had inclosed, as gladdened and surprised that young man exceedingly. Miss Winchester wrote that it was a very great pleasure to do this for him and for his poor Portuguese, and added that " Hope was very happy copying the music and singing the hymns, just as if she could understand Portuguese !" Miss Winchester did not tell Wayne that she had found Hope crying over his letter, she was so thankful and so glad! Neither did she tell him that Hope had never offered to return it to its rightful owner.

Then came the sultry summer days of August, unusually trying this year to Cousin Bess, for she seemed to lose strength and energy in an alarming manner. One day she received a letter, gave it to Hope to read, and asked her what she would think of inviting the old clergyman and his wife to spend the rest of their days in the Winchester homestead.

Hope read the kindly, pathetic letter of Mr. Holland, who had been pastor of the Presbyterian Church at Norriston when Miss Winchester was a girl, and with whom she had ever since kept up an occasional correspondence. Now his wife was ill. He was obliged to give up his charge at Portland, Oregon— not, he said, on account of his wife's failing health, but because he found that a younger pastor was desired by his people, at least by many of them. His wife longed for the sight of the home of their early married life, where their children were buried and where some familiar faces lingered still, and so he had ventured to ask Miss Winchester to inquire for him whether the cottage where the Widow Gray used to live would be for rent, and at what terms. They had a small income, an annuity, left to them only the year previous by one of his elders, a warm-hearted friend of theirs, and so on.

In less than three weeks, Mr. and Mrs. Holland, sweet, lovely old people, were established in Miss Winchester's home. And then Cousin Bess broke down, and once more was very near the gates of death. It was a great comfort to her as well as to poor Hope, that the dear old pastor and his wife were with them then. Mrs. Holland had regained her health under the double tonic of change of air and kindly sympathy, and was able to relieve Hope in many practical ways, as well as to comfort her by her motherly care and tenderness.

The attack was a severe and tedious one of typhoid pneumonia, but at length the crisis was safely over and the patient began to rally. One day she drew Hope down to her, kissing and patting the white cheeks of her faithful little nurse, and said :

"I am afraid Wayne would think I was not fit to take care of you, if he could see this pale face."

The quick color rushed to Hope's cheeks, and she hid her face on Cousin Bess' pillow and whispered :

"I don't know, Cousin Bess ; it is so long, perhaps he wouldn't care now."

Then raising her face, she said, steadily enough : "How good you have always been to me, dear Cousin Bess ! It was dreadful to have you ill, but it is a great comfort to take care of you and to know you needed me."

"My dear child, I shall need you more yet, for I am going to be very cross and crotchety, as I am entitled to be, now that I am getting well ; so you must run out for a walk and get strength for the additional worry of my whims."

The days passed by, the autumn glories faded from the forests, and the maples and oaks around Miss Winchester's home scattered their brilliant leaves upon the grass ; but cousin Bess did not recover strength, and her cough worried Hope more than she would confess.

One day, after Dr. Butler's visit, Miss Winchester said to Hope, quite gaily:

"Do you know Dr. Butler thinks of sending me off for a long sea voyage and to winter in a milder climate, and I believe the voyage to Rio and a few months in Petropolis or Tijuca are just what I need, so I think we had better sail, dear, by the next steamer."

Hope's face was a study of changing emotions. With a flush of eager gladness she exclaimed:

"Oh, that would be too delightful!" but swiftly a shadow fell on the brightness, as she added:

"But, oh—what would Wayne think, dear Cousin Bess!"

"What do you suppose he would say?" asked Miss Winchester steadily. "If he could think any less of either of us," she added severely, "I am very much mistaken in him."

"Besides," she said, teasingly, "he need not know anything about us, if you like. His railroad and his Portuguese are quite enough to fill his heart and his life, of course."

Hope was silenced, but not convinced; although longing to see Wayne again, fought hard with maidenly pride. But the decision did not rest with her, seeing that Dr. Butler and Cousin Bess were firmly convinced that "The Golden South Americas" presented advantages beyond all other places for a convalescent. So Hope ordered and arranged their wardrobes, travelling suits and wraps, made all necessary plans for Mr. and Mrs. Holland's comfort in their absence, and was so busy that she had no time to question the propriety of the step. She knew that Cousin Bess had prayed for guidance, and all she could do was to leave her troubled little heart in her heavenly Father's hands.

The time drew near for them to sail. One stormy day Hope had been fighting hard against the fear that Wayne had forgotten, or at least had ceased to care for her. She had been very busy all day long, and just before tea she was going to the post-office to mail some letters, when Dr. Butler jumped out of his gig, shook hands with her and said: "Run in, my dear, and wait for the sunshine to-morrow for a walk. Oh! letters to post? Well, I'll take them to the office. Oh! by the way, here are your letters. Good-bye!"

"Oh, Cousin Bess!" cried Hope, running back into the house, her face aglow with sudden joy.

She gave Miss Winchester one letter, and escaped to her room to read her own.

Wayne wrote to Cousin Bess that he thought he had now earned a right to speak to Hope. "Every day's absence makes her dearer to me, but I hope now her happiness is more to me than my own, and she must decide. If I have lost her love utterly by my foolish jealousy and desertion, I can only say I have deserved it. I know now that, although my dearest earthly wish should be denied, I shall not despair or throw my life away. There is too much to do in this world! It seems to me life broadens and deepens every day. I write this to you, dear, kind friend, for *your* comfort if Hope refuses me, but you may be sure I am terribly in earnest in pleading for her love and promise. It will be very hard to wait two months before I know my fate. It is well that I shall have to be desperately busy, for work has accumulated in my illness, and I must make up for lost time." Wayne mentioned two lucrative offers he had just received, and said they would remain open to him until Hope's answer came.

Miss Winchester was conscious in reading Wayne's letter of a queer, unreasonable sense of regret, as a mother feels that she has lost her boy, in the full-grown man who bends over and kisses her; but that first emotion vanished in hearty thankfulness for his Christian manliness, and she was ready to rejoice with Hope in her new joy.

When Hope returned to Miss Winchester's room, it was with a very different face from any she had shown since Wayne's departure from Norriston. She hurried to cousin Bess and hid her face on her shoulder, saying: "Oh, I am so glad—so glad!" Cousin Bess held her tight and kissed her, and then said, quietly:

"Perhaps, after all, we had better go to Florida or Mentone, dear! Wayne might think something, or say something if we should go to Rio, you know."

"I should be awfully disappointed if he didn't," answered Hope laughing. "You may tease me as much as you like now," said she, raising her April face to kiss Miss Winchester in merry defiance. "I don't mind it one bit!"

CHAPTER IV.

THE SAME.

So letters were written and posted immediately, by way of England, as well as by the American steamer, and Mr. and Mrs. Holland were told the secret of Hope's happy face.

"Indeed, my dear, you couldn't look like Faith, Hope and Charity in one without giving some good reason for it!" remarked old Mr. Holland, blessing her in his kind, fatherly way.

The next evening brought an unusual visitor to the Winchester House, Wayne's father, Grosvenor Halsey, a noble-looking old gentleman, with much of Wayne's irresistible charm of manner.

"I found two letters from my boy on my arrival here from Denver, and ventured to call, Miss Elizabeth, to say how earnestly I hope that my son's suit will be successful. You have been a better friend to Wayne than I have, Miss Elizabeth, and I am glad to acknowledge it. He is a brave fellow, and a far better man than his father is, or ever will be." Then he asked if he might see Hope, whom he remembered only as a bright, pretty little maid of ten. When she entered the room, with a soft blush in her cheeks and a glad light in her eyes, he met her with a courtly grace and gentleness which made her think of her own dear father.

Hope looked on and listened in a sort of dream while Mr. Halsey and Cousin Bess talked together of

Wayne, and a little of old times and old friends. And the story came back to her mind, how she had heard long ago that Mr. Grosvenor Halsey had once upon a time been engaged to Miss Winchester, and then there was some trouble, and he had married Mary Gould, Wayne's mother, who lived only two years after her marriage, leaving a little boy too young to remember her.

Mr. Halsey expressed his regret at hearing of Miss Winchester's illness, and approval of Dr. Butler's decision that she should take the four weeks' voyage to Rio, and winter in that milder climate. Apart from the benefit he trusted she would receive in restored health, he was glad, for a more selfish reason, that Dr. Butler advised Rio instead of Mentone or St. Augustine, as he himself was going to make Wayne a little visit, and would be delighted to be their escort.

Hope looked up astonished and admired Miss Winchester's graceful tact, saying all that was suitable in her simple, unaffected way. When he left, he held Hope's hands for a moment, saying : " I knew your father and mother well, my dear. Wayne will be a fortunate man if he wins their daughter."

Hope looked up shyly, and, with a quick blush, said, gently: "I am very glad you think so, for he did that years ago ! "

Five weeks from that day, at nine o'clock in the evening, the American steamer was entering the harbor of Bahia, the old St. Salvador.

"We shall stay here twenty-four hours," said the captain, " so you will have time in the morning, Miss

Archer, to go ashore and see the queer sights ; go to Baltimore John's and buy humming-birds, and ride up the hill in a Sedan chair on the shoulders of two darkies. What do you want, Jones ? " said he, turning from the group of passengers to speak to the purser.

" Nothing, sir," answered the purser ; " but a gentleman has come aboard and is going down to Rio, but wants his letters before we reach port."

"All right, isn't it ? " " As long as you are sure of him—of his identity."

"Oh ! he has brought the Consul with him, sir."

The captain and Mr. Halsey walked away with the purser, while Miss Winchester turned to Ralph Howland, who for the twentieth time at least had been pointing out to his pretty little wife the wonders of the southern heavens, and to whom he was now showing some of the familiar landmarks on the dimly lighted heights of Bahia.

Miss Winchester and Hope had been much attracted by the enthusiastic, earnest young missionary and the sweet, bright woman he had just "wooed and married and a'."

Many a pleasant hour on the long voyage had been spent in merry tests of Hope's Portuguese, and in planning pleasant drives and excursions in and around Rio.

"You see," said Mr. Howland, with almost boyish eagerness, " Miss Winchester, I have still two weeks' leave of absence and some of my father's wedding present left, which he specially desired we should spend in holiday pleasure together. So Fanny and I have decided to finish our wedding journey before we settle down to our earnest work."

Miss Winchester thought lovingly of Wayne, but she did not speak of him, for it was Hope's wish that their little romance should be kept quiet until Wayne himself should come.

By a sudden impulse Hope moved away from the group. The young moon had already set, and the light of the stars only seemed to make the shadows heavier on the side of the ship away from the lights of the town. Hope walked to the other end of the deck, and turned, standing in the shadow, thinking to herself: "In three more days we shall see Wayne!"

She noticed some one approaching rapidly from the saloon stairway, a stranger, with strong, erect figure and easy carriage, dark eyes and hair, and an air of repressed excitement as well as authority. He was just passing her. Hope's heart beat so fast she thought he must hear it. A mute gesture of her hand—her girlish way long ago of dissuading him from some impulsive act—and he stopped suddenly and seized her hand. "Hope, Hope! is it possible? Is it really you?" exclaimed Wayne, drawing her to a seat in the shadow of a boat.

"Yes, it is my own self," said Hope, trembling so she could hardly speak. "You know Cousin Bess was ill, and the doctor sent her down here."

"No I did *not* know. Oh! then, Hope, you have never received my letter?"

"Oh, yes," replied Hope, gaining composure as Wayne lost his, "and answered it! I suppose my letter is on board this ship!"

"Tell me, Hope ; have pity on me ! " said Wayne, his face growing white with repressed emotion. Hope thought he must surely know already. A sudden, shy impulse prompted her to say it was almost a pity not to wait for her letter. It was a very nice one, and took a whole hour to write.

Wayne turned away and covered his face with his arms, leaning against the boat. "Oh! Hope, Hope ! " he said, " is that all you can say ? "

" Dear Wayne ! " she said, softly, laying her hand against his cheek, don't you *know* my answer ? "

He raised his head. " Is it yes, my darling ? " he whispered, with a glad wonder in his voice.

" It is yes, yes, yes ! " said Hope, softly, "till death us do part ! "

A few moments later Wayne suddenly made his appearance beside Miss Winchester, kissed her affectionately, and grasped his father's outstretched hand, saying: I was coming to look for you, father. I learned only a few minutes ago that a gentleman named Halsey was on board." Then turning to Cousin Bess and looking at her earnestly, he said "Hope says you have been ill. I am so sorry. I hope you are all right now.

"O-ho ! " laughed Mr. Halsey. "So you found a ' living epistle ! ' That accounts for your dropping interest in the mail-bag. The purser has been distractedly seeking the gentleman who was so eager for his letters for at least ten minutes."

Wayne laughingly declared he was still very anxious for his letters, and trusted to his father to identify him.

How they all gathered on the deck that evening, asking and answering questions and receiving explanations, need not be told ; nor how contented Hope was, just listening to Wayne's voice, whether his words were for her alone or for them all.

"Perhaps you do not realize, Wayne," said Miss Winchester, with merry mischief in her voice, "how very difficult it was for me to induce Hope to come here with me ! I believe she was afraid you might think or say something if we came to Rio."

"So I did ! " said Wayne, heartily, with a glad, frank look at Hope. " I thought it was too good to be true. But, since it is true, you needn't imagine I am ever going to let either of you return to America."

"Pretty well for you, my boy ! " said his father, laughing ;"give an inch and take an ell."

" Father, can you not say something for me ? " said Wayne, seriously, as he took his arm and they walked together to the end of the ship.

CHAPTER V.

THE SAME.

THUS it was Miss Winchester and Hope were left to think and speak of Wayne's urgent wish that Hope and he should be married before leaving the steamer.

" It is so sudden, Cousin Bess," said Hope slowly.

" Yes, dear child. But Wayne dreads further separation for you both, and wishes to have the right to take care of you whatever comes. But you must let your own heart decide. If you had rather wait until he has finished his work in the mountains, tell him so, dear."

"Dear Cousin Bess! I don't want to leave you alone in this strange country."

"My dear child," said Miss Winchester, tenderly, "you mustn't trouble your little heart about me; for it is just to please me, particularly, that Wayne proposes to have the ceremony performed before we land, so as to secure the services of Mr. Howland, whom we both must prefer to any stranger. And then, dear, you would not hesitate a moment if you knew how glad it would make me to know that he has, as he says, the right to take care of you, although I should be lonely and miss my sunshine. But he has thought of all this, too, and said he would like you to be with me a while at Petropolis; and he would run out there every few days. He has so many kind friends there that it would not be like being among strangers, you know. My darling, even if I were to be without the sight of your dear face for years, I could not wish to keep you away from Wayne! I have known enough of the chances and changes of this mortal life, little girl, for myself and others; and the hope of seeing you and Wayne happy together in your own Christian home was the thought that gave me courage to start for these 'Golden South Americas.'"

Hope rested her head on Cousin Bess' lap as of

old, and held her dear hand close against her lips in silent love and gratefulness.

"And now I am going to tell you my little secret, Hope!" The young girl lifted her head with a wondering thought of the old story—the unfinished romance of Cousin Bess' girlhood. Miss Winchester saw her thought even before the hurried words were uttered.

"No, dear," laughed Miss Winchester, happily, "I am not going to marry or be married to anybody. My secret is about that mysterious box which I insisted on your packing in my trunk. We must have that brought up, for it has my dear child's wedding-dress and veil, and gloves, slippers and fan, all ready for her. So I shall see you, dear, as a daughter of your own dear mother's should be—'a fair, sweet bride in white.'"

"Oh, Cousin Bess! Cousin Bess!" said Hope, "I haven't any words in which to thank you, and I cannot love you *more* than I do!"

So when Wayne and his father returned from their walk, Hope laid her hand in Wayne's and whispered: "It shall be as you wish, dear. No more partings, if God please."

"No more partings, if God please!" echoed Wayne, as he took Hope on his arm and walked away with her, while Miss Winchester and his father watched them with proud gladness.

"My darling, I can never thank you enough for this! I knew it was a great thing to ask, but it seems to me I could never lose sight of you again."

"It wouldn't be very much easier for me, Wayne,

to have you go off and perhaps be sick and die in those dreadful mountain camps, and never be able to reach you!" said Hope, with a tremor in her voice.

They were standing alone at the stern, watching the wave's steady plash against the ship.

"Heart's dearest," said Wayne, tenderly, bowing his head and thanking her in sweeter fashion than with words.

"My Hope! Not my far-away star Hope any more—thank God!"

Then in quiet talk they made their happy plans together.

"I will see Mr. Howland to-night, dear. I am very glad you and Cousin Bess like him so much, though to tell the truth I wouldn't object to the stupidest man that breathes, so long as he would perform the ceremony to please you, and tie the knot good and tight," said Wayne, laughing.

"You have fairly bewitched my father, Hope; do you know it? He promises to come down and see us every winter, and then insists on our going and staying with him in the summer! Funny, isn't it? The fact is, I suppose, he doesn't realize that I am a hard worker, and am happy and successful in my work, too. Ah! I have so much to work for now."

Before they said good-night, Wayne stopped to look at his letters in the lighted saloon. "Those are for by-and-by," said he, putting Hope's letter and Miss Winchester's in his pocket. Looking at the address of another, his face changed so that Hope exclaimed: "What is it, Wayne; what is the matter?"

He quickly tore the letter open, exclaiming: "Jack!

It's from JACK. It is true. He is not dead! Oh! Hope and Cousin Bess, Jack is alive and well. Thank God. It seems almost too much!"

Then they read his letter together, and learned how, after floating on a piece of a raft for nearly forty-eight hours, he had been picked up by a bark and carried to Madeira. He had been very ill with brain fever, but had recovered entirely, and was stronger than ever now. He had written to Wayne, to his sister, to the owners of the *Santa Lucia* at Rio, as well as to the firm to which he was going in Valparaiso immediately upon landing at Madeira. The Consul and English residents at Madeira had shown him great kindness, and he had accepted a position in a college recently established there, and had sent for his sister to come and live with him. He had wondered at never hearing from Wayne, but had concluded that he had left Brazil, until, he said, "the other day the boy to whom I had given my letters to post, when I landed, came to me and confessed that he had kept the money, and had destroyed the letters without mailing any of them!"

Miss Winchester's kind letter to his sister had been forwarded from place to place, and had been received only the day Jack wrote. How glad he was to hear of Wayne again, and how grateful to Miss Winchester for writing! Except for her kindly sympathy for his sister, he would never have heard again of Wayne, he supposed.

"God's providence again, dear old fellow," wrote Jack. "I hope you love and trust him now!"

"Help me to be thankful all my life, dear Hope,"

6

said Wayne, earnestly. "God has crowned me with loving kindness and tender mercies. Let us live for him, sweetheart!"

Wayne Halsey's wish was fulfilled in a sweeter, fuller sense than he had dared to dream ; for beneath the Southern Cross, dimmed now by the brighter moonlight, he stood with his fair bride, Hope, on his arm, while in the old sweet words they plighted their troth, bowing their heads under the solemn blessing of their Master.

"Whom, therefore, God hath joined together, let not man put asunder."

And so they entered the harbor together!

> No human life there is, so low or mean
>   But, in its widening or its lessening sphere,
> Impinges on some other life, and leads
>   To good and evil, here and after here.

CHAMOUNY AND THE MER DE GLACE.

I.

GENEVA TO CHAMOUNY.

"Some said, ' John print it ; ' others said ' Not so.'
Some said, ' It might do good ; ' others said ' No.' "

THE quaint lines in the preface to " Pilgrim's Progress," which had greatly taken my fancy as a child, came back to mind, when, in April, during a few days' stay in Geneva, we asked counsel concerning the advisability of a trip to Chamouny.

Cook, the ubiquitous, in the person of his agent, replied promptly: "Too early. We do not advise you to go. There is no regular diligence service now,—only one or two lumbering old coaches. We sell no tickets. Possibly in ten days or a fortnight."

Another said : "Go by all means. The drive there is worth your while, even though you should not be able to make any excursions."

"Don't go with a lady unless she is strong and hardy," advised still another. " You will probably find poor accommodations, and be obliged to rough it. If you can, wait a month and then go."

So—we went.

A lovely bright morning was Thursday, the 19th of April. We discussed and settled the mooted question, over our breakfast, sent for Jacques, our charioteer of the day previous, and concluded a bargain, engaging him to drive us in a light calèche, with his uncle's black mare Cotot, to the Hotel Chamouny that night, remain there Friday and bring us back to Geneva Saturday evening.

At nine o'clock we started, with portmanteau, warm wraps and well-filled lunch-basket; landlord, clerk and porters wishing us a pleasant journey and a safe return.

Jacques was a lively Swiss boy from Freiburg,—famous for its grand organ,—of which the young fellow was justly proud. He amused us much by his bright talk on the journey, narrating to us among other things, how he had, the previous summer, conducted to Chamouny Monsieur le Ministre de l'instruction publique, and Madame. Yes, and with this very mare Cotot; how enchanted Monsieur Jules Ferry was with the excursion, with Cotot, with everything; how many hundred francs he had bestowed upon a bridal party at Salenches; how indeed he had given his purse to Jacques, and had asked him to keep account of all the expenses. All this and much more was told, with evident pleasure in the retrospect and with a charming naïveté, quite proof against Maurice's gentle quizzing.

The suburbs of Geneva are indeed lovely, and deserve all that has been said and sung in their praise. For miles the road, along the blue waters of the Lake, is fringed with beautiful villas and pleasure grounds smiling in the presence of the towering mountains, like children playing around the feet of a king.

It was blossom time—a most charming season in any cultivated, fruit-bearing country, and we had not become weary of the flower-laden trees, though our journey had brought us through the peach and orange groves of the Riviera, and the orchards of Tuscany and fertile Lombardy. The road to Chamouny is excellent; a great part of the way lies along the Arve, and the ascent, for thirty or forty miles is very gradual. Beyond Chène, the Mole, a massive pyramid of a mountain, blocks the view. Perched on the rocks near Contamines-sur-Arve rise the two ruined towers of the ancient castle of Farcigny, a most alluring scene for a sketch, if one only were an artist, and could linger by the way. At Bonneville, Jacques, mindful of his good mare, and also, perhaps, of his own second breakfast, ordered Cotot unharnessed and stopped for two hours. We wandered through the little town, wrote a brief bulletin to distant friends, and gave ourselves up to wondering what the people thought and felt, how they lived in their quiet valley-home, locked in by the Brezon and the Mole. Our unuttered question received eloquent answer from the mute marble. Standing before a monument "in honor of the natives of the Department who fell in the Franco-German war," we could easily guess the story of many a home in that valley of Haute Savoie. We passed also a monument to King Charles Felix of Sardinia, which narrates—I really have forgotten what.

About twenty-six miles from Geneva lies the village of Cluses, nearly half way, in point of distance, between Geneva and Chamouny. At the entrance rises a plain, ugly building, Ecole de Horologerie, for this is a watch-makers' village. It looks drearily quiet and precise. However interesting to the lover of his kind may be the humanity, vanquished or victorious, behind those dull walls, the village itself, to a passing stranger, is not attractive. It in no way fulfils my childish ideal of a Swiss watchmaking hamlet, wonderful and picturesque, and I cannot help feeling as, though I had been cheated.

A few miles further brought us close to the bold precipices of the Aiguille de Varens, where we caught the first glimpse of the beautiful cascade of Arpenaz, shooting out from the rocky cliffs on the left, and descending in graceful swaying curves, broken at last by projecting rocks. We were told that it strongly resembles the Staubbach, in the Lauterbrunner. Another waterfall a little beyond, and which seemed to be unnamed, certainly reminded us of the Yosemite Bridal Veil, so ethereal and fairy-like was its descent from the heights above. We had just passed this second cascade when we met two wagon loads of peasants out for a holiday. Jacques informed us that it was a wedding party bound for the chapel of Saint—somebody,—after which they were to return to Sallenches for their wedding feast.

A veritable bridal veil half hid the smiles and blushes of the peasant maid who sat meekly sandwiched between two attendants on the front seat, while in the following wagon, her mother held a like position of honor.

Upon reaching Sallenches, we found, somewhat to our amusement, that Monsieur Jacques had laid his plans to tarry there for the night. (We remembered Jules Ferry and the wedding feast, and wondered whether Jacques mistook us for the American Minister and his wife !)

"Pardon, Monsieur, would it not be far better for Madame ? She must already be excessively fatigued with the long, long journey, and Chamouny is still far distant, and the way is steep, and it will be dark and dangerous, and Cotot cannot travel fast at night, so it would be late, late before we could arrive at Chamouny. But in the early morning, Cotot will travel like the wind, and Madame will be rested, and Monsieur can start as early as he pleases, and reach Chamouny in good time, and have all the day before him ! "

Poor Jacques ! I don't believe he knew that an immortal countryman of ours years ago sang " Excelsior." I am afraid he wished the two "unpretending American citizens " were a little more like the tractable Monsieur Jules Ferry. At last discovering that Maurice remained unmoved by vivid representations of the perils of a midnight drive along precipices and break-neck curves, and the possible fainting of Cotot by the way, as well as by the pleasant tongue of the bright-faced landlady of the little inn, and the charming novelty of a peasant's wedding feast, "a sadder and a wiser man," Jacques disconsolately ordered Cotot to be harnessed, and we again resumed our journey. We were amused to notice that, even in his desperate state of mind, Jacques could not forego the gallant flourish and crack of the whip and spirited rush of Cotot, which marked our departure from every halting-place on the road.

We had lingered so long that the sun was near the horizon when we left Sallenches. Soon the April daylight faded, and the full moon arose in a cloudless sky. It was the close of a perfect day. A few miles beyond Sallenches, we had a lovely view from the crown of a hill which we mounted only to descend, upon Jacques' discovery that he had taken a wrong road.

Before crossing the bridge over the Bon-Nant, we halted at the door of a little inn, and again the persistent Jacques offered us the opportunity to avoid death and destruction by tarrying over night.

Beyond Bon-Nant, the ascent was perceptible; in many places the road being steep. The views grew wilder and grander as we ascended, at times skirting the edge of a precipice, with a towering battlement on one side, and the gorge of the Arve far below. But the drive is entirely safe, the road being kept in excellent order, and protected by walls several feet high, wherever it runs very near the verge.

Leaning over the side of the carriage through the tops of tall pines lining the sides of the gorge, we caught fleeting glimpses of the river rushing from its birthplace in the glaciers of Mont Blanc, towards the far-off lovely waters of Geneva. The moonlight, wonderful glorifier of scenes wild as well as peaceful, gave an unlooked-for charm to the changing scenery. It brought vividly to mind a night drive over the mountains to the Pluton geysers, with a typical California driver, long ago.

Suddenly we plunged into midnight darkness and heard the echoes of a thousand years roaring through the gloom. Beyond the tunnel at the opening of the valley of Le Chatelard, we had a fine view of the irregular, jagged pinnacles of the Aiguilles du Midi.

But the crowning glory of that moonlight drive was the vision of Mont Blanc, suddenly towering before us in unearthly, radiant whiteness. It was impossible then to regard it coolly, as so many feet high, an Alpine summit, which might be scaled by the little race of men.

Beneath far softer skies, Vesuvius stands guard at midnight, with fiery, restless glow, throbbing like the heart of a demon, eager to destroy. Mont Blanc in the moonlight, is a revelation of the beauty of holiness, unapproachable, soul-searching, glorious in purity. Through the solemn silence, in the presence of that heavenly witness, did we not hear the deep heart-cry of the ages, answered, thank God, in the fullness of time on Calvary: " How shall man be just before God ? "

The night wore on, the views became narrower, and at last we entered the Valley of Chamouny. We passed the glaciers de Gria, de Taconay and de Bossons, and saw in the distance the lower part of the Mer de Glace. The first sight of the glaciers was rather disappointing. I could not realize the immensity of those ice-fields. They shone and glistened in the moonlight, while the edges of deep rifts, intersecting them, gleamed like lapus lazuli or sapphire. The beautiful color of the crevasses is noticeable at a great distance. But we had become tired of mountains and glaciers, and were very glad to arrive at our hotel in the slumbering village of Chamouny, and to fall asleep under the shadow of the everlasting hills.

II.

SOFT SNOW ON THE MER DE GLACE.

A CURIOUS sense of the smallness of the world, together with a conviction of the inexorable nature of mundane needs and human limitations, grows upon the traveler as, again and again, recur the appointed times for all things under the sun. One may grow hungry among the buried cities of the past, thirsty on the summit of Vesuvius, sleepy in the Colosseum itself, and dreadfully tired before the oldest pictures of the very oldest masters. So it was not amazing that, after a dreamless sleep, our earliest waking thoughts in the Valley of Chamouny should be divided between breakfast and the Mer de Glace.

While a solemn-looking butler laid the table in the drawing-room, Maurice descended to make inquiries about possible excursions and a guide. I, Dorothy, remained up-stairs and interviewed His Solemn Highness concerning the same absorbing questions. Now in English, and again in French, he asserted that it would be " *tout a fait,* impossible to cross the Mer de Glace at present, that the recent snows were still unmelted, and that no one would undertake such an expedition. To the Chapeau—oh, that was quite possible ! "

After a short absence, up came Maurice cheerfully, and informed me in confidence, that he had begun by mistaking the obsequious landlord for a guide, on the lookout for a party (I believe that mistake was registered in the bill), but that he had found one, and engaged him to take us wherever he judged it safe and our one day would permit. The guide was an accredited one of ten years' standing and was to provide a peasant with two mules ; they were to be ready in half an hour. The landlord had tried to dissuade Maurice from attempting any excursion, as the day was cloudy, and already a mist was gathering, but to those who have no to-morrow, to-day is precious, even though it be not one of sunshine.

So we ate our breakfast, of which I remember one item, the delicate white honey, for which, as well as the Mer de Glace, Chamouny is noted.

Of course it was very commonplace and by millions of sensations removed from that æsthetic Nirvana, apparently the goal of our exotic Anglo-Hindoo civilization, but it seemed to me almost too good to be true that we were really *there*, at Chamouny, and just about to start for we didn't know what. A vague doubt arose in my mind as to my personal identity, and I told Maurice I felt like the old dame in the Mother Goose of our childhood, who woke up and exclaimed :

> " If this indeed be I,
> As I suppose it be ! "

Before I descended to mount my mule, the kind old landlady questioned me as to the warmth of my wrap and the stoutness of my boots, and solemnly advised me to go no further than the Chalet at the Chapeau. " Even though Monsieur should go, Madame, do not you ! Once I went, and in fine weather, but never again ! "

In the presence of the landlord and servants waiting, continental fashion, around the door, Maurice repeated to Paul that he wished to go to the Chapeau, and if he judged it safe, to Montanvert, across the Mer de Glace, that we desired to see as much as we could in our one day, and must leave the question of safety to him as guide.

We rode through the little village, Paul holding the bridle of my mule, and Blue-blouse walking beside Maurice. It made me feel as though I were five years old again, and taking my first ride, but it afforded an excellent opportunity to practice my French at Paul's expense, and to gain some local information. The mules were evidently used to bridle paths and trained to travel only in single file. After some futile attempts to bring his animal abreast of mine and be sociable, Maurice subsided and jogged along behind, like a smoking philosopher.

Before breakfast, a pleasant-faced Swiss maid had pointed out to me by name the various mountain-peaks bounding the valley, so I felt a little acquainted with the Brevent and the Aiguilles Rouges, and the grand Mont Blanc chain. It seemed to me we were too close to them to see them truly. As we rode through the valley, Paul exchanged occasional remarks with those we met, but they spoke such a singular patois that I could not understand what was said. They looked at us rather curiously, and sometimes shook their heads. I was very sorry that they seemed to disapprove of us, but there was no help for it.

The short and usual route to the Mer de Glace from Chamouny is by the Montanvert, but it was impassable by reason of the still unmelted snows. Paul pointed out the direction of the bridle-path, past the English church and across the meadows, saying : " In the summer we pass up there, but at present it is not possible, we must now make a detour and reach the Mer de Glace, perhaps, from the Chapeau."

Strange that this lovely valley, with its numerous hotels and fifteen or twenty thousand of visitors yearly, should, six centuries ago, have borne such a villainous reputation that no traveler dared sleep a night in any house in the neighborhood ! One cannot but admire the religious heroism of St. Francis de Sales, in forcing his way on foot, somewhere in 1600, into this dark corner of his diocese, to look after the "few sheep in the wilderness of les Montagnes Maudites." I am very thankful our lot was not cast in those "good old times."

After an hour's ride, the latter part of the way up a zig-zag bridle-path on the edge of a mountain, we dismounted and left our mules in charge of Blueblouse until our return. Then we began to climb. The way was rather rough, but jagged rocks may be scaled, and there was some interest in walking on the crust of snow twenty or thirty feet deep—snow which had once fallen in an avalanche and was therefore slow to melt. Maurice went ahead, like a born mountaineer.

"Monsieur needs no guide," remarked Paul. He

was evidently of a contrary opinion regarding Madame.

The Chalet is only a rude little hut, with over-hanging roof, set, for the sake of shelter, in an angle of the mountain. We made the pleasing discovery, that, although open to travelers during the season, it was now closed and locked.

A proposal of the guide, to leave Madame sitting on a plank outside the Chalet, with a lunch-basket, for three or four hours in a fine drizzle, while Monsieur and the guide should attempt to cross the Mer de Glace, was received with small favor. Besides, I cherished the secret conviction that Maurice would run fewer risks if I were along.

"Very well, Madame! Then we will forward by the Mauvais Pas. It is properly called La Roche de Muret, and truly I think it does not merit its evil name."

We paused a few minutes and looked up and down the glacier. Miles away, beyond our sight, the river of ice, like the summer river, has its birthplace among the everlasting hills, and, like other rivers, receives tributaries, forms cataracts, presses through narrow gorges and again widens out into a broader and smoother channel. But it looks like an irregular mass of snowy hills piled up in a lofty gorge, the tumbled massive waves running in a general direction parallel with the sides of the gorge, their monotonous whiteness being relieved at intervals by the gleam of blue rifts intersecting them. Opposite us, back of the Montanvert, rose the Aiguilles de Charmoz and du Midi, and the Dôme and Aiguille du

Gouter, both in the mist ; even the sharp outlines of the Aiguille du Midi were indistinct.

Our path lay along the face of a sheer precipice, the foot of the Aiguille du Bochard (as I learned afterwards), which thrusts itself out to the margin of the glacier. Then and there, I took my first lesson in Alpine climbing, a very easy one it doubtless appears to mountaineers, but it was quite enough for a novice who was not endowed by Nature with the apparatus of a fly, suitable for locomotion along a vertical plane. I admit that there are nicks in the perpendicular rocks, but I rejoice to have the testimony of Prof. Forbes to the fact that those rocks are very slippery.

There is also a slender iron bar, riveted at intervals to the face of the rock, but just where it was most needful, turning a corner, or at a fearfully steep place, was it not sure to be missing?

Paul was in advance and led me, while Maurice followed close behind, but I confess I crept along trembling and nervous. Occasionally I was forced to glance down the sheer precipice to the chilly peaks of the glacier below. Comfortless as it looked down there, I silently echoed the Shepherd boy's song :

> " He that is down need fear no fall ! "

At last I grew dizzy and told Maurice I was going to fall, I could go no further, that he must let me go back to the Chalet, and he could then go on if he wished, with the guide. He quietly assured me that it would be more difficult to return than to go forward, that he was morally certain I could do it with perfect safety, and that he wasn't in the slightest degree dizzy himself. Paul asserted that there was absolutely no danger whatever, and that moreover we were very near the end of that unpleasant path. I reflected that probably thousands of my fellow-women—among them some of our own friends—had traversed that path before me without accident, so I plucked up courage and held on my trembling way, remembering with hearty repentance the occasions in the past, when I had secretly considered very unnecessary the tremors of nervous friends. "Maurice," I confessed, "the pride is all taken out of me; I *used* to think I was a good climber!"

Then we began to descend along a snowy ledge towards the moraine. I tried to walk as Paul directed, in his footsteps, but they were a little too large, and again and again the soft snow around my feet yielded, and Maurice caught me as I was about to take a short route to the glacier. Paul, perceiving the difficulty, turned to make some nicks in the snow with his pick, which made my progress very comfortable. He was, perhaps, fifteen feet in advance of us, Maurice having taken the guide's place in leading me, when we heard a queer, hollow, crackling sound above us, almost as though it were in the sky. Paul looked back and upward, and with a sharp cry, began to run forward along the ledge, calling out with frantic gestures, to hurry us (I think I hear him now!): "'n avalanche, 'n avalanche, avancez, vite, vite, toujours, toujours avancez, dangereux—!"

III.

THE SAME.

FROM the white heights directly above us, tore down masses of rock and snow, tumbling, crashing, leaping from cliff to cliff, falling just where we had been walking, and sweeping every obstacle out of their way, in their final plunge over the brink.

How we ever ran so swiftly along that slippery, slushy ledge I do not know. There was only time for a heart-cry to the Helper, and He surely heard and answered, granting the strength and sure-footedness we needed.

When we reached the spot where the guide awaited us, there was very little breath to spare, for a few minutes. We still heard the rattle of rocks and débris falling down the sides of the precipice. "A few seconds more!" said Maurice.

Paul remarked by way of apology: "It is very seldom that it happens thus. In the summer there is no danger from the avalanche. Only in the spring, when as now, the warm days come at first, and the snow above begins to melt, loosening the earth around the rocks and trees, it needs but the slightest jar to start an avalanche! Ah, in the summer, it is quite, quite safe, and also in the winter, but just now, it is not! We shall have no more now," he added cheerfully.

The moraine was not pleasant to climb ; the route along it stands out in my memory as an appropriate type of the course of true love. Not being notably scientific, we did not pause to examine the structure of the jagged rocks which gave their weighty, silent testimony to the irresistible downward course of the mighty ice-river. All my mental and physical muscle was engaged in scrambling over, jumping across, or squeezing between those disagreeable rocks. "Monsieur should ascend Mont Blanc," ejaculated Paul. "He could do it well, not now, but" (as usual) "in the summer. He is a veritable chamois." I noticed Paul didn't propose that Madame should ascend Mont Blanc! My mind had become reconciled to the idea of scaling rocks indefinitely, and, being much interested in taking one step at a time, I was quite unprepared for the guide's announcement, in his presentation tones: "Behold, Madame, the Mer de Glace."

As Paul would say "in the summer," it would doubtless appear quite different, but under the dull sky that April day, it was dreary and lonely as an arctic snowfield. Looking up and down the glacier, as far as eye could reach,—and of course the range was limited, both on account of the curving sides of the gorge and the mist,—there was no track or trace of man. It was difficult to realize that the billowy frozen sea on which we stood was bearing us along at the rate of twenty or thirty inches every twenty-four hours, toward Chamouny.

Now came the momentous question—should we try to cross the glacier?

Paul cautiously remarked: "The snow is perhaps not too soft. In the summer (!) there is no difficulty. There remain then, only the unmelting snow and ice, and one can well see the crevasses. Now, many are hidden by the lately fallen snows, but—If Monsieur pleases, I will advance and sound the snow."

He returned and said we could at least try; we might go a little way even if we should not be able to cross the glacier. It was like forcing a passage through snowdrifts of various depths, over possible chasms and through, what was to us, an absolutely trackless waste. Paul directed me, as before, to walk in his steps, an experience not always to be desired, for he occasionally sunk to his waist in the snow, and I, unlike George the Third, desiring to "profit" by the example of my predecessor, only repeated the experiment after him. Maurice held in his hand a light olive-wood stick, which had done him pleasant service climbing Vesuvius, and was now useful in gauging the depth of the snow; so he often avoided the pitfalls into which we in advance frequently disappeared. His strong hand was always ready to help me up, but once in a while my foot became tightly wedged in a crack of the rocks and it was necessary for Paul to dig the snow away all around me before Maurice and he could extricate me. It certainly was amusing, though it was pretty hard work too. I could not help thinking what a peculiar series of instantaneous views and disappearances we would have afforded to a photographer. If the moraine yielded special opportunities for climbing, the snow-path across the glacier was as abundant in frantic plunges. The danger lay in the unseen crevasses. Several times Paul cried out just as we were stepping over the verge. The soft snow lies over the mouths of these yawning gulfs, and often only a narrow zigzag line, where it has begun to melt, reveals to the practised eye the hidden danger. Once I began to slip into a crevasse, or moulin,—I don't know which it was. Paul and Maurice were near enough to seize me by my arms, draw me up, and set me safely on the further side, before I was aware that it was anything more than an ordinary plunge. It was not pleasant to think of going down suddenly 600, 300, or even 100 feet out of sight. The snow had been loosened by my plunge so there was an open chasm behind me ; Maurice bent down and looked into it. "There's a hole as big as a house down there, and I don't know how deep. There seems to be a black pool at the bottom, but the sides are as blue as the sky." Paul and Maurice threw some ice and stones down the fissure, I suppose for the pleasure of hearing the hollow rattling sound. It gave me a positively sickening sensation. It seemed as though one of us might so easily disappear and perish, while those left behind would be utterly powerless to help or save.

If one were disposed to moralize, the formation of these blue-lipped glacier chasms would yield a fitting type of the growth of evil. First, the imperceptible downward progress, then a check resulting in a strain, an over-strain, and then a tiny fissure, a line, Tyndall says, too narrow to receive his knife-blade, but it is "the little rift within the lute." And so, day after day, month after month, slowly, slowly but ever surely, it grows and widens and at last becomes a chasm of death. Ah ! it is not an agreeable subject. The only pleasant consideration is that sometimes, under pressure, crevasses have been known to close. We will take the consolatory hope in carrying out the comparison.

At length Paul remarked: " Behold, Monsieur, we are across the Mer de Glace. Before us is the Montanvert."

" How about going up to the hotel," queried Maurice.

" No, no, Monsieur. That is altogether impossible at present. Also, the hotel is still closed."

Between us and the snow-covered side of the Montanvert, lay a trackless bed of snow. Should we go further ?

" Just as Monsieur and Madame desire. We are, in fact, across the Mer de Glace " (a gentle fiction, invented in the interest of safety, I imagine). " Between us and the rocks, there is only the same as you have already traversed,—snow and crevasses, and the snow lies very deep in those hollows. If I had brought a rope, we might attempt to cross there," pointing to some jutting icy crags, " but without a rope it would not be safe." His only excuse for not providing himself with the ordinary equipment of a guide, was that he had not imagined we would desire to venture so far.

With a man's natural dislike to stop short of the goal, Maurice was disposed to go forward. Paul advised in such case, that Madame should remain and await their return. Madame, however, objected, and Paul thereupon confessed that he did not know just where the crevasses lay,—there were fewer on the Montanvert side than by the Chapeau, but the snow had thawed very little, and there would probably be no trace of the lips of the fissures, and it would be necessary to sound before every step.

I looked across the smooth, unbroken whiteness, hiding danger and perhaps death, under so fair and peaceful an exterior.

Much to my relief, Maurice turned to me and said : " Dorothy, the man's afraid himself ; it would be simply foolhardy for us to insist upon going, just for a whim."   And so it was decided.

" Very well, Monsieur, then does Madame desire to rest and take some refreshment before we return ? "

A fine drizzle and a deepening fog rendered us all quite willing to postpone rest and luncheon until later.   Paul showed me the direction in which we had crossed the glacier.   It was a little south of west, by Maurice's compass.   " We must return by another route," remarked Paul, " for we wish not to go back along the path where the avalanches now so easily fall.   Permit me, Monsieur, to go forward and discover whether a short way is possible.   Otherwise we must walk much further on the glacier."   Maurice and I waited for him and looked around us.   It was a desolate scene, a vast moor of ice and snow. Over towards the Chapeau, we could see the shimmer of crevasses even under the deepening fog.   I was glad that dear friends across the sea could not see us just at that moment.   Twice Paul returned saying: " It is impossible.   If I had a rope ! but without a rope, no ! "   The fog seemed to grow heavier every moment.   Paul and Maurice looked at each other in silence.   " We have trusted ourselves to you," said Maurice quietly. "We will follow where you lead. It is for you to decide."

"Then, forward along the glacier. It is far, and Madame must be already very tired, but it is the only way."

I declared myself quite ready, and indeed felt entirely content that I was not obliged to attempt to be a fly again, although by this time possible avalanches and the Mauvais Pas had lost much of their terrors.

It was truly a long walk and a fatiguing one along the glacier, but we had become accustomed to plunging through snowdrifts and jumping across crevasses, and realized that every moment was precious, for the fog was heavy. I wondered how Paul could discover any landmarks, and a story came back to my mind which I had read when a child, about a highland shepherd girl who had perished in the cruel mist close beside her father's door. It did not seem incredible.

Maurice was still behind us. I begged him to speak often, to assure me of his safety. It seemed to me that he was sometimes in danger; he afterwards told me of two very narrow escapes on that homeward march.

I fancy Paul feared that my strength or courage would fail, for he frequently assured Maurice that he might truly be proud of Madame; that she walked remarkably well and possessed marvelous endurance.

After we had fairly recrossed the glacier, he remarked that ours had been a very unusual experience; that not one of a hundred ladies could have made such a success; that the route we had taken was equal to crossing the Mer de Glace three times;

that the passage in the summer was nothing in comparison, and wound up by declaring, in true French
style, that he was perfectly charmed with Madame.

I think he was deeply grateful to me for not fainting in some inconvenient place on the way, which,
judging from my bad beginning on the Mauvais Pas,
he probably imagined quite possible. At all events
we found him a very pleasant and respectful guide.

We left the glacier at a point considerably north
of the one where we had struck it several hours previous. After a very rough climb over the moraine,
Paul pausing a moment on an immense boulder, to
look, although in vain, for some Alpine stones for us,
we regained the path, and soon reached the spot
where we had deposited our lunch basket near the
chalet.

The fog lay thick and white over the snowy valley
which we had left, but on ascending, we found a
clearer atmosphere.

Once again we heard the rushing, hollow sound of
an avalanche, but this time it was a smaller one,
entirely of snow. It lodged on a cliff above us, so
there was no need to run. Thereupon Paul remarked
with emphasis: "Monsieur and Madame are very
fortunate. They have to-day seen something of different kinds of Alpine dangers, avalanches, crevasses,
fog. What more could one desire than safely to
come through them all?"

"Very true!" responded Maurice, and, to me
"Allee samee, he ought to have brought a rope."

But behold, Blue-blouse and the mules quite as
tired of waiting, I fancy, as we were of walking. I

mounted my mule, but Maurice preferred to walk. So in due time, we arrived at the hotel, safe and sound, with a comfortable and reassured sense of personal identity and a grateful appreciation of a good fire, and warm, dry clothing.

So ended our.brief experience of soft snow on the Mer de Glace.

If any one who reads this true record, should ever be tempted to try the experiment himself, let me herewith impart to him, freely and emphatically, the often quoted advice of Punch, though truly not in the spirit of that delightful and unblushing cynic:

"*Don't!*"

HOW GERTY MORSE SAID "YES."

———

"Go away, Joe, please, I'm busy."
"Gertrude Lathrop Morse, spinster, are you deaf?"
"Yes, and rapidly becoming more so!"
"I believe it!   Here I've been

> Croaking, croaking, croaking at your chamber door,
> Like a too, too Poe-tical raven evermore,
> Till I'm ready to denounce the world in general,
> And you in particular, an awful Bore,"

chanted Joe, dismally.   Then, suddenly bursting into vigorous matter-of-fact prose, he exclaimed: "I say, it's downright mean of you, Gerty.   What's the use of having a sister that shuts herself up so?   Do let a fellow in!   I want to whisper something to you. It's a secret really and truly."   The door opened slowly, Joe entered, and coolly seated himself at Gertrude's desk.

"Halloo!   If she isn't writing poetry, as sure as I'm alive!"

"Now, Joseph Morse!"   Wrath shone in Gerty's eyes, and saucy Joe cried out:

"Honor bright!   I haven't read a single line. Come Gerty, don't you be mean.   Do come down, like a good sister;"—kissing her.

"A sister of Charity, I suppose, to pick out your tangles, and make some more flies!   What is the special work you've prepared for me now?—for I know very well you don't coax me with kisses for nothing, you saucy boy," said Gertrude laughing.

"It won't require any particular martyrdom on your part," replied Joe dryly, "or at least it wouldn't, if you girls ever could appreciate a splendid fellow when you happen to see one!"

"Poor darling," retorted Gerty soothingly. "Have the girls been cross to him? He shall be appreciated, so he shall;" and Gertrude patted Joe's broad shoulders with a mocking pity that was as bewitching as it was exasperating. Joe received it with scornful silence. It was very aggravating to him to be two years younger than Gerty, and to have her treat him like a boy. She always seemed to forget he was a Sophomore now. He had learned, however, that he could punish Gerty by keeping still.

"Well!" queried Gerty, at last: "If you don't want anything, please go, and let me rest in peace."

"I shall not," replied Joe, emphatically. "Chester finds he cannot walk far without getting lame, and he won't let me disappoint Tom by breaking up the fishing party. Bother those old Rebs. Don't you remember how he used to run and leap? I tell you though, to see how jolly he is, in spite of it, makes a man with two strong legs feel small," remarked Joe, rather inconsequently. Gerty thought she would like to give him a hug, but restrained her sisterly admiration. Joe continued: "I can't expect you to appreciate him, of course. It takes a man, to do that;" rising in the majesty of his seventeen years, and walking about the room, with his hands in his pockets.

"I am very sorry your fishing party is spoiled," said Gerty, "although you hadn't the grace to invite me to join you."

"Oho! Is that it, my lady gay? Well it *was* a shame, but I never thought of it myself. Chester did say—wouldn't my sister go ; but I guessed not—thought you couldn't walk so far."

"Very well, I consider this a special punishment on you, for your unbrotherly conduct."

"All right," returned Joe, accepting her views on retributive justice with cheerful alacrity, "and now, Gerty, do come down and look after Chester until we come back." Gerty gave a little shrug. "Have Major Chester's endless resources failed him, that he is forced to depend upon a girl for amusement?"

"Come, Gerty, do be sensible." Joe's good-natured face wore a look of unusual seriousness. "I can't, for the life of me, understand why you are so contrary. When we were children, you cared ten times more for Gilbert than I ever did, and nearly cried your eyes out when he went to the war ; and now—you'll scarcely speak to him, and treat him almost like a stranger. I'm sure he was as good as pie to you always, and, just the other day, I thought he would have taken my head off, because I said I guessed all girls flirted, when they had a chance. 'A man,' he replied (Major Chester had said 'a boy '), 'with a good sister like yours, has no right to speak or think so.' Now Gerty come, that's a dear. You know you're the lady of the house."

"Joseph, you have conquered—I surrender. Hospitality is a savage virtue, and as such I admire it, and practice it alike on friend and foe. Be easy. I will entertain your friend," declared Gerty, dropping her grand lady airs as she added, "as soon as I have put my things away."

"Very good; then I'll have Chester in the summer-house on the knoll. I'll be home by five o'clock, whether we have any luck or not. So make the most of your time, my dear Gerty," remarked Joe wickedly, as he swung himself out of the room and down the stairs, singing airily:

> "How doth my pretty sister G.
> Improve the shining hour,
> To sing a song in major C.
> Within the garden bower."

Gertrude's door closed with a bang. "Joe is too outrageous," said she, half aloud, as she pressed her hands to her flushed cheeks."

She is a pretty picture as she stands indignant, rosy, tremulous, by her open window, with its screen of morning-glories. Somebody suggests that writers, who assert their heroines to be beautiful, should be required to furnish their photographs, for the benefit of their readers. For my part, I should not be a bit afraid of the public verdict, if I could only show you a picture of Gerty, as she was fifteen years ago. But the terror of the law is upon me, for I was brought up to respect the sentiment expressed in the ancient couplet:

> "Whoever takes what isn't his'n,
> If he's found out, must go to prison."

Of course, I should be found out—I always am. So I refrain, and the public is thereby the loser, and must be content with the following, in white and black :

Her forehead is broad, low and well shaded by wavy brown hair, very thick and soft; which has never known neither shall ever know, bang, frizz or crimp. Her mouth is generous and sweet, full of humor and character. She has a good nose, and a lovely chin with a dimple in the centre, which just matches the one in her left cheek. But the powerful charm of her face is in the eyes,—expressive, eloquent, true eyes; quick to flash with fun or anger, and ready to grow tender and luminous over some deed or thought heroic. Tell-tale eyes they are, whose honesty is not lessened by the dark lashes, which shade while they heighten their beauty. I maintain that eyes are generally windows of the soul. At least, it was and is so with Gerty's eyes. No shallow, petty, selfish soul ever looked through such star-lit windows. The eyebrows are the color of the hair, well defined—a little too heavy for perfect beauty, but all the more in character.

She is taller than the Venus de Medici, graceful and girlish, with head well set, and figure well rounded.

She can row and ride, make bread and beds, nurse the sick, as well as laugh her father's whimsical patients into good humor; she can sing like a bird, frolic like a kitten, frown like a thundercloud and smile like the sunshine. She does much, by her sisterly fondness and frankness, to keep Joe a good boy; she pets her father, and orders the house. The servants love and obey her, and old Martha is the only one who scolds her, yet she treats her like a young queen. One more line in the picture, for the sake of honesty. O gentle critic, spare her! Once in a while, Joe declares, Gerty lets down her back hair, and tries to write poetry. There is a tradition that she even went so far as to send, to the Bard's Magazine, a Scotch poem, which was declined with thanks, as being in a foreign dialect. There was, however, sweetness mingled with the bitter of this experience. The secret had been confided to Joe, in one of his college vacations, and they had both agreed that it must have been really very good Scotch, quite as good as "Auld Lang Syne," or it wouldn't have been supposed to be a foreign language. This is the secret which hangs like Damocles' sword over Gerty's head, for wicked Joe is a born tease, and she never feels sure that he will not some time "tell."

But while I have been drawing Gerty's picture, the original has vanished from the room, with her scrap book under her arm, and some fleecy knitting-work in hand; and, soon after Joe's departure, she appeared, serenely sweet and hospitable, within the Garden Bower.

"I think I am very good and forgiving," she said, smiling, "to take any notice of you, after you all forsook me in such a shabby fashion this morning, without even giving me the chance to decline going with you."

"It was certainly very cruel to rob you of your natural prerogative, merely on the strength of a foregone conclusion," said Chester with an answering smile; "however, but for our shameful defection, your noble magnanimity would have remained to this moment, like America without her Columbus, an undiscovered continent," he added with a bow.

"Thank you," replied Gertrude frigidly; "if that is all your apology, I am afraid you may speedily be forced to explore a good-sized continent in the polar regions of my nature."

Chester looked up, with a quizzical smile. It seemed so absurd to be making stiff speeches to each other. He placed a chair by the table, where Gertrude had seated herself with her work, arranging it so that it nearly faced her in comfortable *tête-à-tête.* She looked up from her knitting, and met his friendly eyes smiling at her. "I've no fancy for Arctic explorations; besides, they don't take lame fellows. They're only in the way, you know. Don't send me off there, please. I won't do so any more."

"That sounds more penitential," said Gertrude, laughing. "I don't bear any malice."

"Then, as a proof of forgiveness, let me watch you knit that wonderful gauzy stuff—worsted, is it, or yarn? I used to know how to do plain knitting, but I am not very good at fancy stitches," continued he, with gravity.

Gertrude looked up in amazement. There was something to her so incongruous in the idea of that broad-shouldered, bronzed young man, with his strong, shapely hands, doing fancy knitting. "Where under the sun?" exclaimed she, beginning a question more emphatic than elegant. "Oh! I beg pardon, I did not mean to be inquisitive."

"Nothing you could ask would ever be that. I learned to knit in a southern prison, and kept it up in the hospital. We had only two knives among thirty of us, so we hadn't much opportunity to enjoy the Yankee luxury of whittling, even when we could find a stick or a bone to work on. Mother has the only carvings I made, and she has a piece of my knitting, too," said he, smiling as he watched Gerty's soft fingers. "It is nothing like this," touching her work, a marvel of fleecy rosiness.

"What is it like, what is it made of?" asked Gerty, hurriedly.

"It is made of bits of cord, and is like Mrs. Penelope's web, in that it has been raveled and re-knit about a hundred times. You can't imagine how one learns to coin amusement out of such miserable trifles. We used to invent puzzles, and work out problems with pebbles and sticks—that is, while we had brains and energy enough. But, indeed, I didn't mean to talk about those times," said he, wondering a little at Gerty's silence. "I've been an egotistical fool," he exclaimed, catching a glimpse of Gerty's face.

"Oh! no, no!" she said, recovering herself as suddenly, with a laugh; "I'm a terribly weak-minded person in certain directions. Some stories and some songs always make me behave like a goose. But thank you for telling me. Don't you want to copy some recipes for me, or read aloud?"

"Agreed, one or both. What is this book—an album?"

"I hate albums," said Gertrude, energetically.

8

"Then may I inquire what I am to call it, seeing it has 'album' in hieroglyphics on the back? I took it for one."

"I never noticed that before," said Gerty, penitently; "but call it a scrap book,—a sketch book,—a cookery book, or all three in one, please, but not an album."

"A wonderful volume! In the literary line, a parallel to the crew of the Nancy Bell," mused Chester; "I'm truly afraid of it."

"I'd like to have those two recipes copied on that page," said she, quietly. "Then, whenever I make a 'Queen of Puddings' or a celestial, rosy strawberry short-cake—"

"'When this you see, remember me,'" quoted Chester.

"Exactly," said Gertrude, lightly. "Will you purchase remembrance at such a price?"

"I will, if I may do it in pencil."

"Very well, if you don't care whether it is rubbed out or not," said she, quickly.

"I shall trust to your desire to retain the recipes," replied Chester. "Now, while I bend my energies to the task, may I beg that you will not interrupt me by any frivolous remarks."

Gertrude looked up, with a flash of her eyes, half-provoked, half-amused. Don't be afraid. On occasion, a woman is able to keep still. May I ask you, dear sir," she added sweetly, "that you will not disturb me while I count my stitches?" Their eyes met with laughter; for a while both heads were bent, and both were silent. But Gerty's thoughts were busy. She wondered if Chester remembered their parting, seven years ago, when she, a child of twelve, had clung to him, passionately declaring she was sure he would be killed, and she didn't want him to go. Then, how he had kissed her and quieted her, comforting her little heart by asking her to pray God, every night and morning, to bless him, and keep him safe and bring him home. She remembered how she had seen him go off, walking straight and soldierly in his uniform, and she hadn't cried a bit, until he was out of sight. Oh! how good and kind Mrs. Gilbert had been to Joe and herself in that sorrowful time at home, when their own dear mother was taken from them. What lovely letters Chester had written to her, and how gentle he had been when he came to see them, twice during his short leave of absence. Then came the news of his promotion for gallant conduct, and next the report that Major Chester was severely wounded and a prisoner. And when he was at last exchanged and came home, Gerty was away at school. Last year they had met, and he had called her Miss Morse, and said he could scarcely hope to be remembered after the chances and changes of all these years. "How could he think so," cried Gerty's faithful little heart, "when I have kept on praying for him every night and morning, never forgetting him any more than papa or Joe!" It was strange, Gerty thought, to have such a gulf between them, now that she was grown up; but, somehow, to-day she didn't feel shy with him,—only, as she sat there counting her stitches, she wondered whether Major Gilbert remembered how good he had been to a little girl, seven years ago.   She never dreamed that the sight of her young beauty, the sense of her unconscious loveliness smote Chester Gilbert with a pain, which grew the keener as he told himself, again and again, what folly it was for him, a maimed fellow nearly thirty years old, to hope to win her.

Suddenly, she came back to the present, and became aware that her companion was looking up from his paper too frequently for a successful copyist. She dropped her work, and watched him intently. "Treason, treason!" she exclaimed.

Chester looked up, merrily finishing the quotation: "If this be treason, make the most of it."   He laid the book on Gertrude's lap.   Her cheeks flushed, as she looked at the sketch he had made, of a child with upraised arms and sorrowful, lovely face.

"I don't see how you could," said she, in confusion at the unexpected answer to her thoughts.

"I have a pretty good memory for faces, and then I had the original before me, you know.   Here are your recipes, too, on this other page."

"Thank you, ever so much," replied Gerty, gently.

Chester turned the pages of the scrap book with some curiosity.   "A queer medley," he thought to himself;—"The Song of the Camp," "The Wind and the Moon," "Blackberry Jam," "To a Skylark," "Jock o' Hazeldean," "Soft Gingerbread," "Maud Muller," "Sweet Pickles," "Beyond," "The Marseillaise," etc.   "Shall I read something aloud?"

"Yes, please," replied Gerty, with inward trepidation, but external calm.

"Here is something Scotchy, if you won't criticise

my Gaelic too severely. It is half as hard to read as
Burns, though;" and Chester began to read, while
Gerty listened, with her head bent over her pretty
work, apparently deeply interested in the intricate
border.

"What a dear, wilful, little lassie, and what a
charming experience," commented Chester.

"Very improper," answered Gerty.

"I wonder if such an experience would be possible,
outside of Scotland, or whether it is strictly a Scotch
article."

"Indigenous to the soil, like blue-bells and gorse,
not known to flourish elsewhere," declared Gerty,
positively.

"Ah! but there you are wrong, for I have found both
gorse and blue-bells on this side of the water, but
never a Jeanie. Do you think there is any chance
of finding one?"

"I cannot say. You had better take the next
steamer for Scotland," advised Gerty stiffly; "American girls don't usually behave in that fashion."

"You mean," said Chester, slowly, "that a fellow,
scarred and disfigured as Allen was, wouldn't have
any chance,—that naturally he would be only pitied,
or worse, be scorned, by a bright, fair American girl."

"Oh! no, I didn't mean that, at all," exclaimed
Gerty with an eager protest in her lovely eyes. "It
must have been Allen himself that Jeanie cared for—
probably"—replied she, now too interested to be
coherent.

"Yes, of course," said Chester, quickly, "only an
Allen Graeme could win a Jeanie."

Gerty was silent. She wished her cheeks would not burn so. What did it matter? She wondered if she had said anything dreadful. Anyhow, it wasn't fair to think Scotch lassies so much nicer than American girls.

"Do you remember The Initials," inquired Chester, suddenly. "Whose?" replied Gerty, surprised. "Mine, for instance," said Chester, mischievously bending toward her with a monogram he had just drawn in her book.

"Oh! said Gertrude hastily. "How stupid of me! You mean that German story. Baroness Tautphœus wrote it, didn't she?"

"Very possibly—I cannot say. Did she write Allen Graeme too?"

"Very possibly—I cannot say," echoed Gertrude, saucily, yet with a growing conviction that either Joe had "told," or Chester had guessed her secret, and was merely teasing her.

"Well," resumed Chester judicially, "I don't believe any German woman ever wrote that Scotch piece ; now do you ?"—appealingly.

"Why should *any one* have written it ?" answered Gertrude, parrying the question, with a despairing clutch at her vanishing courage.

"Why, indeed," repeated Chester. "If it is a conundrum, I give it up, only I'm glad somebody did write it."

There was a moment's silence, like the lull before the breaking of a storm. Then poor Gertrude, driven to desperation, rose hastily, saying : "Please excuse me, I must see about lunch." In her haste to escape, her fleecy knitting caught on Chester's rustic chair. Her fingers trembled so, she could not loosen it.

"Oh! let me undo it," begged he. Gerty sat down. She could not stand, and she could not loosen the tangle of her thoughts. "Poor child," said Chester, gently. The words were trivial, but the tone was a caress. Gerty's last fortress was destroyed—the tears rushed to her eyes. She wished she were a little child again, to be petted and comforted. Mortified, perplexed, indignant—a rush of contending emotions overpowered her. She hid her face in her arms on the table.

"Forgive me, Gerty—it was mean, I know, to tease you so," said Chester, penitently.

"No I won't," replied Gertrude, suddenly recovering herself, and asked, with a nervous little laugh, "What for?"

"For making such a blundering Rory O'More, said Chester, playfully.

Gertrude felt a wild impulse to escape. What if Joe should come along? Suddenly, Chester spoke again—his voice was tremulous with suppressed feeling.

"Gerty, I must speak. Forgive me if it is ungenerous—won't you let me see your face—if I ought to be silent. I cannot tell you, and you could never guess, what the thought of you has been to me all these years. Do you thing I have ever forgotten how you clung to me, a dear little child, seven years ago? I don't know when I began to cherish the hope, Gerty, that, some day, I might win that little child, grown to womanhood, to be the light of my home—my wife. But, O Gerty, God knows how hard it was to come back, maimed for life, even if it was for our country's sake, to see you in your girlish beauty and loveliness,—to realize what utter folly it would be to think of your ever caring for a maimed fellow like me!"

"O Chester, Chester, how dare you say so?" Gertrude's face was suddenly lifted. In her eloquent eyes, he read the story of her faithful heart. Gaining courage, she tells him he is far dearer for all he has suffered—for being wounded for his country's sake—that he is, indeed, her hero,—a thousand times better and dearer than Allen Graeme.

"And are you sure, Gerty, it is not pity for me—it is not because the Rebs nearly finished me?" said Chester, earnestly.

"And are *you* quite sure," answered she, with a happy laugh, "that it is not just because I wrote about Allen and Jeanie?"

"But, indeed," declared Chester, "if you had not been so much more of a woman than an angel,—if you had not been so sweet and so savage—I don't believe I should ever have dared to tell you."

A certain rosy shawl is treasured, to this day, by romantic Gerty, in memory of a June morning, fifteen years ago. Uncle Joe declares that Chester and Gerty owe all their happiness to him, and occasionally hums the identical refrain which once excited his sister's ire; while he threatens, by-and-by, to give Gertrude, Junior, an embellished account, full and entire, of the true and interesting story of the Garden Bower.

SOUTHERN VIOLETS.

To-day I came across some faded violets, plucked and pressed long ago. A line inclosing them is marked: "Little Phil., April 18th, Aiken, S. C."

How vividly the faint, lingering perfume brings back that far-away, balmy April day—the long, quiet walk through the pines, the delicious aromatic air, and the hushed tones of the children, as we followed to his long home the silent form of bright, beautiful little Phil.

> "Violets crushed—the sweetest showers
> Will ne'er make bloom again."

Something of the pathos and tenderness of the old couplet springs up in my heart, with the memory of that day. Will you think it strange when I tell you that little Phil was only "Lucy's boy"—ungainly, dusky Lucy, who was one of the servants of the house ; that he was half-brother to little Maria, a typical young Ethiop, and to baby Tim, one of the ugliest little pickaninnies you ever saw?

Phil's existence was a living protest against the "eternal fitness of things" under the peculiar in-stitution—a sad memorial of the evils growing out of the old relations of master and slave.

He was a beautiful child, with clear brunette com-plexion, and soft, rosy color, glorious dark eyes fringed with long, curling lashes, a finely formed head, covered with rings of chestnut hair, and such a happy, radiant face when he used to run to meet us at the gate, clasping our dresses in his gladness and glee.

His mother had been "toted" down to Georgia during the war, and had made her way back to her old home as soon as she could, "after freedom came." "My ole fam'ly's all done gone, but 'pears mo' like home here, missy, anyway, than 'twar down in Georgia." So she was glad to do some extra work in the house, and to receive her pay in the use of a little hut in the servants' quarters, and food for herself and her three children.

Phil was a sort of pet in the family. He had the freedom of the old southern house, and used to show his bright, laughing face wherever he pleased, in a manner not granted to the other children of the servants' quarters. Lucy attended to our rooms, and in her lazy, thoughtless fashion was accustomed to lock her two boys in her little hut, while she came over to the big house to do her morning's work.

I was dressing for church that Sunday morning, when I heard a cry and a crash, and saw smoke pouring out of Lucy's house. We rushed down-stairs and over to the "quarters," just as Uncle Pete came out of the door which he had broken down, carrying a little burnt figure in his arms, and muttering excitedly: "I jes' tole her so, dat ar Lucy; I tole her t'oder day dat she hadn't oughter lock dem ar children inter dat house; dey'd shore 'nuff cotch fire dessels. Oh! t'oder boy? He's all right, missy. I reckon Phil had mighty good sense if he toted dat ar little Tim onter de bed 'fo' he sot de brush a-fire a-brushin' up de h'arth. Pore little soul, he's had his last day's play I reckon—"

While he was speaking Lucy rushed towards us, and in utter silence, except for a moan, she took Phil in her arms.

They cut away the burnt clothing, and wrapt him in cotton wool, wet with linseed oil and lime-water; but the worst trouble proved to be internal. They said he must have drawn the flame into his lungs. He was very patient, and let us do all we could, and looked up with a shadow of his old sweet smile, when we called him by his name, and with a look that was pitiful in its gratefulness when we held water to his parched lips. His only cry, all through those suffering hours, was, "water, please." It seemed strange that there was so little trace of fire about his head and face. Some of his brown curls were singed, but his face wore its old beauty, almost unmarred. The doctor came after a while, but said, carelessly: "There's nothing to be done but to give him an anodyne. He may live a few hours at most."

I could not help feeling that, to the refined Southern aristocrat, the life of a poor little mulatto boy was of small account, though professional instinct and natural kind-heartedness led him to desire to lessen pain as much as possible.

Phil lingered until sunset, and then the loving, grateful spirit escaped from the little suffering body. The next afternoon they buried him. There was no occasion for ceremony, and all the arrangements were of the simplest description. The ladies of the house where we were stopping had been very kind to Lucy and her boy, but now there was nothing more to be done.

A small pine coffin was provided by the Freedmen's Bureau, and the sister of one of the officers of the garrison brought a pretty white dress which covered the poor burnt little shoulders and arms, and the children laid flowers about the pillow where rested the curly head. The coffin was closed and lifted into an old farm wagon. Lucy clambered in and sat down beside it, while Uncle Pete (Methodist preacher, sexton and general factotum) drove the old army mule through the woods. Three or four of Lucy's fellow-servants followed, while Miss Helen walked with us and the children, through the pine plantation to the place where the little grave was made. Then a strange thing happened. Uncle Pete jumped out, Lucy followed, and the old man, taking the little coffin in his arms, stepped down into the shallow grave. Resting the coffin across one end of the grave, and baring his gray head, he lifted his face towards the sky and began to pray. Such a prayer, so homely yet so reverent, full of quaint pleading and pathos, human nature and grace! I wish I could remember it all as he uttered it.

"O dear, bressed Lord," he said, "you knows all 'bout dis ere 'fliction. You knows mo'n we do, fo' you wos dere, an' seed pore little Phil cotch afire 'fore even us knowed 'bout it. O bressed Lord Jesus, we's shore you's mighty sorry for dis ere poor Lucy. You knows jes' how awful bad she do feel dat she war so keerless an' disrememberful. Out ob dhy bressed heart o' lub, O heab'nly Father, talk to her an' comfort her. An' make all of us dhy servants an' handmaidens, mighty keerful an' rememberful ob de word wot sez, shore 'nuff, 'De Lord cometh as a t'ief in de night.' * * * O Lord, you knows we's pore ignorant creturs. We habn't any book larnin', an' we'se too ole an' slow to larn now. But we want to know mo' 'bout de lub thou hast in dhy heart for us. Come, bressed Spirit ob de Holy Ghost, an' teach our hearts 'bout de Lord Jesus. We knows he's mighty fond ob de little chillen, 'cos he did say it was not de will of his heab'nly Father dat *one* ob dese little ones should perish.

"O dear Lord Jesus Christ, you does know dis ere chile wos a little one, an' he had de spirit ob a little humble chile, an' we do shorely hope he's a little lamb in dhy bosom now."

Then followed a wild, strange melody—half chant, half refrain :

" An' we'll soon go home thro' de beautiful pearly gates,
    To de glory, de glory eberlastin'.
" We'll hab palms in our han's, an' beautiful white robes
    In de glory, de glory eberlastin'.
" We'll be white as driven snow, thro' de blood ob de Lamb,
    In de glory, de glory eberlaslin'.

For Christ's sake, Amen."
"Then lowering the little coffin into the grave, he clambered out himself, and taking a handful of earth he bent over and flung it in, with the old remembered words, "Ashes to ashes ; dust to dust !" Again raising his head, he prayed : "Our Father which art in heaben, here we lays dis pore burnt body ob little

Phil.   O Lord Jesus, *don't forget him in the mornin' ob de resurrection!"*

With a sudden change of manner, he turned towards us and said: "De services is now concluded. We'se much obliged to all de fren's for comin' here to day.   Now I'se jes' a-gwine to fill up dis ere little grave an' den go home."

So there, under the shadow of the pines, in summer sunshine and winter snows, rests all that was earthly of loving little Phil.   Gladly our hearts echo the confident hope of old Uncle Pete that the soul of this "little one," saved by the dying of the Lord Jesus, is happy forever with the Shepherd of Israel, who "gathers the lambs with his arm, and carries them in his bosom."

THE JOYFUL SUFFERER.

—

"Until the bruising flails of God's corrections
  Have threshed out of us all our vain affections:
  Till those corruptions which do misbecome us
  Are by thy sacred Spirit winnowed from us;
  Until from us the straw of worldly treasures,—
  Till all the dusty chaff of empty pleasures;
  Yea, till his flail upon us he doth lay
  To thresh the husk of this our flesh away,
  And leave the soul uncovered: nay, yet more,
  Till God shall make our very spirit poor,
  We shall not up to highest wealth aspire,
  But then we shall; and that is my desire."
      —[*From " Tribulation," an old English poem.*]

ONE beautiful afternoon in the spring of 1858, I claimed the promise of a friend to take me to see Mrs. E., a sick stranger in the neighborhood, in whom my friend was much interested.

In a cheerful tone of voice we were invited to come in. On a lounge drawn near the fire lay the patient sufferer. She welcomed us cordially; indeed, the warm grasp of the wasted hand would alone have spoken for her.

She was very thin and white, and her dark blue eyes and the rings of flaxen hair escaping from her muslin cap, made the peculiar delicacy of her complexion the more striking.

To our inquiries after her health she replied cheerfully, though when questioned as to whether she suffered much, she said she was never entirely free from pain, but added: "If I can get a bit ease like the noo', I've great cause to be thankfu'."

She spoke with a decidedly Scotch accent, but not in what we call "broad Scotch;" and her language, always simple and appropriate, was clearly expressive of her thoughts and feelings.

The previous year she had sprained her left knee, and an abscess having formed on it, her sufferings had been greatly increased since her removal to C——. When we saw her she was unable to walk, except a little, around the room and out to the porch with the aid of a crutch. Our conversation naturally turned from her to her native country, and she talked very pleasantly of famous "men and things" of Scotland. When we arose to go, after a half-hour's chat with her, she thanked us warmly for the visit, and said she was so glad to have anyone come in and see her, that I felt it a severe, though unintentional, reproach for never having called there before.

A brief outline of Mrs. E.'s life, up to the time I knew her, may not be out of place here, although many of the facts have been gathered since her death.

M. C. F. was born in the village of Scone, Perthshire, a place famed in the history of Scotland, for the coronation of her kings.

She was one of seven children. This wee "lassie wi' the lint-white locks," in form so slight and fragile, that one might have thought the first rude blast of life would lay her in the grave, had lived to see the strong and hearty fail, and to feel slipping from her earthly grasp, link after link of the cherished household chain.

These seven children were early left orphans, but He, who "tempers the wind to the shorn lamb," did not forsake those whom He had bereft of dearest earthly friends, and clearly verified His promise: "Leave thy fatherless children, I will preserve them alive."

A kind uncle and aunt took M. after her father's death, to live with them in Edinburgh. Naturally of a warm, affectionate disposition, and possessing a rare cheerfulness of spirit, no doubt the little orphan niece soon became very dear to her kind, Christian friends. She remained with them in Edinburgh, and received her education there. Owing doubtless, under God's blessing, to their excellent counsels and example, she became "wise unto salvation," learning of Him who was meek and lowly in heart, and according to His promise she found rest unto her soul. At the age of nineteen, she united with the Established Church of Scotland, under the care of the Reverend John Clark, to whom she became much attached, although after her marriage she connected herself with St. George's Church, as it was nearer her home. A short time after she had finished her studies, she lost her excellent aunt. Her uncle broke up housekeeping and sailed for America, intending to send for his niece, as soon as he could provide a home for her. Death, however, claimed him ere he could fulfil his purpose, and the orphan girl was again alone. She soon found a kind home, as lady's maid in a gentleman's family in Edinburgh, where she remained until her marriage with Mr. E., Nov. 29th, 1843. Eight years afterward, they embarked for America, hoping to secure a competence in the New World, which they should return to their native land to enjoy. "Man proposes, God disposes." It is truly "not in man to direct his steps." How often are we reminded of the pathetic words of the weeping prophet: "Weep not for the dead, neither bemoan him; but weep sore for him that goeth away; for he shall return no more nor see his native country!" It is well and mercifully ordered, that God's ways are hidden, for how could we part with the light of our eyes and the desire of our hearts, and send our dear ones away with a cheerful "God speed," if we could see the grave in the far-off land to which we are consigning them?

At C., not far from Montreal, Mr. E. established himself in business; and their object in crossing the Atlantic seemed in a fair way of accomplishment. The following year, however, their extensive mills were burnt down; the fire also spread to their dwelling-house, and they narrowly escaped with their lives. Almost all their personal property was destroyed in the fire, and they recovered only half the insurance on the mills, as one company in which they had insured unfortunately failed. Leaving Canada, they removed to H. in New Jersey, where a similar catastrophe occurred.

Under all these trying circumstances, Mrs. E. was never known to utter a word of impatience or complaint. Her husband, in speaking of her constant trust and cheerfulness, remarked that "nothing of a worldly nature ever seemed in the least to put her out." Earthly treasure was as dross to her whose treasure was laid up in heaven : firmly believing in the promise of her heavenly Father to grant whatever was needful, she was not concerned about the riches of this world, which "take to themselves wings and fly away."

My first impressions of her were deepened by each repeated visit. It was one of my best pleasures to spend an hour or two with her, although she always seemed to consider it a self-denial and sacrifice of enjoyment on the part of those who came to see her, instead of an unwonted privilege.

There was something very touching in her self-forgetfulness. Her kind sympathy with the joys and sorrows of the young, and her appreciation of whatever interested others, contrasted strongly with the egotism and selfishness to which human nature is so prone under the pressure of long-continued pain. Uncomplaining, and grateful for every alleviation of her sufferings, she did not seem like one who had not known an hour's freedom from pain for many months. A little gift of flowers, fruit, or any trifle which we often receive with a careless "Thank you," always brought from her the expression : "I'm sure you're very kind ; aye bringing me some nice thing or ither," while the grateful eye told how truly the words were the expression of her heart.

She was quite often alone through the day, as her husband was obliged to be absent most of the time ; but during the summer, friendly neighbors frequently came in to see her.

She always mentioned these calls as unexpected kindness and attention to her. It happened one day that she was speaking of this, and added laughingly: "I told Mr. E. the other day I hadna eaten anything that was cooked in the house, but a bit of toast or such like, for a two months."

That capriciousness of appetite known to almost every invalid, was not wanting in her. Everybody knows how much better any little delicacy is relished, if sent in to one, than if it is of home production.

Her peculiar sensitiveness of constitution made her feel very keenly every change in the atmosphere. Especially during the frequent summer thunder showers, she suffered the most exquisite pain. After some such occasions she has said: "Oh, I didna think last night, that I could live till the morning; the pain came sharp, sharp, right through my knee, but thank God, I'm far easier now." Never did she speak of past sufferings without an expression of gratitude for present relief. I remember well, one Saturday afternoon, when she seemed to feel quite comfortable, I said I wished she could be moved down to church the next day. She looked as though I had touched a chord which had not yet ceased to thrill her, as she expressed her sense of the impossibility of the thing; adding, that she felt she could not stay through the services even if she could bear to be carried down. The deprivation of ordinary Sabbath privileges was deeply felt by her, especially as we were then without a settled minister. Once during the previous winter, she had been much delighted with a visit from a minister—a countryman of hers—who spent a Sabbath with us, and she frequently spoke with much pleasure of his friendly call, and his prayer for her before leaving.

During the summer, she enjoyed several privileges of this kind, and her delight in these pastoral visits showed how much she had missed and longed for them.

Her sweet sympathy with all in affliction of any sort, was a delightful evidence of the Spirit of Christ which was in her: she was truly mindful of the apostle's injunction to "bear one another's burdens." It was noticeable too, how the scriptural promise, "Give and it shall be given unto you," was fulfilled in her experience. It is seldom, I think, that a comparative stranger, although sick and suffering, wins such frequent expressions of interest and sympathy as were elicited by Mrs. E. Possibly this might be partially due to the charm of a rare heartiness of manner and language; but even those who were personally unacquainted with her were in a peculiar degree interested in her.

An invalid friend, who was spending some time with us, took an especial interest in Mrs. E., as she herself was suffering from lameness of a similar character. Knowing how small a token of kindness would give pleasure to an invalid, she lent her a copy of the "Words of Jesus." That little book had been a comfort to one who had entered the dark valley while the sunlight of bright hopes, and the fair flowers of earthly happiness, and the fond love of a mother's heart all sought in vain to draw her back from the grave. It also ministered sweet consolation to this sufferer in her hours of solitude and pain. She always cherished a most grateful remembrance of this little kindness, and an earnest and affectionate interest in the invalid stranger long after she had left us.

The invalid fully appreciated and enjoyed all that was beautiful around her. I have often found her lying on her couch, gazing through the open door on the dense foliage of the trees, and the wooded hills glowing in the rich tints of a summer sunset, with a heart overflowing with gratitude to God for thus clothing the earth with loveliness. No one could fail to notice her acknowledgment of God in everything, and her unwavering confidence in His promise that *all* things should work together for her good. Early in July, the abscess on her knee was opened, and she experienced temporary relief, although she was much weakened by the discharge. She was still able however to go to and from her room, with the aid of a chair which she pushed along before her, even when too weak to support herself with her crutch. She sometimes spoke of the possible necessity of amputating her limb, and in her weak condition she could not but dread it. "But," she added: "I think aye, when the dreadful pain comes as though 'twould kill me, I'd be willing to have the poor knee ta'en off, if the doctor would say it was best." It was an aggravation of her trial that her physician repeatedly disappointed her, his professional engagements being very numerous. Perhaps we cannot fully estimate her patient forbearance, while enduring such severe pain, and waiting in vain for days and weeks, for her physician to bring relief. She frequently spoke of her failing strength; and the slight cough and pain in the side were symptoms of consumption with which she had been too familiar in her family, to easily mistake. The desire to live for her husband's sake, and to do more for God, was not extinct, although she did not look forward to recovery. She sometimes said: "If God would see fit to grant me a little ease, I would be too thankful to ask anything else." Again she said, in great suffering and extreme weakness: "Oh! if I had my peace to make with God, *I could not do it now.* Often, often, I cannot think a single thought,—not e'en to know that I have a soul,—for the dreadful pain; and it's often late, late at night, after I get to bed, and a little easy, before I can get my thoughts together to pray. Then I lie awake, and say over short hymns and scripture verses and prayers, and feel so happy and peaceful." God's mercy and kindness to her soul were truly loving-kindness and tender mercy. He granted her sweetest communion with him, and gave unto her "songs in the night." Her walk had been close with God in her season of health and prosperity, and He did not suffer her to doubt his love and faithfulness when his hand was laid heavily upon her. She could say with Job: "Wearisome nights are *appointed* unto me," and acquiesce in her heavenly Father's will concerning her. She could "take it on trust a little while," and believe that "these light afflictions which are but for a moment" would work out for her a far more exceeding weight of glory. Thus was she enabled to glorify her God in the fires, and to give a stronger testimony for Jesus by her patient cheerfulness on her couch of pain, than many do by a life of active usefulness.

Her patience was a wonder to many, even to those who knew something of the power of God to sustain and comfort his weary ones. Once, when she was nearly worn out with distress, she said something about being "impatient." I could scarcely bear to hear her reproach herself so undeservedly; and in answer to my hasty exclamation, she said very sweetly: "Well, we know *it's not in us;* we cannot do *anything* of ourselves, but, thank God, we know where to look, and he'll give us all the grace and patience we need. Thus his grace was made "sufficient" for her, and his strength was perfected in her weakness.

Often our conversation turned to the "old country," and her anecdotes and descriptions of life there were very interesting. Now it was the pulpit eloquence of Chalmers or Guthrie, or some other of the "Scotch worthies;" again, some description of the royal family, or a panegyric upon the Queen as a faithful and loving mother, and again, some touching story of the loved and unfortunate. Many times, when listening to such a simple story or heartfelt comment, I have felt the force of Shakspeare's saying: "A touch of nature makes the whole world akin." One cold day in autumn I came in with my hands quite chilled; Mrs. E. would not let me warm them by the fire, but held them in her own till they were quite warm, saying at the time: "I mind well, my mother doing so, when we would come in, wee toddling things, from the cold." Who cannot recall such an instance of a mother's thoughtful love, though her hands may long ago have clasped the "rod and staff," in going through the dark valley?

About this time Mrs. E. had the comfort of frequent visits from a minister who was with us for the winter, and of whose kindness and sympathy she always spoke with deep gratitude—while he felt no less thankful for being permitted to witness the wonderful example of Christian patience and resignation, and to minister to her comfort and peace. The influence, she unconsciously exerted over every one who was much with her, was cheering and strengthening, and the assurance of an interest in her prayers was often like the sighing wind, precursor of the longed-for rain. Sometimes before leaving home for a visit, I have told her of my intention; and her affectionate expressions of sorrow at my leaving, and the hope that she might live to see me back, with a promise to remember me in her prayers, were very touching. After such an absence, her welcome home was often the sweetest part of my return; and the assurance that she had missed me, and had been "wearying" for me, was a proof of her loving heart which attached itself to all around her.

One day I found her delighted with a visit she had received the previous day from our minister, and she attempted to give me some idea of a beautiful hymn he had repeated to her. From her description I thought it might be

"Ye angels who stand round the throne,"

and her delighted face, as I repeated it, immediately

showed that I was right. It was ever a favorite of hers, and even in her dying hours she remembered and loved it. I could not but remark how her thoughts seemed ever turning heavenward, and have often noticed her quickened interest and emotion when we spoke or read of the home to which she was hastening. She was indeed "only waiting" for the summons, that she might joyfully enter through the gates into the city. And as she grew in the likeness of her Master, and "endured as seeing Him who is invisible," I was forcibly reminded of the words of Isaiah: "Thine eyes shall see the King in His beauty; they shall behold the land that is very far off." Thanksgiving day her pastor called to see her, and the occasion brought from her pleasant reminiscences of such days "at home," and the more honored observance of them there. When he said, very pleasantly: "Well, Mrs. E., every day should be Thanksgiving day with us, should it not?" she eagerly assented with a look of pleasure at being thus reminded of God's daily mercies. Truly it might have been written of her:

" Thy life rises upward to God every day like a psalm,
   Which the singer sings, sleeping; and waked, would with won-
      dering eyes say—
  I sing not, nay! how should I sing thus? I only do pray."

Her increasing weakness and cough, as the winter approached, made it evident to us that the time of her departure was not far distant. Of this she was herself fully aware, and spoke of it without any apprehensions or uneasiness, trusting to Jesus alone to bring her safely to her desired haven. Her turns of coughing were quite frequent, especially at night. After such an attack, she has said to me: "Ah! I thought, last night, I should never see you again in this world." During the absence of a young friend to whom she was much attached, she said, "I should like, if it be God's will, to live till she comes back," and her desire was granted, much to the comfort of both.

One day, early in the winter, Mr. E. met with an accident from which he narrowly escaped without serious injury. So often does God remind us that, strong and vigorous as we may be, yet "there is but a step betwixt us and death." Mrs. E.'s gratitude for this sparing mercy was deep and heartfelt, but her wan face and altered expression showed that the shock had been very severe. As the Christmas season drew near, there were more frequent tokens of the approach of the messenger, and her growing spirituality and heavenliness were very marked. I told her one day of a little motherless baby, for whom her tender sympathy had been strongly excited. She said: "Oh! I was thinking of the poor wee thing last night, and hoping that his sufferings would soon be over." We then spoke of the difficulty of always *realizing* the nearness of eternity, of remembering, as minute after minute passes by, that *one* moment of time will bear our unclad souls into the visible presence of God. I could not repress the thought, that she with whom I was speaking would soon, very soon, be sharing the joys of angels and the redeemed, and glorifying "Him who sitteth on the great white throne" with a service forever free from sin and imperfection.

But the wise Lord of the harvest sends not forth His reaper until the grain is fully ripe; then "*immediately* He putteth in the sickle," and the precious grain is gathered into the garner.

Christmas day I stopped for a few moments, not so much to give the "merry Christmas" wish, as to let her know that she was not forgotten. She was very cheerful, and entered into the spirit of a Christmas frolic on the ice which I described to her, and seemed to put her own sufferings out of sight lest they should lessen the enjoyment of others. Two days afterwards, she was much worse, but this attack did not last long. When I saw her in the evening, she was quite comfortable, and listened with pleasure to some of Ryle's "Spiritual songs." One of these which the minister had repeated to her, was the beautiful one of Carey's—"Nearer Home," every line of which seemed to go to her heart:

> "One sweetly solemn thought
>   Comes to me, o'er and o'er:
> I'm nearer home to-day,
>   Than I have ever been before;
>
> "Nearer my Father's house,
>   Where the many mansions be,
> Nearer the great white throne,
>   Nearer the crystal sea.
>
> "Nearer the bound of life,
>   Where we lay our burdens down,
> Nearer leaving the cross,
>   Nearer gaining the crown.

     " But lying darkly between,
       Winding down through the night,
    Is the deep and unknown stream,
       That leads at last to the light.

     " Jesus! perfect my trust,
       Strengthen the hand of my faith!
    Let me feel thee near, when I stand
       On the edge of the shore of Death.

     "Feel thee near, when my feet
       Are slipping over the brink,
    For it may be, I'm nearer home,
       Nearer now, than I think."

From this time, the change in her appearance was very perceptible; she grew weaker almost daily, although she continued to be brought from her bed-room to the sitting-room every morning.

On New Year's day, she suffered very much, but afterward she appeared to rally a little.

Her appetite for the past month had been very feeble, and her throat was so painful as to make it often impossible to swallow anything but liquids. Still she showed the same grateful appreciation of every little attention, and tried to muster a little appetite for whatever was sent to her.

She spoke quite freely of her approaching depart-ure, and with the greatest unconcern as to all earthly things. The same thoughtfulness for others which had always characterized her was evident now, in her efforts to have all the necessary preparations made for her death, so that no one should be inconven-ienced on her account. She spoke with wonder of those who could feel any concern about their funeral arrangements, as if it were little matter to her, how or where the poor frail body was laid, feeling assured that Jesus would guard the sleeping dust, and raise it up at last in glorious immortality.

As she lay on her couch, weak and suffering, she kept beside her two little books—"The Faithful Promiser," and "Spiritual Songs,"—which were light enough for her to hold without weariness.

From these she often asked me to read, or to repeat some hymn about heaven or the Saviour.

Although she was so weak, there seemed to be no apparent reason why she might not linger on for weeks or even months; indeed, her husband was so little prepared for the heavy blow, that he had spoken of taking her to Canada as soon as she should be a little stronger, and of perhaps returning to Scotland. The alteration in her appearance which others noticed, he did not perceive, as he was so much with her.

Thursday after New Year's day, I heard that she was not so comfortable; she had suffered intensely the preceding night, and was quite exhausted when I saw her, but there was still the cordial welcome, the lighting up of the face, and the close grasp of the hand. It was the last time I saw her in her old place on her couch. The next day was very stormy. and she was much worse. In the afternoon, however, she seemed rather better, and Mr. E. carried her out to her lounge. She knew well that her sands of life were nearly run, and in the stillness of the winter evening she spoke calmly and hopefully of the change which awaited her, of death itself as the entrance into life.

Her faith was strong and steadfast in the sufficiency of the Saviour; her hope was as "an anchor cast within the veil." Those hours must have been sorrowfully sweet to both hearts, but to her who was nearest the goal, even the grief of severing earth's dearest, strongest tie could not cause her to linger in the race towards the heavenly crown.

When she saw that Mr. E. was altogether overcome with the thought of her death, she changed the subject and did not again allude to it, except, on perceiving that her fingers were beginning to swell, she herself removed her wedding ring and another one she wore, and gave them to her husband.

She did not sleep much during the night, as her cough was distressing and she was very restless. When I went up to see her Saturday, as I entered the room, I was startled to see the lounge pushed back and vacant. Mr. E. spared me the question which I dared not ask, and took me to her room, telling me that there had been a great change in Mrs. E. since I had seen her. It was indeed so; the sunken eye and attenuated features bore the seal of the destroyer; but by God's mercy, he had not been suffered to disturb the peace of her soul, or to shut out from her dying eyes the glorious face of her Redeemer. Perfectly conscious and composed in view of death, she knew she would soon be forever "where the weary are at rest," in that blissful home where " there is no sin, nor sorrow, nor any more pain." She recognized me immediately, but it was very difficult for her to speak, even in a low whisper, as any exertion made her cough painfully.

I repeated to her part of the fourteenth chapter of

John, and her favorite hymn. She was very quiet afterward, and lay with her eyes closed for some time.

There was a peacefulness in that chamber of death, which stilled every thought of earth ; it seemed as though the angels were even then hovering around the dying bed, awaiting "the loosing of the silver cord," to bear the unfettered spirit to its home on high. Oh ! it was a solemn thought that could not but rise in my soul : the spirit now imprisoned in that frail earthly house shall soon, ah ! soon, "at the opening of the prison doors," soar away to the regions of endless bliss, and I felt as though I could give her joy with all my heart that she was so near home.

Two hours after, at sunset, her earthly sun went down forever ; but we have the assurance that, in the city whither she hath gone, "they have no need of the sun, for the glory of God doth lighten it, and the Lamb is the light thereof."

As peacefully as a little child, without a sigh or struggle, she fell asleep in her husband's arms ; one last look, a mute farewell, and the eyes were veiled from earth forever. The fever that burned in her feeble frame, and made her long for something which could quench her thirst, shall nevermore parch those lips. She has drunk deep of the stream which flows from the throne of God and of the Lamb, that "pure river of life, clear as crystal," and they who drink thereof "shall thirst no more."

Oh ! it is well to go to the river side with the pilgrim who is to pass through the flood, and to hear in spirit the blessed words : "fear not ; thou art mine ! When thou passest through the waters, I will be with thee, and through the rivers they shall not overflow thee."

She has crossed the flood, and entered through the gates into the city. May we, too, live as followers of those who "through *faith and patience* inherit the promises ;" and then unto us also shall be ministered an abundant entrance into the joy of our Lord !

10

THE STORY OF ADJAI.

—

FIFTY-SEVEN years ago, in the little African village of Oshugun, in the Yoruba country, about a hundred miles from the slave coast, lived a heathen boy named Adjai. He was eleven years old when we first hear of him, living with his father and mother, and two little sisters and one brother.

For several years a dreadful civil war had been raging in Yoruba, stirred up and aided by the slave-hunters. The people, whom travelers before that time had found remarkably mild and hospitable, had become savage and eager to sell their fellow-men for gold. The country, once so rich and well cultivated, was fast becoming desolate, as tribe after tribe, and village after village joined in the cruel strife.

Perhaps you may like to know the origin of this war, which had such an influence on the fortunes of the boy Adjai. One day, in a village-market, a quarrel arose between persons of different tribes about a "Cowry's worth of pepper." You will remember that a cowry is a small shell, used in parts of India and Africa, as a substitute for coins of very low value. The savage war which lasted for many years, destroying 145 villages, making a wilderness of a once fruitful country, and throwing thousands of slaves into the cruel hands of Portuguese slave-traders, grew out of a quarrel in market, the money in question being about the value of the fiftieth part of one cent.

To return to Adjai,—one bright morning in 1821, the village of Oshugun was attacked by a neighboring tribe. Adjai's father seized his weapons and rushed out to meet the assailants, and was killed. The village was burned, and Adjai's mother and children were taken prisoners. Adjai and one of his sisters fell to the share of the principal chief. Before sunset the boy was bartered away for a horse, but being exchanged again, he was for a while near his mother and sisters, though they were owned by different masters. After a few months a Mohammedan woman bought the boy. He was in daily terror of being sold to the Portuguese slave-traders, and, to avoid this fate, he tried to strangle himself with his belt. His mistress, seeing him beginning to lose his health and strength, sold him for a little rum and tobacco. His new owner took him to the Portuguese settlement at Lagos, to be sold with a number of other poor captives. They were treated with the utmost cruelty, being dragged about, by means of a chain passed through iron fetters around their necks. After months of misery, on a dark night, the whole gang now numbering one hundred and eighty-five, were hauled down to the beach, and stowed away in the hold of a slave ship, where, in sickness and hunger they passed the next day and night.

But although they did not dream of it, deliverance was near at hand. On the second day, the slaver was overhauled by a British cruiser, and the rescued slaves were carried to Sierra Leone. On reaching Freetown, Adjai, with a little girl named Asano and several other children, was placed in the mission school, under the kind care of Mr. and Mrs. Weeks.

From the outset, Adjai showed unusual ability and eagerness to learn. Not content with the two hours of daily instruction in school, he managed to get an alphabet card, and persuaded another child to teach him his letters, which he mastered in three days. In six months he was able to read the New Testament. When he was fifteen years old he was baptized, and received, in addition to his own name, the name of a vicar of a London church who was a well-known friend of African missions. After this time, we shall know him as Samuel Adjai Crowther. His consistent Christian character and intelligence gave great hopes of growing usefulness. He was the first student of the Fourth-Bay Institution, an establishment for the training of natives for the ministry. In 1829, he married Asano, his little companion on the slave ship and in the mission school. For several years, he was the school-master at Regent's Town, under the superintendence of his old teacher Mr. Weeks.

In 1841, Samuel Crowther was appointed to accompany an expedition, sent by the British Government to explore the lower course of the Niger, with a special view to the suppression of the slave-trade. Nearly all the Europeans died from the effect of the climate, but we cannot call the expedition a failure, since it opened to Mr. Crowther the region which he resolved to make the place of his future labors.

During all these long years, no word had reached him of his mother or family, though we can well believe that he must often have anxiously asked for tidings of them, from the thousands of Yoruba people brought by British ships into the colony of Sierra Leone. We are told he never ceased to pray for his mother, though not knowing whether she still lived. After completing his studies at Islington, where he had been sent by the Church Missionary Society, he was ordained by the Bishop of London, as Missionary to Abbeokuta, a city in the Yoruba country. Mr. Crowther returned to Africa, sailing with his wife Asano, and some other missionaries, in December 1844, for Badagry, the nearest port by which they could reach the Yoruba country. They were detained some eighteen months at Badagry, but lost no time while there. Mr. Crowther preached under the shade of a huge tree to the mixed population who came to hear the gospel from the lips of one of their own African people. While still at his work at Badagry, he was told one day, that, among a gang of slaves from the interior, was a man said to be Samuel Crowther's uncle. The news was true. The old man was ransomed for ten pounds, five shillings. From him Mr. Crowther learned that his mother still lived, not far from Abbeokuta, the mission station to which he was going. He therefore sent a messenger to tell his mother. She could not believe the message, but notwithstanding, she hurried to meet him, and when she saw him, although twenty-five years had gone by, she knew him to be indeed her long lost Adjai. From the lips of her own son, so wonderfully restored to her in her old age, Afala heard the glad tidings of the Saviour, salvation from sin, and eternal life. Among the first fruits of Samuel Crowther's ministry in the Yoruba country, was his own mother. Soon after this, his brother, two sisters and four children were brought to the station as slaves. He ransomed them all for one hundred dollars, so low an estimate is put upon human flesh and blood in that region.

The work continued to gain ground steadily in Abbeokuta, and the neighboring towns. We can believe there was plenty to do, when we learn that, in 1861, Burton estimated the population within the wall of the town at 150,000; and outside 50,000 more. At that date, there were in Abbeokuta 1,500 Christians; the rest were pagans whose religion was fetichism. The pagan priests opposed the missionaries, and with the slave-traders persecuted the native Christians, but failed to shake them from their faithfulness in the midst of dangers, and at the peril of their lives.

We have not time to give, in detail, the work Mr. Crowther accomplished during his missionary labors, of nearly twenty years, among his own Yoruba people, and on the Niger. He had translated a large part of the Bible and Prayer Book into several native languages, and had made four separate missionary tours up the Niger, establishing stations and laying the foundation of new missions on every tour. None but a native missionary could do the work, for the climate was fatal to Europeans. In 1864, he was called to England, to receive ordination, as Bishop of the Niger. No man could have received a nobler welcome than was given to him in England. The Queen gave a special interview to him and his wife

Asano, and the University of Oxford conferred the degree of Doctor of Divinity upon him. On the 29th of June, 1864, the little slave boy and girl of forty years before, stood side by side, in the great Cathedral of Canterbury, while Samuel Adjai Crowther was consecrated first negro Bishop of the Niger.

He sailed straightway after his ordination, and returned to Sierra Leone, where another welcome awaited him. In a fortnight, he was once more at Lagos, where so many years before he, in despair and agony, had been dragged through the streets.

By strange ways God had led him, but, as Joseph said to his brethren, so Crowther could say to his cruel captors: "Ye thought evil against me but God meant it for good, to save much people alive."

The miserable little Yoruba boy, torn from his home and sold as a slave to go into a far country, was brought after many years to high honor, and to stand before a greater than any earthly king, and to receive from Him the best blessedness of life, useful service to his suffering, ignorant fellow-men.   *   *

*   *   *   *   *   *   *

ANDREAS HLAVERTI.

———

AN outlandish name, you say. So it is; for it is the name of one from far-off Hungary, who seems to have been sent to these western shores, just to receive a little gleam of light from Heaven, to learn the truth about Jesus and His salvation, so that he might carry back that blessing to those still in darkness, in his own native land. Last Sabbath, he was with the little flock that assembled to listen to a Bible lesson from our pastor and a Hungarian assistant. To-day, he is out on the broad ocean, but, as he said before he left, "I go home to my country, but I go praying God to bless this work that Christian people do here for my people. I read in my testament, Jesus Christ said: 'I am the light of the world, but men love darkness rather than light because they do evil;' that is the way with my people, but they do not know the Bible—I never heard the Bible in my country.—I pray God to take away the dark out of their hearts, and the anger and the hate, and make them want to know good, and love Jesus Christ. So, the Christian people must not be afraid. God will take care, and He can do what He pleases."

One afternoon, entering the Bible-class room some time before the hour of service, he passed through to a smaller room, where some maps were hung on the wall. While he was examining them, two men entered—one of them evidently under the influence of liquor.—"What are you doing here?" they inquired roughly. "Oh! nothing," he answered. "Yes, but what are you doing?" "I look to see where is the city, Jerusalem, where Jesus Christ was crucified." "You come here to Church—this is no place for you—you are a Roman Catholic." "Well, here I can worship God. For Roman Catholic, Greek Church or Protestant, there is one God. This is a God-House, and here I learn only what is good—so I come."

He walked out of the house, and they followed, evidently abusing him. "You're Roman, Catholic—you must not come here again—you must go to Roman Catholic Church."

"Why not? *You* have been here once—twice; you know what they teach here. You hear nothing but good words about God, out of his Book—no swearing words, no ugly words, about Roman Catholics or anybody—only that God is ready to have all men come to him, and He save them. What harm is there to hear that—for Roman Catholic or Greek or any one?"

They became violent, and threatened him—said he should be stopped—they would waylay him every time he tried to come. "This is America. I shall come where I hear only good things." Then they taunted him with forsaking the Church, called him a bad Catholic, and cursed him. He answered: "You talk about Roman Catholic Church. I think you like 'Dick's church' better than Roman Catholic Church. [Dick kept a beer-shop, much frequented by their countrymen.] You go to mass one hour,—then you come out and go to Dick's two or three hours, and get drunk. Is that good? No! You say if you're Roman Catholics you're safe. If a man gets drunk and fights and swears, and has one wife in Hungary, and comes over to America and has another wife here —all right, if he's a Roman Catholic. God will save him, no matter how bad he is."

This was plain truth, and hit a sore spot, for a brother of one of the assailants answered fully to this description of a good Roman Catholic. The men then became so abusive that Hlaverti feared they would waylay and murder him, as they threatened to do. So, leaving them, he turned into the house where the Hungarian assistant lived, and reported to him the conversation. The latter advised him to keep quiet—to remain at his house for a while, and not go to Bible-class that afternoon. Hlaverti followed this counsel, but was present at the evening service in the Presbyterian Church; and he continued to attend quite regularly, although his knowledge of English was of the slightest.

Before one Communion season, he told the Hungarian Bible-reader that he would like to come to the Lord's Supper, if the Christian people would let him —to mass he could not go. It was strange that he learned so much truth with so little of human teaching. Rugged old man, that he was, he had the humble spirit of a little child—a true disciple of Him who was meek and lowly, eagerly seizing upon the Scripture doctrines, as shown by verses of the Bible, printed on the blackboard Sabbath after Sabbath, in Hungarian, Bohemian and English.

He was very helpful to his fellow-learners, and encouraging to his teachers. Such verses as these were carefully read over, in the different languages, the translations compared, so as to teach the foreigners a little English on the way, and then explained as fully and plainly as possible.

These are some of the verses: "This is a faithful saying," etc. "Jesus Christ came into the world to save sinners;" "God so loved the world," etc.; "It is appointed unto all men to die, and after death the judgment;" "God will bring every secret thing into judgment," etc.; "Then shall the King say unto those on His right hand: 'Come ye blessed;'" "I am the Good Shepherd;" "And other sheep I have, which are not of this fold; them, also, I must bring."

If we can, by an effort, empty our minds and memories of these Scripture words, standing for the whole doctrine of man's sin and Christ's atonement, we may perhaps appreciate, a little, the eagerness and gladness with which this simple-hearted man received the good news of a Saviour *for him*. To him, the story of His birth in Bethlehem of Judea—the years of His life on earth—His pity and help and healing —His agony in the Garden—His betrayal by one follower—His denial by another—abandonment by all—the death on Calvary—came with the freshness of truth told to a little child, and the preciousness of a cooling draught to a thirsty and waiting soul.   *

*   *   *   *   *   *   *   *

A MORNING IN THE HOMES OF CHINA TOWN.

I.

In the heart of the city of San Francisco, only a few stones' throw from large hotels and stores, lies "China Town," where you may walk apparently in a foreign land, and very rarely meet any but long-queued little figures, with dark blouses and slippered feet.   Parts of Sacramento, Dupont, and Kearney streets are included in China Town.   "Barbary Coast," the significant name of a small portion of the Chinese Quarter, is not a safe place to visit, except under the escort of a policeman.   It is a den of thieves and roughs.

By the kind invitation of one of our missionary ladies in San Francisco, one October morning six years ago, I started with her to visit the Chinese Quarter.   "As your time is so limited," she said, " I will try to give you a glimpse, at least, of the different grades and classes of homes. I generally go with Ah Ho, our assistant's wife, as I have not yet mastered enough Chinese for ready conversation. We will call on her first, and see whether she is at liberty to go with us, this morning."

On our way, Mrs. C. told me something of the history of Ah Ho and her husband Tam Ching. Ah Ho was educated in the family of Dr. Happer of

Canton, China, and, under Mrs. Happer's care, became a Christian and married Tam Ching, who had been brought up in San Francisco, but studied for the ministry in China. "They have a little child, a year old, who was baptized a few weeks ago, under the name of 'Oi Chan,' which means 'Love the True.'"

We found Mrs. Ah Ho very willing to join us, as soon as she could make some necessary arrangements about her baby, and change her in-door Chinese dress for the ordinary dress of Americans. So we made an appointment to meet her at Mrs. Lum Zue's, and as we crossed the street, we met Tam Ching going home with little Oi Chan, bundled up and asleep in his arms.

"You have just seen a Christian Chinese home," said Mrs. C. "Now we will call on a little heathen mother, who was born here and understands a good deal of English. Her baby is a few weeks old. Poor little thing! It does not now seem to have much chance of a Christian education, although the mother and grandmother come occasionally to the 'Women's Meetings' at my house, where I entertain them once a month, and they are very friendly and cordial to me when I visit them." So, up we went, to the third floor of a dark, dull tenement house. We were warmly welcomed, and invited into the room where the young mother and her baby were sitting wrapped up. The baby was fretting like any other baby, and the little mother, who looked like a mere child herself, petted and soothed him in a very natural fashion. Our visit was the occasion for a general reception. One woman after another came in, until there were seven or eight, besides ourselves, in that little room. We are told the standard and type of beauty differs materially, among different nations. These China women may have been belles in their own land, but to my eyes they had been, as our old Scotch nurse used to say of herself, "to the hint o' the door, when the beauty was given out." Each one entered with a short little bow and bob of the head, and a variety of renderings of our "How do you do," and "Good morning." The mother understood us pretty well, and answered, in broken English, Mrs. C.'s questions about herself and baby.

"Baby month old Sunday. Then he wear his new clothes. We have feast. Won't you come?" "Oh! Sunday not good day? Why not?" she exclaimed, as Mrs. C. thanked her, and said she would like to come very much if it were not to be on Sunday.

"Oh! oh! Sunday—your Joss' day? You go to Joss House, Sunday!" We assented, and the little mother then offered to show us the baby's "new clothes." While the brisk, proud grandmother went to get them, Mrs. C. explained to me that a Chinese baby always wears old clothes for four weeks. Then, when the family can afford it, it has a complete new suit of blouses and caps, generally made and given by the baby's grandmother,—a person much more universally honored among the Chinese than in our American homes. So much is this the case, that the living grandmother often becomes an object of worship, as well as the more remote ancestors of the pious Chinese. This ancestral worship appears so inwoven into the Chinese nature, that the renunciation of it is often the severest test of their Christianity; it is the last superstition they give up. I could not help thinking how shocked the Christianized Chinese might well be, if they could see the cool indifference towards the "old folks" in many an American home—if they could hear boys and girls vote their grandfathers and grandmothers "slow," and "a horrid nuisance," when their infirmities called for some renunciation of pleasure on the young folks' part.

But while I was thinking and comparing morals and manners of Young America and Heathen Chinee, the grandmother returned with baby's new clothes. They were of handsome material and beautifully made. The under-sacque was of scarlet flannel, the outer, of navy blue serge, lined and wadded, and finished with a heavy cord. The street garment was of magenta-colored brocade and looked large enough for a child three years old. The most singular thing about the suit was the pair of caps. They were little scarlet skull-caps, very much like those we often see on the little monkeys led around by organ grinders. Each cap had a band of ornaments across the front, with medals representing the idol whose care was especially invoked. On one was the inscription, which Mrs. C. translated for me, "May you be rich!" and on the other, " May you have long life!" Poor little baby! It seemed very sad that those who loved him best, could make for him no better, higher wishes.

The women crowded around me, noticing my dress

and particularly examining some oxydized buttons on it.   I thought afterwards they perhaps imagined the buttons bore some image or inscription similar to those upon the baby's caps.   Their questions, in very broken English, were quite amusing.   Sewing and cooking are their only occupations, and their lives are utterly void of outside interests or knowledge.   I noticed an extremely dull, heavy-looking woman sitting stolidly in the corner.   Mrs. C. told me she had been bought by a Chinaman last Christmas, and had not been allowed to stir out of the house since that time. She had not been out of that house for ten months. I thought it was no wonder that she complained of constant headache.   These poor slave wives are in the most abject bondage to their husbands.   Fancy if you can, the life of one of these poor, ignorant creatures, in a Christian country, yet living in the grossest heathenism, with no hope in this life, nor in the life to come.

I was surprised to see, on the wall, a map of the world.   We were glad to point out, to the most intelligent of the women, the places where we came from. It was pleasant to notice how their faces brightened, as they understood us and asked us questions about New York, and tried to say some English words after us.

Most of these women were in the habit of attending Mrs. C.'s "Women's Meetings," and she visits them in their own homes, and tries to win their love and confidence.   It is necessary to do a great deal of apparently fruitless social work, in order to assure them of the true, friendly feeling of our missionaries, for it is a sad and shameful fact that the Chinese have been so grossly abused in San Francisco that it is little wonder these heathen consider a religion which permits such cruelties, to say the least, not very attractive. We took our leave with a good deal of handshaking, and bobbing, and many good-byes, and as we left the room, two of the women followed us to the head of the stairs, saying very pleasantly, "Walk slowly!" "Walk slowly!" I fancied they wished to warn us of some dangerous place on the stairs, but Mrs. C. told me that it was only their pretty, polite way of thanking us for the visit, and expressing regret at our departure.

Our next call was at the house of a Christian Chinaman, "who bought his wife for $700 here in San Francisco," Mrs. C. told me. "He is a merchant in comfortable circumstances, and is one of our most intelligent church members." We were received very politely, as he came into the parlor through a curtained recess. Mrs. C. said she hoped we had not disturbed him. "Oh! no," said he, "I have taken rice." (Which is equivalent to our saying we have breakfasted.) Soon his wife Lum Zue, came in, dressed in ordinary Chinese style, loose trousers, and long blouse with large sleeves. She was young and pretty, with a soft pleasant voice, and most elaborately arranged, shining black hair. The manners of the Chinese at home are certainly very courteous and pleasant. In allusion to the difference between Chinese and American styles of dress, our host remarked that it was a mistake to say that a Chinaman would not be allowed to land in China if

11

he had cut off his queue,—but, that if one returned to China without it, he would be a laughingstock of every one! "Very much the way," said he, "that it was here sixteen years ago, when I came to San Francisco. All the boys in the streets yelled and hooted at me, because of my queue. The China boys would hoot at me there, if I went back without it." I told him I had always thought that our fashion gave a man much advantage over his wife in the ease of dressing, but a Chinaman had as much trouble as his wife, with his long hair. "Oh! no," said he laughing, "I brush and braid mine every morning in five minutes." His wife said, with a little blush and a smile: "It takes me two hours!" and I could well believe it.

Mrs. Ah Ho, the assistant's wife, soon joined us, and, after some pleasant conversation with our host about the church and former missionaries, we took our leave, he and his wife thanking us politely for our call. Then, with Mrs. Ah Ho, we went into some of the opium shops. They are not places where one would wish to enter alone.

Our next call was upon a much poorer class of women than we had yet seen. Up, up we went to the top of a dirty tenement house, past many a door from which squalid, dull faces peered out at us strangers, until we found ourselves at last, in a large open room, on the top of the house. Doors and some merely curtained partitions opened upon this hall. A group of women sat on the floor, or on low stools, sewing on coarse under-clothing, working for a few cents a day, from morning till night, day after day,

and week after week, and month after month. One
of them "took rice" while we were there, in the most
hasty, incidental way, disposing of her saucerful by
means of her chopsticks, in a very few minutes.
Several children, of different ages and sizes, were lying
idly around. One little creature, frightened perhaps
at us, ran to its mother with the familiar cry : " Mamma, mamma ! " One of the women told us that the
preceding day had been a feast day, the Chinese
New Year, as I understood. Before we left, she
brought out a few cakes which their bakers made for
the feast, and some of the singular, sheep-head nuts,
which are great favorites with the Chinese, and offered them to us. She seemed very much pleased when
I told her, through Mrs. Ah Ho, that I should take
them home with me, and show them to my friends.
Mrs. C. told me that she had made many efforts to
get permission from the husbands of these poor
women, for them to come to the " Women's Meetings "
at her house. Only a few were permitted to come.
It takes a long while to break down the strong walls
of prejudice and national custom which surround
these poor creatures.

Before leaving the room where they were working, I noticed that one of the curtains was raised,
and a thin, miserable-looking woman came out,
with a baby as forlorn as herself, in her arms. Mrs.
Ah Ho said to me : " That woman bought that baby
—gave $25 for it." We received no explanation
—no comment. It was an immense sum for that
poor woman to accumulate, considering that their
wages are, at the most, a few cents a day. Poor lit-

tle baby, lowest down in the scale of humanity, of all the children we had seen that morning. I could scarcely wish that it might live, and yet even such a little waif may, by God's mercy and in His over-ruling providence, be as happy and as useful as the little baptized " Love the True," the child of many prayers in a Christian home. This was our last visit in China Town. I thought, as I took the cars for the hotel, what a mighty debt we women owe to the Gospel of Jesus Christ ; for it is that which has given us back the place God gave us first in Eden,—a place which no heathen nation has ever yet accorded to the women of their race.

Since writing this little history of our visit in China Town, I have heard from Mrs. C. that they have decided to provide a home for Chinese women, where they may be rescued from the most disgraceful and degrading slavery, and be taught of Christ and his salvation.

THE ACID TEST.

WE had been looking over some pieces of old jewelry at home, and discussing their comparative weight and purity. The subject interested me a great deal; so one day, soon after, I took a little piece of gold to a jeweler's shop, to be weighed and tested. After weighing it, he said: "You would like to know its quality, I suppose?"

"Yes, please. May I see you test it?"

"Oh! certainly," he answered pleasantly. "It's no secret."

I had some knowledge of the different processes to which gold ore is subjected, but was not prepared for anything so simple and suggestive as the jeweler's gold test. Perhaps some reader may be as ignorant as I was; if so, will you stand by my side, while the pleasant boyish-looking jeweler tests my piece of gold?

"I'll compare it with this," he said, taking a ring from a case and handing it to me. "That is eighteen carats gold, six parts of alloy to eighteen of gold." Then he took a small block of stone, smooth and dark, and rubbed the ring and my piece of gold upon it, leaving two narrow yellow bands side by side on the dark surface of the touchstone.

"Yours is more than eighteen carats fine," he said

looking at the two bands, which were perceptibly different in color.

"How can you tell how much purer it is?" I asked.

"I don't know that I can tell very accurately, for I don't often have occasion to test gold, and it doesn't pay to keep ornamental jewelry of finer quality than eighteen or twenty carats," he said, while he carefully examined a box full of rings.

"I was looking for a twenty-two carat ring which we made to order," he said, after a minute, "but it must have been called for. Where there's much of this testing to be done, they keep little bars of gold ranging from fourteen to twenty-four carats fine—you know twenty-four is pure gold—and, by comparing the streak made by the gold to be tested, with that made by the bar nearest it in color, one who has much experience can tell pretty accurately how much alloy there is with the gold, without the test by acid."

"What is that?" said I, growing more and more interested, as he took a small vial of colorless liquid, and let a drop fall on the two yellow streaks.

"Aqua fortis."

"That is nitric acid, isn't it?"

"Yes'm, just the same. The purer the gold, the less it will change under the acid. The gold itself is not affected, it's only the alloy that changes color and is dissolved." I watched the yellow bands: one turned to a greenish mottled color, the other seemed unchanged. "I must try something better," he said. "Your gold is pretty rich. I have a little pure gold here; at least, it was sold to me as such; I'll test it with that." He broke off a little corner from some soft gold leaf, and rubbed it on the touchstone beside the yellow band left by my piece of gold. "They seem to be just about the same," he said, looking at the two bands side by side.

He poured some acid upon them; both bands dulled a little, but neither of them changed color.

"Yours is just about pure gold," he said. "There may be a little alloy, but I can't detect it. If you would like, I'll take it to an assayer's, and let you know precisely what its purity is." I thanked him, but said I was quite satisfied with his test, and had been very much interested. After a little more conversation, I took my piece of gold and came home, with a lesson in my heart.

The thought came to me, how closely the world watches while God's children are tried and tested; and what a sure touchstone, dark and hard, this mortal life of ours is. Then, too, how truly the mark we leave in life is a part of our very selves— not a whit more golden and pure can it be, than we are in the sight of God. It may look well to our eyes, it may even seem fair to others, but God knows just what it is. Then how human, how natural it is, to compare one Christian with another, instead of taking Christ alone as our standard, the pure, un-changed, unchangeable gold, tried by the sharpest, most fiery tests, and found without alloy. The lam-entation came to mind: "How is the gold become dim, and the most fine gold changed!" Ah! that is written of us, not of Him! God knows we need the acid test, lest we should seem to be, and think ourselves, other than we are. But it is a comfort to know that the acid dims and destroys only the alloy. Christ in us, the hope of glory, is untouched, untarnished. We look on, while friend after friend, our nearest and dearest, are tested and tried. We suffer in their sufferings, for pain is not a whit less truly pain because the sufferer belongs to Christ. But we need not fear for any of them. Little by little, the alloy is dissolved. Under the revelation of so much positive sin, as well as of the possibilities of evil in his nature, the poor sufferer is bewildered and distressed beyond words. He cannot understand how, if he be a Christian, he can be so bad, so unlovely, proud or mean. He feels he is less than the least of the disciples, because he is a disgrace to his Master. By and by, the acid test will be over. God will take care of that ; but purity is more precious to Him than man's praise.

I thought for how short a moment in the long, long summer's day the acid lay upon the gold. " A little while ! " Some brave, strong words I had once read returned to my mind. " Mortification and anguish, that wistful yearning, which, like hope deferred, maketh the heart sick, have but their day. Endure them, lift them up, and carry them as a daily burden, permitted by the Master, though perhaps administered by a fellow-servant ; have faith in heaven and earth ; and the new dawn will rise sooner or later, which will ever brighten into the cloudless morning of eternity."

Should not this certainty give us courage and hope, and make us better comforters than the friends of Job, when we must stand by and see others suffer ;

and whenever the sharp agony appointed for ourselves may come, shall we not remember that it is written: "Behold the end of the Lord; for He is very pitiful and of tender mercy."

CASTING, OR CARRYING?

—

IN these troublous times, of wars and rumors of wars, social wrongs, abounding iniquity, and wide-spread distress, many a Christian heart is burdened with anxieties real and pressing, whether they be narrow or world-wide, in their range. There is but one way of relief from care, borne by servant or by sovereign, for a child or for a country, whether it has come through the weakness of a moment or the wickedness of years. No human heart is strong enough, no human sympathy is deep enough, no human wisdom is wise enough, to carry the burden under which some fellow-traveler beside us has fallen to the earth, despairing of relief.

Probably, all of us have frequently noted the linked precept and promise in the fifty-fifth Psalm: "Cast thy burden upon the Lord and He shall sustain thee, and the still more familiar words of the apostle Peter: "Casting all your care upon Him, for He careth for you." They are echoes of the Saviour's exhortation and assurance: "Neither be of doubtful mind (margin, 'Neither live in careful suspense'), for your heavenly Father knoweth that ye have need of all these things."

"Beautiful words," we think, with a sigh, " and of course they must be true:" yet we go on groaning under our care, unrested, unhelped. What is the trouble?

Paul, the aged, when nearing the end of his course, tells us: "Be careful for nothing; but in everything, by prayer and supplication with thanksgiving, let your requests be made known unto God. And the peace of God which passeth all understanding shall keep your hearts and minds through Christ Jesus." Phil. iv: 6, 7.

These words tell of the unspeakable peace of God, garrisoning the saved soul that casts all its care on Him who careth for it. If we fail of the blessedness of that rest, is it not as with Israel of old, "because of unbelief"? (marginal reading, "disobedience.")

Those of us who have had loving, wise and faithful fathers and mothers may be glad to recall the sense of security, the light-heartedness and content, which possessed us after confiding our childish troubles or desires to those whom we had ever found able and willing to help us. We scarcely needed the cheerful assurance: "I will endeavor to arrange it, my child," or "I will see about it, dear," to send us away happy, "nothing doubting." It may well be that, through the mist of years, we have lost memory of times when even their love and care could not compass the fulfilment of our desires, or remove the burdens which their sympathy lightened, but the hearts of their children "safely trusted in them."

Now, having so undoubtingly confided in our earthly parents, is it not strange and sad that we should be shy with our heavenly Father?

I remember once hearing of an extremely timid

little girl, who we knew had for the first time in her life voluntarily asked her father to bring her some trifle on his return from a journey. It was not strange that, in mentioning the circumstance afterwards, he should show how his heart had been gladdened by her confidence, while he owned that he had often been grieved that one of his children felt so much less freedom with him than the other.

Is not our reserve and want of trust, in our heavenly Father's care and desire for our happiness and good, a dishonor to him who has declared that "like as a father pitieth his children, so the Lord pitieth them that fear Him"?

Again, it seems to me, we may heartily trust our heavenly Father to forgive us our sins for the sake of His dear Son Christ Jesus; and yet is there not sometimes an unconfessed shrinking from casting upon our Lord the care which is the consequence of our sins or mistakes? But we surely need to ask Him what he would have us learn by these chastenings, praying Him to save us from bitterness and hardness of heart, and that this discipline may soon yield to us the peaceable fruit of righteousness. We surely cannot think He does not "care" that we should be made better by them.

I have seen a little child when punished by his faithful, tender mother turn to her with an outburst of love and sorrow, clasping his arms around her neck, unwilling to be parted from her for a moment. How much dearer the little fellow was to her than if he had borne his punishment in sullen silence; aye, and how much less likely was he to repeat the fault.

The confidence that declares: "He hath smitten and he will heal us" is precious to our heavenly Father. Is it not significant that the apostle's exhortation, "Casting all your care upon Him," follows closely upon the command "Humble yourselves, therefore, under the mighty hand of God"? It is spiritual pride, as well as unbelief, which would read, instead: "Carrying at least some of your care away from Him, for He cáreth not for you in certain matters." Ah, it is sadly true that we sometimes make ourselves self-appointed scapegoats to bear away our burdens into the wilderness, into a land not inhabited.

Let us be very sure that *all* care may and should be consecrated, whether it be anxiety temporal or spiritual, for ourselves or for others, for individuals or for nations.

> A heavy load once bowed
> My heart and soul;
> Fainting, I cried aloud
> Beneath my dole;
> Then Jesus said:—Am I not strong to bear
> This burden also—all thy grief and care?
>
> Dost thou indeed believe
> My love and might?
> Ah, then, at once receive
> A dear child's right.
> 'Let not your heart be troubled,' be thy song.
> Rest all upon my shoulder. I am strong.

Is not "care" one of the "all things" working together for good to those who love God? The occasion of anxiety or suffering may remain, yet the burden be lifted from heart and mind. The soul that has cast all care upon the Lord goes on to "commit his way also unto Him, trusting Him to bring it to pass." No need now, to measure and weigh the burden, once and forever cast where, blessed be God, "the government" safely rests—"upon His shoulder."

Years ago, there was a mother dying. Her heart had been torn with anxiety for the little children she was leaving, until she surrendered them utterly to Him who is the Father of the fatherless.

As she lay, weak and worn with suffering, dreading the physical struggle of dying, she clung to the hands of those who loved her, saying: "It seems to help me bear the pain—mine is a very dependent nature; you know how it has been, all my life." Then thoughtfully she added: "Perhaps that is not right. I will let everything go, and look straight to Christ;" and she loosened her hands from the clasp of those beside her, all powerless except for sympathy, and folded them quietly on her breast, and so lay, waiting for her Lord.

A little later, she said, brokenly: "I am so weak I cannot listen, I cannot even pray. The only thing I can do—is to cast all my sins—and my sorrows—and my cares—on Jesus—and just let him take care of me." Faithfully He did take care of her, and so He will, of every soul that trusts in Him,—for life, death and through all eternity.

CHRIST IN ART.

MANY earnest Christians conscientiously condemn pictorial illustrations of Bible stories, and especially any representation of our Lord Jesus Christ, "God manifest in the flesh."

While honoring their sincerity and acknowledging the high reverence for God's Holy Word, and for Him who was emphatically the Word of God, which prompts their condemnation, does it not appear that these pictured parables often set forth truth most vividly and strikingly before the eyes and hearts of the simple and ignorant? Years ago, an earnest and most faithful missionary in Japan begged for illustrated Scripture stories, especially for such as showed the human life of the Saviour, as one of the readiest and most effective means of teaching the gospel to the Japanese heathen.

And in our own land, an incident recently occurred which I think might remove the scruples of the most prejudiced. A simple-hearted woman was employed as servant in a Christian household, and, the first time she was sent to dust the parlors, her attention was arrested by an engraving of Sir Noel Paton's picture of "Christ in the garden, with His three disciples." In speaking to me about it, she said : "I was ashamed to stay in there so long.

I don't know what Mrs. Gray must have thought, but it seemed as if I couldn't get enough of that picture. It was all so real, as if it was just happening there now." I asked her how she had known what it was. "Why, ma'am, don't you remember you read to me once about that night in the garden, when Jesus was in His agony, praying all alone, when He'd asked three of His disciples to keep awake and be company for Him, as if He wouldn't be so lonesome if they was near by and praying too. And there in the picture it was all so true. Jesus had just come to them and found all three of them—Peter, too, that was so forward and sure of himself—all of them under the trees fast asleep, and Jesus looking at them so disappointed. Oh! I knew what it was without asking anybody. Every time I dusted the room, I just used to go and stand there and look at Him."

Some time after, I alluded to the impression made upon Nora by the picture. My friend remarked: "Nora never spoke of it, but I remember noticing, when she was sitting with baby in her arms in the next room, she used to place her chair so she could look through the doorway towards the picture hanging over the piano. I understand it now."

Dark nights of trial, and sorrowful, lonely watching have been Nora's lot since then. I cannot but hope the memory of that garden agony, borne for us "the night on which He was betrayed," has been a comfort and strength to her in her sorrows, and that through Christian art one simple soul has been brought nearer to the Saviour of sinners.

"HE CARRIES THEM UP HILL."

THE other day, the children were learning the twenty-third Psalm, and we were talking together about the Good Shepherd, and how He takes care of the sheep and the little lambs. Impetuous Mary, eager to speak her one thought, said rapidly,—

" He feeds them and drives away the lions and the bears."

" Yes," said Tiny, thoughtfully; "and He carries them up hill."

" *He carries them up hill!*"

The words went to my heart with a strength and sweetness the little speaker did not dream of. Often, often since, their music has thrilled through my tired soul, like an echo of the angels' song.

He, who in the days of His flesh, grew weary with His journey and rested at noontide by Jacob's well— even then not resting from His Father's work ; He, who bore the crushing burthen of our sins so often up the lonely slopes of Olivet ; now, in His glorified humanity, as well as in His divine nature, "fainteth not, neither is weary."

And He it is, who "carries us up hill ;" up every rough and rugged mountain-path of duty and suffering, if we will only cling to Him and trust His strength.

It is such rest to know that He will never be weary of us; that, heavy-laden as we are, we can never tire the Everlasting arms. The Master has not yet ceased teaching us in parables, and sometimes a little child's unconscious touch opens a blessed meaning to us.

Memory with her quick glance, flashing through long years, brings back most vividly to me, one summer day of childhood, with its lesson of happy trust. We were spending the summer at Fort Lee, upon the Hudson. I remember well the long, bright, sunshiny day; such as never comes to us except when we are children and take no thought for the morrow. We had been playing for hours on the beach, watching the little waves roll higher and higher up on the sands, as the tide came in. We longed for evening only that our father might come back to us, and this evening we watched for him with special eagerness, because he had promised when he left, to take us all up the Palisades, to see the sunset, on his return. Some friends from the city arrived with him, I remember, and joined our little mountain party; and as we children crowded eagerly around, impatient to start, one of the party said to my father, looking down at me:—

"Surely you don't mean to take that child up the mountain with you! You would have to carry her half the way." "Better stay at home and play with your doll, Pussy!" said she, turning to me.

How well I remember the words and the tone, though I was only four years old! I felt so little, and the strange lady was so big and important.

Chilled by the threatened disappointment, I caught my breath, waiting only for my father's word.

"No, no," said he, in his cheerful, decided way; "that would never do. *I have promised her, and she shall go, if I have to carry her* ALL *the way.*" And up the steep, mountain-path, in that glorious evening light I went, borne gaily on his shoulder, with my arms around his neck. How I loved my father for it; my grateful hug was instead of words, and with what utter trust I clung to him, sure of his strength, of his love, of his truth.

His noble head rests now in the old church-yard; but, as that bright picture gleams out from the shadows of many years, I thank God for the precious type of Himself, He gave me that fair summer sunset long ago. If my father's promise had failed me then, it seems to me I could never, never again have felt such undoubting trust in him; and I am sure I should have missed the sweetness of the little child's simple words, when years afterwards she said of the Lord, our Shepherd, "He carries them up hill."

HOPE ARCHER'S PARABLE.

———

IT would be a blessed thing if every village had a "Cousin Bess" like ours.   She is the most comfortable and trusty of counsellors, sympathetic as she is wise and good, and so bright and cheery and warmhearted, that her house is the chosen resort of all the young folks of Norriston.   Dearest of all the bright girls who gather around her is Hope Archer, an orphan, a sweet, lovely little woman of nineteen, who is governess in the family of Squire Norris, the great man of the place.   Hope's life this last year has been gladdened and saddened by a great joy and a bitter sorrow.

Cousin Bess knows all about it, and, in the heavy trial through which the young girl has passed, the older woman has suffered and struggled with her.

For the same lack of steadfastness which Wayne Halsey betrayed during his engagement to Hope was shown by Wayne's father towards Cousin Bess when, long ago, he forsook her for the sake of the heiress of old Nathan Gould.

To be sure, Wayne's fickle fancy only flitted away for a while he averred, and he returned, penitent and ashamed, to Hope and prayed her to promise still to be his wife.   When she refused to give him any pledge and returned his ring, though she could not hide from him how faithfully she loved him still, he bade her good-bye, and no one in Norriston has seen him since that day. He wrote to Cousin Bess that if he lived he would come back a different sort of a fellow and, he hoped, a better one. He didn't blame Hope a bit for not trusting such a butterfly of a fellow as he had been.

Wayne Halsey holds that mysterious, magnetic, personal charm, impossible to describe or analyze, but whose possession we are wont to recognize in our "pet sinners," the irresistible winsomeness, through all faults and follies, by which many an unprincipled Absalom steals the hearts of all Israel.

Not that any of us in Norriston, unless it be Carroll Norris or Frank Guernsey, would care to call Wayne Halsey hard names. Indeed, when he went away, we thought with a sigh we could have better spared some better man.

Carroll Norris is especially pleased with Wayne's absence. He confided to Cousin Bess, not long ago, his opinion that "Hope's head was level," and followed up with this syllogism :

"Hope won't marry that good-for-nothing fellow, or any one like him. That he, Carroll Norris, is not the least like him (which is true). Therefore, Hope will be very much pleased to marry him, Carroll Norris."

To which piece of false logic Cousin Bess replies with an emphatic shake of the head, but the conceited young fellow will not believe her. Cool, clever, calculating, miscalculating Carroll Norris.

I find I have not begun to tell you about Hope's

parable yet, and I am tormented with the fear that you will be so tired with my long introduction, like the fine-print pages in the first part of the Waverley Novels, that you will not finish my story. But, really, now I am going to tell it.

The other day Hope came into the pleasant sitting-room where Cousin Bess was reading just at sunset, put her arms around her old friend's neck, and then sat down in her favorite place at her feet, and looked up with a face full of emotion.

"Well, childie, what is it? What does this rain-bow face mean?"

Cousin Bess laid her hand on the girl's soft hair, and kissed her tenderly as she spoke.

"Cousin Bess, do you believe in parables, outside of the Bible?"

"That depends," said she smiling. "I do believe that God in his providence gives many a secret lesson by types, which he sends home to our hearts for private interpretation. But tell me what your parable is, dear child."

"I dare say it will not seem like much when I tell it, though it does mean a great deal to me," said Hope, softly. "You know Mary West has been sick and shut up in the house for ever so long, and the other day I had a note from her begging me to come down on Saturday, and especially asking me to sing and play for her. So, last night I gathered together some music that I knew she would like, and rolled it up ready to take with me. This morning, I thought of those songs you love, that Wayne gave me; I knew Mary would enjoy them, and it seemed selfish not to take them to sing for her. So I made up a little package of those songs and fastened it, as I thought, securely with the others. Just as we were landing at New Brighton, a runaway horse dashed down the street to the boat, and we had to spring aside until he was caught. I hurried off the boat and was walking up to Mrs. West's, when I missed my precious roll. I started back, but the bell had rung and the boat was steaming away. All I could do was to take a car and try and reach the next landing in advance of the boat.

"Well, dear, to make a long story short, it wasn't to be found anywhere. Everybody was as kind as possible and tried to help me, but no one had even seen my missing roll. One blundering, kind-hearted fellow suggested, 'Ye mought ha' drapt it overboard, miss, when yon tearing brute of a horse skairt a' the wimmin folks' wits away.'

"So I had to go up to Mary West's with a heavy heart. Do you think me awfully silly and superstitious? That little roll of songs was the only thing I kept that Wayne had ever given me, and in losing it I seemed to lose him too."

Cousin Bess bent down and kissed Hope's upturned face for her only answer.

"I don't mind telling you," said Hope softly. "I did pray real hard that I might find it somehow, somewhere.

"I sang and played as well as I could, and Mary thanked me so sweetly I felt ashamed of myself. Isn't there something in Proverbs about the cruelty of singing songs to a heavy heart? But I sang to myself as well as to Mary, and somehow the hopeless, miserable feeling passed away, and the old thought came to me that used to give me courage when I was a little child—that the thing I had lost was surely somewhere, *somewhere*, and that God knew all about it, though I didn't. So I had that comfort on my way home, and as the boat neared the Battery the thought flashed across me: 'Ask for it on the other side.' So I asked, and there I found it, kept safely for me all those painful hours. Is it very silly," said Hope with a lovely look in her eyes, "to take comfort and courage from such a parable, to think that I may—that I *shall*—find Wayne, if never before, safe at last on the other side?"

HOW A CHRISTMAS CARD SAVED A LIFE.

———

MERRY Christmas time was drawing near, and I wanted some pretty illuminations to give away, so I went one morning to 150 Nassau street, where I knew I should find a beautiful variety.

While I was looking over a multitude of mottoes, and making my choice, I noticed a lady near me, apparently bent on the same errand. After a few minutes, as she seemed unable to find what she was seeking, I asked her if there were any among those I had chosen which she particularly liked.

She thanked me pleasantly, and said she had selected all she wished except one, and she felt pretty sure of finding it among the unassorted cards, for it had been published, she thought, by the Tract Society only the year before.

"It is one with purple pansies—heart's-ease, you know—and the verse :

'Casting all your care upon Him, for He careth for you.'

I want it for a special use," she said ; and then added impulsively : "Those words saved a life—a soul— last Christmas. You don't wonder they are precious !"

Then in a few words, she gave the outline of the story of one who had, through terrible trials, lost faith in human love, truth and honor, and,—worst of all, in his misery had made shipwreck of his faith in God.

It was a Christmas day. He started to leave the house, with the full purpose of committing suicide. The children were just coming home from a Sunday-school Christmas-tree, eager and happy with their pretty presents. He stole out through a room from which they had passed, so that no one might see him leave the house. Lying on the floor, just where he must step to cross the threshold, was a card, with purple pansies and the words: "Casting all your care upon Him, for he careth for you." Startled, thrilled to his soul, he could not pass by that message from heaven, facing him, as if to drive him back from his wicked, cowardly purpose. Faith in God and His love came back, and with it came courage and strength to take up the heavy burden of a bruised and shattered life. God did care for him, and was a very present help in trouble.

The story touched me deeply, and has often recurred to me since, though I have never seen the lady again, and know nothing further of the circumstances. It always comes back with special force, whenever I have to choose Scripture verses to give away. Since we have the promise, "My word shall not return unto me void," may we not rightly ask God's peculiar blessing on these little messengers, which go to so many homes we may never enter?

I could not help thinking that perhaps some one had been praying "in secret" for God's blessing on that very message.

The hand of God was so clearly in it all, guiding

the choice of the text, providing that this one and no other should be given to the little child,—that her chilled fingers should carry it safely through the streets, and then drop it at the very moment, and in the only place, where it would save a life,—that it seemed to me it would be for His honor to repeat the story of His loving care, which came to me so · strangely.

May it be a Father's message to some other poor troubled heart, assuring him of the faithfulness of Him who "will not suffer us to be tempted above that we are able; but will with the temptation make a way of escape, that we may be able to bear it." May it remind him of One who was wounded for our transgressions, and on whose tender, human heart we may to-day cast all our sins, and our sorrows, and our cares, and be sure that He will care for us.

AN INCIDENT OF THE WEEK OF PRAYER.

DURING the Week of Prayer, I was present with a friend at an up-town meeting, the subject for the day being " Humiliation and Confession—for personal failings, for social vices," etc. After several prayers had been offered, a gentleman quietly arose and said, with emphasis: " ' I acknowledge my transgression, and my sin is ever before me ; ' yet let me never forget that ' the Lord is good and ready to forgive, and plenteous in mercy unto all them that call upon Him.' I have proved this true in my own experience, and as it grows out of and is connected with the Week of Prayer, it seems to me not unfitting that I should tell the story of God's grace now and here. To some of you the incident is already known.

" It was twelve years ago. I was then a confirmed drunkard, an outcast from respectable society, a wreck, soul and body. I had tried again and again to break loose from the evil habit which held me. I had tried pledges, resolutions, the Inebriate Asylum, all in vain. I knew I was going down to death, temporal and eternal, and yet had no power to stop. Already I was suffering in my body the terrible wages of sin. I was very miserable.

" It was Sabbath morning after the Week of Prayer. Special intercession had been made for me

during the week, but I knew nothing of it. I determined to go to church that morning, not from any
sense of sin or desire for pardon, but only with a
longing to be freed from the penalty of bodily suffering which was tormenting me or, at least, to secure
some respite.

"As I walked along the street to the church, my
thoughts were very busy. I looked back on my life,
realizing that I had lost everything which had once
been mine—friends, health, position, good name. I
was miserable indeed.

"Entering the church, I sat down in a pew, and,
while sitting there, the Spirit of God found me. I
thought, 'Would it be possible for God to save me?'
and, like an answer from heaven, came the words of
the Saviour: 'Come unto Me, all ye that labor and
are heavy laden, and I will give you rest.'

"The man of God preached from the words: 'I
am that bread of life.' The sermon seemed intended
expressly for me. Listening to that blessed gospel
message, I repented and believed.

"As I left the church and walked along the street,
I thought within myself: 'Dare I speak to others of
this wonderful change which has been wrought in me?
Dare I call myself a disciple of Christ—so full of
sin, and utterly without strength to resist temptation
as I am?' Then came to my mind God's words to
Peter, which answered my doubt—'My grace is sufficient for thee, for My strength is made perfect in
weakness;' and I trusted His strength and it never
failed me.

"I have lived here ever since, in this city, as some

of those who are present know. The Lord has kept me all these twelve years. He has given me back to friends and home and an honest, honorable life. You can judge whether I have not reason to love and remember the blessed Week of Prayer.

"Let me say to any who are discouraged about those who have gone astray, God has power to save them. I know it, for none could be more utterly lost than I was. The Lord still says: 'Let the wicked forsake his way, and the unrighteous man his thoughts, and let him return unto the Lord and He will have mercy upon him, and to our God, for He will abundantly pardon.' Therefore 'let us come boldly unto the throne of grace, that we may obtain mercy and find grace to help in time of need.'"

We listened with hearts awed and thrilled by the narration. I think no one could forget the deep impression made by the story of God's grace, told in such deep earnestness and gratitude.

The following day, the subject under consideration was "Prayer for families, and for all who have the care of children and youth," etc. We were especially interested when the same gentleman arose and, after briefly alluding to God's rescue of himself, remarked that, although he knew that salvation was entirely of God, he still felt deeply grateful to the human hand which had brought to him the gospel offer.

"We do not honor the Lord the less," said he, "for honoring and loving His messengers. How can I but be ever grateful to that faithful man of God who was such a patient friend through all those years of struggle, who cheered and helped and strengthened my heart in the Lord, giving me wise counsel and a brother's sympathy?

"Nor can I ever forget or cease to bless God for the loving Christian mother who long ago taught me to pray, who when I was only a little fellow led me to the house of God, who stored my childish mind with Scripture truth which came back to memory long after she had been taken away from me.

"God's promises are sure, and I am only one more proof of the security of the old pledge to those who train up their children in the fear of the Lord. They may give sore grief for years by wandering from the right way, yet *when they are old* they will not depart from it."

"I SURRENDER."

In one of our hospitals lay a wounded officer, dying far away from his home. Young, brilliant, and beloved, death came to him as an unwelcome messenger. In his buoyant health and strength, he had, like another young man, turned away from Jesus, clinging to his "great possessions," and unwilling to humble himself to enter into the kingdom of heaven as a little child.

When the shadows of eternity were closing around him, his proud heart was troubled, and he began to seek Him whom he had rejected. Earnestly and eagerly he asked to be shown the way of salvation, but as often he turned away from the free grace of God. His sister and the chaplain repeated the promises of God again and again: "God so loved the world, that He gave His only begotten Son, that whosoever believeth on Him should not perish, but have everlasting life."—"Him that cometh unto Me, I will in no wise cast out." But the habit of years appeared to be strong on him still, and pride of intellect wrestled with the simplicity of gospel truth. His sense of sinfulness was deep; he seemed to feel that he was lost.

"I cannot understand it!" he exclaimed. "I am willing; but I cannot see how *believing* can save me. Oh, help me, help me! I cannot understand it!"

Worn and wearied by mental struggles in addition to his physical sufferings, he yet returned constantly to that one thing. Earnestly his sister prayed and pleaded for him, and would not give him up. He seemed to be brought almost to the threshold of the kingdom; but, unconsciously to himself, his pride, "the strong man armed," beat him back.

At last the simple gospel words, "He that believeth on the Son of God hath everlasting life;" "Believe on the Lord Jesus Christ, and thou shalt be saved;" "Come unto Me, all ye that labor and are heavy laden, and I will give you rest,"—applied to his soul with power by the Holy Ghost, reached his heart. His face grew brilliant like a child's. With momentary strength he raised himself from the pillow; and, stretching out his arms, he exclaimed with thrilling earnestness,—

"I accept the terms: *I surrender!*"

That one cry of faith was his last. In that final "surrender" the soul went out to meet its Maker.

But, ah! how nearly "too late" was it for him! The Arch-enemy, as of old over the body of Moses, "contended" for his soul. But it was, we trust, a "brand plucked from the burning" by an everlasting arm of strength.

Fellow-Christians, should not the language of our lives be, every day and every hour: "I surrender; I surrender"? Every purpose, every longing, every joy, we should bring to Him for the seal of His good pleasure. Life would then be no barren, joyless thing, but an ever-new and ever-strengthening impulse from the one Life-giver. Though, while we look steadfastly toward heaven, some cherished life-work may be parted from us, and the clouds receive it out of our sight, yet let us not fear that we shall be the losers by a cheerful surrender. It may come back to us "after many days," clad with an angel's energy, and consecrated anew with the blessing and the message which were given at Bethany eighteen hundred years ago.

Fellow-sinner, while pardon and peace and a Father's blessing are offered to you, "surrender." Let not your pride be your destruction. If Christ the Lord stooped from heaven to offer you eternal life through His blood, will you be too proud to reach out your hand, and take it from the hand that was pierced for you?

"Kiss the Son, lest he be angry, and ye perish from the way when his wrath is kindled but a little."

A NINETEENTH-CENTURY BARREL OF MEAL.

A TRUE INCIDENT.

ONE bright spring morning, I called at the house of Mrs. Macgregor, a Scotch woman whose acquaintance I had made at one of our little missionary prayer-meetings some time previous. I had been attracted, from the first, by her warm-hearted simple faith and the quaint directness of her language, which, as timidity was lost in earnestness, sometimes lapsed into her native dialect.

She was a little woman, with a small, thin face and intelligent blue eyes. Somebody once described her as a "wisp of straw," and she did indeed look as if a strong gust of March wind might blow her away; but she possessed a tenacity of purpose, an energy and power of endurance, that enabled her both to do and suffer more than many a plump, comfortable-looking woman of greater apparent vigor.

On this occasion, she was speaking of the unfailing kindness of the Lord in providing for her and her family, ever since she was left a widow with four little children—the youngest only three months old at the time of her husband's sudden death. She spoke gratefully of the kind friends who had been raised up, and had supplied her with work at her home, and mentioned repeated instances in which employment had been exactly suited to her ability and the circumstances of her family.

I could not help noticing how constantly she claimed the promises of God, and grounded her expectation of things needful on the Lord's pledged word.

"It has aye been, ma'am, that strength, as well as oor bread, has been gien as the day has had need o' it, so I hae had nae ca' for worry aboot the morrow."

"But have you never been disheartened?" I asked, feeling the unconscious rebuke of her courageous faith.

"Whiles, ma'am, for a bit, but I've always foun' it a guid thing to be sent direc' to the Lord for help an' comfort. I couldna gae to ony man leeving, tho' it be my ain brither, an' tell him o' oor need, but I think nae shame to tell it a' to the Lord. I'm sure, sure, He kens it a' weel eneuch beforehan', but He maun mean we sould hae the guid o' pourin' oot oor hearts, or He wadna bid us be carefu' for naething, but in ilka thing, wi' giein' o' thanks, to mak known oor requests unto Him. An' ye min', ma'am, we hae His ain word for it; gin we do as He bids, His vera ain peace shall keep oor hearts through Jesus Christ."

"Yes, indeed, but it sometimes takes us a good while to learn to do without worry, does it not?"

"Dinna ye think, ma'am, that the Lord sometimes shuts us a' up i' the daurk, wi' oor ain emptiness, to gie us a lesson o' His fulness? I min' weel ane dour time, four yea   sin', an' hoo He shamed me wi' His guidness.

"There had been some trooble or ither i' the mills,

an' the wark was stoppit for a fortnicht, sae the lads had naething but a job here an' there, an' then Kenneth fell sick, an' the rent was near due, an' I had gien my word to be punctooal, especial sin' the lan'lord had put down the rent, considerin'.

"It was the spring-time, sae we had nae mickel need o' fire, for whilk I was vera thankfu'. We had twa loaves o' bread whilk I had bakit i' the morn, wi' the scrapin's o' the meal-barrel.

"Ah, ma'am, my heart sank down, down, when I thocht o' the lads oot o' wark, an' Kenneth sick, an' the barrel empty, an' the rent due on Friday; an' then the de'il gied a twich o' his evil fingers at my heavy heart to gar me lose courage an' my trust i' the guidness o' the Lord.

"I had twa gowns i' the hoose to mak for a young neebor woman, but I hadna been able to sew for three or four days, on account o' Kenneth. But noo I maun begin them, an' by warkin' day an nicht I made sure o' finishin' them, an' wi' the money for the wark I wad pay the rent.

"Sae I wrought a' the day lang, an' a' Tuesday nicht thro', an' a' the next day, savin' to do what was needfu' aboot the rooms an' for Kenneth (we didna hae mickle cookin'), but when Wednesday nicht cam' aroon' the wark wasna half dune, an' I was sae a'thegither tired oot, an' my head was sae bad, I couldna put in anither stitch. I was fair discooraged wi' my fine plans.

"I just laid my head doon on the table an' began to greet. It seemed as though the Lord Himsel' was against me, for a' my strivin' to keep my word was nae guid. Jamie, my biggest laddie—he was near fifteen then—came into the room while I was dryin' my e'en. I'm nae mickle gien to cryin', an' the lad was fair astonished to see me sae o'ercome.

"'Mither,' said he, 'may be the lan'lord wad wait a day. It canna be sae mickle to him as it is to us.'

"'But, Jamie, there's my gien word,' I said.

"'Weel, mither, greetin' 'll do nae guid to him nor to you. We'd mickle better pray.'

"Sae we went to my little room and kneeled down thegither, an' Jamie prayed first, an' then he went awa' to his bed. But I didna rise frae my knees. O ma'am, I canna tell ye hoo close the guid Lord was, just as He was wont to be when He was upo' the earth an' let puir women touch His garments an' pour oot their sad hearts at His feet. I just tellt Him He kent weel hoo I had been strivin' i' my ain strength, an' hoo I hadna keepit a guid cheer i' Him, but had been sair downhearted an' dootin'. But He had aye been forgivin' an' mercifu' to me, an' I had naethin' to do but gae to Him for forgiveness, an' I was sure, sure, He was aye mair glad to gie it than I was to get it.

"I made bold, too, to ask Him if He wad be pleased to let help come to us in a certain way for the morrow, an' then a' the care an' weariness were gane, an' I stoppit thinkin' o' oor need, an' was sae glad o' heart to be at His feet I thocht o' naethin' but a' His loving-kindness.

"I took nae heed o' the time till it struck ane o' the clock, an' then I went richt awa' to bed an slept sweet an' soun' as a baby, wi' nae thocht nor care for the morrow.

"The next day, I finished ane o' the gowns an, carried it hame, but I couldna get my pay for it. I wasna fash't though, for I kent weel eneuch the Lord could hae sent the money that way gin he had a mind to.

"I' the afternune a neebor woman, a kin'-hearted body, though she doesna believe i' the Beeble nor i' prayin', steppit in to ask after the bairn. She said to me suddintly:

"'Mrs. Macgregor, do you know there's a barrel of flour for you at the station?'

"I didna say a word. I wasna surprised, but sae thankfu' I couldna speak.

"'Were you expectin' it?' she asked, kind o' sharp.

"'Yes,' I told her, 'I was.'

"'What made you?' asked she.

"I told her I had need o' it, an' had asked for it.

"'You don't pretend to tell me you prayed for it!' said she.

"'Yes, Mrs. Kean,' I said, I had.

"'Weel, you will have it to-morrow I suppose,' she said, kind o' wonderin', as if she didn't fair believe it.

"I told her I expected to have it that nicht, for I needed it. She didna bide lang, but when she went to the door to gae hame, she cried oot:

"'Well, I never! This does beat all. Mrs Macgregor, here's Sandy Brown wi' your barrel o' flour.'

"An' sae it was. Wi'oot a word or thocht o' mine, the barrel was in my hoose, an' Sandy wad scarce be thankit for the bringin' o' it. He was a kind lad, the son o' an' auld widdy I had nursit i' the fever, an' the lad was aye fain to do some guid turn or ither to his mither's frien's."

"But did you never know where the barrel came from?" I asked.

"Oh! yes, indeed, ma'am; that's the best part o' it. That vera nicht my brither, who is a butcher in New York, knockit at oor door. He askit, maist as sune as he cam' ben, if I had received a barrel o' flour, an' if we had been in need o' it or in distress o' ony sort. Sae, ma'am, I tellt him a' the truth, an' aboot the nicht afore, an' that I had askit the Lord to put it into his heart to sen' me some flour. He got up an' walkit up and doon the room, an' the tears ran down his face. (He was aye tender-hearted, forbye he had sic an' unco' sair trade.)

"'This goes ahead o' anything I ever knew, Mary,' says he. An' then he began an' tellt me that he couldna rest the Wednesday nicht, for e'en as sune as he wad shut his e'en there I stude before him in his dreams, an' he felt sure I was in trooble. I' the morn when he gaed oot for his orders, he stoppit to see an auld frien' o' oors, an' she askit him direckly when he had seen his sister Mary. He said it was near a twal-month.

"'Weel, Robbie,' said she, 'ye maun gae an' see her immejitnly. I'm a'thegither sure she's in trooble.'

"He said he couldna posseebly gae, but she keepit on urgin' him till he tellt her he maun gae to his beeziness, but he wad sen' a barrel o' flour express. But a' the day lang, he said, I was in his thochts sae he couldna rest, till he tuik the train an' made sure o' kennin' the truth his ain sel.

"An', ma'am, he gied me money for twa months' rent, an' wad scarce be content that I wouldna gie my word to let him ken if we sould ever be in sair straits again. Ye may weel be sure, ma'am, I thankit my brither an' thankit the Lord for the guid answer which cam' sae sune.

"Dinna ye believe it was the Lord Himsel' wha troubled my brither's dreams at the vera time I was prayin', an' dinna the Lord sen' him to yon auld frien' o' oors, sae to mak sure he wadna forget my need? Surely He has mony a way to help, by day or by nicht, an' we canna conceive o' them, for His ways are higher than oor ways and His thochts than oor thochts, an' a' hearts are in His ain han'. Dear ma'am, why souldna we trust Him?"

REDEMPTION OF STRAYS.

—

ONE evening, which I shall long remember, I was very tired, heart, soul and body. Life seemed so difficult, and nothing seemed worth while. Sharp pain would have sent me to the Helper, but vague despondency and unrest held me in their coils, paralyzed and dull.

I had been copying some law papers through the day. Mechanically I kept on at the work—an index of subjects of legislation—although there was then no occasion to continue it. No help nor hope for me, as I wrote line after line. But suddenly before my eyes flashed the words, " *Redemption of Strays.*" The words, the thought, thrilled my heart, and wrought a revulsion of feeling, so swift, so complete, that it held me with a sense of awe in the midst of my happiness. It seemed as if the Master himself had stooped from heaven to show me His hands and His side.

The cloud was gone : heart and soul were rested now. I was at home again, safe, safe, and welcome.

What a flood of precious Bible words rushed into mind when those human words opened the way! " I have gone astray like a lost sheep." " But thou hast redeemed me." Was it not truly my Shepherd's voice, calling me through the earthly words of man's work ?

It seemed to me very beautiful that human law

should provide for redemption for God's poor dumb creatures, ignorant trespassers, gone astray from their rightful owners ; but oh ! what a trivial type, at best, of the infinite, everlasting redemption which the Lord has provided for His poor wanderers ! I thought of that beautiful description of those who were called by God from among men to be His high-priests, "who can have compassion on the ignorant, and on them that are out of the way," and of the one Intercessor forever who is touched with the feeling of our infirmities, "being made in all things like unto His brethren." "He hath poured out his soul unto death." "He bare the sins of many, and made intercession for the transgressors." "The good shepherd giveth His life for the sheep." "My sheep hear my voice, and I know them, and they follow me : and I give unto them eternal life, and they shall never perish."

"And He careth for you ! Oh, how He had cared ! " Very sweet was the thought of His good providence that prepared my way before me, leading me in my discouragement and weariness to go on with my day's work after the evening-time of rest had come, and which made ready the words to "restore my soul."

"When he hath found it, he layeth it on his shoulders rejoicing ! " What rest and safety there is in that return to the fold ; not driven, nor even led, but wrapped in the Shepherd's seamless robe, laid upon His shoulders, and carried home rejoicing.

Oh ! if every one would only learn for himself how pitiful and strong, how merciful and faithful this dear Shepherd and Saviour is !

SPENDING-MONEY.

———

"Cousin Ruth," said Ethel Grant one day, "did you ever come to your last cent?"

"Of my spending-money—yes, dear, more than once. Why, have you been in straits lately, like the hero of the 'lone fish-ball'?"

"Not exactly," answered Ethel laughing; and then with a sudden change to earnestness, she added: "I don't know but it would be the best thing for me, if it would make me more willing to help people. It's an awfully mean thing, I know, but I never do want to spend or give away my last twenty-five cents. I feel so very queer and helpless without any spending-money," said she quaintly.

"It's not very comfortable I know, dear, and one day years ago, I realized pretty keenly what it must be for poor wanderers to find themselves penniless and far from home."

"Why, Cousin Ruth? Oh! won't you tell me about it, that is, if you don't mind?"

"I don't mind a bit, dear, but it is not much of a story. Once upon a time, or, to be more specific, when you were running around in baby-dresses, and I was about as old as you are now, it happened that I made my first journey alone."

"Did you have your pocket picked?" demanded

Ethel. "Somebody picked mine the time I went to Brooklyn alone."

"Poor child! I have heard of another traveler who was robbed by thieves of his spending-money. Well, what did you do in your trouble?"

"Oh! I went to Uncle John's office, and had to borrow fifty cents of his clerk, for Uncle was out of town. Oh! how ashamed I felt."

"That was rather a mortifying experience to a young lady of your independence."

"Yes, and to have Uncle John ask about my pocket, every time he saw me, for six months after," said Ethel with a little pout. "But I didn't mean to interrupt you, Cousin Ruth—please go on."

"Well," began Ruth, "I was coming home from Washington after the Grand Review."

"Oh! I heard Uncle John telling Harvey about it —how they marched to the music of Old John Brown. That was just after the war, wasn't it?"

"Yes," said Ruth Oliphant, her face kindling with the old enthusiasm, "May 23d and 24th, 1865. I think I shall never forget, to my dying day, that grand army of worn and tired soldiers, with their tattered, faded flags. No pomp or holiday look about them now! They had been through the fight and knew what it meant. But oh! the thin ranks, the many, many missing! Ah! well, I must not think about that now," said Cousin Ruth, rousing herself to speak cheerfully.

"Don't be in a hurry, please. I like to hear about real things and real people, and what they did and how they felt," pleaded Ethel, with her pretty, coaxing caress. "I don't want to come to the end of it too soon."

"Aren't you afraid there may be a moral tacked on at the end, dear?" said Ruth with a laugh. "Well, I will make my story long to please you, but mind, if you get tired, it will be your own fault."

"I'll take the risk," answered Ethel.

"I stayed in Washington for a week or ten days after the Review. It was not my first visit there, but it was by far the most delightful one. There were always the nicest times in the world at Mr. Lambert's, and Grace was my dear friend. And then, deep down in our hearts, there was now the undercurrent of thankfulness that the war, the terrible four years' war, was really over. You know both my brothers were in the army, dear, and when they were off staff-duty they were very often with us. Poor Grace had one brother in the Northern and two in the Southern army—"

"Oh! how dreadful," said Ethel, with a shudder. "Did they all live till the end of the war?"

"Yes, rather strangely, and now can talk of those sad, terrible times without bitterness. But the Southern brothers were not in Washington then. Each day of my visit, as it came and went, was brighter and fuller of happiness than the one before, until the last of those bright days came to an end.

"Rather against my brothers' wish, I had chosen to take the night train instead of the morning one.

"When the time came to leave the Lamberts', some friends came with my brothers to bid me good-bye, and made quite a grand military escort for a little girl starting off home on her first journey alone. The excitement and novelty of it all kept me from realizing that this was to be really good-bye to the pleasant Washington days. Even when my brothers had arranged everything comfortably for me in the ladies' car, kissed me, and given me my ticket with some parting injunctions, and some nonsense to keep my spirits up, I could not somehow make myself believe that they were not all going with me. But when the train moved off in the faint moonlight, and I no longer saw their waving handkerchiefs and lifted caps, I began to realize that I was alone."

"I think it's horrid, Cousin Ruth, to have to come to the end of nice times," said Ethel vehemently. "Everything seems so flat afterwards."

"I know," said Ruth slowly. "But that is often merely the natural reaction after the unusual excitement. The real happiness of any sweet, pure 'good time' endures and does us good in the memory."

Ethel looked up with a sudden impulse as if to speak, but checked herself, and said:

"It is too bad. I am interrupting you all the while. It is very impolite in me, 'speaking out in meeting,' as the old woman said."

"It does not disturb me at all," said Cousin Ruth quietly; "this is our little talk, and we may as well talk as we please."

"Well, then, Cousin Ruth, did you feel very blue that night," asked Ethel.

"No. I remember amusing myself between the snatches of sleep that came to me with sketching my sleeping neighbors, and writing notes to send back to

Gracie Lambert and my brothers.   I may have sighed a little sigh, remembering the hours and miles that were parting me from them, but I did not think they would forget me, any more than I dreamed of forgetting them.   I was not at all *blasé* nor at all pathetic," said she, a little mischievously.

"I could scarcely believe it," said she, resuming her story, "when an expressman came through the car and I heard him say we were nearing Jersey City. I gave him my baggage check, paying him what I afterwards learned was an extortionate charge for delivering my valise up-town.   I remember I had to empty my little outside pocket-book in order to pay him, and, foolish child that I was, I never looked to see how much change was left in my other purse where my bank-check was safely stowed away.   In those days, you know, Ethel, we had no silver money, nothing but paper and nickels.

"It was four o'clock, a beautiful June daybreak, when we crossed the ferry.   I felt like a traveler landing on an unknown shore, the city seemed so strange and dim, everthing looked so queer and shut up.   I thought how, just two weeks before, we had reached Washington as early in the morning, but then Cousin Joe and Belle were with me, and it wasn't at all lonesome.   There were some pleasant ladies on the boat, however, and I thought I would go with them to the ladies' restaurant at the ferry before I started up-town.

"I opened my purse in the waiting-room to count my money.   Well, I was in a worse plight than even the Harvard professor, for I found I had but just five cents !

" So there was plainly no breakfast for me at that time of day, and I began to wonder how I should ever reach Nineteenth street."

" Poor Cousin Ruth ! " said Ethel. " How did you ever manage ? I wouldn't know what in the world to do in such a scrape."

" I remember walking up Cortlandt street towards Broadway, feeling, I must confess, rather forlorn, and not at all like the brave girl I had thought myself when I laughed away my brother's objections to my early landing at Jersey City."

" But why did you not ride up town in a stage or street-car ? Were they not running in those days ? " asked Ethel, somewhat in the tone she would have used to inquire concerning Revolutionary times.

" Oh ! yes ; but the fare in the omnibus was ten cents and in a street-car six, and I, alas, had only five. I thought of going to the Astor House, but then I had never been to any hotel alone, and I did not feel inclined to try it."

" Couldn't you take a carriage ? "

" No. I did not think that would be as safe or comfortable as to walk, so on I trudged up Broadway, and began to feel a little faint and cold, and oh ! such a longing as I had for the sweet home welcome and rest that I knew were always ready for me at my dear old friend's.

" I remembered, remorsefully, how my brother had asked me, only the evening before, if I were quite sure I had plenty of money to last until I could get ·

my check cashed, and how confidently I had answered, Yes. I thought how gladly I would take one cent now if I could.

"At last I reached Canal street. By that time I felt pretty much like any other demoralized tramp, and made up my mind to pocket my pride, take a Sixth-avenue car, and ask the conductor if he would carry me for five cents." ·

Cousin Ruth stopped to laugh at the recollection, and Ethel asked anxiously:

"Well, did he?"

"Yes, I suppose he thought I looked tired enough to be honest. I remember telling him I would send my full fare to the car-office as soon as I could get a check cashed, so he would not get into any trouble on my account. It must have sounded rather ridiculous, I suppose," said Ruth, "but I was very much in earnest."

"I never should have thought of offering to make it square in that way," said Ethel.

"Well, I did not need to do so, as it turned out," added Ruth, "for a nice old gentleman in the car, who tried hard to look very grave, handed one cent to the conductor, saying: 'Allow me to settle the balance for this lady.' And then when I turned to thank him, he looked at me with such a kind, amused look, as if I had been seven instead of seventeen, and said: 'Oh! no matter, my child, no matter!'

"So you see, my dear Ethel, I have been not only at the end of my spending-money, but I have actually received charity from a stranger once in my life, and know how it feels."

"It was very queer, and must have been very disagreeable," said Ethel, pondering.

"Not so very," replied Ruth, with a twinkle in her eye, at Ethel's extreme gravity. "It was a kind of object lesson to me, on the way to give without making any one uncomfortable."

"And then, after all," said Ethel, "you knew that you had your check,.and that made some difference in your feelings."

"Yes," admitted Cousin Ruth, "but my check was no better for immediate use than little Faith's jewels and precious roll which the thieves happily found not, when they robbed him of his spending-money."

"Oh! I wanted to know what you meant by saying that. It's in Pilgrim's Progress, is it not?" Ethel handed Ruth the old worn copy of Bunyan, and kneeling beside her, so as to look on she said : "I never can make very much out of these old allegories, except easy parts like the Slough of Despond and the steps Christian could not see in the midst of the mire ; and then Doubting Castle and the key called Promise, hidden all the while in Christian's bosom, which was able to open any lock in the Castle. I think that is just beautiful," said Ethel, with the soft, earnest look in her eyes Cousin Ruth loved to see.

"So it is, dear, but I think you will like this part, too," said she, reading aloud a page or two of Little Faith's story.

"Poor man," she said, "you see he was forced to beg as he went, to keep himself alive until he came to his journey's end, for his jewels he might not sell, nor his precious roll, the pledge of his acceptance at the gate of the Celestial City. Those three sturdy rogues, Faint Heart, Mistrust, and Guilt, rob a good many of us pilgrims of our spending-money to this very day," added Ruth, thoughtfully.

"I don't understand," said Ethel slowly, "what spiritual spending-money means. Do you suppose it stands for everything we need to make us comfortable and useful on the way?"

"I suppose so, just that. Not our eternal life— for that is hid with Christ in God, a jewel no thief can touch,—but our hope of it, with strength, peace, heart's ease, and joy."

"But I don't see," said Ethel, "how we can be robbed of such blessings."

Cousin Ruth answered slowly: "Mistrust stole the pilgrim's purse, while Guilt with his club knocked him down and left him bleeding. If we sin, and being of little faith, fail to go to our Father, confessing our wrong-doing, pleading for forgiveness through our Advocate, and receiving the pardon and peace He has promised for Jesus' sake, why then our guilty conscience brings us low, while mistrust of God's mercy and of our right to it, robs us of peace, hope, and comfort."

"Yes, I see now," said Ethel softly. "But we don't need to stay robbed do we?" Ethel's wistful look brought the tears to Ruth's eyes.

"No, dear child," said she, kissing the dear little face. "I think Jesus is ever saying to us: 'Wherefore didst thou doubt?' Faith honors, as surely as doubt dishonors our Lord. We are the children of a King, and it is not our Father's good pleasure that we should go as beggars upon the King's highway, while He says to us: 'Things present, and things to come,—all things are yours.'"

"Good-bye, dear Cousin Ruth, and thank you ever so much for your story, and the moral, too," said Ethel with a grateful kiss and a smile. "I hope I shall not mind being short of one kind of spending-money, while I have a right to plenty of the other."

SPIRITUAL MALARIA.

A LOVELY Christian lady once said to me, when speaking of the way she had felt while suffering from malaria: "I did not care for anything or anybody. I lay on the sofa, and was miserable, and did not care whether my house was kept properly or not. It seemed as if I did not care for even my baby and my husband, for anything on earth, or in heaven. But tonics and change of air completely cured me!"

There is a kind of spiritual malaria very prevalent nowadays, enervating and depressing in its influence, even deadening every noble instinct, all Christian principle. Neglect of secret prayer, indifference to known duty, sluggish apathy when others need our help, selfish discontent with our lot, are not these symptoms of this undermining disease?

Thank God, there is a great Physician, who knoweth our frame, and remembereth that we are dust. His hand upon our pulse brings healing. "He giveth power to the faint, and to them that have no might He increaseth strength."

Health does not always come back easily. "Tonic treatment and change of air," often mean bitterness and sorrow, humiliation, bereavement, losses. But any healthful suffering is better than a living death.

If we ever find that we do not care whether we do

right or wrong, that we do not care whether we hurt or help others, that we do not care to follow Jesus in self-denial, taking up our cross daily, oh! let us go straight to Him who alone can deliver us from this spiritual torpor, who healeth all our diseases and redeemeth our life from destruction.

—

"PLEASE, auntie, tell me a story—a real true story about some naughty little boys or girls, won't you?"

"But, Nan dear, why do you want to hear about naughty children?"

"Oh, I don't know, 'cept I guess they're more interesting, don't you?"

So here is auntie's story for Nan, about

A LITTLE GIRL WHO COULDN'T BELIEVE WHAT SHE DIDN'T SEE.

"Once upon a time, there was a round-faced little girl, with blue eyes and flaxen hair, and she was such a dumpling of a little girl that her aunties used to call her 'Mother Bunch.'

"Well, this little girl's name was Mollie, or pretty near it anyhow, and her grandma and aunties used to borrow Mollie once in a while, for they had no little children at their houses, and they made a great pet of her, and Mollie loved them all dearly.

"One time, Aunt Belle borrowed Mollie for a week or two, and I think she did have a nice time! How surprised Uncle Jimmy would look every evening, when he came home from business, and Aunt Belle would tell him there was a little girl somewhere around!

"What a great time he would have, hunting all

about the parlor, under the tables and in auntie's work-basket, and up the chimney and behind the doors, and at last Mollie would jump out from a little corner by the sofa. Then how he would catch her up in his arms, and sing: 'O Mollie has a beaming face!' in his funny way!"

"But, auntie!"

"Yes, Nan dear, I'm coming to it pretty soon. After Mollie had been at Uncle Jimmie's about a week, there came a storm that lasted several days and Mollie couldn't go out, and she got very tired of her playthings, and I dare say she missed the dear little brother and sisters, and her own dear papa and mamma at home.

"But Aunt Belle was just as kind and indulgent as ever a good auntie was in the world, and had already bought Mollie more doll-babies than she would have had in a long while at home, for I am sorry to say that Mollie was like some other little girls I have heard of, and broke up her playthings and dollies very carelessly."

"O auntie! you don't mean me, do you? You said the other day you thought I was improving my carelessness."

Auntie laughed and said: "I think you are trying to be more careful, dear, and I hope Mollie tried, too. But she grew very cross that stormy morning, and when Auntie Belle said: 'Molly Polly, come here, in auntie's room, and bring your dolly, and you can dress her up with some of these pretty ribbons,' I am sorry to say that Mollie cried out that she hadn't any dolly to play with. Every dolly hadn't any legs or

arms or something—and she did feel very 'uncomfor-
bottle!' Auntie asked her if she thought she would
be happy if she had a new dolly. 'Oh! yes,' Mollie
thought 'she would, to be sure, but then she didn't
think auntie would go out in the storm to get her
one.' But Aunt Belle said, in her lively way: 'Be a
good girl, little Mollie, and auntie 'll bring you a
dolly.'

"And Mollie watched auntie start off, with a big
cloak and rubbers on, and an umbrella, and she
saw her from the parlor window go splashing through
the slush and the snow, until she turned the corner of the street and Mollie couldn't see her any
more. But she stood and watched, and watched,
and watched, until she saw auntie's umbrella bobbing
up and down as she came near the house. But, O
dear! Mollie didn't see any dolly! The beautiful
dolly she had been thinking of until she thought she
knew just how it would look, when auntie should hold
it up for her to see it under the umbrella.

"When auntie came to the door and the servant
let her in, Mollie stood still for a moment waiting to
see the dolly, and then she burst out in a naughty,
passionate cry: 'O dear, you said you'd bring me a
dolly, and you haven't got it. O dear! O dear!'

"Auntie said: 'Why, Mollie! is this little Mollie?'
And the servant took the wet cloak and rubbers
away, and auntie drew the little girl into the parlor
and said: 'Doesn't auntie keep her promises, Mollie?
Auntie said she would bring you a dolly, and here it
is,' drawing it out of her pocket where she had put it

to keep it all safe and dry! Oh, how ashamed and sorry little Mollie was!"

"My! Yes. I should think so," says Nan. "She was a real naughty little girl, wasn't she, auntie? And what kind of a dolly was it?"

"Well, I don't think I could tell you very much about it, but it was just the kind Mollie wanted, and I have heard she was very happy with it, and loved her kind auntie very much for going all through the storm to get it for her."

"Yes!" said Nan. "I'm glad she wasn't an ungrateful little girl, aren't you?"

"Yes, dear, and now, Nan, you see if Mollie had believed her auntie, believed her very hard, even when she couldn't see the dolly, she wouldn't have been so naughty to her kind auntie that rainy day. And that reminds me, Nan, of a little verse I want you to think of, when you remember this story about Mollie and her auntie. Say it after me, dear: 'He is faithful that promised.'"

Nan repeated it two or three times, until she knew it perfectly.

"And now, Nan," said her auntie, "God wants us to believe we shall have what He promises us, even when we don't see the good thing. Do you understand me, dear!"

"Yes'm, I guess so," said Nan slowly. "The dolly was there all the while under her auntie's cloak, so as not to be spoiled, wasn't it? And her auntie meant all the time to give it to her, didn't she? I think I know what you mean about the verse, auntie.

It's like the doll in the pocket, isn't it? But was Mollie always good afterwards, auntie?"

"I'm afraid not, dear."

"Then won't you tell me all the naughty things she ever did, please, auntie?"

"O my! No indeed, I couldn't possibly; besides, how do you suppose I should know of all the naughty things she did?"

"Well!" said Nan, "I'm glad she did that naughty thing, anyhow, and you knew about it, so you could tell me, for I do love stories about bad little boys and girls," added she, with a sigh.

PRAYER-MEETING VARNISH.

IT was a fine moonlight evening. Harry Holland
and his friend, Phil Washburne, partners in " House
Decorating,—Wood-tiling a specialty," passed out of
the lecture-room of the Chestnut Avenue church, and
walked toward their respective homes, arm in arm.
For a few moments, there was silence, and then Phil,
with an impatient gesture, burst out vehemently:

" I say, Harry, tell me honestly—is the trouble
with these meetings, or with *me?* Can you like them,
get help from them? If you do, I reckon it's on the
principle of the old Scotch woman who ' thanked the
Lord she enjoyed vera puir health.' I've been four
times since I came back, and every time I go away discouraged, and far more in doubt than I went. Twice,
Elder Brown has warned young Christians against
being too happy—has told them they needn't expect
to be kept from sin, but they must trust the Lord to
pull them out of the pit when they fall into it. Then
Elder Brace always declares himself a poor cumberer
of the ground ; but somehow it seems to me he doesn't
go to work to do anything else. Two or three times
you, Hal, and some one or two others, have spoken
of God's promises and Christ's fullness. Do you
really suppose any poor sinner, straying into that
meeting to-night, would have been likely to learn of

Christ as a present Saviour from sin, a Friend, a Brother?"

"I am afraid not," owned Harry, sadly, "except for old Sam's prayer."

"Yes, that's so. That was genuine prayer, humble and childlike. But, Hal, this is a vital matter to me," added Phil, earnestly; "I expected to unite with the church next communion. If I should do so, I should feel bound to attend the prayer-meeting, and the plain truth is, I don't want to."

"I understand just how you feel, Phil, but I don't think this stumbling-block should hinder your confessing Christ. I acknowledge I generally go from a sheer sense of duty, often with my head full of business, and of course I am not ready to receive spiritual benefit,—the more shame to me."

"Harry," exclaimed Phil, earnestly, "I don't in the least believe those elders and deacons conscious hypocrites. I have seen most of them in their stores and factories, and know they are leading upright, Christian lives, in the face of temptation. Yet I tell you, when Wednesday night comes around I am inclined to think their religion a sham, for there's such an evident veneering and varnishing,—such a covering up and hiding the solid truth, that it seems like poor stuff after all. It's dreadful to feel so, I know, and makes me very much doubt whether I can be a Christian at all," added he sadly.

Harry Holland tightened his hold on his friend's arm, and answered, earnestly: "Indeed, Phil, I don't agree with you there. You're a very different fellow from what you were six months ago. *Then*, you might have made a joke of it, but now it really hurts your heart, I know."

"Well, that's a fact," said Phil, simply, while Harry continued :

"I believe these meetings are a kind of sop to our consciences, Phil, for we are in a very dead-and-alive state."

"I couldn't help thinking," said Phil, thoughtfully, "how astonished those people to-night would be, if they could be carried off a thousand miles, and be dropped down in the middle of a prayer-meeting at Gordon."

"Do tell me about those meetings, Phil. I wanted to ask you about them when Sam Fletcher interrupted us the other evening. How did they differ from ours ? "

"I suppose it was the spirit, more than anything else, though the manner had something to do with it, too. They were so much more social and informal —more like a family gathering, you know. I don't believe I can give you any just idea of them, though I think I remember every word of the first one. It was then that I got a message straight from God."

"Do tell me, Phil," said Harry, warmly.

"Well, you know, Harry, I went out there to pick up some notions for our business here, and went to Gordon to see my mother's cousin. When I recall the welcome his wife and he gave me,—the warm-hearted, wise, fatherly interest he took in me from the first,—the way he remembered me at worship, just as though I were his own son come home,—I realize what that means : 'Thou *preventest* me with Thy goodness,'—going before me and making ready the best things. But that wasn't the prayer-meeting; only it was my preparation for it, I honestly believe.

"Well, they took it for granted I was going with them, when Wednesday evening came; and of course I went, but I did wonder that they seemed so glad to go. And that fact struck me about every one who came into that upper-room. They seemed to expect some good, and weren't a bit stiff, but looked as cheerful as Cousin Ned and his wife. The minister who conducted the meeting was a stranger, a visitor there. He told them this meeting belonged to them—he shared it, as any other Christian present. He hoped all would take part, either by prayer or singing, or repeating some message from God; and reminded them they had a right to claim His promise that, 'His word should not return unto Him void.' And then he prayed, so fervently, that each heart might be open to receive the baptism of the Spirit. I felt then that this was seeking the Lord with a whole heart, worshipping Him in spirit and in truth.

"Then they sang several hymns: 'I need Thee every hour,' and 'Just as I am,' and 'Still there's more to follow.' While we were singing, there was a slight stir, and a lady dressed in white was led by an attendant to a chair in front of us. When I saw she was blind, I remembered my cousin's mention of a friend of theirs who had recently lost her sight under most trying circumstances, through improper medical treatment of her own husband."

"Pretty tough," said Harry Holland.

"Then there were one or two very brief prayers, and

next, Harry, that blind lady spoke. Well, you know
I had been brought up to think such a performance
altogether queer and out of the way. But, do you
know, it didn't seem a bit strange there. And it
came into my head,—or my heart:. "Why *shouldn't*
Christians have some meetings as simple and informal as this?"

"What did she say?" asked Harry, a little inquis-
itively.

"Oh! she told them she was so thankful to meet
them again, after these strange six months—in which
God had smitten her. She thanked them warmly for
their sympathy and kindness, which had helped her
far more than they could guess. Then she begged
them to pray that she might not dishonor God in this
trouble. The hardest part of it had been that sometimes she was tempted to think this was the Devil's
work, not God's. 'Anything but that,' she exclaimed ; 'Pray that I may not mistake my Father's
hand in the dark!' Then there were some earnest
prayers for her, and afterward, almost every one
present repeated a verse from the Bible."

"That's not a bad notion, Phil. I wonder if we
couldn't suggest that some time."

"Well, most of the verses were familiar ones, but
some of them came with a power I had never before
felt. After several had been repeated, referring to
Christ's free salvation, some one said, with emphasis :
'He *shall* save His people from their sins ;' and then
followed : 'Sin *shall not* have dominion over you, for
ye are not under the law but under grace.'

"Just then, a splendid-looking man, perhaps thirty-

15

five years old, rose up and said, hurriedly : ' Friends, I know that's in the Bible, but I want to know whether it's true, really true to any of you in this life. Most of you know me. You know I've a quick temper and an ugly tongue, and, that if I don't actually swear when I'm angry, it's mighty near it. You know all that, but you don't know, any of you, how hard I have prayed and fought against this be-setting sin. *Easily* besetting ! Yes, indeed. I've traveled that road over so often, I'm sick and tired of it—Repent, confess, try again, and *Sin again !* I don't seem to make any headway against it, and the promises of help in time of need seem sort of hollow. It's dreadful to say so, but *it's worse to feel.* I'm nothing but a stumbling block, and a disgrace. I've just about made up my mind to quit. I *can't* bridle my tongue, and so my religion is vain.' Then he sat down."

"Well ? " asked Harry, eagerly.

" A kind-looking white-haired old man got up and, turning to him, said : ' Dear brother, if you're sick and tired of sinning, that is where God wants you to be. But suppose you just quit thinking your tongue is your own. Give it up, for good and all, to the Lord that bought you, body and soul. It's part of the temple of the Holy Ghost. Tell that to God, and beg the Holy Ghost to take care of it, Himself. Then walk humbly before God, brother, and believe Him. He'll do it, for His own name's sake. I've been through it all, and mine was a drunkard's thirst.'

" Then they sat down together, and some one

prayed. After that, were some more hymns, and then, Hal, came God's message to me. Somehow, all through the meeting my hardness of heart and unbelief had been breaking down, and then— It was the last verse my mother taught me before she died," said Phil, huskily. " I had been learning the 15th chapter of Luke, but did not get any further than that verse : 'And when he had spent all, there arose a mighty famine in that land, *and he began to be in want.'* Harry, it was like a sword thrust in my heart. That last summer evening with my mother came up before me ; her words, her very voice sounded in my ear—the pleading, tender tone, in which she told me of the hunger of heart and soul which God uses to draw us back to His arms. How she prayed for me, and gave me up, heart, soul and body to God, to use as He pleased, for Christ's sake ! "

Phil stopped short, and Harry said, gently : " I don't wonder you feel so about Prayer-meetings, Phil. Let us ask God to show His people here how to come to Him and get His blessing."

" Suppose," said Phil slowly, " we stop for a while, every evening in our shop, with any other fellows who would like to, and have a meeting to ask God about the Wednesday evening meetings."

" All right," answered Harry, warmly. And so they did.

*   *   *   *   *   *   *   *

ENGLAND AT GARFIELD'S GRAVE.

[London, September, 1881.]

In this time of our national sorrow, we have grown very near to the great, tender-hearted people among whom we live. You know, long before this, with what homage and honor to our fallen hero, with what spontaneous sympathy and tenderness, from the Queen down to the roughest fishermen, our heavy sorrow has been shared by these brothers across the sea.

And since it is sweet and fitting to die for our country, as he whom we mourn has done, it is surely sweet and fitting that we love and honor those who have watched with us through these eighty days of hope and fear, and now clasp hands in hearty and brotherly tenderness across his grave.

This thought, as you may suppose, has found utterance in many ways during these days of sadness. One said, on the street the other evening, with a quaint mixture of regret and satisfaction : " Well, it's a pity, but we never can have a chance to return the sympathy of these English people, *for they haven't any man in England like* HIM!" Another said, with a hearty emphasis : "We never, never can fight England again—we never could forget this!" We smile with tolerant good humor at the big way in which these older brothers of ours appropriate and recognize as their own those personal characteristics which gave our dead President such strong and lasting hold on the hearts of our people. It is only another way of saying they love us! We have largely outgrown, during these few sad months, that sensitiveness and restiveness under English comment which arose from imperfect sympathy between the two great nations; and they, in words and deeds, are saying to us: "England and America, at peace forever, ready to work for God and for the world!"

Of the great meeting in Exeter Hall, on Saturday, Sept. 24th, you have little need to hear fuller reports. The building was crowded long before the hour appointed. Words strong and sweet and simple were those in which our poet ambassador spoke of the sad errand for which we had gathered together. Not for praise, for in all praise there is a touch of patronage, as from the higher to the lower, but for *honor*—honor to the noble life and worthy death of our country's heroic son; and to·express our sympathy with those who were smitten the sorest by this heavy stroke.

He said, alluding to the womanly devotedness of Mrs. Garfield, and the manner in which the whole world's heart had been touched by it: "But to Americans everywhere it comes home with a pang of mingled sorrow, pride and unspeakable domestic tenderness that none but ourselves can feel." And again, speaking of those memorable eighty days: "The one touch of nature that makes the whole world kin is a touch of heroism; our sympathy with which dignifies and ennobles." "He was no ordinary man who could die well daily for eleven agonizing weeks, and of whom it could be said at last:

> "'He nothing common did, or mean,
> Upon that memorable scene.'

"The dignity, the patience, the self-restraint, the thoughtfulness for others, the serene valor which he showed under circumstances so disheartening, and amid the wrecks of hopes so splendid, are a possession and a stimulus to his countrymen forever."

I think I have always been heartily thankful for my American birthright; but it grew more precious every moment, as we traveled in thought to that "blessed country" across the sea, the land of the loving and the leal, and we realized, indeed, as Mr. Lowell grandly said of the soil where our hero is resting: "Since such men are made out of it, it is good to be born upon, good to live on, good to die for, and good to be buried in!"

After Mr. Lowell, others spoke, in words less scholarly, but none the less true and tender. You, who know so well what manner of man our President was, do not need the record given on this side of the sea.

When Bishop Simpson referred to the Queen's message to Mrs. Garfield "on behalf of her and her people," saying, "God bless the Queen," the whole multitude arose and cheered. It would have seemed unfitting on such an occasion, if it had not been so natural and spontaneous. It was an impulsive recognition of the tender, womanly words which have fallen during these sad weeks and months on the sore heart of the nation, like the touch of a cool hand on a throbbing brow.

There is no danger of our caring too much for the love and good-will which prompted those kindly words. With the fading flowers on that far-off grave, they shall rise forever as a Mizpeh between the nations. The reverent love which we give to those we hold most noble and most dear is hers to-day, whom for years we have held in high honor as a true mother and wife, and guileless Christian woman.

Victoria Regina, Queen of the greatest empire in the world, she has this day a grander empire in the hearts her womanly sympathy has won for her, in that "blessed country" across the sea!

One circumstance in connection with the memorial services here touched us greatly. In the Sunday afternoon service at St. Paul's, on the 25th, Mendelssohn's funeral march was the voluntary. Dr. Stainer played the Dead March in Saul with wonderful beauty of expression; but the memorable circumstance was the choice of two anthems composed by Sir John Goss, which had never been sung in the cathedral since the death of the Prince Consort, until they were sung over our President. The music, we are told, was exquisite. The words were from David's lament over Abner: "And the king said to all the people that were with him: 'Rend your clothes and gird you with sackcloth and mourn.' And the king himself followed the bier, and they buried him. And the king lifted up his voice and wept at the grave, and all the people wept. And the king said unto his servants: 'Know ye not that there is a prince and a great man fallen this day in Israel?'"

The words, with which the Canon in residence prefaced his sermon, were very earnest and beautiful. At the close he said: "I do not mean to dwell on these things, yet standing as I do now in the midst of the greatest church in the greatest city of the world, I feel sure that I am interpreting the feelings of all who hear me, when I say that we do most heartily sympathize in the public sorrow of the great nation, our brethren lamenting as with one heart and voice the loss of an honored and loved ruler, cut off in so strange and sad a way by such an inscrutable visitation. . . . As for him, the souls of the righteous are in the hand of God, and there shall no torment touch them . . . they are in peace."

Monday afternoon, at 3 o'clock, there was a memorial service at Westminster Abbey.

On the previous afternoon, Canon Duckworth, the Canon in residence (you know Dr. Beasley has not yet been installed as Dean in Dr. Stanley's stead), paid a noble and beautiful tribute to the memory of Garfield, whom he associated, as so many naturally do, with our martyred Lincoln. After repeating the grand words of Lincoln at the consecration of the cemetery at Gettysburgh, Canon Duckworth said: "Who could doubt that the cause, for which the speaker of those burning words died, was reinforced now and re-consecrated by a new sacrifice? The American people was the richer this day, in all that could dignify national life, for Garfield's heroic dying."

And, alluding to our great man's wistful question,

"Do you think my name will have a place in human history?" and the reply of one who spoke for the whole world in his answer, "Yes, and a grander one in the hearts of men," Canon Duckworth truly said : "No sweeter promise ever fell upon a ruler's dying ears; no safer prediction ever passed mortal lips. He was gone hence, and would be seen no more, but his works followed him."

But I must make mention now of the Monday memorial service. Parts of the English burial service were read while our hearts bridged the thousands of miles between us and the far-away burial place beside Lake Erie. The music was very grand and beautiful.

The dirge composed by Sir John Goss for the funeral of the Duke of Wellington was sung, and then Dr. Budge played the Dead March in Saul. It was very thrilling, and unspeakably suggestive to us strangers from that "blessed country" across the sea. The grand wailing music in that beautiful old cathedral, so filled with associations, so rich in memorials in honor of the good and great! It was very precious to us, to be sure that the tribute of glory and honor rendered by the whole civilized world—of which the service in that Walhalla was a fitting type—was given to the noble, heroic goodness, the purity, unselfishness, bravery and patience of one who loved and trusted and honored our Lord and Saviour Jesus Christ. And the thought would come up, how the Lord, who knoweth the hearts, had honored the two great men, our Presidents, whom He yet had permitted to fall by the hands of the wicked.

The two men were those who were in public and in private life emphatically without guile, and whose utterances, "I never yet could hate anybody," and, "With charity towards all, with malice towards none," are human paraphrases of the angels' song at Bethlehem :

"Peace on earth, good-will toward men."

But while I was thinking, the grand music from the Messiah, "I know that my Redeemer liveth,"—the promise of the resurrection glory, sounded through the numberless arches, and fell upon our hearts sad and heavy for our loss, with the glad assurance of "beauty for ashes, joy for mourning and the garment of praise for the spirit of heaviness," for "they which sleep in Jesus will God bring with Him. So shall we ever be with the Lord; wherefore comfort one another with these words."

As we passed out with the dense throng, the bells began to toll. The chimes of Westminster,—"Big Ben" sounding deepest among them,—were caught up and echoed by peals from other churches. But there are no tolling bells in that fair City whose builder and maker is God. The chimes of earth which tell of universal brotherhood, ringing in the promise of the Millennial Peace, are echoed in heaven with the peals of everlasting gladness, "for the former things are passed away."

Monday evening, at half past six, some of our party went to the memorial service at Rev. Newman Hall's, and others to the church of St. Martin-in-the-Fields, where the Archbishop of Canterbury held a memorial service, preaching an appropriate sermon.

At all of the services in connection with the death of our President we, as Americans, were surprised at the crowded buildings. We did not realize until then how almost national was the sorrow of the English people. It was no wonder to us that all Americans should be present at such special services, but, as at St. Martin-in-the-Fields, so in the other churches, the mourning badges of the Americans did not secure the seats freely offered to them in the public papers. But we were more than recompensed for the loss of reserved seats by the hearty sympathy and recognition of mutual loss given by these English brothers. The sermon of Archbishop Tait, while it was scholarly, simple and noble, brought home to my consciousness the fact that, until these last few months, the English people, nay, even the very highest in ecclesiastical position, one of the Queen's councillors, a man of large heart and cultured mind, had little acquaintance with the noblest, most pure and chivalrous side of our American people. It is a wonder to them that such a grand, heroic nature should have developed unknown to them. But we can scarcely wonder, remembering how with ourselves it needed these months to reveal our hero to us, aye more, *he* needed the crucial test, the fiery ordeal to prove the true man he was.

After reviewing the life of Garfield, and his steady rise by self-restraint, energy and courage, through changes and by stepping-stones undreamt of on this side of the Atlantic, he said: " All this I must say was to most of us quite new. It opened up a picture of manhood, such as in this country we were little acquainted with, and no wonder that our affections were drawn forth, and we felt that it was no common man that the civilized world had lost. But then comes the nobler and better lesson."

The Archbishop spoke nobly and beautifully of the evidence of the Christian principle and faith in the life of Garfield, though apparently knowing little of facts in his religious life that are so familiar to us, and closed with a most earnest and eloquent appeal to us all, to be true to the trust committed to us above all other nations of the world, "to carry through the boundaries of the human race a civilization founded upon Christianity." He spoke of that which would make us truly one—"individual, family, social or political life must all have its current in the gospel of Jesus Christ."

No one could help noticing in how many memorial services the hymn so loved by our President was sung. Church of England, Congregational, Presbyterian, Wesleyan, Independent, sung alike, "Nearer my God to Thee."

At the close of the services in St. Martin-in-the-Fields (which for those who do not know London, we might say is on Trafalgar Square and far away from the fields of to-day) the beautiful hymn from the Prayer Book was sung, beginning:

> "Now the laborer's task is o'er,
>   Now the battle day is past,
> Now upon the further shore
>   Lands the voyager at last.
> Father, in Thy gracious keeping,
> Leave we now Thy servant sleeping."

The words lingered in our hearts while the organ sounded to the Dead March in Saul, and we passed out into the moonlight, thinking how that same moon looks down on that far-off grave in the West. It was good to remember the grand old words which we had sung at the beginning of the service:

> " O God, our help in ages past,
>   Our hope for years to come,
>   Be Thou our guard while troubles last,
>   And our eternal home."

As we walked slowly by the beautiful Trafalgar Square, Landseer's lions, the Wellington column and Havelock's monument, those Scriptures in bronze and stone spoke in mute eloquence of the grandeur, bravery and goodness of this great English people. God bless them! They loved our hero and mourned with us in our great sorrow. May they rejoice with us in the Great Day when their Lord and ours shall come unto His own again, gathering those who love Him out of all kindreds and tongues and peoples, when there shall be one flock and one shepherd forevermore.

GUY FAWKES' DAY.

(London, November, 1881.)

NOVEMBER in London is anything but a cheerful month. Dull skies prevail, even when the sun is not entirely hidden by yellow fogs. A general leaden hue steals the beauty from the fairest scene, making it very easy to believe, for the present, in "the light that never was on sea or shore."

But there are happy exceptions even to the dreariness of the "melancholy days," when the sun's round face looks like a good-natured friend returning from a journey, and Hyde Park, despite its leafless trees, is fairly cheerful in the sunshine, and makes the best of it; when children and nursemaids, red-coats and policemen, fine carriages with languid ladies and lazy men, again assemble to welcome the sudden sunny rift in the clouds.

One of these bright gleams fell this year on Guy Fawkes' Day, November 5th. It seems to us Americans a singular instance of British conservatism that the name of one of a number of conspirators should thus be immortalized, even though it be by hooting, effigies and general nonsense. Imagine the celebration of a day in America, year after year and century after century, in ages to come, in perpetuation of the name and memory of Benedict Arnold, Wilkes Booth or Guiteau. "No," say we, the younger nation; "let us remember and celebrate deeds and aims that were noble and pure, and let the dark memories lie still in the silence of the grave." But Guy Fawkes' Day was kept, we are told, as a national thanksgiving for the discovery of the Gunpowder Plot, and the deliverance of Protestant England from the evil plans of the Roman Catholic party.

On the morning of the fifth, before ten o'clock, I met two or three groups of street gamins with their Guys, horrible-looking creatures, dressed in rags and jags, wearing hideous red masks.

One of these interesting spectacles on Wigmore street was drawn in a hand-cart by a hooting crowd, who recited some doggerel which I tried to make out, but in vain. It was something about the Pope, and probably a relic of the old tradition connecting the burning of a wax effigy with the death of the person represented by the figure. One needs to have some pennies in the pocket on such a walk, for swift as thought the manager of the show, seeing me a block away, darted across the street with a request for something to pay expenses and put down Popery! Primrose Hill, an open knoll northwest of Regent's Park, is a favorite place for the burning of these many Guys, with accompaniment of bonfires and fireworks on the night of the fifth. If ever such barbarous fashion of rejoicing is suitable, it would seem that the use of gunpowder on this occasion has some poetical fitness.

It may not be known to some of our readers that, ever since the discovery of the Gunpowder Plot before the meeting of Parliament in 1605, the cellars of the Parliament House are officially searched and pronounced free of traitors and fagots before the meeting opens. Such a survival of an ancient warning shows the steady-going, solid character of our English cousins. In these days of dynamite and fiery Irish agitators, Nihilists and Guiteaux, it seems a sensible precaution at least.

But the day is not given up exclusively to the memory of the past.

At the Alexandra Palace—a sort of rival of the Crystal Palace at Sydenham—on the evening of the fifth, the exhibition for the popular amusement this year comprised thirty or forty Guys, representing and bearing the names of various public characters of the present day, whose supposed demerits might be fitly expiated by a harmless burning at the stake. Among the subjects were Gladstone, in full Highland costume, pulling the wires of a puppet labeled "Land Bill," till it danced with frantic gestures, while under the chieftain's feet were fragments suggestive of Parnell and Treason; then the figure of a burly blusterer repudiating Parliamentary oaths; the inevitable Irish trio with dynamite and swagger; Temple Bar memorial with its "unspeakable" Griffin, hideous enough to be safe without the protection of two solid metropolitan policemen mounting guard beside it; and, in the direction of the fine arts, a pair of figures, a gardener with eyeglass and sun-flower button-hole bouquet, watering lilies and chrysanthemums from a Japanese teapot, while a young lady of sweet sixty stands by, simpering sillily—quite too totally æsthetic for anything but a pair of Guys!

GIFFORD'S WIFE.

"GIFFORD'S WIFE very low, wants to see you. I will meet you at 42d St., 3:20 train.

F. M."

This was the telegram Frank sent to me at noon, one October day. I packed my satchel, sent Jane to ask Miss Hunter to let the children come home from school, took a hurried lunch, and gave the usual directions to Sally, about what she must do, in case of sickness, accident, fire, or company, while Frank and I were absent.

Ruth's little heart was very full, for I think she loved Marian almost as dearly as I did. But she behaved like a real little woman, choked down her tears, when she bade me good-bye, and said : "Oh ! I am so glad that we came back before dear cousin Marian got so dreadfully sick." Tom,—bless his little heart,—promised to be a good boy, and take care of Ruthie and Jane, and not be cross to Sallie ! Then came a few minutes in the horse-car, half an hour on the boat, and a long, slow ride up to Forty-second street.

How I longed and yet dreaded to see my dear Marian again ! I had not seen her since she and Gifford bade us good-bye on the steamer, the afternoon we sailed, four months before.

16

There had been a singular reticence about herself, in all her letters to me, and Gifford's to Frank were not much more satisfactory. One sentence in his last letter had troubled me a good deal: "As for May, one would think she had taken a vow against ease and slumber. She does not seem to rest a moment, night or day."

> "Never a word said she!
> She made no moan,
> She gave no groan,
> But she died right willingly!"

These words kept ringing in my ears, as I remembered how she had sung them a few months before. It was an old ballad Gifford had picked up somewhere, and brought home while Frank and I were visiting them. I believe Marian would rather have gone into a burning house, than have sung that song. But when her husband said, in his nonchalant way: "Sing that doleful ditty I brought you yesterday, Marian, if you please," she took up the music, saying, lightly: "You see, Forrest's gray hairs and sentiment are creeping on together." But how she sang it! One verse runs:

> "He vowed on his bended knee.
> Ah! light is a lover's oath!
> She gave him her life and troth,
> —And she died right willingly!"

I wondered then, whether Forrest Gifford was cruel as well as careless. Such a blithe, merry, dancing girl as Marian was, five years before, with beautiful dark eyes, and such a soft, lovely color coming and going in her cheeks! It was a short acquaintance and courtship. Marian was traveling with her aunt, Mrs. Barrett, the only relative she had in the world except Frank, who is a far-away cousin on her mother's side.

I was always glad that Frank did not give Forrest Gifford a letter of introduction to Mrs. Barrett. I don't know who introduced him, but Mrs. Barrett asked Mr. Gifford to join their party in Switzerland. He was a man of culture, position and wealth. This was the sum of Mrs. Barrett's requirements. He was a brilliant talker, and was considered fascinating. *I* always thought him an egotist, without his peer among men,—and only refrained from sarcastic speeches to him because he was Frank's friend. But then, I never had any patience with carpet knights and society idols.

Well, he fascinated my dear Marian most completely. She never dreamed, poor child, that he could be less devoted and tender than he showed himself in the romantic scenes where he wooed and won her. They were married at the American Chapel in Paris, and two months afterwards Mrs. Barrett died. Gifford and Marian came home in the spring, and bought a charming little place on the Hudson, expecting to spend their winters in the city. Frank and I used to see them very often in those days. Gifford certainly was proud and fond of her for a while. He was proud of her beauty, and spirit, and grace, and seemed well content to be a hero, in her eyes. But that was long ago.

Marian has never seemed like her old self since her baby died. No one had ever said a word about it, but I was as sure as I wished to be, that Marian was not willingly absent from her sick boy the last night of his life. Gifford is just the sort of man to be annoyed by what he would consider foolish fondness and anxiety of a young mother about her baby. Our little girl, Marian's namesake, was very sick when Hugh was buried, and I did not see Marian until both dear little ones had been laid to rest. She never alluded to the circumstances of her baby's death, except that, when I was telling her of our little Marian's sufferings, and how the sight of her pain made me willing to let her go, she said, as if the words were wrung from her: "Oh, you were with her! You did not leave her to die alone." I shall never forget the terrible anguish in her face, and her tone.

We often spoke together of our babies who were gone out of our arms. Hugh was just beginning to walk, and to say a few words. He was a beautiful child, and very winsome. My baby was two months younger, and not as forward as Marian's boy. I think I was the only one to whom she ever spoke of her child. I am sure it was good for her to talk about him. The hard, set lines about her mouth always softened then. But I could not help noticing how her face grew stern whenever her husband made any allusion to their lost boy. I used to think it must be hard for Gifford, for he did love his child, and was very proud of him. Marian seemed to hug her sorrow all the closer, when her husband tried to share it with her. Still it was something with which not even a trusted friend could intermeddle, so I was sorry,—and kept still.

One day, when we were alone, Marian took a little morocco-covered book from her desk and said: "Kitty, if anything should happen to me, I want you to have this little book; will you remember?" I knew well what it was, for Frank and I have one just like it, full of notes about our three dear children. Marian liked the notion very much, when she first saw ours long ago. I remember how bewilderingly pretty she looked when one day she showed me the book she had bought, as she said,—to write about her babies in.

Well—well! Frank met me at Forty-second street, and we went up to Gernheim together. The pretty rose-covered stone cottage,—Marian used to call it her Bower of Bliss,—was lovely as ever, under the October sky. Every turn we took, up the winding path from the stile by the railroad, to the house on the hill, brought back a vision of Marian's light figure beside us. An old rough-hewn seat, near the crest of the hill, was her watch-tower, her favorite place at sunset. Far down below, lay the broad, full river she had loved so well. The sun was only an hour high, but the long, level beams shot across the lawn and over the river, lighting up with some glints of gold the gray walls of the Palisades beyond. How often Marian and I had watched the light fade out of the sky, and the gray shadows fall on the same peaceful scene—and now !

Frank and I were very quiet, as we walked up to the house, for we both loved Marian ; and Frank, I think, loved Gifford too. They had played together when they were boys, had been class-mates in college, and somehow the old fellowship and association had kept Frank from despising Gifford as I did. Besides —my husband is a great deal better Christian than I am, and believes that there is hope for even such careless, self-satisfied sinners as Gifford. We noticed that the carriage-drive was thickly strewn with straw, and, as we neared the house, we saw that the bell was muffled too. Gifford met us at the door.

"Thank you so much for coming ; it is so good of you ! Please excuse my careless appearance, Mrs. Mason, I have been with Marian for two nights, and feel rather knocked up."

Indeed he looked so, and I fancied he had been crying. Well, I thought it was time he did ! With curious distinctness came up before me Frank's face as it looked, after he had watched by my bed eight days and nights, when they all said I must die. Did the two men who walked before me up the stairs, belong to the same species?

Gifford told us that Marian's mind seemed to be wandering a good deal. "At times, she sings bits of songs, and counts, and talks to herself about little Hugh. She can't bear to have the nurse in the room with her ; so either Doctor Halleck, little Hester or I stay with her all the time. She hasn't slept for six nights. Halleck says, unless we can get her to sleep "—Frank grasped his hand, and said something which I did not hear, as they walked away to the window. Only I heard Gifford say distinctly, in that soft voice of his: "That's the worst of it—if it were not my fault, I think I could stand it."

They came back to me, and Gifford said: "I hope it will not be too painful for you, Mrs. Mason, Marian has asked for you so often to-day, in her intervals of consciousness. She is quiet now. I think she will know you. The doctor says, if she is inclined to talk, we must let her. She recognized the physicians who consulted with Dr. Halleck, yesterday, but they thought worse of her case than Halleck does."

I could not speak, except to say it was my great wish to see Marian if it would not excite her. How strange the beautiful rooms seemed, without Marian to welcome us! I went in with Gifford to see her. I never saw anything more beautiful than her face, as she lay there in the evening light. She saw me as we entered the room—"So glad—so glad!" she said, caressing me in her old, loving way. "I am going to see my baby soon. Tell me about it—I can't think, my head aches so. He'll know me, up there, won't he, Kitty? I don't want him to care more for the angels than for me." She looked at me wistfully, for a moment; then a wild look came into her eyes, and she said: "No tears—no tears! I don't cry any more. Dead people don't cry. I've been dead a good while. One—two—three—four—one—two—"

Her husband knelt at the other side of the bed and held her hand against his face. "No, no! May, you're not dead; you're not going to die. My little May Queen!" He laid his hand caressingly on her beautiful hair. I wondered that they had not cut it off.

"Who is it talks?" said she looking right up in his face, without a shadow of recognition in her eyes. "Queen! Queen!" Then she burst out singing a little French song she had learned at school:

> "La Reine est morte.
> Vive la Reine!"

"Reigned in Jerusalem one year and eight months, and *she* died. Go on—what's next? one—two—three—four—"

It was pitiful beyond words, to see and hear her. A spasm of pain passed over Gifford's face. I was very sorry for him, and said : " Perhaps she would be quiet, if I stayed alone with her."

"Thank you—perhaps. She does not seem to know me at all," said he, brokenly. "She asked to have you sing to her,—if you came in time,—and here are some books she wanted to have brought to her, so she might give them to you herself."

Yes, she had remembered. One of them was the pretty, brown book she had spoken about, months before.

Frank and Gifford went into the next room. I raised Marian up, so that her head might rest on my shoulder, and then I sang to her, very softly, old hymns we had often sung together, in Sabbath twilights, in that same pleasant room. It quieted my sad heart, and soon it seemed to quiet Marian too. She stopped that dreadful counting, and seemed to listen. Once she said : "Yes, it is; it is Kitty."

Then her eyes lost their bright glitter, and at last she fell asleep.

Half an hour after, I heard Gifford speaking eagerly to the doctor in the hall. " She is asleep. You said there was a chance for her if she could sleep ! "

I did not hear the doctor's answer, but my heart caught at the hope, and I prayed for her life as I had not dared to do before. The doctor came in, leaned over, and lightly touched her pulse. "Good, good ! Keep her asleep as long as you can. We'll have a fight for her yet."

Frank took charge of the medicines to be given if she awoke, and then I coaxed him to take Gifford down with the doctor, and get their supper, while Hester, Marian's good little maid, stayed within call, in case I needed her. Frank brought up a cup of tea, and managed to hold it to my lips, without disturbing Marian.

The fall twilight deepened in the room, and the night came on, and still she slept. Gifford came in and begged to stay. I said no,—that I would call him if he could do anything, or if Marian asked for him.

" If she awakes, kiss her good-night for me, please, with my love," said he, humbly.

"I will, certainly," said I. "God knows I am sorry for you now." He touched Marian's hand with his lips, but she did not stir. He went away with a stifled groan.

There were no sounds in the house, except the ticking of the old clock in the hall, and the occasional crackling of the open fire in the next room, where Frank was sitting. It was a beautiful night. Star after star shone through the window, and all my childish fancies, about their watchful eyes and friendly guidance, came thronging back to my heart. Bound as I was to one place, by the precious burden in my arms, my thoughts were all the freer in their range. Oh! terrible mysteries of life, mysteries never to be understood, until, in the light of God, we know even as we are known. No wonder—human hope and courage fail, without the clasp of the only Hand, wise and warm and strong enough to lead through the dim, strange paths of life, through the dark gateway of death itself, unto the glorious light of the Life everlasting!

At last, I saw the pale gleam of the moonlight on the river, far away. Eleven o'clock! The doctor came in, quietly. "Courage! nothing could be better."

Frank came in often, just to look at us. It was such a comfort to see his dear, good face! Once he brought me a soft pillow to lean against. "I am afraid your back will be nearly broken, wifie mine," he said.

"No fear, dear. I am really not much tired. I could bear it all night and day, to keep her asleep." Soon after, he brought me a cup of hot coffee. I don't think anything ever was more refreshing to me, for I began to feel a little chilly.

Midnight, and still no change. Gifford's pale face was anxious enough to make me pitiful, when he came in, and looked sadly at Marian.

"Sleeping still. Frank will tell you when she wakes. Do try to rest! You may have a good deal of this kind of work yet."

"I hope so—I hope so!" said he, fervently. Poor fellow. He was not very explicit, but I knew what he meant, and liked him better for not trying to explain himself.

Again the doctor came in. "This sleep will save her life and her reason, too, I trust," he said, softly. I heard him tell Frank that he would stay in the library until six o'clock, and that he must call him, if there were any change. Then all was quiet again.

At last, the moonlight stole in, through one of the windows, lighting up a favorite picture of Marian's. It was a full-length figure, in a palmer's dress of black, with a lavender-colored cape, a girdle with scrip and scollop shell, a staff in one hand, in the other a palm, and over his head a scroll bearing the words:

"In silentio et in spe
Erit fortitudo tua."

According to the Roman Catholic legend, these were the dying words of the holy pilgrim martyr, San Juan de Mycenæ. The grand, pure face, always reminded me of Dante's. It was sweet and strong enough for one belonging to "the noble army of martyrs." I thought of the many talks we had had, Marian and I, over that picture and the legend.

When the first shiver of the coming dawn stirred the trees, Marian woke with a frightened cry.

"May, darling, don't be afraid. It's all right, dear. Lie down again and sleep." She had started up, with a strange look in her eyes, but when I spoke, she turned toward me, and said, just like herself: "O Kitty! how tired you must be, dear! Let me lie down on the pillows, please, and you lie down too and rest." How thankfully I heard her, no word can tell. I slipped a cool pillow under her head, and leaning over her I said, slowly: "Forrest asked me to bid you good-night for him, dear. He left a kiss on this hand, with his love."

Her face quivered. She raised the hand he had kissed to her lips, and said, fervently: "Thank you, Kitty. Tell him please, I shall rest well now." Her lips moved and I heard her say, brokenly: "Our Father—forgive us our debts, as we forgive our debtors." Then she slept again.

The doctor stood at the door, but signed to me that he would not come in. I saw by his face, that he thought the crisis was past safely for Marian. Frank went to tell Gifford her words, and Doctor Halleck came back to me after a few minutes, and told me my husband wanted me, and that he wished to watch Marian for a while himself. I rather suspected it was a ruse on the part of the kind old doctor, to get me out of the room, and make me rest. But I was content to go, since Marian still slept, and I could do no good.

Frank and Gifford were together in the library. They made as much of me as if I had been a heroine. Being a very matter-of-fact, common-place sort of a person, I suggested that we should have something to eat. Gifford's thoughtfulness had already provided coffee, boiled eggs and sandwiches. Doctor Halleck had had his lunch before he took my place with the invalid. I don't believe there were three more thankful people in the world, than we were, that early morning.

Frank made me lie down on the sofa in the library, and Gifford and he talked. They walked up and down in the music-room, next to the library; so I heard distinctly what they said. I called out to them that I was not asleep. Gifford said they would not talk if it disturbed me, but he wanted me to know what he was trying to tell Frank, for I was Marian's friend, and he hoped that, for her sake, I would be his friend too.

Well, he went back to the beginning of his acquaintance. "I realize now," he said, "that I have thought and cared only for myself. It never entered into my head to question whether I, a man nearly double her age, could make the happiness of that lovely child. I took it for granted that any woman, so honored as to be my wife, must necessarily be happy," he said, sarcastically. "I was really very fond of her, but I thought her a sweet, shallow little thing, as indeed I used to think all women were by nature, except those of the dreadfully strong-minded, short-skirted class, who are my special aversion.

"After a while, I wearied of the rôle of devoted lover and husband; then I noticed that Marian seemed changed. She lost her buoyancy and brightness. I blamed her and left her alone. I went back to my club, and, although I cannot accuse myself of intending to neglect her, I see that I never praised her, never showed that I cared to have her with me, except when we were invited formally to some place, where I wished to introduce my beautiful wife. She had her music, and books, her old school-friends, and her housekeeping.

"I had an idea that these resources were sufficient for any ordinary woman. Marian never had any passion for housekeeping, for its own sake. At first, it seemed a pleasure to her, when I used to let her, in her quaint, pretty way, tell me of her mistakes, and laugh over them with her. But I made up my mind that it was beneath my dignity to play David to my Dora ; and once I told her so. I can see her startled, grieved look, now ! Something went from her face then, that has never come back. I told her she could have an excellent housekeeper to relieve her of all domestic cares, if she pleased, as if that would make it any better.

"It is humiliating to acknowledge, but I honestly believe, that, if Marian had not been so utterly alone in the world, I should have been more considerate of her. I gave up petting her, because I thought it made her exacting and dependent upon me. Still I was proud of her, and especially proud of her singing. Whatever she had, or was, belonged to me, and so far as it flattered me, I prized it. Good God ! what a selfish brute I have been, all through ! But, Mason, I never realized it until lately.

"Speaking of her voice, do you remember how Jack Brenton admired her, and how he used to rave about her singing ? I had forgotten that he had ever cared for her, and brought him up with me one night. I heard them singing together. It was like the music of heaven, but you may be sure I stopped it, and afterwards I told Marian it was indecorous to sing with so much expression!

"Jealous? Yes, I suppose I was, in a most mean and cruel fashion. I was jealous of her devotion to our boy. For a good while, Marian had not been well enough to go out with me in the evenings. But when we came to town, for the winter,—Hugh was six months old then,—I told Marian I wanted her to go into society again; that she was becoming a thorough little rustic, shut up in that quaint place on the Hudson. So she went. But still I was not satisfied. I felt that she had left her heart in the nursery. Again and again, I was told that my wife was more beautiful than ever, and I could see it was true myself. Whenever I saw her looking particularly gay and pretty, I knew that some one was talking to her about our boy!"

Frank said: "Don't go on Gifford, it hurts you so!"

"No, no! I must; and it is a relief, too. I can understand the comfort of the confessional now," he said, grimly. "These days and nights of May's delirium have shown me myself in such a hideous light that I cannot bear that you and your wife, May's best and dearest friends, should think better of me than I deserve. For I haven't come to the worst, Frank— *I made Marian go with me that night when our boy was sick.* My sister, who had had four children of her own, promised to stay with Hugh, and so she did. He died in her arms before we reached home—"

"It's of no use. I can't talk about *that* time. I

think I am just beginning to understand Marian. I have been so blind—so blind in my self-conceit! After you were up here at Easter, I sent for Dr. Walker, and had a long talk with him about her. I saw that your wife was anxious about her, when she was here. Walker did not like May's symptoms. There was a suppressed irritability about her, and an unnatural nervous energy in all that she did. He said though, if she got safely through, he thought there would be no danger afterwards. I have tried to be good to her since then. But I can't tell you, Frank, how it made me feel,—to see her shrink from being petted, to see her look of surprise when I called her by her old pet names. She was gentle and courteous, and I saw that she tried hard to be affectionate.

"Once, like a fool, I began to speak about the night of the Charity Ball. 'No! no!' she cried; "Don't dare to speak of that!' I see I have thrown away her heart. It serves me right, but I can't bear to live this way, and it will never do for her either. If she will only live, Frank, I think some time I could make her happy again. God forgive me!"

And she did live.

Frank went home to the children, and I stayed for two or three weeks and helped Gifford take care of Marian. What those weeks of Marian's illness were to them both, such happy people as Frank and I can scarcely guess. I know that all her hardness passed away, and she had plenty of useful work when she grew better, in helping Gifford to forgive himself. She never spoke of the troubled past, as Gifford did; only once she said to me, with tears in her eyes,

" Kitty, I have been very hard and bad. I have not dared to pray, 'Our Father,' all through, since baby died, until now."

Marian has a far finer character than Gifford, but he is wonderfully changed. It is a standing marvel to me to this day, to see Marian evidently consider her husband so nearly perfect as she does. Gifford has redeemed his pledge, for his wife is a happy woman, and I know that the bitterness has been taken away ; else she could not use that same little brown book, lovingly and freely as she does, for writing about her other precious babies.

17

THE WIND AND THE WHIRLWIND.

Poor little Jessie! How well I remember the first time I ever saw her! It was a cold, bright winter morning. We were sitting in our library,—a pleasant, sunny room, and my mother had been giving me some lessons in darning; at which I was practicing patiently, in hope of being permitted to mend a tiny break in one of my father's socks.

Looking up, I caught sight of a bent figure in a gray cloak and hood, as it passed the window, on the way to the front porch.

"Dear me, mamma! There is Aunt Debby. Now she'll talk, ever so long, about everything under the sun," I said impatiently; for my mother had just begun a delightful story, with: "Once upon a time, when I was a little girl"—

"Open the door, dear," said my mother, gently, without noticing my impatience. "Jane is in the kitchen, and may not hear Miss Debby's little knock; and she must not be kept out in the cold."

By the time I had reached the hall, my ill-nature had vanished, and Aunt Debby received as hearty a welcome as she deserved. She came up to the bright fire in the open Franklin, and sat down in an easy-chair which my mother had placed for her.

"It do beat all, Mis' L., to see how different the

Lord do fix folkses in this 'ere world," she said, abruptly, after inquiries had been exchanged.

"What is it, now, Aunt Debby?" asked my mother, pleasantly.

"Well, the fact is, I've come for you, for there's a bad job—in one of the Judge's houses, too. I've just come from there, with the doctor. I done what I could, but I guess the doctor, he's about right. He says: 'This 'ere tangle needs finer fingers to handle than yourn or mine. I guess you'd better tell Mis' L.,' sez he; 'she'll know the right thing to say and do, and she'll do it, too,' sez he. So you see, I'm here; but jest as I come along, and see you and your little darter, a settin' so cosy and comfortable like in your pretty room, full of books an' pictures an' what-nots, it come across me, sudden an' sharp, how this very minute there's a poor mother, a stone's throw away, lyin' in her misery, with a misfortunate little hunch-back of a darter, an' she sick an' sufferin', with a brute of a husband, an' a little dead baby, that never had no welcome, an' hasn't waited for no funeral, neither. The doctor says it's *next door* to murder, least ways."

By this time, I had become so interested that I was rather sorry when my mother remarked, quietly: "Excuse me, a moment, Miss Debby," and, calling me to her, said: "Dear, will you go and tell Maggie I would like her to make some mutton-broth with barley, just as she made it for Jack yesterday; and you may pack a loaf or two of bread, with some butter and cold beef, and a glass of currant jelly in a basket, and put on your cloak and hood and rubbers, and be ready to go with me, if you like."

When my mother came to the door with Aunt Debby, and I told her the basket and I were all ready, she looked very sad, and I wondered that she was not in greater haste to go. I remember how she went back to the bright wood-fire, and stood looking thoughtfully down into the coals. I know, now, that she was truly getting ready to go to that house of misery and sin and shame.

It was not far—not more than a quarter of a mile away from our pleasant home on the knoll. Along the brawling, beautiful river which made one of the chief beauties of our country home, there was a row of tenant-houses, which had been occupied by the employees of a paper-mill situated on the property. When the former owner failed, and my father bought the place, it seemed to him and my mother cruel to tear down the plain little houses, with their hop-vines over the porches, and send the occupants adrift. " If they are obliged to go and seek work elsewhere, I should not feel so strongly about it," said my mother, to an æsthetic visitor who was urging the removal.

But there were two houses, beyond the blacksmith's, under the willows, and the square house with the old cherry trees, whose tenants were always of a less permanent type. It was one of these houses which my mother and I entered, that sunny winter morning.

"Will you please come in, ma'am—I can't quite reach the latch," said a childish voice, in response to my mother's knock.

Oh! pitiful sight! Opposite us, as we entered, stood a little figure, a head and shoulders shorter than myself, with a white, pathetic little face, broad across the honest, bright blue eyes, but narrowing sharply at the chin, and light brown hair, brushed smooth, and braided in two tight braids, which reached only to the poor, misshapen shoulders. The curve of her figure was as marked in the chest as in the back. I had the impression that the poor head could scarcely see over the large, protruding breastbone.

"Jessie, my pretty, give the ladies chairs," said a feeble voice from the curtained bed in a corner of the room. "You're kindly welcome, ma'am; I'm sorry there's not a better place for you to sit in."

My mother went quietly toward the bed, and I heard her soft voice bidding the sick woman not to try to talk now, and not to trouble herself about the children—they would be looked after.

"God bless you, ma'am. The children are my great anxiety, for he's so careless of them, when he's not himself. Johnny, he's gone to cut some wood, the doctor sent—he's coming now—so it'll be warmer soon."

I was left to make acquaintance with the poor little cripple, who had placed a chair for me near the cooking-stove, and, after a moment, seated herself on a bench near by. She seemed like a little woman—not a child like myself. Later, when she answered my mother's few questions, there was occasionally a painful fit of stammering, especially when she alluded to her father or elder brother.

When asked who had been with her mother in the

night: "Me and Johnny were here, ma'am," answered she, convulsively, "until ten o'clock, when father came. Mother felt very bad, and father, he said as how mother could get up and cook his supper if she wanted to, and then he beat her because she couldn't, and I thought he'd killed her. Johnny and I hollered till a woman next door came in, and sent Johnny and me in to her house for her husband, and he said he'd go for the doctor, and we was to stay in his house with the children, till his wife came back from our house."

"And then, twelve o'clock, her baby was so bad she had to leave mother, and we went back there. Father was gone, so we stayed with mother, and she made us get into the trundle-bed, and she said if she wanted anything she'd call me, but she did not call at all, only I knew she felt awful bad, she moaned so— and the man next door came back and said the doctor would be away all night. He didn't come till morning, and then he sent a kind old lady here, and the woman next door, she gave Johnny and me some breakfast—and then, ma'am, you came, and that's all."

"Poor children! It was a hard night for you," said my mother, gently. "You are a good little nurse, I dare say, Jessie, but your mother must have somebody older with her now."

"Please, ma'am, don't send me away from mother. She's so used to me, she's lonesome without me, I do think."

"Very well, dear. You and Johnny may go into the next room, and lie down and go to sleep. I shall be here until the nurse comes ; so you need not stay awake, to take care of your mother."

The children had just gone, and my mother, who had put fresh pillow-cases on the coarse tick, was bathing Mrs. Jordison's head, when a man entered the rear door, and, not seeing my mother and myself in the shadow of the curtain, called out, angrily : "So you're up to your old tricks, are you? lying in bed instead of getting up and cooking your husband's dinner like a decent woman." And then followed some words which I did not understand, but I knew that the tone was brutal. He stood in the doorway as he finished.

"Do not speak, Mrs. Jordison," said my mother, gently, as the sick woman, almost fainting, tried to say : " William, William, don't talk so." My mother left the bedside and walked toward the middle of the room.

" You are Mr. Jordison, I suppose," said my mother, quietly. The man's whole appearance changed. A cringing, astonished, terrified look came over his face, as he realized that a lady was there with his wife.

I do not remember what my mother said then ; I only recall the expression of her countenance. She was a fragile little woman, with a delicate face, beautiful blue eyes, and thick, soft, brown hair. Never in my life had I imagined that she could look *terrible !* The man dropped his bravado, and went out muttering :

" I didn't mean to do nothink, ma'am, but it's rather

hard on a man not to have anything to heat, and no 'ome to come to, and a wife a-blabbin' forever."

My mother said, quietly but with emphasis: "If you are able to understand that the doctor has been here, and that your wife has been silent, you may well be grateful to her, and be glad to remain away until the doctor notifies you that you may return." Then she went back to the bedside, and soothed the trembling woman, until she fell asleep and the nurse who had been sent for arrived.

"What a horrid man, mamma!" I said, during our walk homeward. "Were you not afraid of him?"

"No," she replied, with an amused look; "cruel persons are generally cowards, and I hope he will behave better now, for having been a little frightened."

My mother visited Mrs. Jordison often, during the next fortnight, but I did not accompany her again for several weeks.

Once I said: "Mrs. J. seems so much nicer than her husband, mamma,—I don't see how she can bear to have him about her."

"My child, there is seldom such a terrible state of affairs as we found in that house, without some fault on both sides. It is something I do not wish you to speak of, but I will tell you something of Mrs. J.'s history. She was a wilful girl, and she married against her parents' wishes,—without their knowledge, indeed,—and she feels, now, that much which she has to bear is the consequence of her own wrong, years ago. She is reaping a harvest of the seed she herself has sown. She did not honor her father and mother, and it has not gone well with her."

"Is she sorry, mamma?" I asked.

"Yes, my child. I believe she is heartily sorry for her own sin, as well as for its consequences on herself and on her children."

I was often sent on errands to the little brown house. Mrs. J. was a neat seamstress, and my mother gave her sewing to do, and interested others in helping her in this way. And meanwhile, at home, my mother helped me to make a warm hood and a thick winter frock for little Jessie, and let me take the things to the grateful child.

Johnny, her brother, was six years old,—a bright, rather handsome little fellow, with something of his father's Canadian vivacity about him, but I liked better, plain little Jessie, whose only charm was in her frank simplicity and faithfulness. The children came to Sunday-school, and seemed really happy and merry.

Suddenly, in the spring, the whole family disappeared. Mrs. J. had, without her husband's knowledge, come up the day before they left, and told my mother all about it. J. was a tailor, and he said he had a chance of work in a distant town. He wished to take the two boys with him, and steal quietly away, leaving his wife to struggle on with little Jessie. But the mother was not content to have Johnny with his father. "He'll make him just like himself, and I cannot lose my boy that way," she said, with tears. "Johnny loves and minds me now, but his father has wonderfully winning ways when he chooses (you would not believe it, to see him as he generally is); and he would only teach the child to gamble and drink, and may-be to beg and steal. No, ma'am, I must go with my husband for the sake of my children. But this has been a haven of rest to me. If we could only stop here," sighed the poor woman.

One day, after they had gone, I was enjoying the special treat of rearranging the articles in my mother's treasure-drawer. "Why, mamma, dear, I never saw this pin before, did I?" I asked, taking a handsome, odd, old brooch from her jewel-case.

"Very likely not, dear," she said. "I am keeping it for Mrs. Jordison. I think she has no way to secure anything valuable. It was a gift from her mother, when she was a girl."

It was beautiful and must have been very expensive. I did not know until long afterward that Mrs. Jordison had begged my mother to buy it, and that my mother not wishing to do so, had given her twenty dollars, and consented to retain the brooch, in order to lessen the poor woman's almost painful sense of obligation.

Years passed away. My dear mother went home to God, from a far-off island in the Southern sea ; to the very last giving her life for others, in generous self-forgetfulness, and unfaltering courage. True words were those which my sorrowing, bereaved father wrote in his journal concerning her, the sweet wife of his youth and the crowning joy of his home :

"She was an obedient daughter, an affectionate sister, a true friend ;—a loving, faithful and devoted wife and mother, and an humble disciple of her dear Saviour. She had a noble, generous heart; she could not eat her crust alone. Dearly beloved and honored, as she was, by all who knew her, her loss is to her husband and her children."

One day, I noticed a man with a little boy, coming out from my father's office. I thought the man was Jordison, and imagined the boy was Johnny; and my father told me that it was he, and that he had very reluctantly consented to let him occupy the old brown house again. "If your mother had not felt such an interest in his wife, I would not have the fellow around again," said he; "he is a bad, slippery man, and I dislike to have him in the neighborhood. But you had better go down and see his wife, my dear. She is a respectable, worthy woman, and an unfortunate one."

So, with my father's sanction, after my lessons were learned for the day, I went on my errand alone. How I missed the loving mother, without whose guidance I had never visited the little brown house! All that my mother had told me of Mrs. J., and much that an old housekeeper had casually mentioned, came back to me in that walk, and, with my added years, I understood better the terrible position of the wife and mother whom I was going to see. I remember, too, a feeling of satisfaction that my mother had trusted me with a part of the woman's sad story, and that my father had now sent me to her. It seemed as if it were in my dear mother's stead.

When I knocked, Mrs. J. opened the door. She did not seem to recognize me at first. The child of ten had grown into a girl of thirteen, and I suppose sorrow had added a look of maturer years. When she knew me, bursting into tears she exclaimed:

"Oh! my dear young lady you have lost your dear mother, and I have lost the kindest, sweetest lady-friend I had in the world!"   Her grief and sympathy were such as to break me down, although, usually, when others wept, it made me feel still.

She told me they had been in Canada, for a little, where she earned money and they were quite comfortable, until J. met some of his old acquaintances, and then there was nothing but carousal and shame, and almost starvation for herself and little Jessie. She had begged him to come back to the States—to New York,—which to her meant the banks of the rushing, roaring, sparkling Taronoc; promising to sew or take in washing, and support herself, Johnny and Jessie. Much to her wonder and delight, he had consented.

"I did not know my dear lady was not here, until we reached the station yesterday. If I had, I would not have longed so to come back."

Glancing around the room I recognized the same curtains at the windows, the queer table and some old pieces of furniture. The bed, with its chintz curtains, was in another room, leaving more space in the square, low-ceiling room, with its three old-fashioned windows and small panes of glass. A low chair, near a window facing the road, was Mrs. J.'s usual seat. Behind her was a door, leading, by a crooked flight of stairs, into the garret, where there was only one room partitioned off from the unfinished loft. She told me, afterwards, that she had more than once retreated, with her two younger children, up those stairs, and pushed the bolt—which she herself had put on—when her husband and elder son had come home "wild,"—sometimes bringing boon companions, with whom they would drink and play until they fell to the floor. Then she would creep down, put out the light, look to the fire, and return to her crippled little daughter and Johnny.

"Jordison and Egbert can't bear the sight of my poor little Jessie," said she, one day, when I asked her how long the latter had been crippled. "She was as straight and bright and pretty a darling as you ever saw, until she was three years old. Then, one day, Egbert took her out on a sled. He was seven years old, at the time. We were a good deal better off then than now," sighed she. "But Egbert always was a wilful boy. I told him not to take Jessie out, for Johnny was sick in my arms, and I could not fasten the little one in the sled, as I always did. He disobeyed me, and Jessie was jerked off the sled backward, and from that day she never was well. Her poor little head was dreadfully bruised, as well as her back, and the doctors thought she could not live. She is a good little darling—a real Christian child,—and my greatest earthly comfort, but the misery and ill-treatment the poor child has suffered have made me often wish the Lord had taken her to Himself when she was hurt.

"Well, you see, Miss M., Egbert can't bear the sight of her, for she is a living reproach to him ; and her father can't abide anything misshapen around him, though it be his own poor innocent child. He seems to think he is disgraced by my poor little Jessie," sighed the poor woman, bitterly. "Now, Johnny he is fond of, but I would almost rather he hated him for he will ruin him, as he has Egbert, if he has a chance."

One pleasant summer day in June, I found Mrs. Jordison unusually bright and happy. She was a remarkable-looking woman,—a brunette, with clear-cut features, fine, dark eyes, and delicately marked eyebrows. Her hair was black and abundant, and always neatly arranged. There was an intense and alert look, usually to be noticed in her face,—the token of the strain of years of terror, pain and long endurance. But there was a certain buoyancy about her, in spite of what she had suffered. She welcomed pleasant thoughts, turned readily from her sad lot to consideration for others, and was not beyond seeing and enjoying amusing circumstances in her own condition.

This day, she looked ten years younger and gayer than usual, and I began to understand that she might have been a beautiful girl,—indeed, that now she might be called a handsome woman. I suppose she noticed my surprise at her gaiety. Her dark eyes flashed, as she looked up from her sewing.

"I was away all day, yesterday," said she. "I walked to Barnet and back, and was well paid for it;" and she half drew from her pocket a letter with a foreign post-stamp. Then she stopped suddenly, and remarked: "Your mother knew my whole story, Miss M., and she did not turn away from me. She was like an angel of God, for she helped me see my sins, when I had, before, only been willing to see my misery. May I tell you something of my life? No one here knows, unless your father. I do not dare to speak to any one. If J. knew I had told, I believe he would kill me. He thinks I am too proud to tell how low I have fallen."

By this time, my girlish heart was eager, indeed, and the mystery and secrecy heightened the charm. "My mother did tell me something about you," said I.

"What did she tell you, my dear young lady?"

"That you had disobeyed your parents, and married without their consent or knowledge, and had suffered very much ever since."

She gave a great sigh. "True, true! I sowed the wind, and have reaped the whirlwind. If the suffering only could be all mine, I would be content to bear it, but the evil has gone to my children, and they are suffering and must suffer for their mother's sake. Your dear mother bade me think less of my husband's wrong doing and more of my own; and told me I owed a duty to him, as well as to my children, for I was his wife. It was new doctrine to me, for, these many years, I have felt that he was less than nothing to me; but I do see that she was right, and oh! Miss M., sometimes I wish I could love him again, as I used to. But he has been so cruel—so cruel; he has done his best to give me agony through my children. Sometimes, it seems to me I don't dare to pray: Forgive me, 'as I forgive' him!"

The glow died out of her face, as she spoke, until I reminded her: "But you did not tell me of your good news, Mrs. J."

The bright look came back, and, glancing through

all the windows and toward the door, to see that no one was near, she said : "My letter was from my daughter, Eleanor, in London, Miss M."

"I did not know you had another daughter," I replied, in astonishment.

"Yes, my dear young lady. I have a bright, handsome daughter, sixteen years old ; but she does not belong to me now. I gave her away to my sister, Lady L——t, ten years ago, and she has nothing to do with us, except to write to me, once in a while ; and sometimes she sends me a present for her little sister. She does not know that my Jessie is a cripple, and wonders that I do not send her picture, as well as Johnny's. I have never had the heart to tell them about her misfortune, though it happened nine years ago."

"Have you never seen her, all these years ?"

"Yes, once ; four years ago. My husband had gone off with Egbert, and left me to take care of myself and of the younger children. I did not know where he had gone, or whether he would ever come back. A few days after he left, I received a letter from my sister, enclosing a five-pound note. I took that, and a few dollars I had earned sewing, and crossed with my two children in the steerage. It was not so bad as you would think. Every one was very kind, from the captain down to the steerage stewardess. My poor Jessie seemed to make friends in a wonderful way. She is such a pleasant, patient little creature."

"And then, when you landed, did you see your

daughter, Eleanor, immediately?   Did she meet you at the steamer?"

"No, indeed, dear heart," she answered, with a short laugh. "A fine lady, like Eleanor, must not dream that her mother crossed in the steerage. We took a train for London, and went directly to lodgings. I knew the woman of the house. Her mother had been my mother's maid; and I knew it would be safe to leave the children with her, when necessary.

"And did they see Eleanor, and was she very glad?"

Mrs. J. shook her head slowly. "She never saw Jessie at all. I didn't dare to show her her poor little sister, nor did· I ever tell them that she was with me."

"Why are you so afraid of them, Mrs. J.?   I think she must be a very strange girl, if she despises you because you are poor," I said, hastily.

"My dear young lady," she answered, sadly, "I can't expect you to understand the difference between the two sisters. Eleanor is proud and selfish and petted. Everything painful or unpleasant is kept from her; and she would no more think of loving or kissing Jessie than if she were a little Hottentot."

"Was Eleanor so proud, and so unkind when she was little?" I asked, with indignant pity for poor little Jessie.

"She was a dear, affectionate girl, but always a little haughty and wilful; but, ah! me, if I had thought she ever could have grown so proud, I would not have given her away to my sister."

"Was she willing to be adopted, and to have you

leave her there?" I inquired, in absolute wonder, at the thought.

Mrs. J. wiped her eyes, and said, slowly: "My dear, it *had* to be so. My sister had written she would help me, but she would not give a farthing to Jordison. If I had been willing to leave him, I could have gone to England, and my sister would have taken care of me. But in those days I loved my husband, and he was not so unkind, either; and I had taken him for better, for worse, and I wrote my sister so.

"Then my sister said she would not help me, but if I wished she would take one of the children, provided I would promise never to claim it again, and she sent me money for my passage, first-class, with my children. My husband insisted on my going over to England with the three, to let her have her choice. Jessie was only three years old,—a little darling with golden curls and a sunny face ; Eleanor was six, and Egbert eight. We went to Betty Sampson's, and I went out and bought nice suits for the children and myself—I had more money then, than I have ever had, since."

*   *   *   *   *   *   *   *

"WHEN THE EVEN WAS COME."

(Matthew, viii. 23–28 ; Mark, iv. 35–40 ; Luke, viii. 22–26.)

It was near the close of a hard and trying day.

The Devil had devised two plans for hindering the Lord in His work, and both had failed.

It seems that, in the early hours of this day, the scribes who had been sent from Jerusalem arrived at Capernaum. They came to accuse the Lord Jesus of fellowship with Satan, of casting out devils through Beelzebub the prince of the devils. While Jesus was rebuking them, with fearless words of scathing and searching truth, His mother and His brethren sought Him on a different errand. "Scribes and Pharisees, hypocrites," said "He hath a devil." His kinsman, —for in those days "neither did his brethren believe in Him,"—sought to lay hold on Him, saying "He is beside himself,"—"He is mad."

Whether Mary, His mother, came with them to hinder, or to help them, in their purpose to withdraw Him from His work, we cannot tell. She was only a woman, although the mother of our Lord. She loved Him, and she feared for Him. There may have been much for her to learn, in the two years between this eventime, and the fearful hour of darkness, when she stood by His cross, and when, with the soldier's spear, "a sword pierced through her own soul also."

We are told nothing about the interview between Jesus and His mother and His brethren. But the blessed words are on record: "He stretched forth His hand to His disciples, and said, 'Behold My mother and My brethren! For whosoever shall do the will of My Father which is in heaven the same is My brother, and sister, and mother.'" Yet we know He craved human love and sympathy. How hard it must have been, to be so misunderstood by those who had known Him longest and who should have loved Him best.

But neither Scribes nor Pharisees, mother nor brethren, turned Him away one moment from His Father's work. Through the long hours of that day, He sat in a little fishing-boat, and talked to the multitudes on the shore of the sea of Galilee. To this day's teachings we may refer, at least, the parable of the sower, the lighted candle, the seed growing while the sower slept, the grain of mustard seed—and probably many others. But it had been a long, hard strain on the grand, loving heart, on the fathomless sympathies of the Son of Man. Weary and exhausted, "when the even was come, He saith unto His disciples, 'Let us pass over unto the other side.' And when they had sent away the multitude, they took Him, even as He was, in the ship."

As they sailed, a great storm of wind arose, and the waves beat into the ship. Through the narrow, mountain gorges on the western shore, the wind swept down,—as it does to this day,—with terrific power and suddenness, lashing the sea into fury, and imperiling the little boats on their way to the eastern coast.

" But Jesus was in the hinder part of the ship, asleep, on a pillow."

We know that, in His earthly life, He slept, as truly as He was athirst and hungered, as truly as He was weary, and rested at noon, by the well of Sychar. We are told how He rose up, a great while before day, and departed into a solitary place and there prayed; how, "at night, when every man went into his own house, He went unto the Mount of Olives." We have the record of His midnight watch in the garden of Gethsemane, while His disciples were sleeping. We have a precious record of His thirty-three years—of waiting and working, of His obedience and suffering, of His doing and dying;—but only this once may we have a glimpse of the weary, human-hearted Saviour *sleeping!*

He had no earthly home. He had not even where to lay His head. In the midst of the storm, in a rude fishing-boat on the sea of Galilee, He slept. But it seemed so strange to the disciples, that Jesus should sleep while they thought they were perishing; as it did to a shipmaster eight hundred years before, when Jonah,—obstinate, disobedient and very human Jonah,—on his way to Tarshish, slept in the midst of the tempest, which the Lord had sent for his sake.

Strange contrast and parallel between the type and the anti-type! Jesus doing His Father's will, crossing the raging sea to save two poor demoniacs on the other shore;—Jonah, " fleeing from the presence of the Lord," because he was unwilling to go to Nineveh, and warn and save a city of sixscore thousand souls! Truly, and blessedly for the disciples, " a greater than Jonas was there!" The heathen sea-men in the ship of Tarshish knew that they *must* perish with Jonah in their ship; the terrified disciples with Jesus in their ship, nevertheless feared that they *would* perish. They awoke Him with their cries: "Lord, save us, we perish!" "Master, Master, *carest Thou not?*" That sounds like the cry of Peter,—warm-hearted, hot-headed, impetuous, vehe-ment, impulsive, impatient Peter!

They cared not that they awoke Him from the brief, sweet slumber into which He had fallen. He had said, "Let us go over unto the other shore;" but it seems they forgot all about that, in their ter-ror. Fishermen as they were, living all their lives on, or by the shore of that very sea, it must have been indeed a "tempest from the Lord," that so un-manned them, and even threatened to make ship-wreck of their faith. How nobly calm and grand sound the words of the Master, as He rises and stills the winds and the raging of the waters, speaking "Peace" to the tempest that threatened their lives, and a better peace to the unbelief that would wreck their souls.

Our minister once, in preaching on this subject, told us that there were three lessons to be learned from it:

First. That God often suffers us to get into trouble, even when we are doing His will. The disciples were obeying Jesus when they started for "the other side," and were overtaken by the storm.

Second. That God *always cares*, although some-times our faint hearts may think He does not notice, or is indifferent to our troubles. Jesus slept, but He was in the boat with them ; so they were safe, and *could not* perish.

Third. That God will surely give His people a happy deliverance out of all their troubles. He may suffer sickness to weaken and rack the body ; He may permit the noble mind to wander, for a while, in darkness and dismay. But even out of these sore distresses, what a glorious, happy issue He gives His children in death.

And so, from the troubles which " are not unto death." Though He should suffer any of us to lose friends, and home, and wealth, and even our good name, yet let us be sure that " His compassions fail not," and none " that put their trust in Him shall ever be left desolate." "Wait on the Lord ; be of good courage, and He shall strengthen thine heart." " I had fainted *unless I had believed to see the goodness of the Lord in the land of the living.*"

It is for us to man the oar He gives us in the storm, to do our duty in the place where He puts us, to believe that *He cares*, and will surely, surely, in His own right time, and in His own best way, deliver us out of all our troubles.

" He maketh the storm a calm ;—then are they glad, because they be quiet ; *so* He bringeth them unto their desired haven."

"OH! Aunt Hetty, how *do* you do?" exclaimed a bright, graceful young woman, at the close of the "Ladies' Mission Hour," in the Lecture Room of the church at B., at the same time warmly grasping the hand of an older member, who had spoken at the meeting,—a plain, old-fashioned, loving soul, to whom, "tho' more than kindred knew," many of the younger members "gave a parent's due," as the meed of an unflagging although unpretending zeal in the good cause. "So, you have been to see your niece, and my friend Milly Harper, and the dear little twins! Do come home with me, and tell me all about your visit. I got a letter from Milly,—such a funny letter; she says 'another domestic heathen' is nearly converted, and that 'some of Aunt Hetty's quaintly put arguments' are not altogether innocent of the credit for much of the progress."

So, when the two had reached the pleasant cottage of Milly's friend, and were comfortably seated in the easy-chairs on the shaded porch, Aunt Hetty began:

Well, Milly has told you, of course, all about the little ones—trust her, or any young mother, for that —an' darlin' little cherubs they are, jest as like as two cherries on one stem. Of course, they were wonderful glad to see me—that is, the old folks were, an' if I wasn't glad to see the bawbies for the first time, it was because I didn't ketch 'em up, one at a time, an' both together, an' kiss 'em an' squeeze their little cheeks agin mine, until they an' their mother began to think I was a-goin' to devour 'em.

Then, after I was rested an' come down to where Milly was, a bouncin' around at her work, with the little tots rollin' over the rug an' maulin' the kitten,—why, the old, old, new, new, story began—all about those babies. "The very best babies that ever were, in the world," naturally, an' "so healthy an' cunnin'," an' one of 'em "gettin' a fine row of teeth;" an' every now an' then, she'd turn to me, mother-like, for an approvin' smile.

Just then, a thought kind o' struck me, and so, the next time she come to the end o' one of her fond stories, an' looked towards me, with a pretty blush, an' that smile o' mother-love, I jest kept my face as straight as I could, an' I sez, very serious, "Well, you're a good mother, Milly Harper, sez I, an' you can't help a lovin' your own, but I tell you, there's two sides to every shield, an' I hope an' pray you may be supported under this great burden,—I was goin' to say affliction,—that has been put on your shoulders."

But, my! didn't her eyes flash? And then she jest come a runnin' over to me, an', between laughin' an' cryin' an' wonderin', sez she: "Why, Aunt Hetty! how *can* you say such a dreadful thing about my darling babies?" Then she went and sat down.

"Well," sez I,—trying all my might to look sot an' stubborn,—"when you just contemplate an' consider, remember and recollect how comfortable an' at your

ease you and my nephew James Harper might ha'
been an' continued to be, without stintin' yourselves
here and pinchin' yourselves there, having your days
in peace an' your rest o' nights ; how you might a'lived
in a mansion, an' improvin' yourselves an' your neighbors with your music on the organ and your æsthetic
altar-cloths an' religious fandangoes ; how you might
a'kept your house as neat an' pretty as a pink—an'
now, of course it'll be turned upside down, an' inside
out !   It most generally *is*, for one baby; an' what d'
you s'pose it'll be for two ? "

Milly just sat an' looked at me.   " I think we'd
have grown dreadfully selfish, living that way, Aunt
Hetty.   Perhaps James wouldn't, for he's ever so
much better than I am.   But I don't believe it's very
good for people to live too much at their ease.   I
don't know exactly what you mean by religious fandangoes.   You know we've left St. John's long ago,
—Mr. St. Albans had so many queer notions ; and I
don't mean to neglect my home and James's comfort
even for the sake of the babies.

" Well, Milly Harper, you *do* surprise me," sez I.
" Just tell me true, don't you consider yourself an unfortunate woman, now,—to have two babies, you may
say *thrust* on you to once ? two lively bonny young
ones, and, worst of all, a boy and a girl, an' both of
'em pretty likely to live, so far as I see."

She just gathered them up in her arms, an' hugged
them tight, an' kind o' choked, whisperin' over an' a
pettin' them a minute.   An' then she turned to me,
an' said, so sorrowful and slow : " Aunt Hetty, I
don't see what *has* come over you.   I think Cousin

Jemima and her husband must have done something very queer, to change you so. You always used to say children were blessings, and brought their welcome with them, and you were such a good mother yourself, not only to your own children but to James and his little sister, and to other orphans, I can't imagine why you say such dreadful things."

"Mebbe I have my reasons for it," sez I, "an' I guess you'll allow that you've more 'n you can rightly care for. Stands to reason, two's twice as much trouble as one, an' 'll eat an' cost double; an', as for clothes, you've got to have two whole sets, unless you put one of 'em to bed, spell about; an' the bigger they grow the more trouble they'll be, what with measles an' scarlet fever, an' whoopin' cough, an' mumps, an' doctors' bills, an' schoolin'. An', all through, you've got to love James just the same, an' love an' care for these babies too!"

Milly stood right up,—her babies in her arms (I never quite made out how she could hold 'em both so handy, at once—but she did) an', sez she: "I'd work my fingers off for James, and for them, and you would, too, Aunt Hetty; I know you would, for all you talk so;" an' then she sat down, with a shiny look on her face.

"I s'pose you think the Lord sent em' both, so you've got to put up with 'em an' do your best," sez I, as indifferent as I could.

"No, indeed! Yes, to be sure! I mean; I know the Lord sent them both, but I'm not sorry, but glad, He did. And very likely we shall have trouble with them,—sleepless nights and anxious days, if they are sick or fretful or naughty. But the Lord gives us that to do, and aren't they His little ones? I do believe they've helped us to care more for pleasing Him already;" an' she kissed 'em, warm an' tender, an' laid 'em down in the bassine.

And then she sez, kind o' brave an' bright, but I somehow felt she was disappinted in me: "You can't think how many lovely messages we have had about the babies, and so many presents for them, too! I didn't think people could take so much interest."

"Well," sez I, sort o' meditative: "if they'd only both been boys, it wouldn't ha' been so bad; you can turn boys out, to look out for themselves pretty soon. Or just supposin' you an' James had happened to a' been born in China or Injia! How easy you could a' drowned the little girl in a wash-tub, or let her slip out the window, or set her afloat on the river, or hung her up in a basket on a tree, you know!"

Milly just looked at me one minute—such a look! I do think she believed, for half a minute, I was a lunatic; it most broke me down. An' then if you'd seen the way she flew at me, an' hugged, an' scolded, an' laughed, an' cried! "You dear, dreadful, teasing, precious Home-and-Foreign-Missionary Aunt Hetty!" sez she. "And to think I was so stupid, I never guessed what you meant, nor remembered how I used to talk, and how I was just bound up, soul and body, in St. Johns' and didn't care for anything else—I don't mean that I am very different now, only · the world does seem bigger. Do you remember, Aunt Hetty," sez she, smilin' sort o' sober an' sweet, "you once told me I was holding my little corner of

Christ's big world so close to my eyes that I couldn't see anything outside the edges ? "

" 'Pears to me I do," sez I, "remember you was specially concerned to have the gospel preached to decent folks, that could appreciate it."

" I don't know but I feel a good deal that way still," sez Milly, quiet, an' sort o' searching herself. " It seems such a dreadful waste of life and energy, for good men and women to go to those far-off heathens, and live and die, only to bring a few miserable creatures to a little knowledge of the truth ! "

" D'you remember just what the disciples' marchin' orders was ? " sez I.—Preach the gospel first to Jews, then to Gentiles—Jerusalem, Judea, Samaria ; an' the Lord didn't stop there, Milly, but He said, clear an' plain, 'to the ends of the earth and to every crea- ture.' "

"Aunt Hetty," sez Milly, very sober : "I can't bear to think of the heathen ! There is such a per- fectly dreadful number of them, I get a kind of paralysis, the minute I try to realize the multitude of them."

" I know, child ; I remember feeling just that way, when I was a girl. My father used to pray, always, for the conversion of the heathen world, as if he ex- pected it, too ; just as natural as he prayed for his children. I could a' prayed for one or two, an' worked for a few of 'em ; an' so we children did, but my heart wasn't big enough to take in the millions. I spose it was unbelief, at the bottom,—doubting of God's power and good-will and grace. But I did get a little mite cured of that once,—when 'twas family worship, too : my father prayed the Lord to keep us humble, and make us remember always we all were sinners of the gentiles. That sort o' made me feel as if those fourteen hundred millions perishin' in the dark, were our own kith an' kin, an' I was amost heart-broken, thinkin' of our poor ancestors, who lived an' died before the disciples an' the apostles an' the early Christians got around to give 'em the gospel. 'S far as I can make out, those Britons an' Angler-Saxons an' Picks an' Scots an' Gauls an' Goths weren't so very superior to Indians an' Chinese an' Japanese nowadays.   Mebbe they was a little ahead o' the Fiji Islanders, tho' they do say the old Druid priests used to offer human sacrifices to their gods fifty years ago ; but jest look at those Fiji people *now!* They make us Christian Americans blush."

"Aunt Hetty," sez Milly, her voice a-tremblin' a little, " I can't imagine how you could have been willing to give Cousin Judson up, to go to China,—and he your only son."

I didn't say one word. I couldn't just then, for it all came back to me—what I had to go through, before I was glad to have a son to send to the heathen, to tell them of the Lord Jesus Christ who died for them as well as for me. An' seemed to me I could understand, a little, the struggle in little Milly's heart, that day. I b'lieve she was afraid the Lord might want her children, an' she wasn't willin' to think so—poor child. I knew jest how it felt.

Well, James come in soon, an' we had dinner, an' James an' Milly seemed so proud an' glad to have me there. It made me very thankful, for James was as nigh as could be, to my own son,—being his dead mother was my dead sister Jemima Haselton; an' then Milly, she had to tell James how I teased her, an' James laughed, an' then he looked sober, an' sez he: "Aunt Hetty, to tell the truth, the heathen lie pretty heavy on my heart some times."

"Are you discouraged about them, James," sez I, or do you think the Lord's discouraged?"

"Why, no!" sez he, quick an' earnest; "no man, who sees what God has been doing for the heathen in the last fifty years, has any right to be discouraged. I meant that I want to do more than I ever have done."

"I'm sure you have your boys' band," sez Milly, "and you always attend all the missionary meetings, and do lots of things besides giving freely."

An' then James, he told me about his David-Livingstone-band, of seven bright little chaps, and how interested they were, and how they knew as much about Livingstone as he did. "And Aunt Hetty," sez he, "you ought to see Milly; she helps more than I do, with her singing, and hunting up articles and encouraging the little chaps. The reason she won't allow she cares so much," sez James, half laughing, "is that she has been reading Bleak-House lately, and she's afraid somebody might think she is too much concerned about Borrioboola Gha. If ever you find me sitting in the corner, leaning my head against the wall, like poor Mr. Jellyby, you'll know the reason why!" "Nonsense, James," sez Milly, her cheeks just like roses; "Aunt Hetty, you won't believe a word he says."

"Seriously, Aunt Hetty," sez James, "I'm more interested in those boys than I can express. I've a conviction that some of them are going to be missionaries; that's what I'm praying for and working for, at least. I wish sometimes that I had *my* life to live over again!"

"James!" sez Milly, "you wouldn't go and leave us?"

James looked across at her,—so strong an' gentle he is, to be sure,—an' sez he: "Why, Milly, wouldn't you have married me if I'd been a missionary?"

"I'm afraid," sez Milly, the tears a-coming to her eyes, "I'm afraid you'd never thought of marrying me. You'd have gone off to Holyoke or Oxford for a wife, or may-be advertised for a real, missionary helpmate. I'm sure I'd never have answered that advertisement;" sez Milly, half laughin' an' half cryin'. An' then we all stopped short an' laughed, thinkin' how silly it was to be miserable about what might or mightn't have happened.

But James, he couldn't stop talking of missionary work. "The promises are so grand, and so emphatic, Aunt Hetty! I was looking them up the other day. *It's sure to be done,* and the gospel of the kingdom shall be preached in all the world, for a witness unto all nations. The Son has asked and the Father *has given* Him the heathen for His inheritance and the uttermost parts of the earth for His possession. All the ends of the earth shall—   *

*   *   *   *   *   *   *   *

THE SOLDIER'S COMFORT.

My suffering soldier friend :—If I should now come and stand beside you, minister to your wants, and speak words of tender pity and compassion, to remind you that, though far from mother, sister, or wife, yet there are many hearts bleeding at the thought of your sufferings, would you not believe that I really cared for you? You would not, I am sure, think that a spirit of mere curiosity would lead one to leave home and friends, and all that nature prizes most, to minister to you in your suffering and loneliness.

But suppose I should say, with such earnestness that you would have to believe me: " My poor friend, I wish I *could* suffer in your stead. I wish I could lay down my youth, and health, and vigor for your restoration, who have fought and bled for the country we both love so well." You would then, perhaps, feel a little more impressed with the intensity of my wish to relieve you. But this suffering in your stead, this transfer of pain and loss from one sinful creature to another, is, we know, impossible. I can suffer,— God knows how many hearts do suffer,—*with* you; but we are helpless, further than to strive to soothe and cheer, and implore the Great Physician to heal all your diseases.

But perhaps you may think: " No one can know how much I suffer. The doctors pity me, and so do you ; but really it does very little good."

Did you never hear of any one's curing his own heart-ache by sympathy with the greater sufferings of others? I know this may seem a strange prescription, but it has been found a very good one, by many who were almost crushed by the great grief God had sent upon them. When we see another suffering, without a murmur, tenfold more than we do, we feel ashamed to think so much of our own misery.

And there is *One*, my poor suffering friend, who does know the full measure of your sufferings, and who was " wounded for our transgressions, and bruised for our iniquities ; " who also " took our infirmities and bare our sicknesses." He was " even obedient unto death " for us, that we might have life in Him, and from Him I come now, to tell you how His infinite, tender heart yearns pityingly over you, longing to have you look at His wounds, that you may be healed of your *worst* wounds—those made by sin.

It is not as a stranger that he looks at you. " He knoweth our frame," for He is our Maker, and " He remembereth that we are dust." He is at once your wisest, truest, most compassionate Friend—the " Brother born for adversity," and the " Friend that sticketh closer than a brother." See the wonderful proof He has given of His love.

When the whole world was lying under sentence of death for sin, Jesus Christ, the Eternal Son of God the Father, out of pure pity and love, came down to suffer and die as our *substitute*. And this He did, when we were enemies to Him and His holy law. No higher proof of love can be given than this. A few times in the history of the race, men have been found willing to die for friends, but no mere man has ever yet been found willing to die for enemies. God commendeth His love to us in that while we were yet sinners, enemies, Christ died for us. You surely cannot doubt His love for you, when you consider further, what a *dreadful death* He endured for you. It was not an ordinary death of a man gently breathing out his life among friends and in peace. It was a violent, cruel, lingering death, amid the jeers and scoffs of enemies. His friends all forsook Him, one betrayed Him, another denied Him, and even God, His Father, withdrew the light of His countenance from Him, extorting that bitterest cry that earth or heaven ever heard: "My God, My God, why hast Thou forsaken Me?"

Do you remember how the *whole body* of Jesus was bruised, and torn, and pierced for us? You remember, after Pilate, the Roman governor, had scourged Him, how soldiers wove a crown of thorns and bound it around the Saviour's head. You remember how His tender, compassionate hands, which had ever been ready to help and heal, and His weary, toil-worn feet, were torn by the nails which fastened Him to Calvary's cross. His side was pierced by a soldier's spear, until from the wound there came out blood and water. Thus, head, and hands, and side were bruised and bleeding for you.

But He did still more than this for you. The bodily agony of crucifixion was the smallest part of His suffering. He bore the weight of your sins—the sins of all who will believe on Him. The punishment of sin lay heavy upon Him. In the garden of Gethsemane it pressed Him down to the earth, and "being in an agony he prayed more earnestly, and His sweat was, as it were, great drops of blood falling down to the ground." The penalty of sin was the bitterest portion of the cup which His Father gave Him to drink. He drank even this for you.

My poor friend, should not the remembrance of the infinite agony of Jesus for your sake, and His death from love to your soul, make you almost forget your own physical pains, while from your grateful heart should burst songs of praise "unto Him who hath so loved us as to give Himself for us."

In the great book of account, the recording angel writes down our sins. What a list for but a single day! And think, what must be the record for thousands of days. And each of these sins deserves God's eternal wrath and curse. But look! One stands beside the book—the "Lamb as it had been slain." It is Jesus, the sinner's Friend. He shows you His hands and His side, pierced for you, and with tender, pitying look, He asks you to believe on Him and love Him; and the moment you do, He lays His bleeding hand upon the page and blots out all your sins with His own blood.

Soldier, soldier, oh! trust in Jesus. Repent, confess, and forsake your sins, and love Him who hath so loved you as to give His own life for you. Then, whatever you may be called to suffer, you will be happy, for Jesus pities, soothes and comforts all who love Him far more than does a mother her suffering child. "He healeth the broken in heart and bindeth up their wounds."

May this same Jesus, "who ever liveth to make intercession," send His Holy Spirit with these words, and show you infinitely more of His love, and your need of Him, than any fellow-sinner can! And unto the Father, Son, and Holy Ghost, be all the glory forevermore. Amen.

SOLDIER, A LETTER FOR YOU!

My Brother and Comrade :—Will you listen to a few words from one who is also a soldier, very weak, and entirely unworthy of so high a calling ; yet who is, by the grace and good-will of the Captain, still kept in the ranks, and enabled to fight, in the sure hope of a victor's crown.

My Captain knows you well, and has loved you longer and better than your mother, or your dearest friend. He loved you from all eternity, and He is now looking on you with pity. Do you know Him, my comrade, do you love this Captain of our salvation, who gave his cheek to the smiters, His back to the scourge, His soul unto death, and His body to the cross—for you, if you will only love Him ?

Near two thousand years ago, a band of *soldiers* came one night into a garden, called Gethsemane. They bear lanterns and torches, and are armed with deadly weapons, being sent to seize, as a criminal, the Holy One of God. At the first sight of Him, as He comes forth from the darkness, shining in the majestic innocence which proclaims Him God as well as man, all, even the traitor Judas, with the soldiers, awe-struck in His presence, go backward and fall to the ground. And yet they have the wicked courage to seize Him and lead Him away, "as a lamb to the slaughter." They bring Him to the judgment-hall, and, calling together the whole band, in cruel mockery they put on Him the purple robe of majesty, and give a reed to Him for a royal sceptre. *Soldiers'* hands weave the crown of thorns, and bind it round His head, and smite Him with a reed, and buffet Him. They spit upon Him, and mocking, bend the knee, and cry: "Hail! King of the Jews!" Then they strip Him of the royal purple, put His own garments upon Him, and lead Him away to Calvary. There they crucify Him. Four *soldiers* drive through the quivering flesh the rending nails, less hard and cruel than those hearts and hands for whose sin the "iron entered into His soul." Sitting down, the soldiers watch Him there. They see Him bear the wrath of God in the sinner's stead, and yet these sinful soldiers dare to mock His agony, and offer to Him vinegar to drink, crying: "If Thou be the Son of God, save Thyself!" In view of the cross, they part His garments among themselves, and cast lots for the seamless vesture, type of the spotless robe of righteousness, without beginning and without end, which He wrought out for us in His death. They listen to His earth-rending, heaven-piercing cry for His Father; they hear His dying prayer for His murderers.

O hard and stony hearts! have they no pity, no love? Jesus says: "Father, forgive them, for they know not what they do."

And when His head is bowed in death, a *soldier* thrusts his sword into His side, and from the wound flow out blood and water. Again, by the sepulchre,

where the broken body of our Lord was laid, a guard
of soldiers watched until the early Sabbath dawn,
when the Mighty Angel, at whose coming "the
keepers did quake, and become as dead men," came
down and rolled away the stone from the door of the
sepulchre.   Then the *same Jesus*, who had prayed on
the cross for His murderers, arose from the dead, and
now ever liveth to make intercession for us.

Comrade, can you think of all this,—of the sufferings and death of this great Captain, without feeling
that you, as well as those other soldiers, have an interest, aye, that you have a responsibility in His
death?

Remember that, if you are not a "soldier of the
cross," you are still in arms against Him,—you are
serving Sin, and wearing the uniform of the Devil.
You have been by the holy law of God court-mar-
tialed, tried and convicted as a traitor to your King, a
deserter from your Captain, and a rebel against
heaven.   What hope is there for you, when your case
is in the hands of One omnipotent to punish unto
the full measure of your deserts?   Ah! blessed be
God, that, though your King could not suffer your
awful crime to go unpunished, your Captain, in love
for you, offered Himself as a *substitute* for you.   And
He now holds out to you a *full pardon*, sealed by the
blood which He shed on the cross, by means of the
blessing of the Spirit on these words of a fellow-sinner.
Go to this great Captain, my dear comrade: ask
Him, for His mercy's sake, to be your substitute, and
to make you His true and fearless soldier.   Confess
your guilt, ask Him to wash it away from your soul,

and to make you sure that he has offered a full atonement for you on the cross. Pray for the Holy Spirit to teach you, and to give you the humble spirit of a little child. Jesus is waiting, He is longing to have you and all your comrades join His glorious company. He knows your heart as well as he knew the hearts of those for whom He prayed in His dying hour. He has a brother's hand, to clasp yours in your mortal weakness, a brother's heart to comfort you in your sufferings, as well as a Mighty Arm to rescue you from Hell and Death. Oh! enlist under Him, pledge your heart, and soul, and body to His service, praying Him to keep you "faithful unto death." I am sure you will never be sorry for it.

My comrade, if you are already a " soldier of the cross," be mindful of your Captain. Remember how He "stood guard" for you, how He gave watchword and countersign for you, when the sword of God's justice was pointed at your soul. He answered for you in the roll-call, and pledged His life for yours, and all because He loves you unto death. He died in your place as a deserter, a rebel, and a traitor; He bore the scoffs of men, the malice of the Devil, and the wrath of God, that you might go free; nay, more, that He might thus purchase for you a sure victory over sin, and a seat with Him upon His throne in glory. Can you ever be too brave and faithful in His cause?

You know His first word of command : " *Only believe.*" His second is : " *Follow me.*" He has left a manual for you. He has given such clear and sure directions that you cannot mistake them, if you only ask the Holy Spirit to take His orders and repeat them to you. Be true to your colors, and keep your eye on your Captain. "Standing, each man in his place, by His standard," "endure hardness as a good soldier of Christ Jesus." Do not be ashamed of your uniform and the name of Christ crucified. "Take unto you the whole armor of God," and re-member that all the saints in heaven have worn it during their earthly warfare, and have borne the re-proach of Jesus of Nazareth. *Stand up for Jesus* wherever you are, against sin and Satan, and the evil world. Your Captain's eye is on you, and His arm is ready to help you in your hour of need. Only "be faithful unto death," and then your Captain will surely report you at the great headquarters, and so a glorious promotion and a victor's crown will be yours *at the end of the battle.*

INDELIBLE INK.

I.

"YES, Sue, if you can wait just a minute. I'm sure there are some clothes of Gerard's, that will do for your Samaritan box. Dear me ! there's not much leisure, with half a dozen children like mine. I never *did* see such boys, for getting into scrapes."

Helen Fletcher, round, plump, sweet and pleasant-voiced, did not look as if the world went very hard with her, notwithstanding her six children, and her husband, who she declared was the greatest boy of them all. Sue Harrison, Gerard Fletcher's only sister, seated herself resignedly in the pleasant nursery, while Helen, still talking, opened a cedar closet, and pulled down some packages of clothing, carefully pinned up in linen and camphor.

"Now see, Sue ; these clothes are just as good as ever they were, but since Gerard will persist in getting stout, in spite of misfortunes and hard times, he'll have to take the consequences. If a woman grows stout, she can have her dresses made over,— match the stuff or something, make combination suits and economize ; but it is just a hopeless case when a man outgrows his coats and vests and trousers. So here, these good clothes must go to somebody else, and since your Samaritan box wants them, why, you may as well have them. And here is a set of shirts

—very good, but dear me, they won't begin to fit Gerard now. If Gerard doesn't stop soon, he'll never be able to go deer hunting in Virginia this fall. He'll soon be a subject for Banting."

"Well, I'm thankful," began Sue Harrison, "that my husband doesn't make an object of himself,—in that way. One can stand it in a brother."

"My patience !" exclaimed Helen Fletcher, "Gerard never looked so handsome in his life as he does now ; and he's so tall, he can afford to weigh 180, or 200 even, without being too heavy. I should think you wouldn't object to your husband's following his example."

" There now, Helen—there is no use in our fighting over our husbands ; mine suits me, and yours, I suppose, suits you. But what are you doing now ?" Helen Fletcher was seated, pen in hand, and indelible-ink-bottle beside her, carefully erasing the name, "Gerard Hazeltine Fletcher," from one garment after another. "That tailor always will mark Gerard's clothing in such immense letters !"

"Why, on earth, do you go to that trouble ?" asked Sue, lazily.

"For several reasons," said Helen, coolly. "I am not particularly anxious that Mr. G. H. Fletcher get the credit of giving away his wardrobe, and moreover I don't want strange fellows to go around this country personating my husband."

Sue laughed lightly, saying : "I never trouble myself about such a thing."

"Jane," said Mrs. Fletcher, to her seamstress in the next room, "will you bring me a hot iron from the laundry, to press these marks?   But tell me, Sue, something about this box, and what the Good Samaritans do with the clothing and supplies."

Sue began telling the story of the poor and needy—the story so painfully familiar in these days, when even those who have been until lately generous helpers so often need assistance themselves.   Eagerly and earnestly she talked, and Helen listened and worked, erasing the marks; while Jane pressed the hot iron upon them, to make sure that the erasure should be indelible.   The work was nearly done, when the front door was opened by a latch key—a confused noise was heard, in the hall and on the stairs, and Gerard's voice saying quietly: "Not in there! in *this* room ; don't frighten his mother."

Helen started to her feet, and was out in the hall just as her husband was carrying Frank, her six-year-old boy, into the next room.

"The pony ran away with him, and threw him off. He's not much hurt ; see, dear.   Don't look so white, little mother."

Gerard Fletcher had all his life been used to accidents, and Helen had grown accustomed to take care of bruises and broken bones ; but always, until she knew just what had happened, a sickening fear took possession of her.

The doctor followed close on Gerard Fletcher's steps, and found no serious injury—the collar bone broken, and some bruises.   "He'll be all right in six weeks, and ready for another tumble, Mrs. Fletcher. Your husband and your boys ought to join an accident insurance; you'd have quite an income from the payments."

"No use, doctor," answered Gerard, gaily; "they know us too well, and would ask too high rates to make it pay, for us."

Sue Harrison had been making herself generally useful, while Jane came in and dressed Frank, her special pet, and scolded him merrily for not holding on better.

"Well, Helen, if I can't do anything more, dear, I will go home," said Mrs. Harrison, as she stood with Helen by Frank's bed, where he lay then, smiling up at his mother and his favorite aunt.

"Thank you, ever so much, Sue; you have helped me a great deal, but, now that baby's quiet with Jane, I can stay with Frank, and we shall manage splendidly. If you'll tell Gerard to wrap up those clothes—he's such an excellent packer—they will be all ready when you can send for them. But be sure you don't send anything with his name unerased! I finished nearly all; but there is one suit, I think, not marked,—unless you'll finish the work."

"Very well, I'll see to it carefully," said Sue, "and thank you very much on the part of the Good Samaritans, one and all."

"Mamma, I want to go shooting deers and turkeys, too; I'm sure I could shoot just like papa. I've seen him lots of times, just this way,—bang! bang! bang! You'd like me to bring you home a real, splendid, big turkey for Thanksgiving, and lots of little deers' heads to hang up, like those papa brought last year!"

Helen Fletcher's sweet, bright face smiled down at the eager one beside her. Phil was her eldest, a handsome, restless, impetuous boy of thirteen ; not a marvel in the way of study, for the latent ambition of his nature had never been stirred by words that breathe and thoughts that burn. Now, the instinct of pursuit, the eagerness for the race, the spirit of strife and conquest, lay only in the direction of cricket and hunting. "What would become of all the learning that is to go into this curly head this year, if you should run away from school just in the beginning of the term? And then, Phil, how do you think I could do without papa and you, my big boy, —my right arm when papa's away?"

"That's so, mamma ; forgive me! I never thought of that," said Phil, manfully. "I won't say one more word about it now. If you were willing, I was going to ask father, but it would be awful mean."

"I want you to get me a nice bow, and practice archery with me next month, Phil ; and we'll have a little archery party on grandpa's grounds, when we go out there for a week, when papa is away."

"Oh! that'll be jolly, and you'll ask all the boys and their sisters, and give a prize, won't you, mamma?"

"We'll talk to papa about that, and see what he can do ; perhaps we'll have it on papa's birthday, even if he is not here ; he'd like us to have a pleasant time, shooting at home, while he is shooting away. But mind, don't have any more broken collar bones or sprained ankles before that time, for it might upset your pleasure party."

"We'll be dreadfully careful, mother! I'll tell Jack

and Gove and Fred, and we won't do a thing that's risky. I know it'll be comfortable for you not to be so worried about us, too." Helen laughed, knowing too well the spirit of boys, to be at all convinced that they would not, without a moment's thought risk their heads and heels a dozen times before the archery party. However, after papa had been consulted, among the chorus of eager voices that evening, he gave his unqualified approval, and told mamma to get the prettiest bow and quiver she could find, for a prize.

———◆———

II.

AWAY up in the Shenandoah mountains is a rough log-house, where live the Ervines, a family of hunters and farmers,—quite as much and as many of the former as of the latter,—for, while they work their mountain farm in summer, they all hunt in the winter, and fish all the year round. Sturdy, honest, stalwart fellows they are ; sound in mind and body—all except Harry, who came out of the late unpleasantness with a constitution shattered by fever and hard marches. Five years ago, John, the second brother, married Nannie Gordon, the orphan child of Robert and Elsie Gordon, Scotch settlers who died during the war, leaving their little daughter without guardian or money in this country.

Robert Gordon declared, before his death, that there were lands and kin, in Scotland, belonging to him ; and his great regret, in dying and leaving his little motherless child, was that he had, in wilfulness and waywardness, cut loose from those who would be her natural guardians.

"Dinna ye fret anent yon, i' the noo, gin the Lord's forgi'en ye for that, and for a' the sins, Robbie Gordon," said kind-hearted old dame Ervine. "While we've a poun' corn meal, or an oat cake, or a sup porridge, your lassie shall na gae hungry; an' as for teaching her to fear God and keep His commandments, I'll do that, Robert Gordon, mon. Mair nor you—I'll nae gie my word. Buik larning's hard to win i' the noo, for the gude scholars maist a' deed i' this bluidy war, but I'll do by her as I wad ye suld by mine ain, gin I were in your place, Robbie, mon. Noo, say your prayers, an' leave your worldly cares i' the hands o' the Lord, wha kens a' ye tell Him, an' taks tent o' ye when ye hae no thocht o' Him."

"God bless you, dame, ye're a gude frien'; an' may the Lord reward you, for I can na!"

So, Nannie Gordon grew up in the old log house, a lovely, womanly girl, sweet and true and simple-hearted, like a lily among thorns. At least so Harry Ervine thought, when he came home, wounded and ill. Poor Harry, he had a sore heart to carry for many a year, for John his brother won and wore the bonny lily that each admired so much. Last year, the old mother died; and now, when Gerard Fletcher and his two friends tramped up to the Ervines' door, Nannie and her baby Maggie were the only women folk within five miles.   *   *   *   *   *   *   *
    *   *   *   *   *   *   *   *

20

PINE KNOTS FROM OLD CAROLINA.

I.

IT is a lovely November day. The soft, pure, blue sky is as serene, the sun shines as brightly on the unnamed graves of the thousands who died in yonder fields, as if there had never been sin, war and bloodshed on the earth. It is with no wish to revive bitter memories, or to open old wounds which have healed over—though not without scars,—that I wander among these scenes, and seek to take my reader with me. North and South are brothers ; the family ties have never been broken ; and over the graves of Garfield and Grant we have clasped hands again in a grasp too warm,—God grant ! to be again sundered by scheming demagogues.

Yesterday, I came upon this cemetery unawares. It was a Sabbath morning, and we were going to church. Maurice said : " We will start a little early, and take a walk in the cemetery before service ; " so, walking and talking of many things, and asking no questions as to our destination, I walked on until we halted before a gate. I said : " Why, surely this is a cemetery, isn't it ? " With the answer, came a sudden rush of recollection, linking Salisbury with Andersonville in most painful association. Yonder tall monument to the memory of those who sleep their last sleep, but under shadow of the country's flag, points us to the plateau where eleven thousand un-named soldiers lie on the crest of a slope.

The next day I made a longer visit there,—the one-armed, soldierly superintendent accompanying me explaining most courteously, and giving all informa-tion requested. The cemetery is inclosed on three sides with walls, over which rose bushes and ivy climb, and trees with ivy-covered trunks stand guard around the dead. An old negro is busy, raking the fallen leaves from the graves. There are immense piles of russet and brown ; one cannot but remember how it is written—"We all do fade as a leaf !"

"In these trenches, madam, are buried eleven thousand, seven hundred Union soldiers, who died in the prison-pen over yonder, and were carried here and buried by their comrades, detailed for that pur-pose. You may remember there was a Mr. R. of the *New York* ——, who was taken prisoner and confined there. He took the names of four thousand, five hundred, who to his knowledge, died while he was a prisoner. He escaped, in company with three others, and reported these names to the Sec-retary of War, and those papers are on file at Washing-ton now. That is the only record we have of those who are in these trenches, and of course their graves are not known—only the fact that those soldiers are buried here. You see these blocks of stone. They mark the sections running from the northwestern to the northeastern corner of the plot, from one to eighteen."

The sod is smooth and green as a meadow. No

mound or hillock distinguishes one trench from another. Along the sides of the space where the unnamed dead are buried, are some who were brought here from other parts of the State, many of whose names were marked on a rude head-board which the government has exchanged for a more lasting memorial in stone. These also are numbered. Kentucky, Ohio, Indiana, Michigan and New York have furnished them. But the graves of these soldiers, known and recognized as belonging to their several regiments and States, do not appeal to the heart as does that solid square of unnamed, unknown graves.

We walked around the burial ground,—God's acre, sown with precious seed, in bitter weeping. I cannot but think the fields are white unto the harvest,—God's harvest of peace and good-will to all people and tongues and nations.

> "On Fame's eternal camping-ground,
> Their silent tents are spread;
> And Glory guards, with solemn round,
> The bivouac of the dead."

———◆———

II.

THIS afternoon, I walked towards the cemetery, to make a longer visit. On the way there, I noticed a forlorn old building, weather-stained and unpainted, but which had a sort of belfry as indication of some special use. From an adjoining house, as I passed, rushed a throng of boys and girls, leaping and singing, cutting all manner of capers and antics,—boys turning somersaults into and over a ditch, chasing one another and enjoying themselves with an abandon unknown to any but themselves—children of nature. I was amused and interested with their contortions and frolics, all good-natured and with entire absence of teasing. And, as I paused by the fence, I asked one of the little chaps if this were a school.

"Yes marm, a graded school," answered he, glibly, with evident pride.

I asked them a few questions, which they seemed greatly pleased to answer, and passed on, only to meet an astonishing spectacle—a small darkey carried by four of his comrades, one or two catching hold of each arm and leg, the others dancing, shouting and laughing, and having the best time possible over their successful capture, interspersing their fun with encouraging remarks of this sort: "Aint you gwine to get a lickin'! You'll cotch it, sure's you're a live coon."

"Bring him along, Mary," called a clear voice from the school-room door, where the teacher stood watching the proceedings.

I couldn't possibly help laughing at the ludicrous procession, and watched with great interest to see how they got their prisoner over the fence. "What's the matter?" I asked a little fellow, just to hear what he would say.

"Oh! Sam Markelo, he done run away from school, an' missus tole us to fotch him back. We's aint goin' to let go o' him, I reckon. He's gin us a right smart run, he has,"—grinning. They didn't loosen their hold of him a second, and I rather think he had some pretty severe treatment before he was deposited at the teacher's feet.

As I walked on, I noticed a little cottage standing back from the road a little way, in front of which stood a middle-aged negro woman, shading her eyes with her hand and looking towards the school and the refractory— *   *   *   *   *   *

*   *   *   *   *   *   *

FOREIGN FRAGMENTS.

I.

MARBURG, ON THE LAHN.

SOME one has said: "When you have a pleasure, share it," but how shall I send over the wide waters the picture which I have seen to-day? Artists have much to say about local coloring, lights and atmosphere; and even our untrained eyes appreciate readily the difference between a sun-lit and a moon-lit view—between the brilliance of a day in June, and the soft, dreamy haze of Indian Summer,—between Hyde Park in November fogs, and the same in the height of the "Season."

Here in Germany, the differences seem to lie more in the nature and character of the peoples than in times and places.

Let me try to paint for you the pictures I have seen in my ramble to-day. An old, irregularly built town, by a river side, with narrow streets winding around the hill, and a narrower street turning through an archway, up a short, rough climb, to the Castle on the summit—literally and in verity the Schlossberg, which looks down, in grim and solitary silence upon the life below. Come, walk with me, through the streets of this queer, old town, and see through my eyes, if you will.

Leaving the green pastures and still waters of the

Lahn behind us, we walk from our lodgings in the Bahnhofstrasse, through the main street of the town, passing the Elizabethan Kirche, and then take one of the steep, narrow streets winding up the hill. Queer, quaint old houses, with roofs of many angles, and frequent dormer-windows, — always picturesque,— stand along the scanty sidewalk. At times and places, the two feet we ask for passage disappears entirely. Down the hill, come peasant women, with weather-beaten faces, and curious little, black, pyramidal structures on the tops of their heads, tied under the chin. They wear dresses whose circumference at the hips is astonishing, while their length reminds one of the fate of the old dame in the story, whose frock was stolen and shortened by naughty boys, so that, on attiring herself therein, she was forced, in her mental quandary, to exclaim: "If this indeed be I, as I suppose it be "—　　*　　*　　*　　*　　*

*　　*　　*　　*　　*　　*　　*　　*

II.

THE FACKEL ZUG.

LAST evening, we watched with a good deal of interest one of the sights peculiar to a University-town, —a torch-light procession, in honor of the Professor who served as Rector during the last University year. The hour named for the procession to form, at the Court House or Town Hall, was eight o'clock, but, as we were told, the Students are always a little ahead of time on this occasion, not taking the "academic quarter-hour," which marks the Professors' want of military punctuality at lectures. We had invited a number of friends to share our windows, which over-looked the main line of the procession towards Professor A.'s house, but the torches had nearly passed, before they arrived.

It was a pretty and curious sight,—the students wearing the colors of the various University Societies to which they belong, and bearing banners and flam-ing torches through the dim streets. Certain members in each Society are noticeable for their old-time cos-tume, familiar to Americans in the pictures of the Father of his Country. Some wear highly embroi-dered scarlet coats, with military-looking trappings. Each Society seems to have its own band of music, and the notes of one sometimes overlap those of the preceding.

When they arrived before the Professor's house, they halted and gave three hearty cheers for the Uni-versity and for the last year's Rector, who was much beloved, and, after his appearance on the balcony and the delivery of his speech of thanks, this part of the fun was over. Between six hundred and seven hundred students took part in this Fackel Zug ; and on the homeward march the last were first, and the first, last.

The remainder of the programme was a return to the Saal Bau, the Opera House and Concert Hall of the city, and probably a close contest between the members of the different Societies, as to their ability to assimilate the product of the Brauerei. Seriously, this beer-drinking is a custom which, notwithstanding all that has been said and written in its favor, seems to me to be one of the unfavorable signs for .Germany's future. When a University student trains himself to drink twenty bottles of beer in twenty-four hours,—how to study and be sober becomes a problem which his perturbed brain seeks in vain to solve. But I would by no means say that this is a fact with the generality of the Marburg students. The lectures of many Professors are well attended by courteous, attentive young men.   *   *   *   *   *

*   *   *   *   *   *   *   *

III.

THE JERUSALEM CHAMBER.

I suppose that all have heard of Westminster Abbey, one of the oldest and most interesting churches in the world, but perhaps some may not know of the Jerusalem Chamber, in this same old Abbey,—a square room on the right, as you enter the Abbey by the door—the usual entrance, now.

In this room, to which admission is ordinarily given only by a note from the dean or one of the canons, a good many remarkable scenes have occurred. When we went there, with a note from Canon ——, a few months ago for the first time, the Revisers of the Bible were at their labors. You know how much interest almost every one has felt, both in America and England, in the Revised New Testament, and how much has been written and said both for and against it. So it was very interesting to us to see the long table, with a dozen or fifteen chairs around it, and all sorts of Bibles, of different languages and many dates, lying upon it, just as they were when the clergymen and scholars had ceased using them at five o'clock of the day before, and in readiness for them to resume the work within ten mintes after we left.

Perhaps it will be interesting to you to know—it certainly is, to me—that I am writing this little sketch of the Jerusalem Chamber with a quill-pen which one of the Revisers used in the work to which so many years, and so much loving labor and desire for God's glory, have been consecrated. I do not know which of the number wrote with this particular quill, but I do know that a certain plain, green glass inkstand, which is in my possession, is one which the Bishop of Gloucester—one of the most faithful laborers in the work of revision—was accustomed to use when requiring to mark passages in red ink. I fancy that the reason why the stand had been discarded by his Grace was the loss of the lid, for the sediment of the red ink is quite thick in the bottom.

I would not have you think, however, that we imitated the Goths and Vandals, by helping ourselves to these relics   *   *   *   *   *   *   *
*   *   *   *   *   *   *   *

———◆———

IV.

LORD MAYOR'S DAY.

THE spectacle of Lord Mayor's day is something worth seeing. It is, by general consent, considered the great city's holiday,—a more notable day for London town than the Queen's birthday. Only one year the Lord Mayor reigns, but truly, for that year, he is the great man of London, out-ranking even Royalty itself, as chief representative of the dignity of metropolitan institutions and time-honored pageant.

It would be tedious to describe in detail the procession, comprising the numerous city guilds, the firemen and the boys of the Thames training-school and ship, and a fine display of regimental bands, besides detachments of the Guards and the Victoria Rifles. Some of the groups were very peculiar—mediæval indeed, and new to the time of Wellington and the nineteenth century.

The chief feature of the procession, this year, was the display, on the way to Westminster, of the American flag, specially sent for by the new Lord Mayor, which, as one of the English papers says, was " by a happy inspiration " carried in the place of honor, immediately preceding the Sheriff's carriage, and escorted by a guard from the Royal London Militia. When the procession arrived at Westminster, the flag was carried into the palace yard, and enthusiastically saluted by the multitude, the various bands in the procession playing, in concert, the American National Anthem.   *   *   *   *   *   *

*   *   *   *   *   *   *   *

V.

HYDE PARK.

In the long twilight of these summer Sabbaths, Hyde Park presents a strange scene—many sharp contrasts.   Crossing the drive, which, on other days, would be crowded with carriages, my friend said, quietly: "You see, it is Sunday,—the carriages stand outside, while the ladies and gentlemen take their stroll in the Park, instead of a drive."

Scattered over the broad acres of greensward were hundreds, perhaps thousands of men, women and children, some lying in careless ease on the sweet-scented grass, children running around, lovers walking arm in arm.   Turning towards the first large crowd, where we saw a banner, a platform and a table, we drew near to the speaker.

"It is Mr. C., the evangelist of Hyde Park Hall," said my friend.   "He is going to America, next week. He has done a great work here."   It was not hard to believe *that*, of such an intensely earnest speaker. Every pulse seemed thrilling—every nerve and fibre seemed under extreme tension, as though his whole frame were uttering: "Now, therefore, brethren, we *beseech* you, as ambassadors for Christ, be ye reconciled to God."   On the banner, near the speaker

were the words: "Where shall I spend Eternity?"
The group of listeners at this stand was attentive and
thoughtful, and seemed impressed by the earnestness
of the speaker, and the solemnity of the subject.
He dwelt on the universality of the belief in a future
life, illustrating it by reference to the customs of the
heathen nations in burying their dead—the red men
of the West burying their warriors with tomahawk,
bow and arrows, for them to use in the hunting
grounds of the Great Spirit.

Every pleasant afternoon through the week, the
drive in the park is thronged with beautiful carriages
whose occupants are lords and ladies and other members of the gay London society. But the park is a
gathering place for many besides the higher classes.
Through the past weeks, there have been gatherings
of a political character—speakers on the Irish question, not communists either, striving to set the sore
need and trouble of the hard-pressed, despairing
people before the minds of those who might hear
and heed; reviews of the Guard; parade of the
Highlanders, and other displays.   *   *   *

*   *   *   *   *   *   *   *

———◆———

VI.

FROM RIO TO PETROPOLIS.

LEAVING the city at two o'clock, in the ferry, we
kept up the harbor, fifteen miles, passing islands
decked with palms, bananas and acacias, and landed,

in about an hour and a quarter, at the little town of Maná. Here we took the cars and one hour's ride, through low and marshy ground to the foot of the Serra; then left the rail for the post-coach which runs regularly from this station.

The drive was delightful, in an open *diligence*, drawn by four mules on a full gallop, over a road as smooth as a floor, winding zigzag up the mountains through the wildest scenery; while below us lay the valley, broken into a billowy sea of green hills, and the harbor, with the coast-range beyond, growing soft and mellow in the afternoon sunshine. Palms, acacias, and tree-ferns; parasitic growths, with abundant bloom of the purple Quaresina, the Thunbergia vines— *   *   *   *   *   *   *   *

*   *   *   *   *   *   *   *

---◆---

VII.

BUENOS AYRES.

ONE day we went into an image shop, in the window of which were figures of saints and the virgin, and all manner of carved, ornamental rosaries. As we entered, we saw two workmen, busy with their tools, finishing a delicately carved crucifix. Beside them lay portions of other figures,—the whole scene, and the purely business way in which they worked at their trade, recalling very forcibly the words of Isaiah about the makers of idols.

There were many different styles and sorts of images, all of reputed saints in the Roman Catholic Church. One was a soldierly looking figure,—the palmer's cape and girdle showing that it represented one who had been a pilgrim, in the old days when a journey to Jerusalem was certain to win the title of saint for the pilgrim. 'St. Roque seemed to be a very favorite figure. He is always seen as a vigorous, athletic man, with a worn, earnest face, and one hand lifting the cloak from his knee, where a deep wound appears. I do not know the legend connected with it.

*　　*　　*　　*　　*　　*　　*　　*

VIII.

SUNNY MEMORIES OF MENTONE.

JEAN came with the donkeys, Monte Bello and Blanchette, early one sunshiny afternoon in April, and we started for an ascent to the chapel of the Madonna dell' Annunciata, which crowns one of the hill-tops towards the Western bay.

We rode through the main street of the little town which runs along the Quay, past the Hotel de Grande Bretagne, the circulating library, the English church, the Hotel des Anglais, and the Grande Hotel de la Paix; then past the Hotel Victoria, the Hotel de Mediterranée, and buildings formerly the homes of the Italian nobles, but long since become the dwellings of the peasants; next over the bridge of the C——, always picturesque with its crowd of blanchisseuses standing in the clear, shallow water, busily beating the unfortunate linen committed to their tender mercies, while they keep up a lively exclamatory song, ending in musical open vowels, which mark the mixed speech of the Italian peasants,—although far enough from pure Tuscan, so much more bearable than the French chatter, or English jargon.

We take the T—— road, turning sharply to the right and ride for half a mile or more, on a beautifully graded road, past a garden of some florist and horticulturist, beside an old ruined aqueduct,—one of the many traces of the ancient Romans, and then, entering a narrow, walled lane to the left, we begin a steady ascent.

Here Blanchette, an undersized donkey, too small for any but children, began a series of evolutions with her rider, to indicate her unwillingness to mount with her then-existing load. So, my friend and I changed donkeys, and, after a number of expostulations, threats, and pommelings administered by Jean, who brought up the rear, she condescended to proceed.

We continued our upward way, now winding, like a rough-hewn stairway, up the terraces, and then passing through the olive yards, and between banks of delicious wild violets whose sweetness is a perpetual temptation to me to stop and pick them, even at the beginning of a long ride. They grow over whole hill-sides, with no more care from man than are given to our buttercups or dandelions. In this sunny land, these untrained beauties of the South, free as sunshine and the dews of heaven, make every step a gladness, and life a thing not of thorns and briars only, nor yet a vale of tears, however fiercely the wild winds may rave and the tempests break over our heads,—bearing away lives sweeter and dearer to us than violets in winter-time. And, through the greenness of the unfenced fields, the poppies raise their scarlet heads, and wild anemones, immense buttercups, and crimson-tipped daisies spring up and bloom and pass away ; and everywhere the ivy clings to the gray walls, and the dainty ferns stretch their tiny arms out of the moist earth.

Primroses were past and gone, — the valley of Saint Jacques is the favorite place with them, and the delicate forget-me-nots. Stars of Bethlehem, growing on rough, unlovely stems, lift their lovely lilac in the wildest places, and bring many a precious thought, unspoken, of the land so like this sunny country, with its olives and figs and vines.

But I forget that we are upward bound to the chapel of the Lady of the Annunciation. We come at last, after a long ascent, perilous to any but surefooted little donkeys, to an open arch, and then find, along our way, a succession of shrines to different saints. In the frequent pilgrimages made, in palmier days of Papal superstition, to the chapel on the summit, the devout worshipers always stopped at every shrine along the way, offering prayers and *sous* to their patron saints. Doubtless, one versed in Romish traditions would be able to account for the saints whose altars lined the road, but to me,—with my simple Protestantism, for whom the lives of the saints are contained in the New Testament, there seemed an unmeaning irrelevance in the names which our small guide repeated as we passed each little shrine. To a secular mind, they appear more like little sentry-boxes, than " chapels," though the single pointed arch of weather-stained stone, a few feet wide at the base, is scarcely in the style of our New World architecture.

If, as is quite possible and consistent with the spirit of the times, these " chapelles " were originally niches for the figures of these saints, who guarded the approach to the chapel of the Madonna, the effect must have been quite imposing ; but now, there is not a vestige of a figure in any of these shrines.　　　*　　*　　*　　*　　*　　*　　*

*　　*　　*　　*　　*　　*　　*　　*

REFLECTIONS.

I.

MY JOY.

WE remember our dear Lord's promise, the night on which He was betrayed; we know that the Comforter has come, and that he will, as the Saviour said, "take of Mine and show it unto you." Let us hold this golden key of promise, which unlocks every door of Doubting Castle, praying the Holy Spirit to lead us into an open place, where the sunshine of our Master's joy may warm our sluggish hearts. Let us look unto Jesus, who, for the joy that was set before Him, endured the cross and despised the shame.

Our Lord said, on that sorrowful night: "Tehse things have I spoken unto you, that My joy"—not My sorrow—"might remain in you, and that *your* joy might be full." In the midst of their anguish, at the thought of losing Him from their sight, while He stood in the awful shadow of Gethsemane and Calvary, He promised them peace—aye, more, joy. It was His own peace, His own joy, which He left with them, as a precious legacy. What was this strengthening, supporting joy, but the gladness of the Shepherd, bearing home on His shoulders the lamb which was lost?

Do we truly realize our oneness with our Saviour, in this chosen errand,—His joy? He said: " As My

Father sent me into the world, *so* send I you," and "your joy no man taketh from you."

On that memorable day, on which He led them out as far as Bethany, when, after giving them their gospel commission, He lifted up His hands and blessed them, and a cloud received Him out of their sight, there was then no mourning for their absent Lord, but the disciples worshiped Him and returned to Jerusalem with great joy. During those forty days of frequent communion with their risen Lord, they had so grown into His life, had so learned of Him, that only adoration and gladness were in their hearts, though then their work of preaching the gospel had not even begun.

To-day, nearly the whole world lies open to the feet of those who bring the glad tidings. Surely He has set before us an open door. If we keep His word, and do not deny His name—Jesus, Saviour—we are sure that no man can shut this door. There is a deep truth in that question of a heathen woman of old: "How canst thou say, 'I love thee,' when thy heart is not with me?" If our hearts throb in unison with His mighty heart of love, will not everything we have be His—thoughts, words, purposes, prayers, influence, money, time? Of everything which we gladly give back to Him, we may hear it said, as to one of old: "The Lord is able to give thee much more than this."

None of us can hear and read of the glorious ingathering of the Gentiles, and see the beacon-lights of the gospel gleaming afar amid the gross darkness, without heart-throbs of gladness. What must be the satisfied joy of our Lord, in the travail of His soul?

He had compassion on the multitude because they were as sheep having no shepherd. His is the true shepherd-heart, caring for and knowing each sheep by name—the same Jesus, in heaven as on earth.

So, when His great love fills and floods our shallow hearts and lives to overflowing, when, as the little Syrian child said, we love our dear Lord Jesus "as much as the sea," shall we not rejoice with Him, in His salvation "unto the ends of the earth?" And when, by and by, we go to be with Him, we shall enter fully into the joy of our Lord.

———◆———

II.

Unto You Gentiles.

Not long since, I was forcibly struck by an expression, used in prayer at family worship, which carried home the conviction, as I had never before felt it, that all of us, there kneeling in prayer, were "sinners of the Gentiles."

Swiftly some subtle, unsuspected pride of 'Christian ancestry prompted me to look back for many generations, as far as I could trace the line of descent. But ah! beyond the earthly record I could not go; and the sad thought of a lost ancestry was forced upon me. Far back in those years of darkness, before the One sacrifice was accomplished at Jerusalem, our ancestors were offering those sacrifices which are "an abomination unto the Lord."

Beneath the oaks of Britain, amid the mysteries of Stonehenge, with Druid rites and human victims, or in the unknown worship of savage Celts and Scots—*thus* we know that our forefathers, in their heathen blindness and sin, confessed their need of an atonement. Poor heathen ancestors ! to whom it was not given to see the beautiful feet upon the mountains, and to hear the gospel of peace ! Sorrowful pity for their lost souls stirred such gratitude for the salvation which we have so fully received, that it seemed to me I had never before known what " saved " meant.

The sovereign and unmerited grace of God never appeared so precious as when I began to realize that it was as utterly sovereign in its message to me, as to the heathen to-day. It is sweet to owe everything to Him whose love is infinite as His might, and to remember that, in the councils of eternity, He gave us unto His Son for an inheritance.

But the knowledge of God's grace to sinners comes, in God's appointment, by means of fellow-sinners saved by grace. If the early Church had been possessed of that evil spirit of apathy and cool indifference to the perishing heathen, which is a sad mark of the visible Church to-day, we, sinners of the Gentiles, would still have been without God and without hope in the world.

But there was no lack of Foreign Missionaries then. Those early Christians, well remembering the command to " preach the gospel beginning at Jerusalem," never imagined that the widening circles were to cease, until that gospel had been preached in all the world and to every creature. Paul, the heroic

Christian who, by his learning and logic, and wit and eloquence, together with that mighty moral force which we call *character*, was fitted for the high places of the earth—Paul, we know, was a Foreign Missionary, and gloried in his work, and greatly magnified his office. We do not ask for another Paul, though there may be one now among the persecutors of the Church whom the Lord will meet on the way and mightily bless, in sending as a light unto the Gentiles.

The *work* is still here; the heathen are perishing; and to-day, the Master says to His Church, as to the little band He left at Bethany: "Go ye into all the world and preach the gospel to every creature." Who will say: "Here am I, Lord; send me"? "The preparation of the heart in man, and the answer of the tongue, is from the Lord." God grant that the manhood of our land may have this spirit of consecration to the Master, which is the crown of all nobility, and that, by God's grace, many of them may be, to heathen nations, the blessed messengers of Him "who is able to save them to the uttermost that come unto God by Him, seeing He ever liveth to make intercession for them!"

III.

"HE SAVED OTHERS; HIMSELF HE CANNOT SAVE."

IT was a singular and involuntary testimony of the Jewish world to the unselfish life of the Saviour whom they crucified. The words are recorded by three of the evangelists, as uttered by chief priests, rulers, scribes and the people that stood by.

The Roman soldiers placed over the Saviour's head the accusation,—strange accusation, in its positive and emphatic wording,—written in all the languages of the civilized world: "Jesus of Nazareth, the King of the Jews;" and then, in heathen unbelief, they shouted, as they offered to Him the vinegar: "If Thou be the King of the Jews, save Thyself!" The very thief beside Him bitterly cried: "If Thou be Christ, save Thyself and us!"

Envy and unbelief and pride did not die with those who, more than eighteen hundred years ago, stood beside the cross; neither has the offence of the cross yet ceased. The Father, whose infinite love moved Him to give up His only begotten Son to die for our sins, is arraigned by His creatures for injustice, and, we might almost say, ungodlike cruelty, in permitting a vicarious atonement. Our dear Lord Jesus, who humbled Himself to become obedient unto death, even the death of the cross, is robbed of His divine nature,—the one great fact which made the death accomplished at Jerusalem a virtue for our salvation. "Save Thyself!" is still the cry of the skeptic world;— "Our sins are light; we need no God-man mediator, to die for us, to rise from the dead, and to intercede forever." "Come down from the cross, Jesus of Nazareth!" still shout the Jews, with the stinging scorn of unbelief, "and we will believe."

But the words remain forever true, with a fullness and force and preciousness, which none but a sinner saved by that one Saviour can feel. He saved others ; He saved me ; but only by the sacrifice of Himself. When Caiaphas counseled the death of Jesus, saying : "It is expedient that one man shall die for the people," he did not intend to give the Saviour to the world which was perishing with need. The doctrine of Christ's Atonement was as hateful to the Jews who waited for the purple-robed Messiah, as it is now to the rational heart, which cannot see the wondrous beauty of the face which was bruised and beaten and spit upon, in His humiliation on the cross.

He saved others ! a sweet, strong truth it was,—undoubted by multitudes of lame and halt and blind and deaf, and by those too who had been brought to life by His hand and voice. And yet the scoffing world cries out : " Himself He cannot save." Aye, Jews ! your words are true ; and blessed be God that, in an hour of agony unfathomable, in the quiet olive-shade, the utter depth of self-denial was reached, and, after the "If it be possible," came the " Nevertheless, not as I will but as Thou wilt ! " Then and there, did Jesus make forever true the cry of the Jews.

Because He saved others, He could not save Himself. And with such love as this, which the Saviour bore and bears to-day to us, He says we are to love each other. " That ye love one another, as I have loved you." And then follow the touching words : "Greater love hath no man than this,—that a man lay down his life for his friends." Who of us may stand this test : " Inasmuch as ye have done it unto one of the least of these, My brethren, ye have done it unto Me " ?

IV.

ONE FAITH.

" I believe in the Holy Catholic Church, the Communion of Saints."

This confession of the unity of the faith, at the close of the Apostles' creed, has always seemed especially beautiful to me. I remember learning it, when a child, and repeating it to my mother, on Sabbath afternoons, along with Brown's catechism and Bible verses. I recall, too, our gentle mother's simple explanation of the word " Catholic," which had evoked a protest from my innate Presbyterianism. I sometimes wonder if the little Episcopalians, who hear the Apostles' creed from their earliest years, and unconsciously become familiar with it, understand the word any better than I did.

The precious truth of the oneness of faith of all lovers and followers of Christ must be peculiarly emphasized, when one hears the same dear old gospel of God's grace preached, in far-off lands, to dissimilar peoples, and under such contrasting surroundings, as missionaries often acknowledge and appreciate. But in a narrower range, the same truth is still forcible.

*   *   *   *   *   *   *   *

V.

LITTLE HELPERS.

I wish to tell you something I have just heard at the Children's Mission Hour. After a good deal had been told about Africa, and the thrilling story of a missionary's life had been repeated to the children, our pastor said he thought the boys ought to have the privilege of working in bands, as the girls did. He believed they would do it well, and it was a pity not to give them the chance.

Then the superintendent told how, when he was a boy, he used to go to house-raisings:

"Boys, in those times, they did not build houses as they do now, leaving the work all to hired carpenters. They had great beams, and a whole side of a house was put together on the ground; then great crowds of friends and neighbors met, to raise it bodily. I remember, when I was a lad of fourteen, seeing an old gentleman, who was always present wherever there was a raising. I had a considerable idea of my own importance and strength, but didn't think that old gentleman could help at all. 'My boy,' he said, 'suppose they have men enough to lift all but a pound of the weight of that side of the house! I can lift that pound, I reckon. So, I go, on the chance of their needing just my little strength, to help.'"

Then our pastor said that he remembered house-raisings, too, up in his native State, and the greatest fun he used to have, as a boy, was at these raisings. "I used to go, though I was not more than six or seven years old. And I remember just how they used to fasten those frames together. It was done with great, wooden pins. Well, there always was a man on hand, whose whole work was to make these pins; and the way we little fellows helped was by carrying the pins!

"And now, little boys who read 'Children's Work,' you cannot now put your small hands directly to the heavy work the dear missionaries and teachers are doing among the heathen ; but brave, earnest, hearty boys can do grand, good work, in ways just as helpful as in old times of house-raising, when their willing hands carried the pins."

VI.

THE LION AND THE ADDER.

THIS morning, I heard a most helpful sermon by Dr. G., on the temptation of Christ. His sermon to little children was on the same subject, and was supremely simple and earnest. The milk for babes was undiluted, and children of a larger growth might well be nourished thereby. He spoke of Jesus in the wilderness, with the wild beasts, and reminded them of the promise in the ninety-first Psalm : " Thou shalt tread on the lion and the adder." This was a part of the very Psalm which Satan had misquoted to Jesus, when he tried to make Him presume on His heavenly Father's providential care, and dared Him to prove Himself the Son of God by casting Himself down from a pinnacle of the temple.

The speaker told us that some sins were like lions, and some like adders, but if we love the Lord Jesus, we shall conquer them all. Our very worst tempers and passions, which rend the soul, like raging lions, as well as the temptations to falsehood, and deceit, and meanness, which slay the soul as surely as the crawling, deadly serpents slay the body, were conquered by the Lord Jesus, when He was in the wilderness of this world ; and the enemies He has trodden under foot and destroyed cannot hurt His little children, who truly trust themselves to Him, and wish, most of all things, to please Him.

* * * * * * * *

VII.

GIVE PLACE.

IN the sermon this morning, there was a thought which was quite striking. The subject was the raising of Jairus' little daughter. The words were: "Give place," etc. It was said that, at times, all we could do—all that God wanted of us—was that we should give place to Him ; the Holy Spirit as Comforter, alone could reach the heart of our grief in bereavement or distress ; and the truest kindness was to acknowledge this, and let the Lord speak to our friends' hearts.

And again, in seeking the salvation of others, while we must not undervalue the influence of human hearts and lips, we must, above all, *stand aside*, and let the Master speak—seek this blessing directly from Him.

I AM NO POET.

I AM no poet.   No ! a wingless bird
Is not a bird at all.   Dull eyes that turn
Though longing, still unseeing, up to heaven,
Are not the eyes, which, having seen the Truth,
Bend down their glances, from the heights serene
Upon the earth, to lighten it from God.

But Thou canst open, with Thy blessed touch,
These sightless eyes.   Anoint them as of old,
When, Life and Light, Thou walkedest on the Earth !
And, by Thy fingers on my spirit's lips
Thou canst so purify them, though it be
By baptism of fire, and with sacred seal
Of suffering, that their silence shall be burst,—
When, through my weakness, Thou hast wrought Thy
      strength.
Thou *canst*—Ah ! *wilt* Thou glorify Thyself,
And make me sing of Thee, and praise for aye ?

THY HOMESICK CHILD.

—

" Why cannot I follow Thee now."—John, xiii. 37.

HOME, home ! dear Father, take Thy poor child home,
   And let me rest from sin and strife and sorrow.
Lord Jesus, tarry not ! Oh, *quickly* come !
   Bid me to sleep, to wake in heaven to-morrow.

'T would matter little how severe the pain,
   How fierce the mortal struggle,—hard the dying ;
Once o'er, I ne'er should taste of death again,
   Nor sin, nor grieve,—in Jesus' bosom lying.

Yet, Lord, Thy holy eyes, which try the soul,
   Must see in wretched me such depths of sinning,
That, while I hoped my feet were near the goal,
   Thou'dst know me but the race to be beginning.

And so I leave it rather *all* to Thee,
   One only prayer, dear Saviour, Lord, preferring :
Do what Thou *wilt*, I know that best for me
   Thy ways are ;—altho' hidden, yet unerring.

Yet I would meekly pray Thee that I may
   Live ever at Thy feet : Thee thus beholding,
Like Martha's lowly sister, day by day,
   I may, by sight, grow like Thee,—e'er unfolding

Germs of resemblance, which, at last,
   Shall burst to full perfection, in the hour
When the long years of seed-time shall be past,
   And Thine own hand shall cull Thy perfect flower.

HOMELESS.

A SPRAY of clinging seaweed, floating o'er the wave,
  Still turning pleading tendrils to the rocky shore;
A little boat, cut loose and sent adrift to brave
  The storm and whirlwind, 'mid the restless ocean's
      roar:

A bird that turns at sunset, with a weary wing,
  To seek the happy nest she left at early morn;
But ah! her quest is fruitless—all her wandering
  Ends in an empty nest—a heart bereft, forlorn:

A hungry, shivering child who lingers mute, without
  The homes of gladness, in the merry Christmas
      time,
And hears, with strange distinctness, many a childish
    shout
  Borne down from happy heights he knows he may
      not climb:

Or,—sadder still,—the outcast, warmed and clothed
      and fed,
  With faithful care for all his lower nature's needs,
Yet evermore denied the happy children's bread,—
  The tears and kisses for the heart that aches and
      pleads !

22

LIFT UP THE CHRIST.

———

"And I, if I be lifted up, will draw all men unto me."

Lift up the Christ of God
　Who came to save the lost,
Whose arms are opened wide
　To poor souls, tempest-tossed!

Oh! lift up none but Christ!
　He died for you and me;
Then, Brothers, lift Him up,
　So all the world may see.

Tell how He lived and loved,
　Tell how He loved and died
With piercèd hands and feet.
　And spear thrust in His side—

When He was lifted up
　In pain on Calvary,
And bore our guilt and shame,
　And died for you and me.

Lift up this Christ, and crown
　Him King of heart and life,
Whose love is more than friend,
　Than mother, child or wife.

This Jesus Lord of Jew
　And Gentile yet shall be,
When He is lifted up
　That all the world may see.

He *is* exalted now,
  To save and to forgive;
Oh! look ye dying ones!
  Look unto Him, and live!

Tell the Glad Tidings,—how
  From sin He sets us free;
His Spirit gives us life,—
  New life and liberty.

Oh! Holy Spirit! teach
  Of Jesus crucified,
That every one who hears,
  May love the Lord who died.

Dear Lord, we lift Thee up!
  Thy promise now we claim:
Draw all men unto Thee,
  And glorify Thy name!

————◆————

MY JERICHO.

———

A city clay-built; yet how fair
  It was,—with streaming banners splendid,
And dear-bought treasures, rich and rare—
The shrine before which many a prayer
  Was breathed, and many a knee was bended!

Not Baalbec nor Imperial Rome,
  Nor the fair theme of Homer's story,
No minaret nor Persian dome,

Nor city sprung from ocean foam,—
　No western pride, nor eastern glory.

Unseen by mortal vision dim,
　Its silent guilt from men was hidden ;
Its mystic site known but to Him
Whose pure eyes pierce thro' seraphim ;
　Whom naught escapes—allowed, forbidden.

It was within my heart I built
　This City, graceless, God denying.
The walls were laid in woe and guilt ;
My reddest life-blood, too, was spilt
　To seal my Babel, Heaven-defying.

*　*　*　*　*　*　*　*

WHO AND WHENCE?

Not from Jerusalem, alone,
　To Heaven the path ascends ;
As near, as sure, as straight the way,
That leads to the Eternal Day,
　From further realms extends :—
　　Frigid or torrid zone.

What matters, how or when we start ?
　One is the crown to all ;
One is the hard but glorious race,
Whatever be the starting place :
　Hark ! round the Earth, the call,
　　To each—Arise, depart !

From the balm-breathing, sun-loved isles,
  Laved by the Southern sea,—
From the dread North's cloud-shadowed pole,
We gather to one gladsome goal—
  One common home in thee,
    City of sun and smiles!

The raging billow hinders none,
  Nor aids the tranquil main;
Alike the crags of Norway's gloom,
The verdure of Tahitian bloom,
  The sands of Mizraim's plain,
    Or peak of Lebanon.

From out the green land of the vine,
  Eke from the snow-wastes pale,
Behold an ever-open road
To the dear City of our God;—
  From pagan Burmah's vale,
    And terraced Palestine.

For sorrowing soul, by Jordan's stream,
  Or Indus' swelling tide,
Where Danube rolls, or Thames, or Rhone,
Or glides majestic Amazon,—
  A Home, where joys abide,
    Shines with celestial gleam.

Not from Jerusalem, alone,
  The Church mounts up to God.
Strangers of every tongue and clime,
Pilgrims thro' every age of time,
  Throng the well-trodden road
    That leads unto the Throne.

THROUGH MY SKYLIGHT.

———

(Mid-Ocean.)

Dark waters underneath me,
　Blue heavens overhead—
Between them, I am resting
　Without a thought of dread.

For One abideth *nearer*,
　At sea, as on the land ;
Who measured out the waters
　In th' hollow of His hand.

Tho' often, angry surges
　Shut out the glimpse of sky.
Have patience, soul, awaiting
　The sunshine, by and by !

Let wild winds rave about me,
　The storm its fury pour ;
I ride the flood as safely
　As patriarch of yore.

What tho', as men may reckon,
　The voyage prove too short ;
Tho' God hath willed the haven
　Be not an earthly port?

"Lo, I am with you alway"—
　Holds, for Eternity ;
He with me, I should fear not
　To go to heaven by sea.

But oh! the weary watching
    For never-coming ship!
The thought, to eye brings tear drops
    And tremor to the lip.

To Him a prayer arises,
    To guide us safe to land,
Who measured out the waters
    In th' hollow of His hand.

No billows may o'erwhelm me
    Whose weight He does not know,
Since Christ himself hath tasted
    Infinity of woe.

A human hand, once piercèd,
    Holdeth supreme control
Of me, in life or dying,
    Of body and of soul.

SYRIAN CHILDREN.

(A. D. 33; A. D., 1880.)

I WAS reading in the Bible,
    How, long ago, our Lord
By young Judean children,
    In the temple was adored;
Their glad Hosannas ringing
    A welcome swift and sweet
To Messiah, riding lowly
    Along the palm-strown street.

How, once, when the disciples
  Disputed, on the way,
Which one should be the greatest
  In His triumphal day,
No word of blame He uttered
  To hearts by pride beguiled,
But, entering a dwelling,
  Called unto Him a child.

Close in His arms He held him
  Saying, " Except ye be,
As little children, humble,
  Ye cannot reign with Me."
The place that is the highest
  Is that of minist'ring.
The loving, lowly-hearted
  Stand nearest to the King.

To-day, the little children
  In distant Syria's land
The arms of faith are lifting,
  To clasp the Saviour's hand ;—
Who, when, from loving teachers
  Of Jesus they have heard,
Pray earnestly in secret,
  To understand His word.

When Mualima Hallun
  Their childish hearts would win,
She told the sweet old story
  Of Bethlehem's crowded inn,—
The dear Lord Jesus, cradled
  In manger hewn of stone,

And how His mother, Mary,
  Was humble as their own.

Then one, among the youngest,—
  Whose home had been beside
The deep, blue inland ocean,
  With ebbless waters wide,—
Unto the teacher, asking
  The group about her knee,
How much loved they Lord Jesus,
  Said quickly, " *As the sea.*"

When Mualima Hallun,
  Caressing, as she smiled,
Asked, "Why do you so love Him?"
  Replied the little child,
Clasping her hands for gladness,
  In faith's simplicity:
" I love Him, oh ! I love Him
  Because He does love me."

Sweet baby-lips, that silence
  The words of scorn and dread ;
Dear childish hands, that gladly
  Would crown the Saviour's head !
Ah ! in that day, when cometh
  The King unto His own,
Shall not these little children
  Stand close beside His Throne ?

THE RIFTED CLOUD.

DARK the cloud that now hangs o'er thee,
Shrouding all thy path before thee :
But with eye of faith uplifted,
See, dear child, the cloud is rifted !

Gleams from that fair home of brightness,
Where the ransomed walk in whiteness,
Downward to this earth have drifted—
Jesus' hand the cloud has rifted.

So, whene'er thou walkest dreary,
Keep this token nigh to cheer thee ;
Thou, with "faith and patience" gifted,
Soon shall't see the dark cloud rifted.

Earthly grief shall grow to gladness,
Singing shall replace the sadness, ·
Shadowy scenes, for aye, be shifted,
When *at last* the cloud is lifted.

SPES SALUTIS.

EVEN the summer breeze,
That steals with noiseless step o'er vale and hill,
To kiss with wooing lip the gurgling rill
To sweeter melodies,

Bears on its balmy breath
The power to wake the sad Æolian harp
To wailing minor notes—to strike the sharp,
    Shrill, anguished key of Death.

O Earth ! for our sake
So laden with a burden not thine own,
Beneath which thou must ever toss and groan
    Till God thy bondage break !

For thy sake, toiling Earth,
We wait, with patient hope and strong desire,
Until the promised baptism of fire
    Shall gladden thy new birth

With peace as pure and deep
As that which fills the tideless, ebbless sea
Of God's own heart, in whose immensity
    Earth's circling changes sleep.

The lamb that once was lost,
Won back, receives the Shepherd's tenderest care ;
So thou, lost Earth, wilt seem more dear and fair,
    For what thy saving cost !

And, from that Isle of Bliss,
Which seemeth now so far away and dim,
The white-winged throng of glorious seraphim
    Shall ever pass to this :

The mystic Ladder's bars
Once more be traversed by the angel guild,
And Israel's dream shall yet become fulfilled
    Upon the path of stars.

CUM SCUTO, VEL SUPER.

———

"Go, boy! thou son of patriot vows,
  Go! in the glory of thy youth—
With God's own sunlight on thy brows,
  Battle for God and Right and Truth.

"My child, I laid thee in God's hand,
  When first thy baby heart had life—
Now, when His frown is on the land,
  He calls thee to the field of strife.

"His will, His holy will be done—
  In heaven above—so on the earth—
Though, if they slay my only son
  They quench the fire in heart—on hearth."

"Nay, mother, God will guard me well;
  Is not the Lord his people's shield?
With Him as my strong citadel,
  I shall be safe on bloodiest field."

"God bless thee, darling,—tender, brave!
  God keep thee safe from ill and scath!
Oh! sooner fill a nameless grave
  Than lose this precious shield of faith."

"My mother, trust me in God's hands
  To keep me faithful tho' I die."
--Amid the clang of martial bands,
  He heard his mother's last "Good-bye!"

Far off beneath a Southern sun,
   He fought and, bravely fighting, fell.
Mother, oh! say, " His will be done! "
   "My mother," breathed he, "all is well! "

They bore him to his home again ;
   His white brow wore God's kiss of peace—
A tender, trustful look, as when
   Death brings the soldier glad release.

They told his mother how he fell,
   Still praying on the battle field :
"God heard me ;" said she, "it is well—
   They brought him home upon his shield."

1865.

I DREAMED a dream : beneath a May-day sun,
Behold a host of homeward-marching men—
Of such as never we shall see again ;
   For now the fight is won,

And gleam of bayonet, and sabre's flash,
And flaunting flags, all torn and faded now,
Are only laurels for our country's brow,
   After the battle's crash.

But all the glory of this blessed day,
Long, weary years of dubious conflict cost ;
And many a desperate charge was made and lost,
   To pave the veterans' way.

Full oft, the shot that, swift as falling star,
Pierced to the heart, beneath the gray or blue,
Swept on its deadly course, and entered, too,
    A loving heart afar.

For many a loving mother's tender hand,
In parting blessing, touched her darling's brow;
And many a lonely mother watches now
    The remnant of his band.

We wist not when the sombre cloud arose,
Nor thought, at first, our Father had decreed
That skies should darken till the slave was freed,
    And, from the Nation's throes

Of agony, should spring a joy more great,
More Godlike than all triumphs of the past—
The joy of bringing light and hope at last,
    AT LAST—but not too late.

Yet, mid the darkness, for the trustful heart,
Faint gleams of sunlight shot athwart the sky;
For some who met, in struggle fierce to die,
    Were near, tho' far apart;

And o'er the horrors of the battle field,
Whence angels turned askance, with saddened eyes,
Were open flung the gates of Paradise,
    To those who bore the shield

Of faith in Jesus;—tho' in mortal strife
Each resolute, and armed with courage grand,
They fought and fell, yet, dying, hand in hand
    They entered into life.

So, with the hosts which pass in Grand Review,
True soldiers, tried by march and scarred in fight,
Another army, clad in robes of white,
    Before me passes, too!

From soldiers' graves, broadcast o'er all the land,
From prisons, whence their blood cries up to God,
From Southern plains, and from the church-yard sod,
    They come—a victor band

Of Christian heroes, without fear or blame,
Who, tho' the world looked coldly on, and scoffed,
Still bore their banner and Christ's cross aloft,
    And won a heavenly fame.

GARFIELD.

(ENGLAND—AMERICA.)

Toll heavily, sad bells, toll!
Across the surges of the throbbing sea,
A nation's voice is borne, in majesty
    Of mingled love and dole.

Roll back this sobbing wave!
The People's heart has grown too full for tears;
They will not leave their Hero, thro' the years
    Of darkness, in the grave.

He lives! He is not dead,
For love holds empire mightier than death.
His true life failed not when the anguished breath,
    'Mid Elberon's darkness, fled.

His country's heart is warm :
Safe-guarded there, not buried, let him lie.
The Nation lives—how should her Hero die?
    Nor earthquake-shock nor storm

Avails to rend him thence.
Thro' million veins his true life throbs to-day,
In pulse heroic, thrilling 'neath the sway
    Of God's omnipotence.

Yet why, at splendid noon,
Came nightfall?   Thro' the darkness o'er the land,
Brothers, long parted, clasped each other's hand,
    Craving one common boon.

God gave His answer—Rest.
A patriot's fallen, and the flags are furled ;
Sad-hearted bells ring out around the world :
    " God reigns—His ways are best ! "

Yes, God hath bidden cease
The torture and the struggle—all the strange
Sad mystery of pain.   No chance nor change
    Shall mar his endless peace.

Wild waves, that surge and sob !
Roll back in silence from this peaceful shore.
Thro' agony comes strength, and evermore
    By throes the vital throb.

Not dust, alone, to dust,
But love to love, and life to risen life.
Shout " Victory ! "   For ended is His strife,
    And God has crowned the just.

AT EVENTIDE.

To-NIGHT, I lingering watched th' incoming tide
  Roll up, with gathering might along the shore,
As if, with eager impulse, swift to hide
  Our footprints, which the sands at sunset bore.

Thou mighty sea, that coverest, day by day,
  Of human wanderings full many a trace!
Type of thy great Creator, whom we pray
  To blot our sins out with His pardoning grace.

MINISTERING.

SWEET is the story how, once, long ago,
  The Son of Man,—his mission near complete,—
At even, before supper, bending low,
  In meekness, washed His own disciples' feet.

O Night to be remembered thro' all time,
  The theme of praises in Eternity!
Love, service, sorrow—trinity sublime—
  The upper chamber, and Gethsemane!

Last hours, deep-fraught with human tenderness,
  Wondrous ensample of humility!
"As I have done, do ye." O Master, bless
  Us with the grace obedient to be!

A CHRISTMAS CAROL.

FAST, fast they are flitting—the dark shapes of sin,
And God's shining angels are hastening in ;
Evanished in gloom is the last sullen gnome,
And Christ is the Lord of our hearts and our home.

Then joy-bells, oh ! ring, and ye ransomed ones, sing !
Our sins are forgiven, and Jesus is King.
He comes ; to His footsteps the gates open wide,
Rejoice in His love, on this blest Christmas tide !

BALSAM—BALM—EVERLASTING.

IT has no bloom of roses, nor the lily's fair estate ;
No eye may mark its lowly head among the grand and
    great ;
It boasts no midnight glory, that must die at break
    of day,
Nor fleeting glow of morning, in the sun that fades
    away.

Yet is there something winsome in its fadeless, simple
    dress—
A beauty, speaking to the soul of loving steadfast-
    ness :
Thro' tempests, hail and sunshine, thro' the fervid
    August heat,
The little white-faced flower holds a fragrance,
    strange and sweet

As healing balsam of a love that's trusted, true and
    tried,
Safe-garnered up, in patient souls which faithful e'er
    abide.
—Dear Heart! with trust as constant as this flower's
    fadeless hue,
Thro' life and death, oh! hold embalmed my change-
    less love for you!

GOLDILOCKS AND SILVER HAIR.

A LITTLE maid sits on the post, by the gate,
   And merrily sings, keeping time with her feet:
"Dear Sun, shine forever—don't let it grow late—
   Black Night, stay away, for the daylight is sweet!"

The shadows grow long, in the still afternoon,
   'Neath the old latticed porch, where the elm
      branches meet.—
A silver haired woman sighs: "Dear Night, come
   soon,
   For I am aweary, and rest would be sweet!"

MY LOVE.

A GENTLE, loving, trustful heart,
A woman's wit, and childhood's grace,
The pure soul shining in the face—
   A nature above art.

Quick, wistful, keen to sympathize
With weakness, tho' so far from weak ;
A life whose fearless actions speak
    Truth, scorning all disguise.

Yet is she strangely coy and shy,
Shrinking from careless word or touch.
God shield her.—I, who love her much,
    Am passed unnoticed by.

I love her, but I will not paint
Her with unearthly aureole ;
A woman, with a human soul,
    Is better than a saint.

I cannot touch her garment's hem,
Yet, as the magnet owns the North,
Draws she my nobler nature forth.
    She wears my diadem,

Unconscious as a child, whose brows
Are kissed in sleep by gentle lips,
While love, that makes apocalypse,
    Is mute, nor seeks to rouse.

My dreamer, with those veilèd eyes !
Your changing dreams I yet will watch,
If, after years, I may but catch
    One look of glad surprise—

A wistful, recognizing glance ;
While in my heart I hold you, till
You learn to trust the loving will
    That woke you from your trance.

God knows I cannot love you less—
He gave the love.   Tho' now concealed,
It guards you with earth's trustiest shield—
  A strong man's tenderness.

Dear child, whose hands enclasp my fate—
Wearing the purple of the crowned !
Love's angel watch your path around,
  I love you.   I can wait.

But, let heart-trying sorrow come—
Should summer blossoms, chilled by frost,
Fall fruitless,—friends of yore be lost,
  Ah ! could I then be dumb ?

Grief, touching thee, would swift unseal
The lips where love was silent long :
Hearts are, that braver grow—more strong,
  In woe, perchance, than weal.

The fluttering bird, with broken wing,
Tho' timid, nestles trustful, too :—
So, darling, it may be when you
  To me shall, turning, cling.

------♦------

MY REST.

God's warl' is fu' o' glory—wi' the snow-capt moun-
    tain gran',   .
An' the mighty sea, He holdeth in the hollow o' His
    han' ;

But the heart that's like a birdie, aweary for its
    nest,
Hears the sea an' hill-top singing—Return unto thy
    rest!

I' the secret o' His presence, a' the restless waves
    o' doubt,
An' the skaith an' dool o' strivin' for aye are shutten
    out:
As the ingleside is dearer i' the cauld an' wintry
    nicht,
So, the daurkness o' the warl' mak's the sweeter
    heaven's licht.

A NIGHT WATCH.

"He abode two days still, in the same place where He was."—
John, xi. 6.

Ah! long ago, I used to think
    That we might understand
God's purposes to us and ours,—
    The reason why He planned

A sorrow here, a gladness there,—
    Now glory, now disgrace:
The heights of Tabor yesterday,
    To-day a desert place.

But now, it all is hid from me,
    Or else, my heart is blind.
Out of the dark, I cry to God,
    And reach my arms to find

The Hand whose clasp I dare not miss:
　　Help Thou mine unbelief!
My very crying, Lord, for Thee
　　Brings something of relief.

I know not, and I will not ask
　　Thee what it means; but bless,
Oh! loving Father, for Christ's sake,
　　This mystery of distress!

Jesus! Thou seem'st so far away,
　　When hope of Thy relief,
Thro' lonely hours of night and day,
　　Has almost died in grief.

Watching so long beside our dead,
　　Our hearts grow faint with fear:
He often came to Bethany—
　　Why will He not come here?

Do not I seek Thy will, not mine?
　　Lord, teach me how to wait,
As wearied child, until Thou come—
　　Thou ne'er wilt be too late

To save from sin, to raise from death.
　　Master, I would be still,
And cease to murmur when Thy work
　　Seems different from Thy will.

He comes! He comes! It is His voice
　　Once more, that calleth me.
Oh! Resurrection and the Life!
　　I leave *my dead* to Thee.

THE LAST THING.

———

It is a precious thing.
'T is mine.   For years, I've worn it on my hand,
Upon this finger—Ah ! you understand—
　　It is my wedding ring.

By every word or sign
That seals possession of a thing of worth—
By gift, acknowledgment and use,—on earth,
　　'T is mine and only mine.

And yet it tortures me
To think that, in a very little while,
One—friend or foe—might come and, with a smile
　　That I could never see,

Might take this ring away ;—
While I, to whom it surely now belongs,
Who count such act the basest of all wrongs,
　　Would have no word to say !

I know—I know, 'tis true—
The vanity of vanities ! Love's gold
We clasp, until our fingers grow too cold ;
　　Then drop it—as I do.

I yield, without a word,
The little treasures of my childhood's years,
The gifts of those I've mourned with silent tears,—
　　My pictures and my bird.

I've given everything
To those who love me, and would care to keep
Some waking thoughts of one who's gone to sleep :—
    But not my wedding ring.

    I think that, for my sake,
Some hearts will grieve, and some will lonely be—
How long, no matter!   Not for love of me
    May heart of any break!

    I say it.   It is truth,
Thank God : not often break the hearts that grieve :
That is an early fancy which we leave
    With many dreams of youth.

    I should be sadder now,
This day,—to leave you all, O tried and true!
Were I to know that any one of you
    With hopeless grief would bow,

    After I'm gone away.
—I love so many things—the sounding sea ;
High hills of God, enwrapt in mystery ;
    The swift cloud-shadow's play

    Over the daisied grass ;
All helpless little ones ; poor souls in pain,
That learn, thro' present loss, heaven's blessed gain :
    —Yet soon, they say, I'll pass

    Beyond all earthly things !
My legacy is LOVE,—that claspeth tight
This world of God,—its darkness and its light,
    Its winters and its springs.

Faith shall make parting light.
My own dear friends—my dearest above all !
Let not the shadows from my grave that fall
　　Make God's fair earth less bright.

I think—I think you know
That not in terror, now, my soul is brought
Here, facing Death. Christ won that fight. He fought
　　My battle long ago.

You wonder that I hold
With such a jealous grasp material sign
Of human love, when heaven is nearly mine ?
　　—My heart has not grown cold.

Must it be strange and true ?
What meaneth "strange" ?   Ah ! am I still a child,
From precious present things to be beguiled
　　By future, fair and new ?

Ah ! no more questioning—
For, drop by drop, my cup is emptied low.—
Take, dearest heart, who gave it long ago,
　　My ring, my wedding ring !

———◆———

THRO' GLOOM TO GLORY.

———

' My flesh and my heart faileth."—Ps., lxxiii. 26

The heart is faint, the flesh is frail ;
I fear to glance adown the vale.—
With faith too weak to clasp the rod,
How meet the messenger of God ?

The angel comes and bears this token :
" The golden bowl shall soon be broken ;
The Master calleth thee !   Lay down
Thy life-long cross, and take the crown."

O shrinking heart, O trembling soul !
Why falter now, so near the goal ?
Alas ! mine eyes but dimly see
The crown of glory waiting me.

I near the brink ; the darkling wave
My toil-worn feet anon shall lave.
I trembling cry, 'mid death's alarms,
" O Saviour, hold me in thine arms."

Death's surges roll across my breast ;
They bear me to a peaceful rest.
My cry was heard—His arms are thrown
Around His fainting, trembling one.

My grasp is weak ; His hold is strong ;
He will not let the strife be long :
I'm nearly home.   At last, I see
The haven where I long to be.

The shore is won, my eager feet
Peace-sandaled, tread the golden street :
I gain the great, white throne, and cling
To Him thereon, my God, my King.

—Alas ! 'twas but a moment's dream
I linger still, this side the stream :
But now I tremble not, to think
I'm on the swelling river's brink.

I know on whose dear arm I lean—
A Saviour, near me, tho' unseen.
His touch makes mortal weakness strong,
Turns grief to gladness,. sighs to song.

IMPOTENCE.

FOREVER we are pondering and learning ;
    From childhood unto age, we ceaseless grope,
And cry " more light "—the quenchless spirit's yearn-
        ing
To look at God through human theoscope ;

We feel earth's winding folds our eyesight dimming,
    And hands, sin-palsied, strive to tear them thence.
Angels around us, all unheard, are hymning
    Anthems of joy,—while, in our impotence

To learn, or see, or hear the things eternal,
    We wait at some Bethseda, till the word
Of grace and truth comes down with power supernal,
    And stagnant spirit-depths are angel-stirred.

Will, knowledge, sight, Immanuel's word createth,
    Unseals deaf ears to hear His precious name.—
O longing heart ! Who on His promise waiteth,—
    His trembling trust shall ne'er be put to shame.

The soul that walks in gloom, yet meekly heedeth
    The Saviour's voice, still reaching for His hand,
Ere long shall clasp it, as He gently leadeth
    Through desert drear, unto a glorious land.

DUMB.

Born dumb!   In songless cries, my lips I ope
My heart with tidal surges swells and aches :
But never, in its wildest tempest, breaks
A doorway to the blessed land, where Hope
Sings in the sunshine.   There the dull sounds grope
In wintry dark, beneath the blinding flakes
From stormy heavens falling on the earth,
And swelling it to fruitful toil and pain ;—
    Then shoot to light amid the spring-time mirth
Of robins and of bluebirds.   Not in vain
My heart, shut up in silence, dreads to lose
The blessed speech of others !   Yet there's use
For God's dumb creatures.   Oh ! how long, how long,
    Before this heart of mine breaks into song ?

PEARLS AND PEBBLES.

GOD'S WORD—MAN'S WORDS.

Pearls wondrous pure and precious from depths di-
    vine are brought,
While pebbles lie by thousands along the shore un-
    sought.
Yet faith makes pebbles precious : sometimes a little
    stone,
By hand of youthful David, from sling of faith well
    thrown,

Doth slay a boastful giant.   A power from above
Makes human accents potent, when energized by love.
A child's sweet voice may vanquish the Babel-hosts
        of sin ;
A word, for Jesus spoken, a wanderer may win.

Thus musing, and yet trembling, the while I strove to
        sing,
I threaded pearls and pebbles upon the self-same
        string ;
Remembering Israel's vision, beneath the midnight
        stars,
When heaven's angels traversed the mystic ladder's
        bars,—
When earthly stones, transfigured beneath seraphic
        feet,
Became the pearly arches that guard the golden
        street.

———◆———

UNDER THE SNOWS.

———

UNDER the snows, the deathly snows,
   My treasures are hidden from mortal eyes ;
Death's icy hand holds them ; God knows, God knows
   How much of my heart and my life there lies—
   Of sepulchred love, that never dies,—
Deep buried beneath the snows.

They were taken, and I was left ;
   Theirs is the glory, and mine the gloom.
Death plucked the flowers that grew in the cleft,

And bore up to heaven their rich perfume,
While he spared the poor vine, without scent or
    bloom.
God knoweth, I am bereft!

And yet, what matter?   Sweet is the rest
  Of each of the silent slumberers there.
Weary hands folded across the breast,
    White brows no longer by care oppressed,
    Nothing but tokens of slumber they wear,
Under the snows, at rest.

Under the snows and under the sod,
  Lilies and hearts-ease are waiting for spring.
One day—as, of yore, the bare almond-rod—
    The seed sown in tears, a perishing thing,
    Shall burst into beauty and blossoming,
At the touch and fiat of God.

Deathliest snows and earth-wrought bars!
  Ye cannot fetter the body's guest.
The warrior-victor, in spite of his scars,
    Bears earnest of glory within his breast;
    The legend of conquest engraved on his crest,
He soareth beyond the stars.

Sleep belovèd! no earthly moan
  Over your snow-mantled grave I make.
Rest well, earliest, dearest mine own!
    Death bruised the heart-strings that life will not
      break:
    God their hushed music one day will awake
Unto a heavenly tone.

BONNY DOON.

OH ! min' ye o' yon lee-lang day,
    Fair as a rose in heart o' June,
We wandered past auld Alloway,
    An' lingered by the banks o' Doon ?

Nae hush was on the mavis' sang,
    An' still the braes bloomed fresh an' fair,
Tho' silent noo he sleeps, for lang,
    Wha sung the praise o' Doon an' Ayr.

Far frae auld Scotia's hills an' glens
    The daisy smiles beneath the pleugh ;
"A man's a man," the wide warl' kens,
    An "Hieland Mary" leeves anew.

Cauld blasts frae weary wastes o' snaw,
    Saft zephyrs whisperin' thro' the vine,
Wild winds, frae east to west that blaw,—
    Hae ye forgotten Auld Lang Syne ?

Puir heart ! sae human in its guid,—
    Alas, maist human in its wrang !
The warmth an' grip o' britherhood,
    Wi' jest an' tears, rin thro' his sang.

Yon shaft a' carven wi' his praise
    Maun some day crum'le to the groun',
But ilka Spring shall deck the braes
    Whaur flows the tide o' Bonny Doon.

The gowan's bloom, the river's flow,
  Are mair than tribute graved on stane :
For aye, O Bonny Doon ! sound low
  Thy echoes to his voice alane !

POPPIES GROWING ON THE RUINS OF A ROMAN VILLA.

(Morton—Isle of Wight.)

They come and go,
Or swift, or slow !
This morn, the scarlet poppies glow
Where Caesar's legions whilom trod—
Short-lived usurpers of th' Almighty's crown,
Whose dust may tremble in this thistle-down,
Or nourish English daisies, that bedeck the sod.

Come weal, come woe !
The poppies glow ;
Blue gleams the sea as long ago ;
Blue heavens, arching o'er my head,
Bent, erst, o'er warriors from sea-sundered climes :
Thro' the vast silence sound the solemn chimes—
The tolling knell of Briton, Roman, Norseman,
      dead !

24

OUTWARD BOUND.

In sunset glow lay earth and sea :
　　With glancing sail and pennon gay,
Only a little year ago
　　Swiftly a ship sailed up the bay ;

And in a quiet harbor cast
　　Her anchor,—careless to the tide,
Until the signal came to-day
　　To seek the outer waters wide.

It was a vessel outward bound ;
　　No summer-sailing pleasure-bark,
To drift all day by sunny isles,
　　And seek her moorings ere the dark.

No days are these, for aimless lives,
　　For soulless words and idle will ;
And none but those whose lives are low
　　Need miss a grand, heroic thrill.

To dare to sail by God's own chart,
　　Defend the truth and right the wrong.
To stay by sinking hulks at night,—
　　To keep this pledge, O ship, be strong !

A precious freight is thine, good ship,
　　For, standing on the shore to-day,
I see a mother's hopes and prayers
　　Into the future sail away.

And we who watch with earnest eyes
   May only cry with heart and lip,
As white sails glisten far away;
   "God speed the ship! God speed the ship!"

Tempests are near when skies are blue,
   Soft glow may swiftly change to gloom,
And ever, through the gathering night,
   The pirate's deathly shadows loom.

But storms may burst and billows crash,
   And shapes of darkness do their best;
They strive in vain to sink the ship
   Where Jesus has a quiet rest.

Still, as of old, His word of grace
   Rings high above the billows' roar,
Hushing the craven cry of doubt:—
   "We sail unto the other shore."

The other shore! Oh! speed thee well,
   Brave ship upon this troubled sea!
Who *bears the Lord* shall surely reach
   The haven where he fain would be.

TWO SUNSETS.

I watched the winter sunset, and the glow
  Fast fading.   It was twilight in the room ;
  Where warm red embers battled with the gloom.
She raised her head, that had been resting low
Upon his breast.   " If there might only be
  A window in this heart that beats so fast,"—
She softly said—" for then my loving eyes might see
  And catch some bright-wing'd thought, before it
      flitted past ! "

A girlish wish was hers—a daring thought !
  But perfect love is very brave, we know,
  And, singing, climbs where fear could never go.
Her heart had known no fear, had not been taught
Sad wisdom.—" Love, were open window there
  For guileless eyes of yours, a day or more "—
  He bent and, smiling answered—" I should ask,
      before
You looked ; so all things might in order be, and fair."

Ah ! then I would not care to look at all."
  Her voice sunk low, and in it was a sob,
  Half hushed—I felt my heart rebellious throb—
She climbed so high, poor child ; and must she fall ?
—And yet he loved her, while he said the truth :
  " Alone before the pitying Lord, laid bare
We leave our hearts !   Not even for your eyes, my
      Ruth
Would I forever have an open window there ! "

Her hands grew weary in life's harvesting ;
    And so God took her.   Years and years have fled,
    Since the June sunset when I saw her *dead ;*—
The sweet lips mute, that used to laugh and sing.
I loved her all my life,—He, for a fleeting year !
    She gave him her whole-hearted tenderness,
And I,—I was their friend, for both to me were
        dear :
    —Thank God, they neither dreamed that I should
        love her less !

No window ever opened in *my* heart, ·
    For her true eyes.   In that sad sunset light,
    I knew that God would lead my soul aright,
Tho' in a desert, thus, to dwell apart ;
Till love, uncrowned, had won the victory,
    Thro' crucifixion for dear Honor's sake.
    —Wake, Hope !—In yon sweet Home, no hearts
        will ever break
With longing for a blessedness that must not be !

DECENNIAL REPORT OF THE P—— FOREIGN MISSIONARY SOCIETY.

IT may seem a little out of order, perhaps, on this birthday party of the ten-year-old daughter of our Philadelphia mother, that the younger children should have equal share with the older ones, in the general rejoicing. But on this happy day, the old-fashioned rule—that children should be seen and not heard—is to be honored in the breach rather than in the observance. For we all belong to the blessed family whose elder brother is our Lord, Christ; and the weak and the strong, alike, share His loving sympathy and blessing.

As our kind presbyterial secretary bids us, we shall strive to tell the story of the past years, with its failures and struggles and encouragements.

On the last day of the year 1873, there was organized in our church a Ladies' Aid and Missionary Society. It was the duty and pleasure of the Foreign Missionary Committee to bring before the Society the needs and claims of heathen women and children. Although having no distinct organization, we were told that we might consider ourselves an auxiliary of the Presbyterial Society if we would pledge ourselves to give twenty dollars yearly to "Woman's Work."

Between the years 1873 and 1878, we collected money mainly through the envelope-system, our yearly contributions varying from thirty to forty dollars. We found, as do all others, that we grew to love, more and more, the cause we worked and prayed for ; and we felt sure that, if we could only persuade our friends and neighbors in the church to join the missionary circle, they would soon be as interested as ourselves. But this sometimes was hard and disheartening. With the wish to relieve missionary work of its distant vagueness, and to render it a vivid reality, we invited Mrs.——, of Syria, to visit us, and talk to us of the trials and triumphs of laborers in the Lord's own land. Another year, we invited Dr.——, for years a resident of Yokohama, Japan, to show us his fine curios, and to tell us of that wonderful land, whose doors have been flung open so marvelously for the light of the gospel to enter.

Little by little, as we look back, we can see and believe that the missionary cause was gaining ground among us. It surely did, in the hearts of those who met to pray for the coming of the King to His inheritance. Often, I think, we should have faltered and lost heart, had it not been for the messages which every month brought to us from our toiling sisters in heathen lands. "Woman's Work," "The Missionary Link," and occasional letters from the field, kept us from forgetting the needs of the absent, in the midst of very urgent and imperative claims at home. Sometimes, a little word, straight from a heathen woman's heart, thrilled ours with sympathy, and intense desire, for Christ's sake, to give those poor dark souls the gospel which has made us so blessed. Often, often, we have been ashamed of ourselves and our half-heartedness, when we knew how much our dark-browed sisters who have learned of Christ have borne and suffered, for the sake of their and our Lord, Jesus. During these five years before our organization as a society, we held a little missionary prayer-meeting on the first Wednesday of every month. I am sure that monthly concert holds a warm place in the memory of all who were wont to attend it. Some who were most faithful and interested have moved away, yet, from time to time, we hear they have not forgotten those informal, pleasant meetings. One of our number has gone home to our Father's house. Perhaps she too remembers it, and is glad.

In March, 1878, the Woman's Foreign Missionary Society of P., auxiliary to the Presbyterial Society, was organized with a membership of eight ladies. Through all the years before and since our organization, our pastor has been the warmest friend and most efficient advocate of foreign missions, interested not only in such work as must be done by man, but also in that which is open to woman, and to woman only.

If we, as a church, are but half alive to our duty and blessed privilege in this direction, it can never be said that the fault lies at our minister's door. His library of current missionary literature, containing twenty or more periodicals issued by societies in America, Great Britain and the continent, is always open to us, when we seek information concerning any special field. It makes the glory as well as the burden of this work that we are continually proving the truth of the Master's words—"The field is the world;" white already to the harvest, but oh! the laborers are so few.

In looking back four years, and striving to gather up memories worthy of mention here, it seems as if there had been very little of unusual or peculiar interest. We have worked together in love; officers and members have been alike interested. We have tried to learn something, every month, of the field, and the workers forming the subjects suggested for our study and prayers. The ladies who have served on the committee to prepare the programmes of each meeting have grown fond of the work, and have found it a great mental and spiritual quickener. The letters we have received from foreign fields, from missionaries among the Dakotas and the Senecas in our own country, from India, China, Africa, Siam, Mexico and Syria have been very interesting. The visits of our former president, our vice-president, and Mrs. ——, formerly of Ningpo, China, have been, not simply pleasures, but also blessings to us,—sometimes coming, too, just at the time we were greatly discouraged over our small things.

The way in which a missionary spirit has sprung up among the children and young people is one of the strongest encouragements to us.

*   *   *   *   *   *   *   *

On looking back, it seems as though we had accomplished very little—not nearly all we might have done, if we had been more unselfish, and eager to find ways to help the work with prayer and effort. But it is done, and we can only pray the Lord to forgive us for all we have left undone, when we know He is waiting to have us carry on this blessed work for Him, and He has given us the promise of His perpetual presence and blessing.

Now, for a little while, we see Him not, for, as of old, He has gone up into a mountain apart, to pray. But He is watching us still, while He sends us on His own chosen errand to the lost. Often, our hearts echo the homesick words of the disciple whom He loved: "It was now dark, and Jesus was not come to them!"

From the far-off hill, He sees us toiling in rowing, the wind being contrary. At last, when the Lord comes to us in the power of His spirit, shall we not know His voice, though, in the early twilight, we may not see His face? Is it not now the fourth watch of the night, and near the breaking of the day? Of us, may it also be true—"Then they willingly received Him into the ship;" and it should be no marvel to us that, "immediately the ship was at the land whither they went." No more toiling in rowing now; no more contrary wind nor wild sea-waves. Surely, surely, though the faith of His disciples be sometimes weak, and their courage small, they are on the errand dear to their Master's heart; they are bearing Him to the multitudes waiting to touch the hem of His garment.

———◆———

FOR THE MASTER'S USE.

(London, November, 1881.)

I HAVE jotted down some thoughts from what I remember of a sermon we heard in the Congregational "Chapel," at Hythe, on the Kentish coast, last summer. The pastor, Rev. Valentine Ward, is a kindly, gray-haired, scholarly gentleman, whose pleasant voice has sometimes enough of the north country burr in it to make one fancy him Scotch instead of northern born. I am sorry not to do justice to his sermon in these jottings, but trust its simple, earnest teachings may not be without use on the other side of the sea.

2 TIMOTHY, II. 21.

Scripture illustrations are often very homely, such as the humblest and youngest may understand. Take this one, for instance. If a maid is called to bring a cup, and she brings one that is not clean, it is sent away as not fit for the master's use. So, in this verse and the context, we are taught what things unfit us for the King's service, as well as by what means we are made ready for His use. It is a great thing to be used by the Lord. Whether we realize it or not, it is true that He has appointed unto each of us some work.

It may be that, in the eyes of man it seems very

humble service, but it is honorable to the Master, if we do it *for Him*.

But if we are not ready, when He calls us by His Spirit and by His providence to the service, He will pass us by. Oh! what an infinite loss and disgrace to us!

When, a great many years ago, the Spanish Armada threatened our country, Queen Elizabeth called for volunteers to repel the invaders. Men sprung to arms at the call of their country; ships and sailors, as well as soldiers to man the forts, were offered freely, heartily. Hythe did her part bravely; some say three, others say five ships, with sailors for them, were sent from our own harbor of the cinque ports. (I thought of the scene when, the other day, I passed Tilbury, where Elizabeth bade Godspeed to England's fleet, and used those brave words, which were no empty boast: "That though she was a woman with a woman's feeble body, she had the heart of a King, aye, of a King of England, too!")

Ah! was there not shame and disgrace in that day for the town and the port which had sent no ships nor soldiers in the country's time of peril?

But how much more if, when the King of heaven calls, we are not ready to fight in His cause, under His banner, against the traitor archangel and the enemy of man!

Prompt obedience and whole-heartedness are characteristics of a good soldier. It was a grand thing for Paul, the aged, to be able to say: "I have fought a good fight, I have finished my course, I have kept the faith!"

Do you remember how he answered when the Lord Jesus revealed Himself to him on the way to Damascus? There was no reluctance, no parley, but the sudden, whole-hearted response: "Lord, what will Thou have me to do?" Emptied of his pride, his Phariseeism, his plans, he is ready for the Master's use. When Ananias received the command to go to Saul of Tarsus, and putting his hand upon his eyes to restore his sight, the Lord said these words: "He is a *chosen vessel unto* me, to bear my name before the Gentiles and kings and the children of Israel."

Let us see what we are taught, first negatively, and then positively, about this preparation—this fitness for the Master's use—what hinders and what helps it.

We are taught to shun profane and vain babblings and youthful lusts; to follow righteousness, peace, charity. If we have our hearts and our minds filled with our own conceits about life, and draw our conclusions and form our plans without reference to the teaching of God's word, we shall not even hear His call, we shall not be ready for His work when it waits for us to do it.

Again, lust includes, besides the sins to which the young are especially exposed, all desires for everything or anything unlawful and rebuked in the word of God. Covetousness is lust. I have been grieved with a prevailing tendency I see to discontentment with our lot. Each man wishes to be something other than he is, or to have something that is denied to him. Do you know this hinders our preparation for the service of the King? Those who are seeking great things for themselves are not those who are the humble-hearted, ready for whatever work the Lord requires.

Then we are taught positively what way of life, what principles cherished and carried into action, are a means of preparation for the Master's use.

" Follow after righteousness, faith, charity, peace, calling on the Lord out of a pure heart." . . .

It is a grand thing to be fit for God Himself to use, set apart by Him. Pray the Lord to make you holy, to keep you from all that grieves the Holy Spirit, to make you hate sin, to increase your faith, humility and love.

Our dear Lord loved us so well that he became poor for our sakes and came to die for us. He tells us, as He loved us, *so*—mark that—we are to love one another. And the fruit of this warm and faithful love will surely be peace. We shall then not seek our own glory, but God's. The cry of our hearts will be that He would use us as He pleases, and that He would show us what we can do for Him and for those He died to save. What high happiness and honor for us if we can in any way advance His glory, and hasten the coming of His kingdom in the hearts of men !

But, oh ! there are some who cannot do this work. They are still living in sin and loving it. Oh, don't go on so ! Do you not want to be ready for God to use you ? You say, "Yes, next month I will work for Him." But who tells you you will be alive next month ? Go to Him now and confess your sins. Ask Him for His Spirit. You can plead God's prom-

ise for that. Pray day and night that He would cre-
ate in you a clean heart, until He gives it to you. He
never, never turns any one away. Then when your
sins are forgiven for Christ's sake, pray Him to make
you a vessel sanctified and fit for the use of the
King, that henceforth you may live the happy life of
loving, humble service, and to Him shall be praise
forever and ever.

HAMPTON-COURT VINE.

PERHAPS it may seem strange, but the one memory
carried away from Hampton court, which I think will
survive all the others, was not of the many brilliant
beauties of the time of Charles II., nor the finer,
braver faces of those of William IV.'s day; not any
of the numberless relics of Wolsey and his royal master, the gems of the picture gallery, the fine stained
window, nor the beautiful flower gardens; not the
chestnuts of Bushy Park nor the bewildering Maze itself,—but the great Vine, more than a hundred years
old, and still in apparently immortal vigor.

I cannot tell you how eloquently it spoke to me of
our Master and ourselves. After seeing all the pomp
and glory of the old palace, built in human pride and
vain-glory,—remembering how all those associated
with it,—their jealousies and loves, their hatred and
envy,—had been cut down like the grass, it was a
sweet relief to come to the long walk leading to the
House of the Vine. It is a wonderful sight. The

massive trunk and its far-reaching branches, laden
with luscious purpling fruit, forming a beautiful leafy
network over the roof and sides of its transparent
dwelling-place.

We walked silently under the shadow of the Vine,
noting how carefully the branches were pruned ; how,
while every branch bore fruit, those nearest the trunk
were fuller, and heavier and more luxuriant. It was
a marvel to me that the branches so far away should
bear fruit at all. No wonder, if they should not
bear much fruit. But the life of the Vine is in every
branch, however far away or feeble. As I walked
back to the entrance, it seemed to me we should all
pray that we might be of the branches close to the
Vine ; else how shall we bear much fruit to the glory
of the Father?

There was another little sermon for me in the fact,
that this is a royal Vine, and all the fruit belongs to
the sovereign. She may give it to whomsoever she
will,—to the poor, who never would taste such fruit,
except it were bestowed by the royal bounty. But
no single purpling, juicy grape is there for its own
glory ;—it is all and only for the King.

Y. M. C. A.

———

Sue and Emily walked, one day,
  In the streets of a—nameless—city;
They plotted and planned, in their own sweet
    way,
—Tho', really, I couldn't pretend to say
  That either was wise or witty.

Suddenly Sue, with her face aglow,
  Exclaimed, as in startled wonder:
" How stupid I am! To-night we go
To the Y. M. C. A., Dick said, you know—
  How could I make such a blunder? "

" See what? Go where? " cries Em to Sue,
  " And what said Richard, your brother?
If you only would finish one sentence through,
Perhaps I might know what you mean to do.
  One should certainly tell your mother

You are quite bereft,"—with a laugh :—but Sue
  Retorts, without answering glee :
" I am sure I think you are crazy too ;
For I only said what is soberly true—
  To-night is the Y. M. C."

" I give it up," said Em, with a sigh,
  " You have told me three times, already ;
But I'd like to know, before I die,
What is to-night, and *what* I must spy ;—
  My brain's in a hopeless eddy."

25

"Oh! dear," cried Sue, with a look of despair,
　As she came to the end of her patience—
—Both girls looked up, to the awning where
A sign swung gaily: "To-night, the fair
Of the Y. M. C. A."—And Em said: "There,
　So much for abbreviations."

CENTENNIAL.

THE shades of eve are falling fast;
Ghosts, goblins, ghouls are flitting past,
My few ideas are all aghast,
　　　　　Centennial!

No words of mine can fitly tell
The horror of the mighty spell
Which, with thee, on our country fell,
　　　　　Centennial!

Thy brand is on our coats and frocks,
Beds, blacking, frying-pans, bonds and stocks,
Tea-parties, hair-dye, babies, blocks,
　　　　　Centennial!

Oh! when this nightmare once is o'er,
Relieved, we'll shout: "Ah! what a bore
It was! I'm glad there is no more
　　　　　Centennial."

BACHELOR'S SOLILOQUY.

———

My stars ! this is comfort,
Though may-be 'tis selfish.
How happy I am,
That no womanite elfish
Is here to disturb me,
When (tailor's boy dodging)
Undunn'd I have reached
My bachelor-lodging !

This little low chair—
('Tis not worth the mention)
Is very convenient
For ease in extension :
I bought it at auction,
Last year in November ;
I thought may-be some one—
But, fudge ! I remember
I was really quite glad .
(No ! 'twas late in October)
That no one was here,—
Be she silly or sober,—
To borrow my meerschaum
Or steal my nice peaches ;
To call me a stupid,
And laugh at my speeches :
And then, if I venture,
Forlorn and despairing,
To take my departure,—

My purpose declaring,—
My patience! what torrents
Of tears and of temper
(Old Virgil just hit it,—
Mutabile semper)!

They *say* there *are* prizes
(I'm given to doubting)
Who won't call you horrid,
Or lapse into pouting :—
If home comes a fellow
Cross, may-be, and surly,
These angels won't tell you
You're somewhat too early,
But gladly and gaily
Will run out to meet you,
And with a sweet welcome
Most cheerfully greet you.   (muses.)

A nice little supper
In a parlor so cosy!
I wonder—I wonder
If that little Josie,—
The witch with blue ribbons,
And eyes even bluer,
Would give me the mitten
If once I should woo her?
I wonder—I wonder—
The evening is pleasant ;
My back hair's brushed nicely
No time like the present!   (Exit.)

DOUBLE ENTENDRE.

———

" Ah, do not go ! " her blue eyes say,
    Caressingly pathetic ;
He lingers, yet he looks afar,
    Alert and energetic.

" Come walk with me along the beach
    And past the silver maples ;
I prize no bay like yours, my own,—
    Not e'en the bay of Naples.

" But no ! you long to leave me still,—
    So obstinate and dogged :
My will could fetter you, but go—
    Unhindered and unclogged

" And eager as a young M. D.
    To shine at learned clinique !
Alas ! I've learned to think there is
    No sin in being a cynic.

"Ah, go ! but now you turn, and give
    Me tenderest caresses,
As one who, sinning all the while,
    Still kisses and confesses."

" Alas ! my words detain him not,
    My tears are unavailing.
—Ho ! John, look out ; that dog has gone
And jumped the garden-railing ! "

THE TROOPER'S DEATH-SONG.

THE weary night is o'er at last ;
We ride so far, we ride so fast,
　　We ride where death is lying ;
The morning breezes coldly pass—
Landlord, we'll take another glass,
　　Ere dying—ere dying !

Thou springing grass, that art so green,
Shall soon be rosy red, I ween,—
　　My blood the hue supplying.
I drink the first glass, sword in hand,
To him who for the Fatherland
　　Lies dying—lies dying.

Bring quickly, now, the second draught,
For that shall be to Freedom quaffed,
　　While Freedom's foes are flying :
The rest—O Land, our hope and faith !
We'd drink to thee with latest breath,
　　Tho' dying—tho' dying.

My Darling!—Ah ! the glass is out—
The bullets ring ; the riders shout :
　　No time for wine or sighing !
There ! take my love the shivered glass.
Charge on the foe ! No joys surpass
　　Such dying—such dying !

APPENDIX.

(*A Letter from Mrs. S. K. B.*)

(1888.)

At your request, I will try to give some reminiscences of the few months that Mary Lee and I spent together in Army Missionary Work. The Wire-bridge of memory must be stretched across the space of a quarter of a century to do it. Where, and with what shall I commence?—From the very moment at which our lives began, through a mutual interest, to be interlinked.

I, returning, with a heart overburdened by the memories of a few weeks spent in army nursing, at the front, just after McClellan's unfortunate seven days' battle, when so many of our soldiers were lying captives in the Southern prisons, suffering, starving, dying: we had gone within the enemy's lines, and brought home to Northern hospitals many of these our suffering, dying brothers—how could I, with such memories upon me, take up the ordinary routine of daily life?

Would I be willing, I was questioned, to go to David's Island, where nearly two thousand of our

(391)

sick soldiers were lying in tents, and work for them in the "Diet Kitchen," with other ladies who had volunteered to do so?   I would, and at once; and I went.

It was an October twilight of 1862, when I entered the low barrack-building named the "Pelham Diet Kitchen."   David's Island is only an island of sand, situated on Long Island Sound, about 21 miles from New York City; no structure of any kind being upon it, saving an old frame building, which was used by summer picnic parties for taking their refreshments, after the beautiful sail up the Sound.   The U. S. Sanitary Commission took possession of this barren island, in the name of the government, and hundreds of tents were there pitched, for the sick and wounded soldiers whom Government was now sending to Northern hospitals.

They also erected there four barrack-buildings, which were denominated "Ladies' Diet Kitchens," to be supervised by four different townships: Yonkers, New Rochelle, Pelham and Glencove.   I was assigned to the Pelham Division, being acquainted with the lady there in charge.   After giving me a kindly welcome, she showed me to a very small room, containing two iron bedsteads and a moiety of furniture.   "*This* will be your room, which you will share with a Miss Lee, of Croton Falls, who has come to join in the work."   I was too full of the cause, to stop and think how desolate an appearance it all presented.

I was glancing over some books which had been sent for the soldiers, when a graceful, willowy-figured young lady, in deep mourning, entered, to whom I was introduced as my room-mate, Miss Lee. She was not especially pretty, yet this quiet, low-voiced young lady, in deep black, with a wealth of soft, natural curls shading her face, interested me greatly at once; we seemed to strike a kindred chord from the beginning. She had been there several weeks, and quite readily took me in charge, to initiate me in my new duties. We slept together, and in the early morning she said: "we ladies (four) take charge of different branches of the work, some staying in-doors to prepare delicacies, receive orders from the doctors, etc.; some going outside to see what is wanted, and do the missionary part of the work. Which will be your choice?" "Oh! the missionary work, by all means; it was that I came for," was my reply. "So did I," she responded, "and we will go this morning together," which we did.

And what a labyrinth we found ourselves in! A perfect network of tents on all sides, with no distinctive landmarks of any kind, for we were living literally upon an island of sand. In and out, in and out of this labyrinth, this quiet, gentle lady led me, stopping now at this tent, now at that, to see what was most needed by those sick and homeless men, that the "Diet Kitchens" were able to provide; resting from our work only long enough to return to our Kitchen for a hasty noonday meal.

So we worked, until the shadows of evening fell; but we had done something that day, besides visiting sick soldiers. We had touched each other, heart to heart, and commenced a friendship, one of the dearest and noblest (to me certainly) that I ever formed. I think it was mutual.

This was the beginning of many such or similar days, each one of which was fraught with some event of peculiar or stirring interest. We often talked together of the brave boys at the Front (both of us having dear brothers doing duty there). Her innermost being was stirred within her, as was mine, at their sufferings and patient endurance. I can see her now, as we talked it all over, as though it were but yesterday—I telling her of that which had come directly under my own observation, in the few weeks I had spent at the Front. Sometimes those deep liquid blue eyes would fill with tears; sometimes they would seem to be looking inwards, and neither words nor sighs nor tears would come; then, unexpectedly, she would break out into some involuntary burst of patriotism, or some almost agonized words of irony, at the apparently needless delay of the General-in-Chief of the Army. But this was only in the evenings, after the work was over for the day. After our first day of work together, we would only start together—separating as soon as we reached the division of tents assigned to us.

The four Kitchens endeavored to make an equal division of the tents, in order that, as nearly as possible, all might be visited. Ours being the most northerly Kitchen, we took the northernmost sections of tents. Our work was very laborious, and yet it did not seem so to us; the cause and its needs appeared so entirely to fill our hearts. Our ladies were all of the same stamp, a set of self-denying Christian workers, most of them having come from homes of luxury, only too glad to volunteer in this service for their country, no matter at what personal sacrifice.

How well I remember saying to Mary Lee, one day: "M., to be honest with myself, this work does not seem to be a work of self-denial to me." Her singularly sweet, expressive eyes looking right into mine, with their most penetrating look (it used to seem to me as though little rays of light were dropping from them), she answered: "Oh! do you feel so too? I am so glad that you do, for it has appeared, at times, almost strange to me that I could so forget my home, with all its attractions, in the joy that this work affords me." It was not very long before we began to be accustomed to this labyrinth of tents, and to learn to know which were our own especial charge. The men in themselves, as a rule, were not of any remarkable interest of character, few of them having any degree of education (all privates), yet there were exceptional cases among them, some who interested us in their own individuality—aside from the interest they bore as sick soldiers. But if there was one man who chanced to be less interesting than another, one, in fact, whom we would rather turn aside from, that would be the very man whom Mary Lee would seek out and hold fast to. I remember one just such case. The man, though a worthy young man, being so uninviting in his personal appearance that we all involuntarily turned away from him. One day I said: "M., how can you hold so fast to such a repulsively uninteresting person?" "Because, dear," she answered in her tender way, "he *is* so almost repulsive that I fear, if I should give him up, nobody else will go to him."

She was, I think, one of the most entirely truthful persons that I ever met. Without striking against any one's antagonisms, her own trumpet would give forth no uncertain sound, but such quiet, deliberate, well-thought-out judgments, that no one could fail to see that they proceeded from a well-balanced mind and heart, as well as from inner soul-purity. There was no shirking of truth or duty, ever, in her case. She would neither force herself nor her views upon any one, but if her opinions were called for, there was no hesitation in giving them, in her clear, impressive, truthful manner. Her words were both deliberate and measured, yet not stilted in the slightest degree. At times, she would be so lost in thought as to apparently forget her subject; then we would laughingly say: "Well, M., are you going to sleep?" "Oh, no, no! but I am so afraid of giving a wrong judgment, ever." Then her sweet smile would break forth, like the sun through the clouds. Yet she was not the least depressing in her method— rather the opposite, but she ever seemed overwhelmed with the solemnity of this work, and of life in all its bearings. She never would permit herself to question God's dealings in any way, no matter how great might be her disappointment in His method. I remember questioning her on a certain subject that had been a sore trial to her. I spoke of the strange mystery of God's dealings in the matter. "Don't, please, don't; it is a great mystery, I know, but it must be right if He does it." I can seem even yet to hear her cheerful, musical laugh, as we would relate the amusing experiences that we might chance to encounter in our work.

She was entirely above small or petty jealousies of any kind. Her large soul could not comprehend such things. We ever worked together without antagonisms of any kind. A case in proof comes clearly before me, of a young soldier whom I had become acquainted with, and was much interested in, and at night would tell her of. As much as possible, we avoided visiting each other's patients, simply because there were so many who needed us, that we were enabled by this method to include a much larger number in our visitations.

The weather had now grown cold, and government had erected large barrack-buildings, which were termed Pavilions, to take the place of the tents, each Pavilion holding eighty beds; thus putting the men all under proper shelter. We were now, consequently, better able than before to systematize our work; could know, by the number of Pavilion and bed, just how to reach each man under our care; we ladies only visiting from 9 A. M. until 4 P. M., the other hours being used by the doctors for their visits. To return to my story, M. said to me, one night, about this time: "I have been in such a Pavilion and had a conversation with your sick soldier, M—— B——. He is a very interesting young fellow" (he was both reticent and thoughtful, which traits always pleased her). It so chanced that she stopped by his bedside, several times, to converse with him, while visiting in the Pavilion where he lay. One night she said to me, with a troubled look: "I have done that to-day which rather troubles me, in regard to M—— B——." "What is it?" I queried. "Well, you know that I have chanced to stop at his bedside a number of times; he interests me greatly, and I hope that at length he has become interested in religious subjects." "Well, are you not glad of that?" "Yes, dear, but there is something further which I *must* tell you. You know that we are not all constituted alike, and he wishes me, for the future, to visit and converse with him, instead of you; he says that I can help him as you cannot, and that troubled me,—to seem to be trying to take the work out of your hands, when you are the one who first sought him out, and labored patiently with him." "No, no, M., a thousand times, no. We cannot help our preferences, and I am truly thankful that you can help him if I cannot, and gladly pass my care of him over into your hands." Which I did; she laboring most faithfully with this thoughtful young soldier, until he hoped that he saw the truth for himself; her method of reasoning was so clear, so biblical, so persuasive. I went, in the meanwhile, to see him, telling him how glad I was that he could open his heart to Miss Lee, if he could not to me. "I could not bear to hurt your feelings," he said; "but she did seem so well able to help me out of my doubts, with her slow, quiet earnestness." The boy seemed almost to worship this refined, gentle, Christian lady. How could these sick, homeless boys help doing so—her goodness and purity shone out in her every word and action.

Thus we lived, talked and worked, day by day, our

love and respect for each other growing daily. The
large picnic-building, to which I have heretofore alluded, had been secured, and improvised for Chapel
purposes. It was a long walk, to reach it from our
Kitchen home, but with what pleasure we talked over
our work, on our way, each Sabbath! One of our
ladies always presided at the melodeon, and M.'s
sweet voice never sounded so sweetly as when she
joined in that music. How fond she was of that
hymn, which they sang from their little army hymn-
books:

> "Come sing to me of heaven,
>   When I'm about to die;
> Sing songs of holy melody
>   To waft me to the sky."
> There'll be no parting there;
> There'll be no parting there;
> In heaven above, where all is love;
> There'll be no parting there."

One day, she handed me a large card, with a hymn
printed upon it, such as they were then using in the
army, requesting me to give her my opinion of it.
"It does not strike me as anything remarkable. Why
do you ask me?" "Because I have just been reading something an Army Chaplain says of that hymn.
'I have never given out that hymn in any prayer-
meeting held among the soldiers, that, after the meeting, some soldier has not come to me to inquire the
way to Christ,—the result of that hymn.'" "It is
one of my own composition," she added, "but it
does not seem to me worthy of having received such
a blessing; yet I am so rejoiced to hear of it." It
was called "A Recruiting Song."

There was not the slightest affectation in her modesty. She was truly humble, ever self-depreciating, in all she did. One day, she turned to me with a wearied look, saying: "I have about given it all up —I "—"Given what up, M.?" "Why, trying to be like any of you. First, I tried to be like Miss B——, but soon gave her up; then like E—— C——, with a like result; then I tried to be like you, and now, I think I shall have to give you up too." "The sooner the better, M.! I think you had better go back to the only true model, the Lord Jesus Christ." "I think so too; and I will." Truly, she did follow closely in the footsteps of Him whom her soul loved.

So our work went on for months. I can only think of it as an oasis of joy, in the wilderness of woe by which we were surrounded. Sometimes it would be interrupted by a return to our homes, for an interval of rest or call of duty; but, each time, coming back to it with renewed zest, and never wearying of the work, or of each other. After a term of months, I do not remember exactly how long, various duties called us both to our own homes. Most of the men with whom we had been laboring had been sent to their homes or back to the seat of war. Some had gone to their long home. Government was taking control of all the hospitals, and David's Island was now being used for the sick Southern prisoners of war, as well as for our own soldiers. So, one after another, we dropped away from the work, others in turn filling our places; and this strongly marked epoch in our lives was over. Not so, however, with our friendships then and there commenced. We kept up a close and warm intimacy, occasionally passing a night with each other, and then how all alive she would seem, as we talked over the past together.

Just here, I would like to quote from a letter received from one of our disabled soldiers who had been sent to his home. He was a man of sad and dreamy temperament, yet full of strong manhood—had lost an arm, and was much depressed. He struggled out of darkness into the light, with a conflict that seemed to be with Apollyon himself, and became a noble specimen of manly Christianity. This, accompanied with his poetic temperament and his fine physique, rendered him a valuable coadjutor with us in our work. How many hours have both M. and I spent pleading with this manly fellow, to find his true life in Christ. The letter which I speak of was dated, "Cincinnati, Ohio," after the war was over. He was speaking of his love of the twilight hour, for meditation. "At such an hour," he writes, "and in such a place, the soul almost forgets its mortal dwelling-place in sweet communion with Him; it has seemed to me, at times, as if earth and heaven met and combined." His letter breathes only of this spirit, and he closes with an earnest inquiry concerning his friend, Miss Lee.

Now, let me quote from a letter which I received from M. herself, years after the close of the war : "Do you know, dear, that I think one of my great joys in heaven will be our converse together, over the weary, sin-sick souls we together tried to help to the dear, loving Saviour." She always wrote, and I think only wrote, when she was so overcharged with thought that she could hold it back no longer. I think one of the most intense poems written during the war, was her poem, "A Voice from Belle Isle." An officer at the Front read it from "Littell's Living Age," in which it was published. "I would so much like to know," he said, "who wrote that very remarkable poem." On my replying that it was Mary Lee, he could scarcely be made to believe that a poem of so much merit proceeded from her pen. I said to her afterward : "Please tell me what induced the writing of that intense poem ? " "Why, my whole being was so wrought upon, with the sufferings of the starving prisoners of war, that I could not eat ; one night, sitting down to a plentiful repast, I could not swallow; the food seemed to choke me. I arose, left the table, went up-stairs and wrote those lines." Surely, that was born of soul agony.

At one time, I was preparing for publication a brief record of Army Work, at David's Island and elsewhere. M. came to pass the night with me, and I read her some of the manuscript, as she lay on a lounge by my side. Slowly, as I read, she raised her head from its resting place, her eyes kindling with a light that I always loved to see in them. "Is it exaggerated, M. ? " "Ex-ag-ger-ated ? No, no, no ; but I seem to be living it all over again." That was enough ; I needed no further criticism.

She frequently would talk to me of her home, of her almost idolized, deceased parents, her fondly loved brothers and sisters. At one time, she was telling me of the death-bed scenes of a dear sister, who had recently passed away. Then she dwelt upon the aloneness of each individual soul. "C——," she said, "when dying, called some member of the household to her bedside, saying: 'Take hold of my hand, I want *one* of you to hold me fast, I am so weak.' But soon, she dropped the hand that tenderly clasped her own, saying: 'No, no, I must go alone—alone—with my Saviour; you cannot, one of you, go with me. I must not look to human help now; I must go alone.'"

After her young brother, who had gone on a voyage for his health, went down at sea, she talked to me of it, with a pathos all her own. She was ever a great lover of nature, especially as it is manifested in the ocean. "But," she said, "I cannot bear to look at the ocean, now. I cannot seem to see those great black waves, without seeming also to see my dear brother being swallowed up by them, all alone. I have tried to hope that some passing vessel had rescued him, and that he would yet be heard from; but now I have almost given up even that faint hope, and it seems as though I could not bear it." And her deep blue eyes, with their far-away look, would fill with tears, no longer able to be held back. Nor could she find any comfort until she stayed herself upon the thought, that Christ, his loving Saviour, met him, His own dear child, and clasped him in His own loving arms; no deep waters being able to engulf his soul.

And now, those far-away, blue eyes, her soul's eyes, as they ever seemed to me, are gazing upon the King himself in " His ain Countree." To use her own sweet words:

" I've His gude word o' promise that, some gladsome day, the
     King
   To His ain royal palace His banished hame will bring:
   Wi' een an wi' hearts running owre, we shall see
   The King in His beauty, in our ain countree."

ALPHABETICAL INDEX.

[Includes statement of names (where known) of publishers, by whose courtesy articles heretofore printed are now reproduced; also approximate dates of publication; and dates of composition of certain of the other contents.]

Acid Test, The (*Illustrated Christian Weekly*, May, 1879) 165

Adjai, The Story of 146

Andreas Hlaverti 152

Appendix (*War-Letter*) 391

At Eventide 353

Bachelor's Soliloquy (186—), ... 387

Balsam—Balm—Everlasting, ... 354

Bonny Doon (1887),. 368

Buenos Ayres (*South America*, 1870), . . . 319

Casting, or Carrying (*Ill. Christian Weekly*, Sept. 1885), 170

Centennial (1876), ... 386

Chamouny and the Mer de Glace (*Presbyterian Journal*,

 June, 1887), ... 83

China-Town, A morning in the Homes of (187—), . 156

Christ in Art (*Ill. Christian Weekly*, April, 1886), . 175

(405)

Christmas Carol, A 354

Christmas Card, How a, saved a Life (*Ill. Chr'n. Weekly*,
Dec., 1878), ... 185

Cum Scuto, vel Super (1862), ... 348

Double Entendre (1874), ... 389

Dumb (1876), ... 365

Eighteen hundred and sixty-five, . . . 349

England at Garfield's Grave (*Presb. Jour.*, Sept., 1881), . 228

Fackel Zug, The (*Germany*, 1883), . . . 312

Garfield (1881), ... 351

Gerty Morse, How, Said "Yes," . . . 106

Gifford's Wife, ... 241

Give Place 334

Goldilocks and Silver Hair, ... 355

Guy Fawkes' Day (*Presb. Jour.*, Dec., 1881), . . 238

Hampton-Court Vine, ... 383

He Carries them up Hill (*N. Y. Observer*, March, 1871), 177

He Saved Others; Himself He Cannot Save, . . 328

Homeless (1864), ... 337

Hope Archer's Parable (*Ill. Chr'n. Weekly*, Aug., 1878), 180

Hyde Park (*London*, 1881), ... 317

I am No Poet (1860), ... 335

I Surrender, ... 192

Impotence (1861), ... 364

Indelible Ink, ... 299

Jerusalem Chamber, The (*London*, 1881), . . . 314

Joyful Sufferer, The (*Presb. Bd. of Publication*, 186—), . 127

Last Thing, The (1876), ... 360

Lift up the Christ (*American Messenger*, Nov., 1885), . 338

Links (*Presb. Jour.*, July, 1882), . . . 3

Lion and the Adder, The, ... 333

Little Helpers, ... 331

Lord-Mayor's Day (*London*, 1881), ... 316

Marburg on the Lahn (*Germany*, 1883), . 311

Master's Use, For the (*Presb. Jour.*, Nov. 1881), . . 379

Ministering, ... 353

Mission, A Domestic, ... 280

Missions Report, Foreign (188—), ... 374

My Jericho (186—), ... 339

My Joy, ... 324

My Love (1864), ... 355

My Rest, ... 357

Night Watch, A, ... 358

Nineteenth Century Barrel of Meal, A (*Ill. Chr'n. Weekly*), 195

One Faith, ... 331

Outward Bound (1865), ... 370

Pearls and Pebbles (1863), ... 365

Pine Knots from Old Carolina (1885), . . . 306

Poppies growing on ruins of Roman villa (*England*, 1885), 369

Prayer-Meeting Varnish, . . . 221

Redemption of Strays (*Am. Messenger*, April, 1878), . 202

Rifted Cloud, The, ... 346

Rio to Petropolis, From (*South America*, 1870), . . 318

Soldier ! A Letter for You (*A. D. F. Randolph, & Co. ; A leaflet, during the war,* 186—), . . . 294

Soldier's Comfort, The (*Presb. Bd. of Publication ; A leaflet, during the war,* 186—), . . . 289

Southern Violets, ... 121

Spending-Money (*Ill. Chr'n. Weekly,* May, 1881), . 204

Spes Salutis (1862), ... 346

Spiritual Malaria (*Ill. Christian Weekly,* Oct., 1878), . 214

Story for Little Nan, A (*Ill. Christian Weekly,* Oct., 1871), 216

Sunny Memories of Mentone (*France,* 186—), 320

Syrian Children, ... 343

Thro' Gloom to Glory (1859), . . . 362

Thro' My Skylight (*Ill. Chr'n. Weekly,* June, 1886), . 342

Thy Homesick Child (*A. D. F. Randolph & Co. ; " Way-side Hymns,"* 1860), ... 336

Trooper's Death Song, The (186—) . . 390

Two Sunsets (188—), ... 372

Under the Snows (1862), . . . 366

Unto You, Gentiles, ... 326

Week of Prayer, An Incident of the (*Ill. Chr'n. Weekly,* July, 1884), ... 188

When the Even was Come, . . 275

Who and Whence ? 340

Wind and the Whirlwind, The, . . . 258

Y. M. C. A. (1876), ... 385

www.ingramcontent.com/pod-product-compliance
Lightning Source LLC
Chambersburg PA
CBHW050902130726
47900CB00015B/1699